Hope U like the story & arts

ELDRITCH

Investigations

LOVECRAFTIAN TALES OF OCCULT DETECTION

Curated & Edited by Tim Mendees

Illustrations by Jasiah Witkofsky

& Graveheart Designs

First Edition
Published by Mythos Press
An ímprint of Nordic Press
Kindlyckevägen 13
Rimforsa, Sweden.
2023

Eldritch Investigations
Lovecraftian tales of Occult Detection

Cover Design by Graveheart Designs
Illustrations by Jasiaha Witkofsky & Graveheart Designs
Edited by Tim Mendees
Ebook: 978-91-89853-12-6
Paperback: 978-91-89853-13-3

CONTENTS

WHERE DREAMS COME TRUE

Simon Bleaken

I held my breath as I stepped into the kitchen.

The place was huge, too full of shadows and corners. Sounds echoed across the hard surfaces despite my attempts to move silently. It was impossible not to feel watched. There was also a faint stench, acrid, with an unpleasantly metallic undertone.

The building had formerly been a three-star hotel, though it had closed down over six years ago and was meant to be empty. My torch beam flitted across an array of scuffed worktops and a grimy, cracked tile floor, the windows covered with yellowed blinds. It all seemed utterly deserted, but I knew better than to make dangerous assumptions.

Besides, my gut was telling me that something was very wrong here.

As I moved deeper in, my beam picked out some disturbing items, and my gut feeling achieved instant vindication.

The cult was here. I'd recognised their mark scratched onto the door: The Children of the Green Flame. Judging by the gutted and skinned corpses now dangling in the light of my torch, they were getting ready for a ritual. I'd guess a summoning of some kind of lessor servitor, or something equally unpleasant.

Can't say I was surprised, this place had all the hallmarks of one of their hangouts—secluded, full of malign odours, with liberal scatterings of body parts and corpses in various states of dismemberment. Oh yeah, not to mention the sigils on the doors and windows disguised to look like gang symbols and mindless graffiti. I'd neutralised those easily enough before picking the lock, but there was always the worry that they'd leave a little surprise that I might miss. Luckily, these guys were either lazy or they'd grown complacent.

I had a strong stomach, hell, you had to in this line of work, but even I felt sick at the sight of those ravaged corpses. The bodies swayed gently, torn shreds of skin flapping above congealed blood and discarded entrails, all the parts they didn't need. They'd taken the eyes, the tongue and the heart by the look of things. I guessed they were symbols of vision, communication and feeling, but for all I knew they may just have been the tastiest parts, assuming whatever they planned to call up even needed food. There might have been other bits missing from within those bodies, but my skills didn't lie in anatomy.

The only thing I could glean for certain, from a quick inspection of the accompanying piles of bloodstained clothing and personal items, was that these were the missing people I'd been investigating. I took no joy in finding them, not like this, but honestly, I'd have been amazed to have found them alive.

There was something else too, I realised as my foot slid in it, some kind of slime; thick and tacky, a nauseating phlegm colour. It covered parts of the floor and walls in a wide spray. I had no idea what had made it, I just prayed it was nothing more sinister than a cultist with a bad cold (as if I was ever that lucky). I took a sample for later analysis, making a mental note to burn everything I was wearing when I got back to the Lodge.

We'd been monitoring cult activity in the area for a while, and had gotten wind of a few civilian disappearances that bore all the signs of increased ritual activity. Our hidden informant within the police department had secretly slipped us the details, which was how I now came to be skulking around this filthy slaughterhouse of a kitchen, ruining my good shoes.

These guys were on our watch list, but they'd been quiet for months. There'd been none of the usual indicators that they were about to step up their activity, and I hadn't been able to pin down any red flags–celestial alignments, propitious dates, or any omens or prophecies–that suggested any reason why they'd suddenly kick in with a summoning like this. Something had changed, that was for sure, and I needed to know what.

Thankfully, I had all the resources of the Lodge at my disposal; a boon most other investigators lacked. Its official name was The Order of the Celestial Consciousness, but we just called it the Lodge, less pretentious and more down to business, reflecting our new way of working.

It had been founded clandestinely in the late 1800s. Originally intended as a magical order akin to the Hermetic Order of the Golden Dawn, it had eventually branched its considerable resources outwards, taking on cases that most other agencies were not equipped to even understand.

In short, we monitored occult threats. We didn't have any official legal standing, but those who needed our services knew of us, and we had wealthy patrons ensuring we got all the support we needed.

It was dangerous work, but somebody had to do it.

I felt the reassuring weight of the gun against my hip

as I moved deeper into the building, though I knew its aid wouldn't stretch far beyond cultists.

The odour was stronger in the hall just beyond the kitchen. I stood for a moment, listening, before following my nose to a steep flight of stairs heading into the shadows of a basement. Occult activities and mephitic stenches went hand in hand far more than most people realised.

It grew worse as I reached the bottom and approached a door at the end of a short hallway. There was a dance of candlelight from under it. The silence around me had become as intense as the smell that was now scouring skin cells off the inside of my nostrils.

I turned off the torch before reaching for the handle.

The door moved soundlessly on well-used hinges, and an inner sanctum opened before my eyes.

The room was wide. The black-painted brick walls and concrete floor were softened by hanging drapes bearing a stylised green-flame symbol. In the heart of the space, before an altar adorned with offerings of eyes, tongues and hearts, was a large circle of candles and...

...for a second, I froze at the sight of the kneeling forms around the edges of the circle, and then I let out a slow, uneasy breath. There were twelve of them, clad in heavy robes, hands bound and heads bowed as if in prayer. But, no god or entity that I knew of could hear prayers from heads that had been utterly hollowed out.

Shit. This wasn't good.

The air felt charged with static as I approached those corpses. They looked like discarded puppets whose strings had been severed. The cuts to their craniums were precise, surgical, and clean. The brains had been taken. Not a drop of blood had spilt onto the floor or stained the bodies of the victims.

This was no ritual gone wrong; this had been a hit from a rival cult. I guess that answered the curious ease with which I had disabled the sigils on the doors and windows upstairs. Somebody had beaten me to it.

There was a charred book lying a few feet away from the altar, its blackened state contributing to the assault on the back of my throat. I crouched and turned the few surviving pages. There wasn't much that was still legible, but I could make out some faded Latin. I carefully pulled the pages free and folded them into my jacket pocket to study them later. Latin always gave me a headache, so this might be a job for the scholars at the Lodge. They loved old tomes, the more recherché and esoteric the better.

I took one last look at the kneeling bodies. The cult of the Green Flame was rumoured to continue to live beyond death, supposedly dwelling forever in rotting carcasses in hidden places, bound in eternal servitude to their deity. I for one failed to see any appeal in that kind of an afterlife. Each to their own, I suppose. Sadly, for these few, it looked as if that strange destiny was going to be denied to them. I wasn't sure if I should feel sorry or relieved.

I retraced my steps carefully. I figured there was little point searching the whole joint, it was clear the basement had been where the main action had taken place. But, as I returned to the long service hallway I heard the sound of something coming down the stairs further along.

There was no tread of feet, but rather a heavy sliding-thumping, clumsy and slow.

I drew my gun and edged to the bottom of the staircase.

I glanced up just as the thing came around the bend.

It lurched forwards, the shockingly monstrous form matched only by the hungry and demented mewling coming from its throat. My jaw slackened and my world swayed. I'd seen inhuman before, things that had shaken me to my core, things that still gnawed at my sanity in the early hours of the morning—but this? This was a nightmarish hybrid formed in the most barbaric and cruelly twisted of intellects. The mouth parted and a white, wormlike tongue protruded. It seemed to be scenting the air.

Whatever it was, it wasn't the product of any summoning ritual, but of a kind of hellish augmentation and experimentation. Its eyeless, twisted face was speckled with blood as if it had just been feeding, and its misshapen body shivered as it extruded several questing pseudopods that began exuding more of that yellow-green slime. It opened its mouth and a guttural howl erupted from that lipless slit.

There was a metallic webbing of silver across its skin that seemed wired into the side of its cranium. It was as if several dozen different organic specimens had been genetically fused and then further enhanced with technology; a blasphemous melding of alien machinery and re-animated life.

Cold horror flooded me, threatening to ice my feet to the spot—but I forced myself to run. I was lucky I did because, at the sight of me, it began to move faster, pouring itself down the last few steps and spilling into the hallway.

Momentarily forgetting the way out, I shouldered my way through the closest door into the dining room, cursing myself for wandering so blindly into this trap.

There was a loud scraping from the hall and a moist pseudopod slapped against the wood. It seemed it hadn't worked out handles yet. Pale folds of glistening flesh bubbled from beneath the door and oozed around the edges, before it burst inwards as the greater bulk of the beast surged inside.

I hurried through the room, half-springing and half-sliding across the filthy tables, barging through the first door that I found. I could hear the entity behind me, charging madly across the room, scattering furniture.

I slid the flimsy lock on the door shut. It would only buy me seconds.

There was another corpse in the next hall, a man in his mid-forties. He was lying face down, his tattered body thickly coated with sludge. The guy's left leg and arm were chewed down to the bone. I wondered if he'd still been alive at the time. It looked like he had been trying to get away, and sure enough, there was an external door at the end of the hallway. I almost kept moving, until I saw something scrunched in his right hand. I prised it free just as the lock gave way and the door to the dining room flew open.

With no time to stop and examine my slimy prize, I slipped it into my other pocket and fled down the hallway and out into the damp foulness of an alleyway.

Fortunately, there was no indication that anything was pursuing as I stumbled through the shadows towards my car.

I drove a circuitous route back to the Lodge, stopping at least once to grab a coffee from a late-night diner, all the while keeping a careful watch for any signs I was being followed, either by other cars or by anything else out of the ordinary. I had to pull over a few times to steady myself, and I thought I was going to puke more than once. I forced the coffee down, which helped. I considered myself a seasoned Lodge investigator, but nothing could prepare you for some of the things we ran into out here. Bodies were easy, they were just dead meat–well, most of the time–but, some of the other things? Let's just say there was a reason why I wasn't teetotal, and leave it at that.

When I was sure it was safe, I made for home.

The Lodge is a grand old house, deeply secluded in sprawling grounds behind high walls, trees and thick hedges in a neighbourhood full of similar large houses, all basking in the fading echoes of past glory and days long gone.

We never go in by the front; it's far too easy to be observed from the road. Instead, a tree-shrouded back drive permits a more secluded ingress and egress for all Lodge agents. The trees around the entire building all bear concealed warding sigils, as do the walls, and the magical defences are as strong as we can get them; though I'd not want to hedge any bets on how long they'd hold up if put to the test. We also have several secret safe houses scattered around the city. We've learned to be careful.

I hurried inside, checked in with the guard at the front desk, and made my way into the secured and restricted areas in the heart of the building. I stopped by the towering stacks of the library to drop off the pages I had recovered with our head scholar, Robert Ashton. He assured me that I would be the first to know when they had something to report. My next stop was to the Inner Chamber, to detail what I'd found at the hotel with the Illuminated Council. It was clear we'd need a full clean-up crew to take care of the mess.

One of my fellow investigators, Jackson Colby, greeted me as I walked back out into the front lounge. I must have looked a sight, my clothes and shoes spattered with stinking slime and my hands still shaking from my recent brush with eldritch abominations.

"Busy night, Dredson?" he raised an eyebrow.

"You've no idea." I wanted to drop into one of the comfortable chairs and get myself a tall brandy, but I couldn't. Not yet anyway.

"I know that look. What's up?"

"Any idea what this is?" I handed him the crumpled paper and he took it carefully with a look of disgust. It was still dripping.

"Not sure," he frowned, turning it over in his hands. "It's not a rune or an alchemical symbol. Doesn't look like a cult marking either, unless we've a new player in town?"

"Possible," I nodded. "Somebody's just taken out a room full of cultists. That was on one of the bodies."

"This is all you've got to go on?"

"There were some charred pages, though I'm not sure they'll shed any light on anything relevant. But that," I nodded at the crumpled paper, "was clutched in a dead guy's hand. He'd been running for the door."

"It's modern paper, and this looks printed. It could be a fragment from a flyer?"

"Yeah, I wondered that."

"You should have the seers take a look."

"No, this one's mine. It's bugging me, there's something familiar about it."

"Now that you mention it…"

"Come on," I clapped him on the shoulder, "let's go for a drive."

"Where?"

"There's someone I need to talk to, but I'd rather have you watching my back while I do; bad part of town."

He handed the paper back. "Alright, let's go."

The old square just south of Hollowston's Bridge is somewhere most sane people avoid. It sits in a part of town that should have been torn down decades ago, and yet somehow still clings to the city like a dead limb. The buildings are mostly boarded up and dilapidated, little more than chilly squats for the homeless or drug-addled; or places where criminals lie low. I don't think I've seen a cop in those streets for over five years now. The few homes still with legitimate inhabitants are tiny oases of light in the darkness, but each year the number of those lights slowly dwindles.

"Bad part of town? Hell, I wish I'd known you meant here," Colby grumbled as we pulled up. No street lights were working and it was hard to see if anyone else was around. "I'd have brought a bigger gun." He pulled a small metal amulet from his pocket, turning it slowly in his fingers. It glinted like copper. "My lucky amulet," he said. "I always carry it with me. Think we'll need it tonight."

"Does it work?" I raised a sceptical eyebrow. It looked like some cheap trinket.

"Hey, don't question the magic. It works for me because I think it does," he shrugged.

"This shouldn't take long," I said, climbing out of the car. The wind felt colder and stronger here, and litter skittered through the streets adding to the sense of desolation. Somewhere in the darkness a dog barked and I shivered. I had no desire to spend any longer here than I needed to.

"It stinks of piss," Colby muttered as he joined me.

"Just watch our backs," I advised, leading the way across the cracked pavement and up to a grimy doorway. I knocked twice and said loudly: "It's Aaron Dredson. I'm here to see The Dreamer."

Despite the considerable resources of the Lodge, there were times when visiting outside informants was the only way to get answers that evaded even our agents. People like The Dreamer walked in circles that we couldn't safely access, and they weren't bound by the rules of the Lodge when it came to their methods of acquiring that information. I'd visited The Dreamer many times over the past few years, and I trusted the things he told me–though I wasn't foolish enough to let my guard down around him. Truth be told, I wasn't even entirely sure he was human.

There was a shuffling from the other side of the door, and a sound like flabby fingers pawing at the lock before it creaked inwards. In the dim light of a single candle burning a few feet further down the hall, I saw a stocky, hunched shape standing in the doorway.

"Dredson?" a thin voice wheezed. "You have something for me?"

"Can we come in?"

He didn't answer, merely turned and shuffled back inside. I motioned for Colby to accompany me.

We followed The Dreamer's shambling form down that narrow hallway. The bare boards groaned beneath our feet, and the musty walls were speckled with mould where the tattered paper had sagged and slipped. Strange sounds came from all around the house: whispering, whimpering, and a curious wet gurgling that seemed to come from within the walls themselves.

There was a heady scent pervading the air, like some kind of noxious incense. It got stronger the further we went. My eyes grew drowsy and a headache burned behind them.

"What's that... smell?" Colby frowned. He went to put a hand against the wall to brace himself, and then thought better of it.

"The lotus works a subtle magic," The Dreamer grinned, his leprous face breaking into another sharp-toothed smile. His black tongue flicked across peeling lips, and his milky-white eyes followed me, even though

I knew he was quite blind. "It guides my dreams and carries my mind beyond my body; sometimes into distant Cimmeria, other times to the charnel shores of future Zothique, and through all the ages between, around and beyond. Sometimes, my dreams take me to places strange, dark and terrible. Oh, I have seen the shadowy stretches of Leng, the white towers of Nuub-Surghaakt in the hollow wastes, and I have witnessed what happened on the shores of dim Carcosa where black stars blaze."

"Sounds delightful," Colby muttered.

"I've glimpsed what dwells in the hearts of dead worlds," The Dreamer continued, "and what crawls and festers in the farthest nebulae in deep space. And, I have seen the dancers and pipers that attend the writhing chaos that burns at the heart of everything."

"Any chance you've seen something a little closer to home?" I asked dryly.

The shadows pressed in as we edged down that hallway, as though we moved between worlds ourselves rather than merely between rooms. The pungent incense drugged our senses even as it whispered into our minds, redolent with promises of other times and places, of worlds between worlds and of dimensions that waited only a single step away. The squalor and decay of that rotting house seemed as intangible as thought, as though the physical world was nothing more than a figment of some tormented imagination, and only that incense–and the dreams it promised so seductively–were instead the true reality. The sounds from behind those closed doors were getting louder and more insistent. I reached for one of the tarnished handles.

"Do not open the doors!" The Dreamer hissed, eyes wide with alarm. "You must only follow me."

Finally, we reached the end of the passageway and he guided us into a back room. It was bare apart from a bed and a candlelit table upon which a small burner lay, a thick clump of dark incense smoking atop it. The light that speared through that swirling coil of dense smoke took on prismatic qualities, like a rainbow of colour in the air. Some of those hues were utterly unknown to me, and I shivered at the sight of them.

"Show me!" The Dreamer demanded, and I handed my crumpled clue to him. It was still dripping, the slime refused to dry.

He took it and licked the paper slowly, a shiver of what I assumed to be pleasure running through him. "You always bring me the best," he chuckled.

"Glad you like it," I tried to hide my revulsion. "It's yours if you can tell me what that symbol means."

He sniffed the air. "The shoes too?" he asked hopefully. "There's more on them."

"Don't push it," I warned him.

He shrugged and licked the slime once more before deeply inhaling the foul curling smoke. His eyes rolled back to the whites and the strange folds of skin at his throat twitched. His hand tightened around the paper and he began to moan.

"Things are shifting, moving. The sands of time are flowing faster now, casting a shadow over all of us."

"What shadow?"

"An ancient power, flexing its muscles... is awakening from dormancy, or seclusion."

"Alright. So, why are they attacking the other cults?"

"The Messenger seeks to unite all under his tattered wings. The Eye is open. It seeks. It sees. Those who will not come, will not join, will be swept away."

"Which cult? Who's behind all this?"

"The Brotherhood of Whispers is among us, and all will hear its words."

"I thought they were based in Cairo?"

"Their reach has grown. Their voices echo in many lands now."

"And the missing brains, why'd they take those? Why cut open their heads like that?"

"The Messenger's acolytes are not without allies of their own. The demands of that alliance are many, and unusual."

"What allies?"

"They come from far away. You would be wise to avoid them."

"So, where are they?"

He blinked those sightless watery eyes at me.

"Where are the Messenger's acolytes?" I clarified.

"Closer than you think. You'll find them where dreams come true."

"Dreams?" I frowned. "What do you mean? I need more."

"Go home, Dredson," he laughed. "Go home, but keep your eyes open. You'll see it. You'll know it when you do."

"Home? But..."

"Go now," he urged. "Go quickly. Time is against you."

I turned to leave, but he grabbed my sleeve, twisting the cloth frantically in his pale fingers.

"But, tread with care. You are expected."

My head was spinning by the time we stumbled out into the night air, but the effect of the incense was already wearing off; the world was solid once more, and the experiences within that house were fading like smoke on a breeze.

"What was in that stuff?" Colby grumbled, rubbing his forehead as we climbed back in the car. "My skull's pounding."

"Probably best not to ask," I answered.

"You've… experienced that before?"

"More than once," I nodded, feeling my senses gradually realigning. Everything still felt as if it was swaying though, and I didn't dare start the car until it stopped. "It passes quickly, and you kind of forget it in time."

"Glad to hear that. Feels like my eyeballs are bleeding." He sat back, took a deep breath, and then gestured wearily at the road. "How about we get the hell out of here now?"

"No argument here."

"So, any of that make sense to you?"

"Not yet, but I'm hoping it will soon."

"Think he's right about the Brotherhood of Whispers making a power grab here in the city? How come we missed that?"

"I have a feeling there's a lot we haven't seen," I said grimly. "Let's try and get some of those answers."

Colby fell silent after that, and I was glad. I had my own thoughts to deal with, crowding in my mind like a swarm of agitated bees. But more than that, I was watching the city, keeping my eyes open as I drove just as The Dreamer had advised.

The buildings flashed past the windows. In the darkness, their lights looked magical, even welcoming, but they only deepened the shadows and hid the ugliness festering unseen all around us. The heart of the city was rotten, and it had been spreading slowly outwards for years.

It was sixteen minutes later that I saw it on the other side of the street. I braked so hard I would have caused an accident had the road not been empty apart from us.

"Son of a bitch..." I muttered.

Colby stared at me like I'd lost my mind. "What the hell are you doing?" he barked.

"Look over there," I pointed across the street at the darkened hulk of a building.

At first, he didn't get what I was gesturing at. This was a seedy part of town, close to the red light district, and had the hour been earlier, the pavements would have been crawling with hookers. Then he drew in a breath, and I knew he'd seen it, the red and gold sign above the main door that proclaimed:

The Celephais Gentleman's Club
Where your dreams come true.

"Think that's it?"

"Look at their logo," I said softly. "It's the same as the symbol on that flyer we found."

I had driven past that damn place every night for years without paying it much attention, but The Dreamer's words left me in no doubt that we'd found the source of the new cancer spreading through our city.

We couldn't go to the Lodge though, not yet. We needed actual proof.

We pulled up around the back, parking in the garbage-scented shadows of an alleyway that was dark enough to have been a mugger's paradise.

"We really wanna go in there?" Colby asked uneasily.

"We have to," I said, checking my gun. "Something big is brewing, and I'd feel happier knowing what. So, we'll go in carefully, scope the place, and be out before anyone knows."

Colby shifted uneasily in his seat. "What about us being 'expected'?"

"Well, if we're expected, who are we to disappoint?"

"This is why none of us ever make it to retirement age, you know that right?"

"You'd only get bored. Come on."

The night was chilly, steam rose from vents like lost souls fleeing the shadows as we approached the building. Every window was black, giving the outward appearance that the place was empty, but it didn't take long for us to notice the subtler signs—cult symbols and hidden sigils that would have gone unnoticed to the untrained eye or average civilian.

"Looks like the place," Colby muttered grimly. "You know this is a trap, right?"

"Of course it is. I'm just hoping they weren't expecting me to bring you along."

"And, if they were?"

"You got a gun?"

"Yes."

"That's plan B. Let's go."

The door was locked tight but we found a window that wasn't properly secured, I doubted by accident. The sigils around it were tricky and well hidden, but even so, they were still just a little too easy to neutralise for my liking. Colby hung back as I worked, watching the entrance to the alleyway. All our agents, whatever their speciality, had some degree of magical training. The most adept worked and studied within the Lodge's Sanctum and rarely ventured out on assignments. Magic had limited practical applications in the field; it generally took too long to set up.

I held my breath as I opened the window. When nothing unpleasant happened, we quietly let ourselves into a rear hallway.

"Hang back a bit," I whispered to Colby once we were inside. "I'll go on ahead. Hopefully, if anyone is waiting for me, they might not see you."

"'Hopefully' and 'might' are never comforting phrases," he remarked, but he held back as I edged deeper in. We both knew we'd gone too far to turn back now. We'd crawled into the gullet of the beast, it was time to see what lay at its heart.

I crept through the low lighting of the club, listening carefully. The decor was gaudy; Art Deco meets cheap whore's boudoir, complete with hanging red silk drapes, bowls filled with rose petals, and an underlying odour of residual lust that seemed ingrained in every surface, as though the desperation of a thousand lonely patrons had soaked into the structure of the place.

I moved past private booths and small side rooms that despite being empty were somehow still haunted by the hollow ghosts of the carnal pleasures frequently enacted within. This place was a gilded temple to baser desires, baptised in sweat and ejaculation, but it was also a pale mask concealing a deeper and darker purpose. I wondered how easily someone might vanish inside one of those secluded rooms or behind all that hanging silk never to be seen again. With so many lost and isolated souls in this city, they'd have no shortage of victims desperate to get inside.

I knew immediately the building was not as empty as it looked, I could hear someone talking from somewhere up ahead. I strained to listen, but the words were too faint to catch.

I followed the sound, grateful for the thick carpet that swallowed the noise of my footfalls. It led me through some hanging veils and into a larger side room, the dim lighting reflecting from a shiny dark tiled floor. Overhead the high ceiling was hidden by even more folds of hanging silk that moved softly as if in some breeze that I couldn't feel, like a gently undulating sea of red.

As my gaze fell upon the centre of the room I drew in a sharp intake of breath at the sight of the brutal sacrifice of three men and three women on the smooth floor before me. They were naked. Their battered bodies were hacked and twisted, and their blood had pooled into small channels cut into the floor. These weren't the impossibly clean and clinical wounds I'd seen on those hollowed craniums back in the old hotel, these were savage and brutal, more force than finesse. Beyond this cruel carnage lay an altar of smooth black stone, flanked by two burning braziers set atop tall metal tripods.

"I had started to wonder if you were ever going to get here," a voice from the shadows announced, the tone jovial, as if greeting an old friend. A man stepped into sight from behind more of the hanging silk. He was tall and dressed in black. His sallow face seemed almost preternaturally pale against his dark clothing and his green eyes were the only point of colour about him. "I'm afraid the blood has entirely coagulated by now. It spoils something of the effect."

"And who are you?"

"I should probably ask that question of you. You're the one who broke in."

"Call the police then," I gestured at the room, "though you might have some explaining to do."

His smile deepened. "Shall we waste our time with word games, or worry about names? Although, I do know yours, Aaron Dredson, and I know who you work for. As for me, I'm just a priest, in a manner of speaking, nothing more."

"Fair enough, let's get to it. What do you want?"

"I have a better question for you—why do I want you here? Can you guess?"

He was far too chatty. The talking was just a distraction, and I knew it. He was playing for time, it was the only reason why he'd engage me like this. I tried to keep an eye on the shadows as much as on the priest. It was obvious he wasn't alone. My fingers itched to plant a bullet in his arrogant face, to wipe that smug smile off his lips permanently. But I needed answers, and he didn't seem to know about Colby yet, so I was hoping I still had an ace up my sleeve.

"Yeah, I'd heard I was expected. It's nice to be wanted. But what I'd like to know is why you're hunting down other cults?"

"The ones you were also hunting, you mean? I would say we solved your problem for you. You should be thanking us."

"Somehow, I doubt I'd like your motives."

The priest shrugged. "Nothing more than a simple business takeover."

I wondered how long it would be until that included The Lodge, if it didn't already.

"So, you're stealing brains now? What's the deal with that?"

He chuckled. "Our associates have use of them."

"And, where are they now?"

"They had business elsewhere, sadly. Though luckily, I did manage to persuade two of them to remain behind. I require their special skills tonight."

There was a soft rustle of movement from behind the silken curtains to my left as something pushed its way through from the shadows beyond; a twisted lobster-like thing, about five feet long, with a pinkish-grey crustaceous body and multiple articulated appendages. At the top of its body was a writhing clustered mass that I assumed to be a head, where moist feelers flexed as though sensing the air, producing a thick, insect-like vibration. Behind it, two large membranous wings carried the beast clumsily aloft, though it was clearly struggling with our gravity. In its armoured claws, it held a bizarre coil of strangely-greenish metal, which it pointed at me like a gun.

And so, the trap closes.

I wondered where the other one was.

"You know," the priest sighed, "your Lodge has no jurisdiction here, and no official standing in this city. You're nothing but a mob of vigilantes with more knowledge than is good for you, and not enough sense to use it wisely."

The creature had fully entered the room now, and its strange writhing head flickered dimly through a succession of pale colours.

"I'd put down your gun," the priest advised. "It will be easier for you that way."

"If you wanted me dead, I already would be," I replied.

"Frankly, you're not that important. But, your Lodge's reliquary holds many rare items that are of great interest to us. Oh, we could storm your building, tear it apart and slaughter everyone inside, but we'd risk losing the prizes we seek with such a clumsy approach. It's far easier to get inside your mind and uncover the gaps in your armour."

"I don't buy it, all this just to find a way past our defences?"

"Two birds, one stone, as the old saying goes. It's not all about you."

"And your associates, what exactly do they gain from all this?"

"You ask a lot of questions," the priest said. "But now we'll get some answers from you."

The alien monstrosity aimed the bizarre coil of metal and I felt the air about me thicken. I turned, trying to sprint for cover, but it was like trying to run through waist-high water.

The priest was coming around the altar now, one hand raised and twisting through a series of subtle gestures as he readied some kind of spell, his gaunt face splitting into a diabolical grin...

...that promptly slipped from his lips as Colby burst into the room and shot him. The bullet slammed into the priest's shoulder and sent him staggering backwards. He stumbled into one of the tall braziers, which collapsed with a dull crash, scattering glowing coals across the floor and setting several of the hanging silks alight. The priest screamed as the sleeve of his shirt burst into flame, and he writhed on the ground, trying to put it out.

The winged horror turned and directed its bizarre device at Colby now. He gasped as the thickening air dragged him to his knees, his arm trying to lift his gun and his lungs struggling to draw breath. The creature adjusted some kind of setting on the device, no doubt intensifying the effects.

So I aimed a bullet of my own and shattered it.

The device sparked and then exploded in a violent sparking spray that sent the winged monster tumbling backwards in a cloud of smoke, two of its long arm-like appendages hanging limp and twisted.

"Jesus!" Colby gasped as I helped him to his feet. "What was..."

There was an angry sound from overhead. I realised that the second creature was hidden high above the layers of silk festooning the space below the ceiling. It dropped swiftly, sharp claws shredding the thin fabric. I had time to shout out a warning to Colby, and then it descended like an angel of death, membranous wings spreading wide amid a rain of tattered red silk. It clutched a weapon that looked like a strange length of twisted yellow bone.

"Move!" I shouted, half-dragging Colby out of the room before this new threat could attack. Flames were already reaching greedily up the walls and licking at the ceiling as more of the drapes went up. Colby regained his strength and balance as we darted into a side hallway. We could hear a furious buzzing echoing through the air behind us, but we didn't dare stop or look around.

We raced towards the back of the building, intending to escape as we had entered; instead, bright lights blazed in through the windows where only the darkness of the back alley had been before. We heard the murmur of a chant on the night air, twisted syllables of some alien tongue, guttural and harsh, spoken as best as human vocal cords could manage. As we neared the window and chanced a sly glance outside we saw a sinister line of robed figures standing before the headlights of four parked cars. Then shots rang out, shattering the glass of the window as they narrowly missed us, and we ducked back out of sight, knowing there would be no escape that way.

We were trapped.

We were also being hunted. We could hear that insect-like drone echoing through the darkened rooms, but the acoustics made it impossible to judge where it was coming from. For all we knew, the priest was still out there too, gun ready to cripple or kill. To top it all off, the roar of the flames was getting louder, and dense smoke was rising through the building.

If we didn't find a way out soon, we were never leaving.

"This way!" I urged, finding a staircase leading upwards. I only hoped that if we could access the roof, we might get across to the neighbouring buildings.

"Those things fly, you know!" Colby cautioned.

"But the cultists don't," I reminded him. "Got any better ideas?"

He said nothing, his lips pressed in a thin grim line.

We reached the next landing and carried on up, our ears alert for the sounds of pursuit from below us. By the time we reached the next floor, the first coils of smoke were already waiting for us, and I glanced around in alarm, spotting the vent on the wall that had allowed it to travel up so rapidly.

There was also a clawing, scraping sound coming from inside it.

We barely had time to dart for cover before the vent cover flew off and one of the winged horrors scrabbled out. Once free of the vent, it stood upon its hindmost 'legs', the feelers that clustered around that strange globular head twitched with a clicking hum. It was the injured one, I realised right away. It had somehow discarded its two damaged limbs, and I wondered if new ones would eventually grow in their place.

Colby flashed me an anxious glance from his hiding place. The entity was between us and the staircase up to the roof level, and the smoke was getting thicker. We could feel the searing heat rising with it.

I reached for my gun, wondering how much use it would be, unsure if bullets would even affect it at all, when I saw Colby pull out something small and shiny from his jacket pocket. It took me a second to realise it was his lucky amulet. He gave it a quick kiss, and then hurled it over the top of the creature and down the hallway. I saw it pinwheel through the air before clattering against the wall and floor.

We braced ourselves to run, but the creature was smarter than that. Instead of taking the bait, it whirled around and went straight for Colby's hiding place, as if figuring out where it had been thrown from. Colby gave a strange choked cry as it sprang at him, a cry that turned into a scream as one of those thick armoured claws clamped around his hand, bone splintering and flesh tearing.

As he collapsed back against the wall, the creature barrelled into him, claws tearing at his upper body and reaching for his throat.

Without thinking, I stepped out and pressed my gun against the side of its head near the top of the neck. It looked fleshiest there, the least protected by the exoskeleton.

When I pulled the trigger, a spray of grey-pink matter exploded across the wall, and the entity dropped heavily to the floor, limbs twitching and feelers writhing. It made no other sound.

I don't know if it was dead or merely stunned, but we weren't waiting to find out.

Colby staggered past it, his face pale with pain. His mangled hand had lost at least two fingers, and I tore a strip from my jacket and quickly bound it around to staunch the bleeding.

"We have to go," I said. "The other one will be coming."

We hurried up onto the roof, the fresh night breeze a welcome relief. Below us, smoke was streaming from the windows as flames danced wildly on the first three floors. The sound of sirens was drawing closer upon the air, both fire engines and police, likely summoned by the exchange of gunfire. We crept to the edge and risked a glance, only to see the cultists in the alleyway were dispersing ahead of those incoming sirens, like roaches scuttling back into the shadows once more.

That was when the bullet slammed into my shoulder.

I cried out as I dropped to my knees.

"You think you've escaped?" the priest shouted as he marched across the rooftop, his shirt torn and soaked with blood. "You think you have anywhere left to run?"

I turned my head, waiting for the next bullet. Beside me, Colby was frozen with his good hand reaching for his own gun.

"One of you is coming with us," the priest assured us.

Behind him I saw something dark against the blackness of the night, swooping low over the rooftop. Colby spotted it too; I heard his breath catch in his throat.

It was the second creature, no doubt, come to extract our brains so they could dissect our secrets at leisure and learn all that we knew to bring down the Lodge.

In that instant, trapped between action and inaction, with a gun pointing at us and an unknown fate sweeping towards us on alien wings, Colby and I both reached the same unspoken conclusion.

We chose to go out fighting.

As one we drew our guns, but we never got the chance to fire.

The swooping shadow hadn't come for us after all. It seized the priest from behind and dragged him up into the air, kicking and screaming. His gun dropped uselessly as his arms flailed and beat at his attacker.

We watched as it carried him up into the night, wings flapping clumsily, until they were lost from sight amid the blackness of the pre-dawn sky where stars blazed like the crazed eyes of wrathful gods.

It seemed the alliance was broken. Such things were often fickle at best, fraught with conflict and unspoken tension–or perhaps, that final act of betrayal was on the whim of the greater power they both served, displeased at the priest's failures and at the loss of the club, a lucrative source of sacrifice. In the end, who could say? I wasn't going to waste too much time worrying about it.

We made our way over to the next roof, and then the one beyond that, just for good measure.

The dream was over. The Celephais Club was doomed, lost to smoke and flames. It would claim no more victims. But, the cult was still out there, growing in the shadows and spreading its tangled roots through the fertile ground of the city.

Next time, I feared they would be far more direct in their attack against us, and there would be a next time, sure as day follows night.

I helped Colby across onto the next building, his mangled hand little more than a bloody claw clutched tightly against his chest.

We collapsed onto the damp rooftop watching the club burn, a pyrrhic victory hanging over us and the taste of ashes in our mouths.

The Lodge would survive for another day, but the Brotherhood of Whispers had found a voice in our city, and it would not be easily silenced.

"Let's get to the hospital," I told him.

Colby looked at me; his blood-flecked face seemed to have aged ten years overnight. "Was it worth it?"

I stared at the burning building just as the first of the fire engines pulled up, and sighed. "At least now we know they're coming."

"Can we do anything about that?"

I left the question hanging unanswered as I searched my jacket for my cigarettes. Instead, I found only the torn pocket where they used to be.

"Come on," he said, offering me what passed for a smile under the circumstances. "Let's get out of here."

The flames still danced as the sky began to turn a golden red.

Another day was dawning, and we were both still standing.

But the shadows in the city were growing too.

Simon Bleaken lives in Wiltshire, England. His work has appeared in magazines, ezines and podcasts including Lovecraft's Disciples; Dark Dossier, Tales of the Talisman; Lovecraftiana; The Horror Zine; Schlock! Webzine; Night Land (Japan), Weird Fiction Quarterly, and on The NoSleep Podcast. He has also appeared in the anthologies: Eldritch Horrors: Dark Tales (2008); Space Horrors: Full-throttle Space Tales #4 (2010); Eldritch Embraces: Putting the Love Back in Lovecraft (2016); Kepler's Cowboys (2017) Best Gay Romance 2015 (2015), Twilight Madhouse vol. 2 (2017) and HellBound Books' Anthology of Science Fiction Vol.1 (2023). His first collection of short stories: A Touch of Silence & Other Tales was released in 2017, followed by The Basement of Dreams & Other Tales in 2019 and Within the Flames & Other Stories in 2019.

By day he works for the NHS but divides his free time (when he should be writing) between reading, combating a severe case of Skyrim addiction and even the odd spot of ghost hunting. He is also a full-time slave to two cats.

Aaron Dredson is an original creation for this anthology, and this is his debut tale. However, the author thinks that he and the Lodge have a few more stories in them, and has some ideas for a follow-up...

THE IDOL OF DAGON
STEPHEN HERCZEG

I remember it well. It was a hot August night. One of those nights when the still air seems to suck the moisture from your skin, and the life from your bones. London had almost succumbed to the heat. Tempers were already frayed as tensions still ran across the continent, but as the temperatures remained high, anger built within the populace of our fair country.

Sitting in my study, I pored over several volumes of arcane lore, the likes of which the average man's mind would shrivel to a prune if he had access to the information they contained. Sketches and diagrams of otherworldly horrors stared back at me from the pages. Their names; written in unintelligible scripts and unpronounceable from our mouths.

As I read, my old bones felt as though there were rumblings in the ether. My mind was only too aware, and several messages from close sources indicated that the followers of the elder gods were assembling their might on Earth. Something was coming. Something that would change the face of our planet, and the destiny of mankind. For the people of the world, barely a year had passed since the greatest and bloodiest conflict that humans had ever known, but now many years later, I realised that there was an even greater threat to come that if unopposed could have removed our species completely.

My study of those arcane texts was interrupted by a cry from my study door.

"Good Lord, Iff, what are you playing at?"

I turned to see my long-time friend, Miles Sistenka, standing in the doorway. It took me a moment to realise why there was a look of abject horror upon his countenance. A small grin crossed my face as I finally discerned the cause for his shock.

Knowing full well that I would be alone and, hopefully, undisturbed, I had taken it upon myself to strip down to my underwear. My feet sat in a pail of cool water, and the window was wide open with the curtains drawn back, begging for any hint of breeze to waft its way into my room.

"Apologies, Miles, it's this detestable heat. I did not expect to be disturbed." Creasing my brow, I added, "In fact, I thought I had given Wilkins direct orders to that effect."

"Ah, sorry about that, yes, your man did mention your wishes, but this is important."

Sighing, I slowly closed the thick leather-bound tome, careful to ensure the thin vellum pages did not crease and wincing every time the ancient leather cracked and threatened to split further. Once the book was closed and the horrid face that stared up at me was at rest, I turned towards Miles.

"Where in the world did you retrieve a copy of the Necronomicon from?" he asked, standing by my right shoulder.

Staring down at the ancient and evil tome, I took in the features of the tortured face, peeled from its original owner and tanned to form the front cover of the text, and said, "I have my ways, old friend. This book has taken me years to find and its cost was immeasurable, for one does not simply purchase its like. A portion of my being was transferred as part of the exchange."

"But why?"

Turning towards Miles, I answered, "Something is coming. We may have recently endured the horrors of war, but there is worse to come. I can feel it." I placed my hand on the book. "There are secrets in here that call out to the void. I am simply trying to translate and comprehend them."

"Then it is good that I came by. I have a puzzle for you that smacks of a similar vein."

Miles had a car waiting outside, and once I'd dried off, and changed into something a little more respectable, we were away. We both remained silent as Miles's driver wound his way through the busy London thoroughfares. I'll admit that the car itself bobbed around almost as frantically as a horse-drawn hansom cab but at a far increased rate. By the time we reached Kensington, my stomach churned as if I had endured a rough ocean crossing.

Stepping from the horseless carriage, I said, "I'll never get used to these automobiles. Far too rapid and jarring."

"Yes, but modern times require modern conveniences. That trip would have taken almost an hour before the war, and we are here within twenty minutes. I know you are busy, so count that as time recovered."

I wasn't convinced and turned towards the three-storey terraced house. Miles's friend was obviously well-heeled.

"You haven't mentioned whom we are seeing?"

"No, I wished to keep that knowledge between us. I respect and trust my driver, but there are some things I don't wish for him to know." Allowing me to ascend the short flight of steps to the front door, he added, "This is the house of Sir Edgar Aliste-Socard."

I stopped mid-flight. I'd heard that name before. Searching my memories, I asked, "Socialite? Businessman?"

"Yes, that and more."

Tracing the trails and threads of my internal remembrances I found the details I sought. "Historian. Specialises in arcane and esoteric religions and their presence in the modern day."

A broad smile broke out on Miles's face. "Well done, my friend. Given the volume you were entranced by earlier, I believe you and Sir. Edgar will be well acquainted before long." His expression became dour. "That is if we can find him."

Before I could ask further, Miles stepped up to the door and rattled the large brass knocker several times. After a few moments, an ancient corpse-like man answered. "Ah, Chance, my good man, I've brought a friend to assist with our little problem."

The old butler stepped back, allowing us to enter. "Right, you are Sir."

Miles strode inside without another word as if he was well acquainted with its layout and had visited many times in the past. I followed through the labyrinth, descending with him into the basement. I was intrigued, in most houses such as this, the downstairs area was reserved for the servants and sundry household tasks such as laundering clothes and preparation of meals. Within a moment we stopped before a solid wooden door. It was painted in several layers of black paint, but the most striking feature was the large carving that stretched across the top half of the door.

"This is Sir Edgar's study. He has been missing for the last two days, but Chance here, and the rest of the household are sure he hasn't left the premises in all that time. I am afraid that he is inside and quite unwell, or …" Miles's voice trailed off, but I understood his intent.

Staring at the design, I said, "This is a unicursal hexagram. This form is a one-way binding spell. Why would anyone purposely carve one into their door? It can only be used once and will keep anyone from entering until reversed." Miles brought a lit candelabra towards the door. The extra light revealed more to my aging eyes. "Ah, now I see."

I soon realised that the carving had not been created for decorative purposes. It was much cruder than I at first thought. Running my fingers along the multiple crisscrossing lines, I noticed that the carving dug deep in places, but then almost disappeared in others. Whoever had created the design had done so in a rush. The lines themselves were slightly wavering and not as dead-straight as an artist would have created.

"You know what it is then? You know how to reverse it?"

"Of course. As I said it's a simple binding sigil. Thelematic. I didn't even realise they were still around. I lost contact with Crowley and his Thelema crowd many years ago. As I learnt more about them, I found their intentions a little abhorrent and their magic lacking in any true power."

"Well, this has stumped me." He pointed at the key poking out of the large brass lock. "The door will not open, but it isn't locked."

I tried the handle, and then the key. Both turned easily. Pulling on the door resulted in nothing. The door, even without any mechanical locks in play, would not budge.

Shrugging, I said, "Magical then." I stepped back for a moment, as something occurred to me. "I'd seen this before. A door. Magically locked by a hexagram sigil." I smiled. I may be getting old, but when coincidences from my youth replay in my mind, I do find it amusing.

"As I said, simple magic."

Pulling a small pouch from inside my coat pocket, I stepped over to a nearby side table and unrolled it, revealing several tools used for lock picking, and other more nefarious acts. Retrieving a metal scribe, I returned to the door, running my fingers down several of the lines of the design, until I found one point of convergence. Using the scribe I added a few deep lines of my own to the design. Once finished, I stepped away and muttered a small chant under my breath as I rolled up my lock picks. When finished, I said, "You should be able to open the door now."

I heard the creak of the door followed by a gasp from Miles and a rush of feet. Turning back I saw, through the doorway, Miles hunkered down over a shape on the floor. Following in his wake, I found him attempting to rouse a prostrate figure. I could only assume that this was Sir. Edgar, but had no other information to go by.

From Miles's desperation, I realised that the man was still alive. If he had been dead, my friend would have been more devastated and had moved away. It was as I observed Miles's ministrations to the unconscious man, that I noticed the lines carved into the wooden floor.

Another hexagram.

"Miles," I said, moving towards my friend and placing a hand on his shoulder. "Please move away. If you disturb or move him, there could be dire consequences." My friend did as requested.

"What is this about?" he asked, a confused look on his face.

I simply pointed at the lines. "It's another unicursal hexagram."

"A binding spell? Like the one on the door?"

"Similar." My extended finger pointed to the circular line running between the points of the hexagram. "This one is a containment spell. It should be etched into the surface before placing a person or object inside. The essence of which is intrinsically linked to the design. If you try to remove the body, then its life force will remain even though its substance has been moved. Essentially, you would kill Sir. Edgar."

"Good Lord. Can you dispel it?"

A slight grin came to my face. "Of course, old man, of course. A simple matter."

Once more, my tools were whipped from my pocket. I used the scribe to carve lines across the circle, effectively breaking its path and nullifying the spirit-binding spell.

A simple trick. Replacing my tools, I helped Miles sit Sir Edgar in a padded chair located on one side of the room. Chance appeared at the doorway with some water and a cloth. While Miles administered a cool compress to Sir Edgar's forehead, and brought him back to wakefulness, I scanned the room.

Within seconds I found myself impressed to the point of fascination. Sir. Edgar was indeed a fellow student of the arcane. The small room was a study of sorts. A desk and chair sat in one corner. The other padded chair, he now occupied, appeared to be a reading chair as it sat beneath a light. One entire wall was taken up with bookshelves and display cases, the contents of which had snatched my fascination.

Idols and statues adorned the display areas, with volumes of thick, leather-bound books taking up the shelf space. The idols were of a rough and ancient style, some may call them brutal in their portrayal of ancient deities virtually unknown to modern man. I was impressed. Sir Edgar had curated an intriguing collection. I noted Innana from ancient Mesopotamia, Chinnamasta from the Nepalese arm of the Hindu religion, Sheela Na Gigs from our own British Isles, and even a depiction of Huitzilopochtli from the Aztecs. As I moved along the shelves, I noticed a space between two of the statues. A clean area sat amongst the fine layer of dust, suggesting that something had recently been removed. Glancing at Sir Edgar's desk, I found the surface devoid of any idols or statues.

Turning back, I became intrigued by the collection of arcane volumes. The spines depicted a myriad of languages and scripts. A part of me wished for them to join my own collection, they would complement my own studies suitably. My musings were broken by a frail voice from behind me.

"Ah, you are a student of the arcane as well?"

I found that Miles had roused Sir Edgar from his slumber. His sharp eyes viewed me from within the folds of skin that adorned his face. Lying on the floor, I hadn't taken in how large a man he was, now that he sat upright, the flesh had reformed into its regular appearance. This was a man taken to a very sedentary lifestyle, possibly one that rarely left the desk in this very study.

Stepping towards the man, I held out my hand, "Yes, Sir Edgar, Simon Iff. I am pleased that you have recovered from your expedition into the unknown."

His face grew slightly confused. "You have me at a loss, Sir, what expedition would that be?"

"You were placed under a binding curse. I have heard tales that the mind experiences a strange disassociation with this plane during such a state."

"Now that you mention it, yes. I had the strangest of dreams. It was as if I was in a perpetual state of peril, while unseen terrors lurked just on the periphery of my perception. A most agitated state of mind."

"Do you have any idea who may have cursed you?"

Shaking his head, he answered, "No. I was alone in here, as I often am. I didn't even hear the door open. It creaks you know, so I can generally hear it. The next thing I know I'm in that horrible nightmare world until I awoke here and observed you and Miles."

I stepped across to the hexagram and pointed. "Do

you know what this is?"

Sir Edgar shifted and stared in the direction of my finger. He remained quiet for a while, mulling over the design before speaking. "No. I can't actually say I do. I mean, I have seen such designs as part of that strange religion that flowed through England many years ago, but I think that they exhibited a rose or flower of some sort in the centre, and there was no circle. This is vastly different."

With one last glance at the hexagram, I nodded and stepped across to Sir Edgar's desk. Looking down, I noticed the open book for the first time. Staring at the strange diagrams and hieroglyphs I realised it was the Grolier Codex, an ancient collection of writings gathered together from the Mayan civilisation. An intriguingly interesting book, but not worthy of the act perpetrated on Sir Edgar.

Looking back at the shelves, a thought occurred to me. Stepping across, I pointed at the empty space. "Sir Edgar, if I may ask, this is a fascinating collection. This gap on the shelf, has something recently been removed? For study or restoration perhaps?"

The large man's eyes followed me and grew wide as they spied the missing piece. "My word, no," he gasped, attempting to rise, but was held down by Miles.

"You're still a little weak, Edgar, calm yourself."

"But, but the idol. It's gone."

"What idol?"

"Dagon. The idol of Dagon."

"Dagon?" My mind raced. Memories exploded across my inner eyes. "Ancient Sumerian god of the seas. Also appears in other religions, most notably, the Cthulhu Mythos. An Earth-based elder god of immense power, especially within his watery home."

Sir Edgar's gaze drew up towards my face. "My word, Sir, you are well versed." Staring back at the shelf, he added, "But that idol. It is a one-of-a-kind rarity." Pointing at the bookshelves, he added, "There is a passage in the Grimoire de Nyarlathotep, that states Dagon can be summoned if one recites a certain incantation, using the idol to cast the waters into a roiling tumult. How I don't know."

Glancing at the shelf, Sir Edgar indicated, I noticed a series of volumes, all bound in similar leather, and annotated with the same spidery script style. The fine layer of dust indicated that all had sat on the shelves undisturbed for some time, except one. A slight sense of fear gripped my chest as I reached for the one volume, the dust before it had been moved as if the book had been pulled from the shelf, and then returned.

Pulling it out, I immediately realised it was the same grimoire that Sir. Edgar had spoken of. Moving to the desk, I placed it down and gently opened the ancient leather cover, carefully leafing through the aged pages. The sketches and lines of text neatly replicated the same style as that which I'd been reading only an hour or so earlier. The authors of the Necronomicon and this Grimoire were either the same or from the same school.

And then I found the disparity. My slight gasp alerted Sir Edgar and Miles. "What's wrong, Iff?" my friend asked.

Running my finger along the tattered edges of several

adjacent pages, now missing, I replied, "There are two, no three pages torn from this volume."

A loud sudden creaking and expiration of breath accompanied Sir. Edgar rising from the padded chair. His bulk joined me at the desk, accidentally nudging me aside as he pressed forward. I spied a look of terror on his face as he stared at the book.

"Oh, Lord, the incantations are missing."

"Who has left this house in the last two days?" The question blasted the old butler Chance, momentarily causing him to lose all understanding and blubber an incoherent answer. I felt the need to intervene. From what I had detected already, Chance's age had wearied his faculties some, to the point that I wasn't sure he understood half of what was going on around him.

"Miles, if you please," I said, placing a hand on my friend's shoulder and gently pulling him aside.

We had moved into the parlour upstairs, a more comfortable room by far than the study, but Miles's temper had increased as we realised further that everything revolved around Sir Edgar's confinement and the theft of the idol and incantation pages. As our host settled himself in a comfortable chair in the corner, Miles left the room, returning momentarily with a slightly distraught and very confused butler.

Chance was forcibly moved into a seat and set upon by Miles's questions. A tactic that only proved, to me, that the butler had no idea about the circumstances behind it all.

Taking over the questioning, I pulled a chair up and sat before the perplexed servant. "Chance," I said, staring into the older man's eyes, "You know the inner workings of this house more than anyone." The butler nodded but remained silent. "Have there been any visitors, other than me and Miles, in the last two days?"

Shaking his head, Chance added, "No. No deliveries either."

"Have any of the residents left the premises in the last two days?"

"I…uh…I don't think so." His voice hung on the last syllable for a moment before growing silent. His eyes were wide in fear, they flicked from my face to Miles's across to Sir. Edgar reclining in a chair in the far corner. I wasn't sure if it was due to our presence or some unspoken threat from another. "I just don't remember." He dropped his head into his hands. "It's happening more often."

"It's all right, Chance. We only wish to determine what happened to Sir. Edgar. I don't believe it was someone from this family, I only wish to establish whether another party was involved."

The butler's old, watery eyes tracked back to stare into mine once more. I wanted to try another technique and waited a moment. Holding up a single finger, I asked Chance to stare at it for a moment. Slowly I shifted it from side to side, tracking the movement of the old butler's eyes, and the subsequent motion of his head. Then I placed my chin on my steepled fingers and stared directly into his gaze.

"Did the cook, Mrs Weston, isn't it?" He nodded slightly. "Did she leave to perhaps fetch groceries?"

Chance's face remained unmoved. "I don't think so."

"Did Lady Catrina leave?"

No movement in those irises, only a slight shake of the head.

I tried the name of Sir Edgar's son. "Was it Maxwell?" Again nothing.

Once more, I waited a moment before using the final name. "Did Ardella step out for a while?" And there it was.

At the same time that Chance said, "No", I saw a widening of the eyes, a rise of the eyebrows, a quick dart of the pupils towards Sir. Edgar, before returning to gaze at me.

I smiled. The old man wasn't lying, his deep conscience knew that someone had left, but his higher memory had lost track. "Thank you, Chance, you may go."

Confused, the aged butler rose and after checking on Sir Edgar's well-being shuffled off into the bowels of the house.

"What was all that about, Iff?" asked Miles.

"We need to talk with Miss Ardella."

"Ardella dear, can we have a moment?" Sir Edgar's *knocking* and verbal requests were met with the *scraping* of a wooden chair and the sound of heavy footsteps across the floor. The knob rotated and the door creaked open, revealing a formidable figure behind it. Ardella Aliste-Socard shared her father's physical stature, but the dour look on her face gave her a slightly fiercer aspect.

"Father." Came her curt reply. "What is this about?"

"You may not have noticed," Sir Edgar said, "But I have been missing for the last two days. Your dear mother put out a request, and these gentlemen found me unconscious in my study. Under some sort of spell. We just wish to find out if you know anything about my predicament."

"Why would I know?" The tone of Ardella's response grew even more glacial. "I have been in my room for the best part of the last two days. Ask Chance, he has delivered my meals here."

"Yes. We have discussed this with Chance. He barely remembers who is where at the best of times. We won't take up too much of your time, dear, but if you could please chat with Mr Iff and Mr Sistenka here, I would be most appreciative. It seems some items were also taken from my study, so with their help, I wish to investigate all lines of inquiry."

Her eyes narrowed as they moved from my face to Miles's, but eventually, with a shrug and a sigh, she backed away and allowed us to enter.

Introducing myself, I asked Ardella to sit in a comfortable armchair, whilst I took a small stool before her. My initial line of questioning was to gauge her reactions and mindset.

"Miss Ardella, I understand you haven't left this house for two days, is that correct?"

She snapped back. "I just told you that. So, yes."

"Do you know if anyone other than your immediate family has come to the house of late?"

"No. None that I know of."

"What about Mr Hermanes?" Sir Edgar piped up from behind me.

Ardella's eyes grew wide then narrowed; her lip slightly curled in anger. "Oh, yes, sorry. My suitor, Georgio Hermanes, came to the house recently. But not for some days. If father says he was unconscious for two days, though I'm struggling to believe that, then Georgio had nothing to do with it."

"He didn't attend to you over the last two days?"

Anger brimmed on her face again. "I've told you. Is this some sort of interrogation? Am I under suspicion of something?"

I held up my hands in supplication. "No, nothing like that. I'm simply establishing any events or visitations that have occurred recently. If you have not left or know of no one that has visited, then I am satisfied with that." I halted for a moment, hoping that my statement would satisfy her. After a while, her face relaxed, and her gaze settled once more on mine. "Good. Now, this may be a strange question. Do you know what a unicursal hexagram is?" I smiled. Her face remained passive, but as she shook her head, her eyes darted up to one side. An indication that her conscious mind didn't have any knowledge, but something deep within did.

When I remained silent for a while, she asked, "Are we finished?"

"Almost." I reached into my jacket pocket and pulled out a tear-drop-shaped crystal that hung from a small silver chain. Letting the crystal drop from my palm to the length of the chain, it snatched her attention. As the crystal spun, I asked, "Have you ever seen one of these before?"

Her eyes remained fixed on the spinning crystal. Her speech sounded slurred as she spoke. "Pretty."

"It is, isn't it? Look deeper. The light almost glows from within." She repeated the affectation, drawing out the word as her mind became fixated on the light glowing through the crystal. I relaxed my voice, delivering a soft, soporific monotone. "It's almost as if there is a world within the light. A world that we would all love to visit. Why don't you visit that world? It is deep within you. It is within us all."

"Yes."

Ardella's eyes grew wider for a moment as they relaxed. "Close your eyes. Visit that world within. Seek out its wonders." Her lids grew heavy and closed, her head dropping slightly to her chest, and her breathing became slow and deep. "Good. Good. Now, Ardella, in that world you will know things. Things that you cannot normally see."

"Yes."

"Do you see yourself over the last two days?"

"Yes."

"Where were you? Where did you go?"

"Outside." I heard Miles and Sir Edgar shift behind me. I held up a hand to bring silence.

"Where outside?"

"Georgio called for me. He took me to the nearby park. We sat beneath the trees in the shade. He was ever so nice to me. He's always nice to me."

"What did you talk about?"

"He told me he wished to take me away from all this. He wanted to marry me. To make me his wife. I only had to do one small thing for him."

"And what was that?"

"He said he needed Daddy's idol. The crystal one. And some pages from one of Daddy's books."

"Did he ask you to harm your father?"

Her face became concerned. "Oh, my no. He told me how to help Daddy sleep until Georgio came back and released him. Daddy wasn't to be harmed, goodness no."

"Do you know why Georgio needed the idol?"

"Yes. He was going to our future home. He wanted it to decorate the main hall. I must admit, I didn't think it was that attractive, but Georgio has strange tastes."

"Where is this home? Your future home?"

"Geg Tafarndal. I'm not altogether sure where it is, but I know I'll be happy there. I'll have Georgio with me."

As I looked around at Miles and Sir. Edgar, I shrugged. I had never heard of the place. Miles was likewise blank-faced, but Sir Edgar nodded.

Feeling that I had all that I needed from Ardella, I spun the crystal once more. "Ardella. Come away from the light. Come back to us. Come back to the world."

Her eyelids flickered several times until her eyebrows creased up and she stared around at the three of us. "What have you been doing? What is that crystal for?"

Whipping the crystal and chain away, I quickly secreted it in my pocket. "Nothing at all. I simply thought you may find it charming; it has been in my family for generations." Her face showed disbelief at my statements.

"What do you want with me?"

"You were telling us about your last two days in the house. But, I still have a couple of questions. Do you know what a unicursal hexagram is?"

Her mouth curled up into a grimace. "A what? I'm sorry but mathematics has never been my strong suit. I detest the manipulation of numbers and shapes. Quite beneath me."

Suppressing a smile, I then asked. "What about Thelema?"

"Is that another shape or something? I have no idea what you are talking about. Father? Why do you have these men bothering me?"

"Iff?" asked Sir Edgar. "Do you have all you need?"

"I believe I do, thank you, Sir Edgar," I said over my shoulder. Turning back to Ardella, I bowed slightly in my chair before rising. "Thank you, Miss Ardella, you have been most helpful."

Behind my back, the last thing I heard from the young woman before I left the room was, "But, I didn't say anything."

"I don't think I've ever seen Sir Edgar that incensed before. He looked fit to burst when you explained that Ardella has been hypnotised by her suitor and coerced into subduing him and stealing the idol and incantation."

"Yes, I was a little afraid that he would have a seizure or something."

"Still, he made a very generous offer to you to retrieve them back."

I nodded. "Though the money is nothing of concern compared to what may unfold if we don't stop the ritual."

Miles took a deep breath. The events of the previous day had obviously affected him as well. "This Hermanes fellow? You know him?"

"Yes, Miles," I answered, my voice almost drowned out at the train's whistle let out a raucous howl as we moved out of Paddington station. Miles had booked a first-class berth for us. With the doors closed we were siloed from the rest of the passengers, but not completely from the noises outside. "I knew him years ago as an acolyte of Thelema. He was one of Crowley's most diligent students. Once I left, I no longer had contact with him, but he obviously kept up his studies, and seems to have expanded them."

"Poor Ardella. She'll be heartbroken, won't she?"

I shook my head. "Yes. Yes, I think she will. I believe she has been an unwitting pawn in his detestable little game to gain ownership of the idol of Dagon and the pages containing the incantation. Once she understands she'll recover quickly."

"What's it all about? Why are we headed to this Geg Tafarndal? I've never even heard of the place."

"I don't know much of it either, but revisiting Sir Edgar's books on the Cthulhu cult, there was a small note that mentioned Dagon and a town called Innsmouth in Massachusetts. Again I have no idea of the place, but the hand-drawn map in the back of the book indicated it was a very isolated place, possibly with an insular population and dependent highly on fishing for its livelihood." Drawing a small book from my valise, I opened it to a pre-marked page. It showed the coastline of south-eastern Wales. I had marked a ring around Geg Tafarndal. "This is pretty much the same. Isolated. Coastal. Probably in a rich area for fish. If you were to attempt to contact and raise an elder god from the sea, then it would be a pretty good place to try."

Miles visibly shivered. "I've never encountered anything of this like before in my life."

A small grin sprung to my face. "Sadly, I can't say the same."

To answer my enigmatic response and pass the time, I related the tale of one of my journeys abroad in my early thirties. Whilst travelling through Cairo I encountered a strange little man that dealt in ancient curios and oddities. At the time, I was more interested in arcane books of lore, rather than trinkets. It was the early days of my lifelong search for a copy of the Necronomicon, but none were to be found, such was their rarity.

The old man's brow creased upon hearing of my quest. He mentioned that he had once possessed a necklace that made the wearer invulnerable to death. I scoffed at his claim until he named it. *The Rondure of Cthulhu*. It was the stuff of legend. Too many, simply a mere trinket with an outlandish design, it pictured the great god, Cthulhu, on its front. To those that knew of its purpose, it was both a boon and a curse. Those that wore it were indeed protected by invisible forces that would see off any assailant, but if the possessor were to ever remove the pendant, then those same forces would turn on them. Death was immediate.

I journeyed to the home of Muhammad Kalfic, the current owner of the Rondure. From conversations with some other locals, it became clear that Kalfic was a rogue and scoundrel. He used the power of the necklace to build a criminal organisation across all of Egypt. But, with that dominion came enemies, many of whom had succumbed to the capabilities of the rondure.

My interest was simple. A man that knew of the rondure would surely know of, or at least be able to guide me in the direction of where I could obtain a copy of the Necronomicon.

I found Kalfic to be quite genuine and affable, not what I had expected from the gossip of the streets. He wore the rondure proudly and I found its simplicity alluring, but the depiction of the elder god was almost terrifying in its detail.

After some brief formalities, I got straight down to my business. Kalfic said he didn't possess a copy of the book I was after but would give me details of a man who did, but not before we dined so that he could convince himself that I was genuine, and I supposed, glean any further knowledge about other artefacts that I'd encountered in my journeys.

The meal was a simple affair, which suited my tastes quite well. I had expected some lavish display of Middle Eastern exotica, but Kalfic had ordered an array of food aimed at my English sensitivities, possibly to ensure I was not distracted while we talked.

As a way of compensating for his generosity and seeking favour so that he would give me the name I sought, I regaled him with stories from my adventures. I admit that I did embellish much to make my stories sound more exciting than they were. My host smiled broadly as I spoke, mentally storing any significant details of places I'd visited and the mysteries I'd seen. It would be up to him to digest whether the names I sprinkled into the conversation, of deities from the pantheon of ancient gods mixed with place names would come to anything if closely scrutinised. Truth be told, nothing I mentioned was an out-and-out lie, but any serious study of our conversation could quickly unravel the slight fabrications sewn into my tales. I banked on Kalfic merely accepting and storing any facts and examining them in detail once I had departed.

As I reached the end of another tale, involving a recent trip through the French countryside, our revelry was disturbed by shouts from outside the room. Kalfic stood, moving towards the door, but stopped short when three men, dressed in black robes, burst into the room. Each had a rifle and levelled them at my host. Seeking safety, I dropped to the floor and crawled towards the wall farthest from the pending conflict. I was too shocked at the intrusion to contemplate any heroics, but as events unfolded, I held no thoughts of blaming myself for cowardice.

One man stepped forward, levelling a pointed finger at Kalfic and shouting in a strange guttural language. I realised it was about the amulet, as my host's eyes dropped towards the pendant, before staring back at his accuser. A slight grin came to his face, which seemed to urge the robed man into action. He quickly brought up his rifle and aimed at Kalfic.

In my memories, all time seemed to slow down, the way it does during a crisis.

The rifle bucked as it fired. The man to Kalfic's right joined his leader. Each cocking the bolt and firing as quickly as they could.

To my incredulous eyes, the bullets stopped in mid-air, mere inches from Kalfic's smiling face. As each man readied their rifles for the next shot, the air turned into a blur as something unseen moved towards them at blinding speed. Flashes of motion were followed by sprays of blood as unseen blades slashed across their bodies, opening deep rents in their flesh and turning them from armed men into blood-soaked corpses within a matter of seconds.

In the tumult, the third man raised his rifle and fired, just as the unseen assailants reached him, the air turning into a hazy cloud of activity resulting in his disembowelment before my eyes. As he fell to the ground, I heard a cry of despair from Kalfic and turned my gaze towards him.

The stray bullet had found its mark, but instead of smacking into my host's flesh, it merely snapped the chain around his neck. His hands flapped in dismay, trying to find the rondure as it spilt from around his neck. I saw it drop to the tiled floor and roll away. The *tink* of metal on ceramic preceded the screams from its owner.

He stood staring in abject horror at some invisible fiend before him. I could see nothing physical, but my mind's eye filled with visions of the void between worlds. A void crammed with indescribable horrors. Of creatures that if viewed fully would tear at the very fabric of one's mind. I blinked the images away and stared back at my host.

All I could see was a cloud of red as the assailant turned their attention to Kalfic. I looked away as my former host's body was torn asunder. His lifeblood sprayed and misted into the air, bathing all around in crimson.

As silence fell, my curiosity urged me to turn back. There was nothing left that resembled the man I had met only hours earlier. I have seen things and believe in my strong constitution, but even I had to hold onto the meal I recently ingested and turned away once more to contain it.

I decided that discretion was the better part of valour. I had nothing to do with this episode, and would only be tied up for an indeterminate time if apprehended by the Cairo police.

As I stood and readied to leave, another figure appeared at the doorway. Like his compatriots, he was clad from head to toe in black robes, with only his dark pupilled eyes showing. He reached up and pulled the scarf from his mouth, revealing a dark-complexioned, but handsome face.

In extraordinarily good English, he spoke. "You are English? Yes? You have found yourself in the wrong place, my friend." The newcomer stepped across to where the rondure lay, and snatched it up, staring at the prize and then at the remains of Kalfic. Nodding in that direction he added, "This was never his. Only evil did it bring him. Now he has paid his dues. Nevermore will this foul thing be used in that way." Without another word, he spun and strode from the room.

I took that as my cue to exit.

Miles's face was a mask of concern. "My word, Iff, what a horrible story. You're lucky to be alive."

I smiled at that and nodded. "I am. I'd be the first to admit that. In that short sequence of events, I learnt more about the cult members and the hideous deities behind them than I had absorbed through all my years of studying texts and artefacts. Whatever those unseen assassins were, they were insignificant compared to their masters. And that's what scares me even more."

Reaching down, I picked the heavy bag up from the floor and handed it to Miles. "That is why I had you bring this. I'm far too old for any physical confrontation, but we may need to enact violence to stop what is coming."

Not long after the train arrived in Cardiff, we stepped out onto Penarth Road. The area was a veritable madhouse as passengers embarked and searched for cabs to take them onwards. I slowly worked my way along the line of cars, seeking a driver that was prepared to help us. After an exhausting interrogation of over a dozen of them, I chanced upon one that was up for the challenge.

Daffyd, he called himself. A young sprightly lad in his middle twenties. I proposed that he take us to the West coast of Wales, to the little town of Geg Tafarndal, and stay for up to three nights until we were ready to return. At first, he was talkative but wary until I suggested a price. My offer was met with a beaming grin, and when half was handed over, he began to treat us as gentry.

"I'm from Llanwnda, which is about twelve miles north of Geg. If we can't find anywhere to room, we can always head home. I'm sure my ma would put you up, and her fish pie is the best in the village," a garrulous Daffyd said.

"We may take you up on that offer, get us there first and we'll see."

As we bumped along the trail that formed the road west from Swansea, I could only imagine we were racing against time. Hermanes had a few days' start over us and would have been preparing for the ritual for quite some time. The previous night I had noticed the moon waxing into fullness. I didn't think such an event would be necessary for what the cultist had in mind, but any person driven by such a ritual would indeed favour such a coincidence.

Stopping in Haverfordwest for a brief luncheon and to plan our approach to the little village, I asked Daffyd as much as I could about it. He happily professed all his knowledge over the pickle sandwiches and watery beer that we found in a small public house.

"It's just a little village. They fish. That's about it." Taking a draw from his drink, he went silent for a moment as he remembered more about the place. "I haven't been for a while, but from what I can remember, the people are a little strange. They have a look about them that I haven't seen anywhere else. Large eyes. Small noses.

You could say they come from the fish themselves." Slapping his knee, he let out a raucous laugh. "It comes with the territory, I suppose. A lot of people would say friends from my village look like the sheep we herd. Though most look at me and think I look more like a bull." I smiled and had to admit the same to myself. Daffyd was a tall and powerfully built man. Probably be useful if there was any physical conflict.

Pressing on, we reached the tiny village by late afternoon.

Despite Daffyd's time away from the place, he was able to find the public house quickly. As we drove through the tiny village, we received stares from the residents who seemed to view the motor car as some sort of craft alien to their world. I realised it was possibly true. Vehicles of this sort had only become prevalent in the larger cities, but out here in the deeper country areas, they would appear only sporadically and be strange contraptions to the eyes of the locals.

With that thought in mind, I examined the faces that stared back at us. They did possess a strange quality, as our driver had mentioned. Their eyes were larger than normal, and their noses were less prominent. Despite their curiosity about our jalopy, they also appeared to be insular and solitary, withdrawing their gaze if looked upon and skulking into the shadows to avoid attention themselves.

Daffyd brought the car to a stop outside of the pub and led us inside. It was late afternoon, so there were few patrons in attendance, they sat in the darker corners of the pub. I noticed their faces turn and regard us for a moment before withdrawing once more.

The publican was a large man, with watery eyes and very little hair. Daffyd conversed with him in Welsh and procured three rooms for us. I handed over some money and picked up our keys. We needed information, such as a possible location for the ritual, or who in the town may be involved.

The pub was a prime possibility for that, but if no one spoke English, my talents may be useless. Daffyd may have to play a greater part in our efforts, but I was unsure how much I should divulge to him. As it was, he managed quite well, just because of his genuine nature.

We agreed to meet back in the bar an hour later. Regardless of our nocturnal endeavours, we needed to eat and drink.

Stepping into the main room, I was surprised that it was empty. Daffyd stood at the bar with a fresh pint of the local brew and was chatting amiably with the publican. A young girl hovered by the door leading through to the rear, where I assumed the food was prepared. Her large, doe-like eyes strained to move away from our tall, handsome driver. I could tell by his surreptitious glances that the feeling was mutual. I smiled; this could prove useful.

Moving to the bar, I joined the two Welshmen. Daffyd introduced me to the publican, who simply nodded in my direction and said, "Croeso."

"Beer?" Daffyd asked me. After I nodded, he held up two fingers, galvanising the barkeep into action.

"Where is everyone?" I pulled out my pocket watch to find it was well after six o'clock, a traditional time for people to begin flooding into local pubs after their evening meal.

"Don't know," said Daffyd. "I asked Owain here, and he simply mumbled something about a town meeting."

"A meeting? I don't suppose he mentioned why he and his daughter weren't at this meeting."

Shaking his head, Daffyd downed the last of his pint. "No. He didn't. Why do you wish to know?"

I leaned in closer and spoke only enough to be heard by him. "That's why we are here. We are afraid that something is going to happen. Something that will affect, not just this little town, but possibly the whole of Britain."

Daffyd's brow furrowed. "What exactly?"

"There is a man from London. He stole something from those I work for. Something that could prove deadly in the days to come."

"Sounds mysterious." A broad smile crossed his face. "And dangerous. What do you need from me, I'm up for a bit of fun."

Oh, to be young and brave again.

I couldn't help but smile at that comment, but something tugged at my thoughts. There was danger here and madness.

By the time Miles joined us, we had moved to one of the vacant tables. Myfanwy, the publican's comely daughter, came by and asked if we'd like anything to eat. She was bored and looking for some distraction but couldn't keep her eyes off of Daffyd. We placed an order for the simple fare on offer, and as she moved back to the kitchen, I prodded our driver and said, "If you'd like to assist, then that's your first task. Find out where and when the people of this town are meeting."

"Leave it to me." The young man gave me a wink before moving off towards the kitchen. I noticed the suspicious gaze of the publican staying with him as he sauntered across the floor.

Miles hadn't quite caught up on the conversation and was scanning the room, a confused look on his face. "There's nobody here. How are we going to find out about this supposed ritual? Do you need to do some of that crystal magic with the publican?"

"No, I've employed magic far older than anything I've ever learnt," I replied, a sly grin on my face. Sitting back, I drained the last of my beer, a nice brew that needed to have company. Eyeing the barkeep, I held up three fingers and pointed to the table. Over an almost permanent sneer, he nodded and retrieved three glasses.

By the time the beers arrived, Daffyd was back sitting with us, a wide, satisfied smile on his young face. When the publican had removed the empty mugs and was settled back behind his bar, I piped up. "Well? Any information?"

"Oh, yes, she's a very attractive young girl, even with those oversized eyes. We plan to meet later tonight."

"About the town meeting, I meant."

"Oh, that, yeah, they's all meeting out at Portmynawyd beach at about nine o'clock tonight. Some end-of-summer festival or something. I've never heard of it. She said something about the Dagonite. Myfanwy reckons that she and her da were told to stay and keep watch on us. I told her I'd be happy for her to keep watch on me." He chuckled to himself.

The Dagonite. Must be the name of the ritual?

"Do you know this beach?"

"Oh, ya, we can be there in about five minutes. It's not far. Though the trail may get a bit bumpy."

"Excellent."

The comely, Myfanwy, brought out three bowls of a thick fish soup, with bread. It was all that was on offer and would more than keep our hunger at bay. She couldn't keep her eyes off the tall lad, which served more of a purpose than I could ever have hoped.

As we neared the end of the meal, I checked my pocket watch. It was drawing towards eight-thirty. Time to move. I wanted to investigate this ritual and its acolytes for as long as possible.

"What's the plan, Iff?" Miles asked.

"Leave one at a time. I'll go last. Miles, go to your room and retrieve your bag. Daffyd, stop at the kitchen and confirm your meeting with Myfanwy. If she has that on her mind, she won't worry much about our whereabouts. I'll deal with the publican. We'll meet at the car in ten minutes."

"More hocus pocus, Iff?"

I nodded. "It works, Miles, that's all you need to know."

The other two moved away with a few minutes between, leaving me alone. I downed my beer, it had grown flat and warm whilst I saved it for just this purpose. Standing, I moved to the bar. "How much do we owe you, Sir?" The dour-faced man gave me a figure that I duly paid. As I reached back into my coat to replace my purse, I pulled out my trusty crystal and, holding my hand up, let it drop before the man's eyes. The transparent bauble caught the light and reflected it across the publican's face. "We plan to spend the entire night in our rooms. We won't be leaving at all and will be there in the morning. Do you understand?"

His eyes were fixed on the crystal, the pupils dilated and his entire expression of a dreamy quality. He spoke in a long, drawn-out drawl with a thick accent. "Yes. Sleep. Morning."

Snatching up the crystal, he snapped out of the trance and blinked several times, his gaze resting on my own. "Good. I will see you in the morning then Sir."

Daffyd was correct in his estimation. Within about ten minutes of assembling by the car, we were within sight of the Welsh coast. The pathway had other plans for us. We drove as close as we could, but only came up to a small area where several horse-drawn carts had been left, their animals complaining and nickering as much as our motorised one did.

Leaving the car, we trudged across the six hundred yards of open ground, studded with thick gorse and spindly grasses. The night was deathly still with just the slight roar of waves crashing against the limestone cliffs and beach to be heard. The sky was clear, with no moon to add light. The orange glow of open fires hovered above the secluded beach below the cliffs. Presuming it was the gathering, we headed for that area.

As we closed in, I became aware of the chanting. A low moan almost. A single word hung in the air. Repeated by dozens of voices. "Dagon. Dagon. Dagon."

We had found them.

Skirting to the south of the beach, we found ourselves on a cliff looking down on the sandy inlet. I was a little surprised and taken aback by the sight. Dozens of figures, wearing dark robes, stood in a semi-circle around a central figure, similarly dressed.

I could only guess it was Georgio Hermanes.

He stood at a wooden lectern, something that looked very out of place on the sandy beach. A small fire sat ablaze, between him and the shore. It cast orange light across the immediate area. And then my eyes focused on the weirdest object of all.

On what seemed to be a metal frame straddling the fire, the idol of Dagon sat. The flames beneath flickered up towards the statue, setting it aglow in a cascading radiance of colours. From yellow to orange to red. The concentrated and refracted light flickered out from the idol illuminating the immediate area.

Miles opened his mouth to ask a question, but I put a finger to his lips. Hermanes's voice had grown louder. I crawled forward in an attempt to hear better. As the cult leader's speech filtered up towards us, the hairs on the back of my neck began to crawl.

"R'luhhor ot gn'th ng gn'thor l' nog c."

I knew that language. I had heard it before. The cult members that killed Kalfic had spoken such a language to each other.

"What dialect is that? Welsh?" asked Miles.

"Not any that I know," answered Daffyd.

"Shh," I spat.

"Ymg' mgep mgepfhtagn. C' c' mgahnnn yg'bthnknahh l' ymg'. C' mggoka liahe ymg' gof'nn."

As I listened, my mind raced off. Black spots grew across my vision, replaced by nightmares from another realm. Eyes stared back from the abyss. Thousands of eyes, their gaze piercing my mind, tearing my thoughts asunder.

I snapped my eyes open. I had to concentrate on the ceremony.

At that point, Hermanes paused and reached into his robes. He stepped to the fire and threw something, dust, dirt, leaves, I did not know, into the flames. The colours changed to vibrant greens and blues, casting a horrible pall across the area. Then the idol's brilliance transformed. All the refracted light withdrew and concentrated into a single greenish beam that shot out of the idol's centre, piercing the waters several yards off from the beach.

The priest returned to the lectern and his chanting began again, his voice rising with each incantation.

Then the waters of the little bay grew calm. The waves diminished to nothing but tiny ripples on the shore. The serenity where the beam of light entered the water was met with an opposite level of turmoil. Small bubbles rose, growing larger with every line of the spell until a veritable tumult boiled in the ocean.

"Something's coming," I said.

"What?" asked Miles.

"Dagon. It can only be Dagon."

As if in response to my whispered answer, the brethren surrounding the spectacle increased the volume of their chant. "Dagon. Dagon. Dagon."

My eyes searched everywhere. The broiling mass of foam in the water. The line of acolytes. The priest himself with his pages of incantations. Then they settled on the idol. That was the key.

"Miles. The idol. Shoot the idol. We have to stop this."

"I'll never make that shot," he said, retrieving the bag I had forced him to bring and pulling out a long hunting rifle.

"You have to try. What is coming cannot be fathomed by mortal man, and cannot be allowed to step onto land."

I heard the cock of the bolt. The slight metal-on-metal sound of a bullet pushed into the breach, then of the bolt sliding home and *clacking* closed.

"Okay, I've never made this distance before. Watch your ears."

With my gaze darting between the idol and the commotion in the water, I clamped my hands over my ears.

The retort of the hunting rifle was deafening even with my ears covered. I kept staring at the idol and almost cheered as it disintegrated.

"By Jove, I got it," shouted Miles, chambering another bullet. "I'll get her ready, just in case."

He didn't need to. The *crack* of the rifle across the little beach had caused insanity to break out below us.

The robe-wearing acolytes ran as one towards the climb up from the beach. The gunshot had broken whatever spell they had been under or had triggered their own self-preservation instincts. Soon, only one figure stood on the beach, bathed in the orange glow of the fire. His face turned slowly towards us, an orange mask beneath his dark hood. I may have imagined it, but his eyes glowed with all the fire of hatred that any man could muster.

Ignoring him for a moment, I stared out at the sea. It was calm once more. Whatever was rising from the depths of the ocean had returned. At best we were safe. At worst, we had only helped delay the old God's return to our world.

"We returned in the morning, but apart from the fragments of the statue and the remains of the fire, there was nothing else to be found."

Sir Edgar regarded the crystal shards before him and nodded. "No sign of the pages?" I shook my head. "No sign of that rotter, Hermanes?"

"No. And when we returned to the village there was nobody present either. Strangest thing. The barkeep and his daughter had disappeared, leaving the pub unlocked, and searching the village in the morning we found it deserted."

"That is very strange."

"Yes, and what made it more mysterious was that every boat had gone from the harbour. As if the villagers had returned and set sail during the night."

"And there's been no word from the Welsh authorities

of dozens of people turning up at other villages or towns?"

"No. They have either resettled or found a home elsewhere."

Shaking his head, Sir Edgar picked up a piece of the idol. "I shan't be able to repair this, though given your story, I don't think I should." He stared across at his bookcase. "It may be best to give my collection to the British Museum. The world, and I, it seems, have come close to the brink of death or worse."

"Yes. And this Hermanes and his followers are still out there somewhere. Who knows what their next undertaking will be."

Stephen Herczeg is an IT Geek, writer, actor, filmmaker and Taekwondo Black Belt from Canberra, Australia, who has been writing for well over twenty years, with sixteen completed feature length screenplays, and numerous short and micro-fiction stories. Stephen's scripts, *TITAN, Dark are the Woods, Control* and *Death Spores* have found success in international screenwriting competitions with a win, two runner-up and two top ten finishes. He has had over two hundred short stories and micro-fiction drabbles published through *Hunter Anthologies*; *Things In the Well*; *Blood Song Books*; *Dragon Soul Press*; *Oscillate Wildly Press*; *Black Hare Press*; *Monnath Books*; *Battle Goddess Productions*; *Fantasia Divinity; The Great Void Books*; *DeadSet Press; Belanger Books* and *MX Publishing*. In 2021, his collection of stories – *The Curious Cases of Sherlock Holmes* was published through *MX Publishing*, plus his novellas, *After the Fall Part 1 and 2* were published by *Black Hare Press*. He lives by the creed *Just Finish It*, and his Mum is his biggest fan.

Simon Iff is the product of the notorious Occultist **Aleister Crowly**, some say a mirror of himself. Iff is portrayed as a mystic, magician, world traveller, high society figure and great detective who is advanced in years but possesses a thorough insight into human psychology.

FRUITING BODIES
GAVIN CHAPPELL

PROLOGUE

The body was found at 3am. The smell had been distressing the tenants of the other bedsits for some days. It had got so bad it was worse than the smell from the basement flat, where some poor half-senile old guy had lived in squalor for years. Finally, in a sober moment, one of the tenants had rung 999.

PC Sherlock saw at once that this was nothing juicy like a murder. Nothing that might lead to promotion. The slashed wrists and the hypodermic told their own story. Which was more than the two brothers his colleague questioned were capable of—they were too hammered to comment. The blind man with a voice like Anthony Hopkins had obviously seen nothing. And the old lag had been in HM Prison Chelmsford until that very morning. As for the guy in the basement, they couldn't raise him. But it was unnecessary. The cause of death was obvious.

"But my boy didn't do drugs," cried his mother when they informed the parents later that morning. Oh but he did, madam, Sherlock thought but didn't say. It was the only explanation. That, or the house was cursed.

PART ONE: THE CURSED HOUSE

Tracy pulled up outside and yanked on the handbrake decisively.

"Here we are," she said, peering up at the dilapidated building. "I spent twelve months here before I got my job on the force, and I got out by the skin of my teeth. I wish you the joy of the place."

Unenthusiastically, Jason Steele followed her gaze. The house was a redbrick Victorian villa that had seen better days. It had started out life as a home for some prosperous businessman or doctor by the looks of it, but that had all vanished. Instead, it had been split up into bedsits, maybe in the Sixties. Multiple occupancy, and a landlord who cared about nothing except for squeezing housing benefit out of his tenants, had left its scars.

As Jason struggled through the main door, weighed down by a mattress and a rucksack full of bedding, he caught a distinct, stomach-churning odour, reminiscent of unwashed socks but mingled with it was a strange fungal compost reek. Pulling a face, he gave his ex a look. "What's that smell?"

Tracy followed him, carrying a cardboard box of crockery. Halting outside Flat 2b she said, "That's Roger the Lodger. Lives in the basement. Wait for the next sunny day and you'll see him out in the garden, sunbathing in nothing but a pair of ladies' knickers and a hankie on his head. But remember there's been a corpse on the premises."

Jason dumped what he was carrying, produced the key the landlord had given him, and unlocked the door. He was rewarded with a view of a bare room, although a carpet had been laid since he had previously viewed it. Hauling the mattress inside he dropped it down in one corner, throwing the bedding on top of it. Tracy put the cardboard box down carefully in another corner.

"So your mum's friends told me," said Jason, remembering his encounter with the grieving couple. "Their son. He died in here?"

"He killed himself," Tracy corrected. "Uniform said there was no suspicion of foul play."

"I don't see what there is to investigate, then," said Jason, scratching his head.

Tracy put a finger to her lips. She went to the door, opened it, and looked out into the hall. She listened. A television was audible upstairs. Acid house was pounding the floorboards elsewhere.

Jason watched Tracy impatiently. She shut the door and leant against it, arms folded. "But I told you that there were deaths when I was here," she said, voice lowered.

"A girl who cut her wrists open leaning against a window that shattered because the old landlord had used greenhouse glass instead of window glass," said Jason. "An old biker who took off like a bat out of hell one evening after a row with his girlfriend and hit a wall by the cottage hospital doing a ton. Yes. And there were others, I found out from the local paper archives, before you were living here. Going back to the Sixties. But those were just tragic coincidences. Not murder. Nothing I could investigate."

"You forget," said Tracy. "Mr and Mrs Johnson think there must be some kind of… paranormal explanation. And you've got yourself a reputation as a paranormal investigator."

Jason made a face. "Paranormal!" He laughed scornfully. How he hated that word.

"You were in the Occult Crime Division," Tracy reminded him. "And then there was that business in Dunwich last year. Don't shake your head at me, Jason, this is a job. They're paying good money. And what's more, you're no longer sleeping on my couch and outstaying your welcome. We split up over a year ago, remember?"

Jason sighed and went to the window, looking out over an unweeded garden. Tracy's lemon yellow Ford Fiesta was parked in the road. "The Occult Crime Division was what led to me being booted out of the force," he said. "As for last year, I don't want to think about it. Anyway, if I'm here undercover, I don't think we should be talking about this. Someone might hear."

"Right," said Tracy. "Let's get the rest of your junk carried in here and then I'll leave you to it."

Half an hour later, Jason was back at the window, watching with relief mingled with a sudden sense of loneliness as Tracy drove off. The sun was beginning to descend over the roofs of the house over the road. He went to sort out his few belongings into something like order.

He had just finished when he heard a knock at the door. After shutting the drawer of the desk in the corner, he went over and opened it.

An old man stood there. He wore a pair of shorts and a striped cotton shirt that entirely failed to conceal his bloated stomach. His face was flabby, his hair white. A welcoming smile was on his weather-beaten face. He was holding out his hand and something was in it.

"Hello," said Jason. "My name's Steele, Jason Steele. You must be Roger."

"How-de-do," said the old man. Jason had heard all about Roger from Tracy. An ageing eccentric who lived in the basement, he had provided her with a fund of bizarre anecdotes. A slight smell of mould lingered about him. "Have these. They're good."

Fastidiously, but wanting to be polite, Jason took what looked like three or four grapes wrapped in kitchen paper. They were wet and slightly warm. He would have accepted the man's severed testicles with greater enthusiasm. "Thank you," he said curtly. "Nice to meet you. I'm the new tenant."

"I know who you are," said Roger placidly. "Welcome to my house."

Shortly afterwards he departed. Jason took the grapes and threw them in the bin. It was by no means the first time he had felt sceptical about the government's 'care in the community' policy.

He went over to his second-hand microwave, took out a ready meal from the fridge, and put it in. As he ate the cottage pie at his table, washing it down with a can of

Carling, he went over what he knew about the situation.

Val Johnson had not been the first to die. As well as the deaths when Tracy had lived here, several more had been reported in the local paper, going back to the late Sixties. All the time the house had been in multiple occupancy it had been the same—although before that point it had been as innocuous a dwelling as you could want. None of the deaths had been murder, just accidents or sometimes suicide. Death by misadventure was the usual verdict.

The Johnsons were paying his living expenses. That was good, it got him off the dole, not to mention off Tracy's sofa. For over a year he had struggled to get his private detective agency up and running, with the heavy-handed encouragement of the DHSS, but until now with little luck. He felt a bit queasy about taking the Johnsons' money, though. After all, what was he likely to discover?

After finishing his meal, he decided to explore. Locking his door behind him, he glanced up and down the corridor. The side door was at the other end of a short hall. Stairs led up to the next floor. A payphone was located next to the door. Under the stairs was a doorway. It was from here that the compost and mould odour emanated. Roger's basement flat was down that way, he guessed.

A TV was audible upstairs. From one of the flat doors drifted the sound of loud snoring. After examining the drab, shabby toilet-cum-bathroom, he went upstairs to find the kitchen in a cramped, garret room up amongst the eaves. The place was filthy. Unwashed crockery and pots and pans filled with stagnant washing-up water lined the kitchen working surface. On the lowest wall, the paint had bubbled into a shape that resembled a staring face. Jason grimaced, vowed never to attempt cooking in here, and went back downstairs.

The following morning he was just finishing his cornflakes when he was alerted by a pounding on the door. Flustered, he went to the door and opened it.

Two men in shellsuits, with an air of youth despite noses red with broken veins, gazed at him. Something about them reminded him of rats. A close family resemblance suggested they were brother rats.

One of them had a can of Tennents Super lager in his hand, and his breath reeked of beer and ciggies. The other was holding onto the doorjamb to avoid falling over. "You just moved in?" he asked. "Landlord said there'd be a new tenant. In…" He lowered his voice. "In the murder room."

His skinny brother punched his shoulder. "Don't be like that, man." He grinned a gap-toothed grin at Jason. "Wanna drink?" He beckoned Jason in the direction of the flat next door.

Jason could think of a thousand and one things he would rather do. He was fairly sure he had arrested the skinny one back when he was in the police for being drunk and disorderly, long before his secondment to the OCD. But he doubted the guy remembered that far back.

"Okay," he said, following the two rat brothers back into their den.

But it turned out it wasn't their flat after all. Sitting in a chair by the window was a bald, slovenly-looking man whose white, rolling eyes told Jason that he was blind.

"Here's your new neighbour, Chas," said the bigger of the two rats. "He's living in the murder room."

"Good morning!" said the blind man. His voice was rich, powerful. He might have had a career in radio with a voice like that, Jason thought. He certainly had the face for it. "Have a drink."

Jason checked his watch. Just after ten in the morning. Tentatively he sat down on a sofa, accepting a can of cider from the blind man, Chas. The two rat brothers nestled on chairs and got down to the serious business of drinking.

"You were here when the guy died?" Jason asked.

"It was sick, man," said the younger rat, who was called Vince. "This place stinks enough already. Stinks of shit. But that smell, it was bad. Like if you leave mince out of the fridge on a summer day. And the flies! When the pigs bust down the door, there was fucking dozens of them. I wouldn't live in that flat if you paid me."

"Don't have nightmares," chipped in Luke, his brother. "But Vince's right. It was well sick. The place stank worse than one of Vince's farts. And that guy, we'd not seen him for a week. Thought he'd moved out. He must have topped himself days ago."

"I heard there've been other deaths," said Jason, sipping from the can of lager. "In the past, I mean. All kinds of people living here died."

"Yeah, like the place is cursed," said Vince. "Reckon it was built on an old Indian burial ground."

"Don't be a dick," said his brother. "You don't get Red Indians in Essex."

"They call them Native Americans now," pronounced

Chas. "You can't call them Red Indians, it's not right-on."

"I don't believe in curses," said Jason. Even if there was a curse, what was he supposed to do about it? "All that paranormal shit, it's rubbish. Don't you reckon?"

Luke shrugged. "But you're right. Lots of deaths. Only way you come out of this place is feet first, unless your name's Roger. He's been living here thirty years and he's not dead yet."

That night, Jason curled up on his mattress and, despite the overpowering smell of rot, tried to sleep. It was a long time coming, and for several hours he dozed at best, or at worst lay awake. Eventually, he drifted off.

At first, his dreams were jumbled, chaotic, flitting from one strange scene to another with no apparent sense. Several times he woke abruptly from dreams that vanished like fairy gold in his mind, only to drift off again.

He was in the house, walking up the stairs. A strange glow came from the basement door and he seemed to hear a distant whispered chanting. His feet were caught in something and he felt as if he was wading through treacle. Eventually, he reached the kitchen on the top floor. The bubbles in the wallpaper were moving as if something was trying to get out, swelling, straining against the wallpaper. He went to the window.

Outside, a single figure stood bathed in the moonlight. Roger, stark-naked but for a brief pair of knickers, which his blubbery gut almost concealed. He had his arms outstretched, head held back, eyes closed. A knotted handkerchief was on his head as a kind of hat. It was as if he was sunbathing, but that couldn't be. The word 'moonbathing' flitted through Jason's confused mind.

Then he was back downstairs, in front of the basement door. His hand stretched out. The door opened at a touch and he was descending a flight of steep steps. The chanting was louder here. The walls oozed moisture and were blotched with great black patches of rot. Jason brushed against the wall as he went. At a tickling sensation, he looked down to see that his arms were both streaked with the same black patches as the wall. His skin crawled.

After so long he thought he would come out in hell itself, he stumbled into the basement. The small room was lit by a single naked bulb. Shadows swallowed up the further corners. A strange stone altar stood in the centre of a packed earth floor. Kneeling before it were three cloaked and hooded figures. Jason couldn't see their faces, but it was these figures that were chanting. He reached out to tap one on the shoulder.

Again he was in the kitchen, but such is the confusion of dreams, it was the kitchen at Tracy's house. The same bubbles bulged in the wallpaper. *Tracy's not going to like that*, he told himself; she was very house-proud. The wallpaper bubbles were moving again, straining. More of them appeared on either side, like two sets of fingers pushing at the paper. Something was most definitely trying to get out.

The smell of rot was overpowering. He was in the

basement again, his naked body streaked with mould. He reached out to touch a hooded figure and it swung round, hood falling back to reveal its face, which was a mass of mould.

He was outside again, gazing up into the sky, his arms outstretched. A shooting star plummeted towards him.

He awoke, sweat soaking his body, with the words, "Fun guy from yogurt," on his lips. They seemed to be of immense significance. He grabbed a pen from his bedside cabinet and scrawled down what he remembered of the phrase on a bus ticket. Then he got back into bed, rolled over on his side, and slept again.

This time no dreams disturbed him. He awoke with the sun streaming in through the windows. He had no curtains. He'd have to do something about that, he told himself as he got up and checked the time. Today was Friday. Friday was a work day.

Every day was a workday now, he reminded himself as he spooned cornflakes into a bowl and poured milk on them. He was being paid to investigate this building, although he still had only a vague idea of what he was looking for. But today was the day he worked for Professor Flint.

After eating he went back to his bedside cabinet, picked up the bus ticket and tried to decipher what he had written on it. With a bewildered grunt, he thrust it into his pocket and promptly forgot it.

A quarter of an hour later, he was in shirt and tie, hurrying out of the otherwise silent house. But as he went up the drive, he noticed curtains twitching on the top floor. Someone was watching him.

Work was only a ten-minute walk away, so it was not long afterwards that he was knocking on Professor Flint's door.

"Come in, come in, Jason," said the professor, leading him into the study. Glancing around at the big house, Jason guessed that it had been built about the same time as where he was now living, perhaps even by the same builder. This was what the house would have looked like in its glory days, before it was so cruelly filleted.

He sat down at his desk while the professor went to the sideboard and poured two generous Scotches. Newspaper clippings had been heaped on the desk, from local and national papers. Each one had some connection with the Satanic panic that now seemed to be gripping the nation. Or was it just the silly season?

"And how is your new investigation progressing?" asked the professor, placing the Scotch beside him.

"Well…" Jason temporised. He began sorting through the newspaper clippings. Flint was an independent researcher, having been kicked out of the University of East Anglia after suffering a funny turn. He had several peculiar obsessions.

"That's wonderful to hear," Flint replied. "Of course, I realise you can't talk about an ongoing investigation. Client confidentiality and so forth." He sat down at his own desk and flicked through an academic journal. "But," he added, not looking up, "I took the liberty to conduct a little investigation of my own. The folklore surrounding that house is quite magnificent for leafy suburbia. And I turned up some interesting little facts."

He looked up and blinked myopically at Jason. "I hope you don't mind," he said mildly.

"No, not at all," said Jason. "There's not much I can tell you because I've only just started. Some peculiar characters there, that's all. Place is disgusting, but no worse than most student accommodation. What have you found out?"

"I went down to the local archives," Flint said, "and asked the charming girls there to provide me with whatever information they could on the house. Much of it was inconsequential. But the archivist herself remembered hearing about what she called a shooting star, a meteor strike."

"It was hit by a meteor?" asked Jason, frowning. A flash of his dream returned to him. "How come it's still standing? I mean, it's a bit of a mess, but…"

Professor Flint shook his head. "The meteor didn't hit the house," he said. "But it did come down in the park next door. You can still see the impact crater as a small pond, according to the most recent maps. I've seen it myself, but a long time ago. This happened back in the 1960s, before I came to live in the area."

"The 1960s…" Jason murmured. He'd have been in nappies. "That was when the house was turned into bedsits."

The professor chuckled. "Bedsitting rooms were all the rage back then. I lived in one myself for a while."

Jason remembered something else. He took the crumpled bus ticket from his pocket and smoothed it out. "Do the words 'he's a fun guy from yogurt' mean anything to you, professor?"

Flint stared at him. "Fungi, as in mushrooms and toadstools?"

"Oh!" said Jason. "I hadn't thought of that. The way they keep that kitchen you'd probably get toadstools. But why yogurt? What kind of fungi comes from yogurt?"

"Where did you hear these words?" the professor asked slowly.

Jason shifted self-consciously. "In a dream," he admitted. "It seemed so important I woke up and wrote it down. Made no sense in the morning. Probably just nonsense."

"Are you sure it wasn't Yuggoth you heard?" the professor asked gravely.

"Yuggoth?" Jason asked. "Maybe. Who's Yuggoth?"

This is the hour when moonstruck poets know
What fungi sprout in Yuggoth, and what scents
And tints of flowers fill Nithon's continents,
Such as in no poor earthly garden blow.

The professor recited the words solemnly. "It's from a cycle of poems I've recently read," he said, "that has links with the esoteric Kutulu folklore and its associated cult that I have been investigating. It also describes a strange grey world, Yuggoth, 'past starry voids.'"

"Another planet?" said Jason.

The professor shrugged. "Who can say?" he asked. "Who can say? Now, could you sort these clippings into the different folders? It's a new system I've devised. Red for domestic crime, green for political figures, blue for police or Masonic involvement..."

On the way back from work Jason took a detour by the park. The pond was surrounded by birch saplings.

Ducks and other waterfowl bobbed contentedly on its grey waters. A mother and a toddler were feeding them bread.

Jason watched for a while. It looked as if the pond had been there since time immemorial, perhaps even longer. He couldn't believe it had been the site of a meteor impact. Such things were very rare, almost unheard of. Most meteorites burn up in the atmosphere.

As he was coming back in through the side door, he heard a voice from behind him and the metallic squeaking of a badly oiled bicycle chain. Jason glanced back to see a heavyset man in his late thirties sprinting up the drive, wheeling a ladies' bicycle.

"Can I help you?" Jason asked.

"Who are you?" the man demanded. He was wearing a denim jacket and tracksuit bottoms, had a broken nose and looked like something of a bruiser. "I live here."

Tersely Jason introduced himself as the new tenant and gave his name. "Bill," said the big man. He wheeled the bike inside. There was the sound of someone vomiting in the toilet down the hall. When Jason unlocked his flat door and went in, Bill tried to follow.

"Come on, I need somewhere to hide this," he pleaded. "It's hot." He had a Northern accent, Mancunian or Scouse, maybe.

Before Jason could explain that he had no intention of allowing bicycle thieves to stow their loot in his flat, Bill was already leaning it against the wall by the fridge.

He flung himself down in an armchair. "Got any beer?" he asked.

"You can't leave that thing there," said Jason. "Keep

it in your own flat."

"Nah," said Bill derisively. "That'll be the first place they'll look, mate. They'll never look in here." He seemed to take it for granted that Jason would join him in his little conspiracy. He leaned over, opened the fridge door, took out two cans of beer from a sixpack and threw one to Jason. "Have this on me," he said, then opened his own can and drank deep. "Ahhhh!" he said, and smacked his lips. "Hits the spot. Got any weed?"

Jason sat down in the opposite armchair. "No," he said. "I don't smoke."

"Okay. This'll have to do," said Bill, waggling the can.

"Look, I've just got in from work," Jason said. "You'll have to go. See you later, okay."

"Okay," said Bill, and stood up. Suddenly, he gave a theatrical cry of pain and clutched at his leg. Sitting down with a thump, he explained, "It's me old war wound. Bit o' shrapnel from the Falklands. Gives me gyp from time to time. Let me just sit here."

He took another swig of the beer and proceeded to regale Jason with a series of unlikely tales. He'd been a soldier, survived several tours of Northern Ireland, the Falklands, the Gulf too. Then a mercenary, or special forces or something hush-hush. Then he'd done time. Now he was out of prison, and heading rapidly back there, judging by everything Jason had seen.

Jason listened absently. Maybe Bill would let slip something of value. He could get the thief's confidence and later subject him to a subtle interrogation. But nothing too blatant yet...

"You know," Bill said suddenly, halfway through a story about the brutal nuns at the Catholic school he had attended, "the others are on to you. They know who you're working for."

He fixed Jason with a beady, bloodshot eye.

PART TWO: THE UNCARING CARER

Jason knocked on the blind man's door. His rich, rolling tones answered.

"Can I come in?" he asked.

Bill pushed past him, an expression of scorn on his face. "Just go in!" he said, shoving the door open. Jason followed Bill inside.

The TV was showing some Australian soap opera. Chas sat in a chair by the window. His blind white eyes rolled in a face that was very pale. Lounging on the broken-down sofa, a half-drunk bottle of Merrydown cider on the table between them, were the two rat brothers. They looked up in confusion as Jason entered and Vince tried to hide a spliff.

"What's all this about me being a dole snoop?" he demanded.

Vince grimaced at Bill. "Ahh, fuck, man! Why did ya tell him?" he whined.

"If people are talking about me behind my back," said Bill frankly, "I want to know. Same goes for everyone.

So I told him."

"But no one would talk about you behind your back, Bill," said Luke, confused.

Jason tried again. "Why have you been saying that I'm an informer for the DHSS?"

Chas looked blindly in his direction. "They don't mean anything by it. It's just that Luke saw you going out of the house in a suit."

"I've got a job," Jason announced. Silence fell. Everyone stared at him. He felt a need to qualify his statement. "It's just a part-time one," he added.

"Why are you living in this shithole," asked Bill, "if you've got a job?"

Jason turned to look at him. "I told you, it's only part-time. Doesn't pay much. I was sleeping on my ex-girlfriend's couch until I moved here. You could say I was homeless."

Bill shook his head sympathetically. "I was homeless for six months," he said, "after leaving special forces. I was living in a…"

"Bullshit Bill," muttered Vince. "Look, Jay," he said to Jason. "We were just trying to work out why you were living here but leaving the house each day in a suit. Luke reckoned you were a dole snoop."

"We're all on benefits," said Chas. "I'm on the sick. Because of my eyes, you see. Luke gets carer's allowance. Vince and Bill are on income support. Give him a drink, Vince."

Grumbling, Vince got up and got a can from the fridge. Jason took it and sat down in an armchair. Bill perched on a stool. They all watched the television for a while.

"People think this house is haunted," Jason announced when it came to the adverts and Chas turned the sound down. "D'you reckon it is?"

"Told ya," said Vince with a giggle. "Old Indian burial ground."

'Sorry,' said Chas suddenly, lurching to his feet and staggering towards the door.

Luke tried to get up to help him as he collided with the furniture, but Jason was there first. He opened the door and Chas blundered down the hall to the toilet, leaving a smell of decay behind him. Vomiting sounds ensued.

"Is he okay?" he asked, sitting down with the others. Luke shrugged.

"Reckon he's feeling a bit ill," he said, taking a slurp from his can. "He drinks too much. It made him go blind. Seriously, that's why he's blind. *Toptic opsic neurothapy*, the doctors call it."

He followed up that pronouncement with his party-piece: farting the first two bars of the Deep Purple classic *Smoke on the Water*.

"I saw a ghost once," Bill announced. "It was in a cemetery at night. I was coming down the road and the full moon was in the sky. I saw this shining figure standing there in the middle of the cemetery. Like a monk it was, but glowing silver. And shrunken, like a dwarf or a monkey. I never went that way at night again."

"It was the reflection of the moon on a marble gravestone," said Luke.

"Bullshit," said Bill.

"You should know," said Vince, and the two brothers smirked knowingly.

The vomiting sounds continued down the hall. "I think someone should do something about him," Jason said. "You're his carer, Luke. You should be looking after him."

Home and Away was back on. Luke produced the TV remote and turned the sound up.

Chas returned from the toilet and carefully sat back down in his chair by the window. His face was pale and slick with sweat. No one seemed to care, particularly not his so-called carer. Jason slipped away before the next advert break, returning to Flat 2b for a think.

There was nothing here to suggest that the place concealed anything but squalor. He had almost gagged at the smell from Chas. If Luke was his carer, he should make sure the blind man washed more often. Luke was taking the money and doing nothing in return. Jason ought to report him, but he had bigger fish to fry.

There was a knock on his door. At first, he ignored it, thinking Bullshit Bill had returned. It came again, though, and he got up and went to answer it.

"Hello," said Roger. In his hand was a half-full can of cider. He handed it wordlessly to Jason who took it, thanked him, and waited.

"It's a hoot!" Roger added, with a nod towards the other room. Jason noticed that the same smell of rot clung to the old man. "Oh well," Roger added. "Nice talking to you."

He turned and went back to his room. Jason shut the door.

Sitting down again he racked his brains for a strategy. Something was wrong here, that much was clear. He remembered what Professor Flint had said about alien fungi. Sounded like something from a B movie. Or possibly a punk band.

Talking to these inebriates was getting him nowhere. Except in the case of Bill, but you couldn't believe a word of it. He could try searching their rooms when they were out, but they never seemed to leave. They must go to the off-licence at some point, surely. Then again, what would it turn up? Something might be found in Roger's room, but probably nothing very pleasant.

He glanced at the stolen bike, still leaning against the wall. That would have to go before he was had up for theft himself.

Frustrated by his inability to find any kind of lead in his assignment, he locked his door that evening and proceeded to get drunk. After finishing off his remaining cans of beer, he sat in a miserable haze.

He was turning into one of them.

Bored and drunk, he went to bed early and soon was snoring.

The next morning, he woke to a pain in his crotch. Inspecting it, he found a red rash on the inside of his legs and a slight stickiness. It smelt of rot. He tried scrubbing at it with soap and water, but that only made it worse. A visit to the doctor's led to the suggestion he had ringworm, a fungal infection also called jock itch.

"Do you lead an active life?" the doctor asked. "Football, rugby? Work up a sweat? It thrives in those conditions."

"No," said Jason, mystified. "Not these days.'"

The doctor sighed and started writing out a prescription. "I want you to take this antifungal cream for the next month. Keep taking it even when the symptoms clear up."

"It's fungal, is it?" asked Jason. "Like athletes' foot?"

The doctor nodded. Jason went to the chemist with his prescription, then walked home through the sunlit streets.

Fungal. The word seemed to reverberate around Jason's hungover brain. *Fungi from Yuggoth*. The smell of rot in this place.

There was a knock on the door just as he was applying the anti-fungal cream. After pulling up his trousers, he opened it. Bullshit Bill stood outside, grinning.

"Come and look at this," he said and led an unwilling Jason to the bathroom where a window overlooked the back garden. Standing in the middle of the overgrown lawn, exactly like in Jason's dream, was Roger, eyes closed, face turned up towards the sun.

"What's he doing?" he said. It was almost as if the old man was waiting for something.

Bill shrugged. "Sunbathing? Come back to my flat and we'll have a beer." As Jason turned he caught another waft of rot. It came from Bill. He wondered if everyone had ringworm.

Chas's door burst open and the blind man came lurching down the hall. Jason and Bill hurried down the way to help him.

"Toilet," he said. They steered him into the small room and stood outside as he vomited.

"He drinks too much," said Bill. "Come back to my flat and… Where are you going?"

"For a walk," said Jason. "I want to clear my head."

He had a vile taste in his mouth. Something lingering from his hangover. As he reached the park gates, he surreptitiously hawked and spat. The spittle landed on the ground nearby. To his shock, it seemed to be flecked with blood.

A small voice inside told him that he should worry about that. It also suggested he shouldn't be walking with a fungal infection of the crotch. But he was finding it hard to think. That was why he had left the house. Its atmosphere was cloying, oppressive.

He had needed to get outside, away from vomiting blind men, storifying drunks, and old men who sunbathed semi-naked. Something was wrong with that place, seriously wrong. But nothing he could put a finger on. Nothing conclusive he could report back to Mr and Mrs Johnson.

He had almost forgotten that he was there on assignment. It was as if he was beginning to believe his own cover story. He needed to get a grip, get down to the serious business of private investigation. But he couldn't concentrate properly. He guessed it was the result of the hangover, but surely it shouldn't still be… hanging over. Besides, he'd only had four cans of lager.

Feeling queasy, he sat down on a park bench and put his head in his hands. Everything seemed to be swimming. He wanted to vomit. Had he caught the same thing as Chas? Waves of nausea rolled over him.

When they receded, he sat up, becoming more aware

of his surroundings. First, he saw that a young mother and her child were both watching him warily. Secondly, he noticed that the bench he was sitting on was right next to the pond he had seen before.

The pond that had once been the crater after a meteor strike. He sniffed. Could he detect a slight smell of rot? He wasn't sure.

The mother ushered her child away hastily.

That night his dreams were long, complicated, and confusing. Familiar objects and individuals washed up in unfamiliar places or guises. Sooner or later, however, they were reduced to a few simple things. The house. The kitchen. The bubbles in the wallpaper, now even more like a human face and two grasping hands. The outlines of a torso were now starting to show.

He stood outside the door to the basement. An eerie pallid glow emanated from within. He reached out a hand. Suddenly he was past the door, making his way down the steps. He saw the room below, a cold, dank, mouldy cellar without so much as a stick of furniture and lit only by a single bulb. Standing in the middle, as naked as the lightbulb but for a pair of knickers, seemingly rooted to the spot as if he grew out of the packed earth floor, was Roger, arms flung out, head back, eyes closed.

The smell of rot was overpowering. Jason detected that strange coppery taste in his mouth as if he had been drinking blood. His head throbbed, his eyes seemed to bulge from their sockets. He looked down. His arms were furry with mould.

He was by the pond in the local park. The waters were glowing. Dead ducks floated on them, dead fish too. A mother and child stood looking out at the water, backs to him. As he approached them they turned. Both were covered in black streaks of mould, both glared at him out of empty eye sockets. Both grinned the toothy grin of a skull.

He was running, scrambling, staggering, crawling down long lightless corridors underneath the earth. He kept looking back. Something was following him, something silhouetted against a glowing light. He ran and ran but somehow he could go no further.

He looked down from the bathroom window. Roger stood outside, on the lawn in the back garden, again rooted to the spot, sunbathing, soaking up the sun's rays as if he needed them to survive. Jason saw that his head was shaking slightly, throbbing, almost as if it was going to explode. He gripped hold of the window ledge and stared down at the old man in nauseated horror. Roger's eyes flicked open suddenly and he was looking knowingly up at Jason. His eyes glowed with the pallid light from the basement, but they were the hollow eye sockets of a skull.

Jason was with Tracy again, in her kitchen. She was subjecting him to some kind of harangue, but it seemed to be mainly in another language. Then she made some strange statement in English about a black goat.

He was awake, lying in bed with a nasty taste in his mouth. The moonlight streamed in through the curtainless windows. And with it was another light. A blue light that washed across the ceiling. He could hear men's voices, the crashing of big feet.

Rising, wrapping his dressing gown around himself, he crept to the door. Raised voices, one of them Luke's. "But I've got to see his body…!" he was protesting.

A powerful, authoritative male voice replied: "You're not going in there. Only next of kin."

Jason tried to peer out of the keyhole, at first seeing nothing that made any sense, only that the lights were on and men in uniform were standing outside Chas's door. He opened the door to a crack. Luke was there too, cringing before a big man, who was dressed in the green uniform of a paramedic.

The side door opened with a crash and two more paramedics came in, struggling to carry a stretcher down the cramped hall. They reached the door and forced it open. Soon afterwards, they struggled back out again, carrying the pale form of Chas. Luke was pawing at the door, trying to open it, but the paramedic told him to desist. Luke paid no attention, and after a short, futile struggle was hustled off by more uniformed men who Jason realised were police officers.

Anxiously he looked back at the stolen bicycle in the corner of the room. Shutting the door as quietly as possible, he went looking in the pockets of his bundled-up jeans for his key.

A pounding came from the door. A cop knock. Jason should know, he'd used that knock more than once in the old days, when he was still on the force. Whimpering like a frightened animal, he jumped into bed and pulled the covers over his head.

The door opened, and the light came on. He sat up, staring at the policeman framed in the doorway. From here the bike was out of the intruder's sight.

He leapt up out of bed. "What's going on?" he demanded. "I was asleep."

"Just a routine check," said the officer. "I must report to you that your neighbour has passed away. We received a call to say that he wasn't answering his door, so we gained entry to the property and…"

"Can we talk outside?" Jason asked. "In the hall?"

Shrugging, the officer complied. Outside, Jason stared at the door to Chas's room which had clearly been forced and now had a padlock on it. The officer was staring at him. Jason stared back. He recognised him suddenly.

"Sean 'No-shit' Sherlock," he said. PC Sherlock had joined the force at the same time he did. "Still in uniform, I see."

"Jason Steele," said Sherlock grimly. "I remember you. First, you were seconded to some creepy paranormal division, then you were booted out. There was a rumour you'd set up as some kind of private investigator, but that can't have worked out for you. Not if you're living here."

Faces were appearing at the other doors. Roger dithered in the basement door. Bullshit Bill thrust his jowls outside, took one look at the copper, and vanished back inside. Vince staggered out of his room. "Where's Luke? Where's my brother?"

"He attempted to gain entry into the deceased's room," said Sherlock, "for purposes unknown. When we tried to stop him, he fought like a cat. He's cooling his heels down in the cells at the local nick. I suggest you all go back to your rooms."

He turned to Jason, looked him up and down. "That's the second corpse I've had to deal with here in recent weeks. What's up with this place? You ought to move out, Steele, or you might leave feet first."

Jason beckoned Sherlock closer. "I'm here undercover," he said. "Investigating the deaths. How did Bill die?"

"Can't say," said Sherlock. "It's under investigation. All I can tell you is that his body was covered in some kind of mould."

Jason awoke groggily around noon. The house was silent. Only the occasional sound of cars from the road outside broke the funereal hush. Chas was dead. Luke had been arrested. That left only Bill and Vince. Oh, and Roger. But Roger was… different.

That nasty taste still lingered in Jason's mouth. He crawled out of bed with an effort of will and went to the wash basin to clean his teeth. When he spat out the toothpaste, he saw it was pink with blood.

Some kind of gingivitis? He ought to see the dentist. He washed his mouth out, gargled, and looked in the mirror. Cleaning his teeth had not got rid of the taste. Pulling down his lower lip, he examined his gum. White mould was growing on it.

Shuddering, he scraped at the mould with his

fingernail. It came off in little gobbets but where it did, his gums began bleeding.

He sat down in his armchair, wrapping his dressing gown around for warmth. He ought to see a dentist, a doctor... someone. He ought to get on with his investigation. He ought to find that anti-fungal cream and put it on his ringworm. But he couldn't remember where he put it. Instead, he sat there staring into space.

It took a real effort of will to get up on his feet. He was tired, and it wasn't just the sleepless night. After the police had gone he had slept well, without any more weird dreams as far as he could recall. He got up and got dressed. Then he went to knock on Bill's door.

"Er, you'd better get your bike shifted, mate," he said when the bruiser poked his face out. "I'm not looking after your stolen property."

"You keep it," Bill said, looking hurt. "I left it you as a present. I don't want it back."

"A present?" Jason laughed. "A stolen ladies' bicycle, and with the police coming round every night?"

There was a knock on the side door. Glaring at Bill, Jason went to answer it. Luke stood there, beaming.

"What are you looking so cheerful about?" Jason demanded.

Luke grinned. "Just spent the night in the custody suite," he said, "and I can tell you, it ain't sweet and there's no custard." He seemed to be waiting for applause. Somehow Jason knew he'd spent all night and half the morning dreaming up that crack.

"What did you think you were doing?" Jason asked. "Why were you so insistent on getting into Chas's flat?"

"I was after Chas's life savings," said Luke unabashedly. "He didn't need them any more. He kept them in a tin box by the wash basin. Pigs'll have got them now, I expect." He brushed past and went upstairs whistling. The whole experience had done wonders for his insecure ego, Jason could tell.

Jason went back to his room. He wheeled the bike out into the hall, then propped it against Bill's door. He rapped on the door, saying, "Here it is. I'm not keeping it."

Bill opened the door suddenly, and the bike toppled over with a crash. It landed on his foot and he stared at it stupidly. Then at Jason.

"Take it," said Jason. "I'm keeping it no longer."

He turned on his heel and headed for Flat 2b. Something flew through the air behind him and struck him in the back of the legs. He went down, with the bike half pinning him.

Flinging it off, he turned to see Bill glaring at him.

"You fucking cunt," said Jason, shoving the bike in his direction with a kick.

"I told you I don't want it!" shouted Bill petulantly.

"Give it back to its owner, then, you thief," said Jason.

A feral gleam glinted in Bill's eyes. He sprang for Jason, seizing him by the folds of his shirt. Jason shoved him away. Bill threw a punch at Jason, who dodged it and Bill's fist connected with the wall. With a howl of pain and anger, Bill came at Jason.

In the confines of the narrow hall, there was no room for Queensbury Rules, nor taekwondo for that matter.

Jason dealt Bill an uppercut that sent him staggering back. He seized him and flung him in the direction of his room. Bill got up, wheezing with pain, and bent double. He lurched towards Jason.

"You've broke me ribs," he wailed piteously. Then lunged at him and tried to force him back. Jason grabbed his leg and hauled on it. Bill fell to the floor, groaning, then got up and tried the same tactic again. Finally, Jason was willing to take no more. After Bill went down a fifth time, he straddled him and punched him several times in the face.

The next thing he knew, he was being dragged off by Vince and Luke. Roger appeared in the door to the basement and watched censoriously. Jason shoved the rat brothers away from him, breathing hoarsely.

The payphone began to ring. Frowning at Jason and Bill, Vince went to answer.

"Yes? Who is it, please?" he asked in best telephone manner. He listened, then said, "I'll get him."

Looking up, he offered the receiver to Jason. "Wants to speak with you."

Jason took the receiver. "Hello? Jason Steele here. Can I help you?"

The voice on the other end of the line was tinny, hard to follow. "This is Mr Johnson," it seemed to be saying. "Your client. Have you found out how my son came to die?"

Jason gulped. "I'm making some progress," he said quietly. "Can't talk now. I'll ring you back."

"Eh? What's that? Speak up, speak up." Someone else was talking in the background. "I'm sorry to say we can no longer afford your services. Please send a report of what you've learnt so far to our address. Sorry, but we've just lost a lot of money on a timeshare in Spain."

PART THREE: THE NEW TENANT

He couldn't blame them.

That was the thought uppermost in his mind as he put down the receiver and went back to his flat, brushing past the rat brothers as they gaped at him gormlessly. He couldn't blame them.

He sucked at his bruised knuckles. What had he found out during his investigations? For a start, that he was useless at investigating. He knew nothing about the paranormal, he didn't even believe in it. Dotty Dorothy had, back in the Occult Crime Division. But he had just been the muscle. It had been a hardship posting, due to a previous cock-up. And when the OCD went tits up, he'd been sacked. Now he'd made a balls up of this investigation as well.

He shouldn't have taken on the assignment. He wouldn't have done, except Tracy twisted his arm. She'd just wanted him out of the house, off her sofa. He couldn't blame her, either.

He sat there staring into space. What was he going to do? He didn't want to go back on the dole. But what hope was there of getting a job, with the country in the grip of another recession? He should have made more of an investigation. Dotty Dorothy of the Occult Crime Division would have held seances, rigged the place up with mics, ghost detectors, god knows what dodgy bits of pseudo-scientific tat.

No hope of that. Especially not now.

He struggled up out of his armchair and went out of his flat. The hall was silent. No sign of the rat brothers or of Bullshit Bill. He left the house and went down the road to the nearest bank, where he checked his bank balance. He still had enough money to pay his way for a week or two.

Next door to the bank was a branch of Safeway. He went inside and bought some food. Reaching the wine beer and spirits aisle, he added several cans of lager to his trolley. After some due consideration, he added a bottle of cheap cider. Might as well, he told himself, while the going was good. He went home and proceeded to get drunk.

This set the scene for the next few days. He'd get out of bed late and start drinking early. Drink to forget. Forget his failure. Forget his lack of employment. Most of all, forget the weird fungal rash around his crotch and the strange white strands he kept finding in his mouth. The alcohol went some way to washing away the bad taste. He just wished he had enough money to buy a TV, in which case he'd have something to do while he drank.

The landlord found a new tenant for the blind man's flat, but Jason made no attempt to greet him. It wasn't until a few days later, when he went into the kitchen, his microwave having burnt itself out the previous evening, when he saw him.

A middle-aged man, dressed in shabby, tattered clothes. Bearded, with a seamed, flushed face, he clearly hadn't washed for days. He stood by the filthy cooker, nonchalantly cooking baked beans in a battered pan. Bread was toasting on the grille. The smell made Jason salivate, although he had no wish to strike up a conversation.

The man looked up. "Hello Jason," he said genially.

"Wh-what?" Jason had trouble forming words. "What? Who?"

The man turned down the gas and put the pan down on the hob. "You don't recognise me? My disguise must be a good one. That's heartening. When you didn't turn up for work and didn't answer the phone I became worried, and decided to pause my own studies and begin my own investigation."

"Professor Flint?" Jason scratched his head, dislodging a blizzard of dandruff.

"Yes, of course," said the professor. "What's wrong with you, Jason? You seem unwell."

But he wasn't looking at Jason. He was gazing at the bubbles in the wallpaper. They had grown much larger, and were taking on an almost human form.

Jason started guiltily. "They stopped paying me. I'm out of work."

"You're 'off the case' then?" Flint asked. "Just like all those detectives on TV?"

"I'll be on the streets pretty soon," said Jason bitterly. "I've got no money left to pay the rent. Spent the last few coppers on booze."

"You have been conscientious in maintaining your cover," Flint remarked, "but I think you may have exceeded your remit. Would you like beans on toast? You look like you could do with a square meal. Then we can go down to my flat and discuss the investigation."

One of the rat brothers entered the kitchen, fag in mouth, and Jason turned away as if he had never met the professor.

A quarter of an hour later, over beans on toast and a mug of tea in the professor's flat, Jason found himself discussing his dreams. "But what's all this got to do with the investigation?" he asked.

The professor put down his tea. "It could be you have some latent psychic powers. Dreams may be our way of accessing a world of knowledge unavailable except by esoteric means." Jason didn't understand a word he was saying.

"D'you mean the spirit world?" he asked. "Palmistry, astrology, seances, all that cobblers? I saw plenty of that while in the OCD to know it's fraud."

"Sentimental tripe for the most part," said Flint. "But some of the darker strains of occultism tap into hidden powers, unknown modes of existence. Like the Kutulu cult with which we've both had dealings in the past. Show me the pond."

"Pond?" said Jason. "Oh, you mean where the meteor struck. Yeah, okay. Do you have any bread left?"

"Are you still hungry?"

"No, but the ducks will be."

They walked through the park and solemnly fed the ducks. It was a nice sunny day, or most people would think so. "You think this is where it all began?" Jason asked, wincing. The sunlight was giving him a pounding headache. The squawking ducks didn't help either.

"I think that meteor had its origins on the edges of the solar system," said Flint. "In the Kuiper Belt, perhaps. That it originated on a planet that, perhaps, has broken up. That the planet in question sustained a particularly virile form of fungal life."

"Fungal," said Jason uneasily. He scratched absently at himself. "You still think that this is all something to do with some kind of alien fungus? But what, I mean, how… I've really seen nothing to back up that theory." He scratched himself some more, then stopped guiltily as he saw Flint staring at him. "Just a bunch of low-lives behaving badly."

"Don't you think it strange that they should all be acting in such an appalling manner?" Flint asked.

"No I don't!" said Jason loudly. A courting couple looked up in his direction, surprised. He lowered his voice. "I don't think it strange. They're just scum. Alcoholics and thieves and dole scroungers." He was sick of the way the sun was blazing down at him, he wanted to get back in his flat and have another drink.

"A somewhat intolerant attitude," remarked Flint calmly. "That's not like you, Jason."

Jason turned around moodily. From here he could see the house. "I'm on borrowed time," he said. "I'll be evicted if I don't pay my rent. And I'm not going on housing benefit. I don't want to feel like I'm turning into one of them."

Flint placed a hand on his shoulder and Jason flinched. "I'm taking over the investigation," he said, "and I'm hiring you. I'll pay your rent and living expenses. We're going to remain in the house until we find out what is going on and, if possible, stop it. Now let's get back inside."

When they got back, Roger was standing in the middle of the back lawn as he did on most sunny days. They watched him covertly from the side door. As usual, he wore nothing but knickers, and had his head tilted back towards the sun and his eyes shut. The side door stood propped open, as it did on most warm days.

"So this is the famous Roger, is it?" said Flint. "It's almost as if he is some kind of vegetable life form, deriving nourishment from the sun's rays."

"Either that, or some kind of old weirdo," said Jason impatiently. "Let's go indoors, I've got a headache."

"Don't you see? This gives us an opportunity," said Professor Flint. "While he is occupied outside, we can gain access to his room."

"You mean snooping?" said Jason in horrified tones as Flint led him inside.

"You are supposed to be a detective," said the professor.

The door to the basement flat was locked. An almost palpable stench wafted up from the depths. Flint took out a large key ring. To Jason's surprise, he recognised a set of skeleton keys.

"Where did you get them from?" he asked, as Flint

searched for one in particular.

"Oh, I've had these for some time," the professor said. "You should get some. They open a lot of doors, so to speak. Ah!"

He inserted one in the lock and turned it. The lock clicked.

"What are you doing in Roger's room?"

Bullshit Bill had appeared at the end of the hall. He shambled forwards and Jason was reminded of a killer gorilla in an old Tarzan film. Bill's eyes were redder than usual and a sickly smell of rot came from him. "Trying to rob the old man? Fucking thieves!"

He banged on the door of Vince's flat, and it opened after some muted cursing. A puzzled rat face poked out. Like Bill, his eyes were bloodshot.

"What? What? Fuckin' hell, Bill, what's up?"

'They're trying to break into Roger's room, mate.'

"What?" said Vince, outraged. "Fucking tea leaves! That poor old guy, and you're trying to rob him."

"Try to make sense," Professor Flint urged him. "What valuables is he likely to have? Why would we want to steal from him?"

"I seen ya trying to get in his door," said Bill. "I fucking hate thieves."

"You're a thief yourself, you hypocrite!" Jason snarled. Flint seized him by the shoulders as he tried to fling himself at Bill. Vince squared up to him. Luke came thundering downstairs, wanting to know what was happening. Like the others, his eyes were bloodshot.

"This is all a misunderstanding," said Professor Flint, his voice loud, with an air of authority gained during years of lecturing anthropology undergraduates. "We found the door open and wondered if Roger was in, wanting to invite him round for a drink. Now let's all settle down and return to our own lodgings."

Flint ushered Jason into the sanctuary of his flat, firmly locking the door behind them. As Jason slumped down on the settee, a pounding came from the door. His headache had reached migraine proportions. He felt exhausted. He lay his head back and, conscious of Flint's anxious gaze on him, passed out.

Jason dreamed, but he didn't know he dreamed. In his dreams, he rose from the settee, passed out of the professor's flat, right through the three tenants clustered outside, including Bullshit Bill who had found a sledgehammer somewhere. Then he was outside. The sunshine streamed down from a cloudless sky. In the middle of the unkempt lawn stood Roger, rooted to the spot, head back, soaking up the rays. His head was quivering slightly as if it was about to burst.

Jason was tramping up the steps now, soon finding himself at the kitchen door. Inside he saw the same squalor of unwashed dishes and the grease-stained cooker. But it was the opposite wall that drew his eyes. The bubbles had taken on a fully manlike form, and it was swelling, swelling outwards. As Jason watched, the wallpaper figure extended a wallpaper leg. A manlike shape of wallpaper and paste lurched towards him, wallpaper arms extended, wallpaper hands grasping for him. Jason distinctly saw the floral pattern of the wallpaper imprinted on the being's skin.

He was going down the steps to the basement now, down and down into the depths. Chanting echoed from the reeking gloom. His head was pounding in time to the chanting. He wondered if it was going to explode.

He was down in the cellar, and Roger was there, standing rooted to the spot, bloated flesh quivering as three cloaked and hooded forms knelt in worship before him.

They were outside, on the lawn. But only Jason was there, cloaked and hooded, chanting as the Roger-thing shook uncontrollably. Suddenly its head burst and a shower of gossamer exploded into the air, to drift away on the summer breeze.

The pounding in Jason's head was louder now, much louder. A monotonous, repetitive booming. He wanted to put his hands to his head, afraid it was about to explode like Roger's, but for some reason, he couldn't move them. He struggled and struggled....

...and woke to find himself sprawled across the settee. Professor Flint stood over him, watching in concern. Jason's scalp and face were wet with sweat.

The pounding from the dream continued into waking life, sending lances of agony through his brain. He looked up. The door shuddered with every thump. Suddenly it all clicked into place.

"Are they trying to smash the door down?" he mumbled. He remembered Bill had got a sledgehammer. But that was a dream, wasn't it? He could no longer tell dreams from reality.

"You're awake!" Flint said. "How you can fall asleep at a time like this…!"

With a terrible splintering noise the door burst open. Bill stood framed in it, eyes crimson, a sledgehammer in his hands. Was Jason still dreaming? Had he ever been dreaming? The two rat brothers crowded around Bill, eyes red, skin blotched with mould, arms outstretched, hands grasping like the wallpaper ghoul from Jason's dream.

"Get out before I call the police," said Flint.

Bill laughed. "How you gonna do that, old man," he said threateningly, gripping the sledgehammer menacingly, "when we're between you and the phone?"

Jason was half delirious, but anger swelled in his aching skull. He staggered to his feet and grappled with Bill, who had lifted the sledgehammer as if he meant to dash out the professor's brains.

The rat brothers forced their way past, laughing maniacally. Vince leapt over the settee in his eagerness to get to grips with the professor. Jason and Bill were struggling on the floor now, the fallen sledgehammer lying beside them. The professor backed away until his backside was brushing up against the bay window. Still, the rat brothers menaced him.

Jason scrambled to his feet, sweat dripping from his brow. When he lifted his fists to defend himself he cried out in revulsion. The backs of his hands were black with mould. Bill rose into a crouch, seemingly about to spring. Streaks of mould mottled his neck, some reaching as far as his chin. He was sweating too, and it was in the runnels of sweat that the mould was at its most fecund.

Bill's eyes were bloodshot and inflamed. Jason's own eyes were itching. His scalp was itching, his skin was itching. The stink of rot wafted from him as it did from everyone in the house.

Except the professor.

Flint was fending off the two giggling rat brothers who were trying to touch his face with their mould black hands. "You're the only one of us who's not affected," Jason said angrily. "Why's that? Why are you singled out?" The pounding in his head was growing louder. An unreasoning anger rolled over him.

"It's happened," Flint said, forcing down the rat brothers' hands. "What you feared. What I feared. You've become one of them!"

The roaring in Jason's head was so loud he barely heard the professor's words, but he knew what Flint was saying. "I am not one of them!" he snarled, wheeling around and sending Bill flying with a roundhouse kick to the chest. As Bill's head collided with the doorjamb, Jason turned to the rat brothers, gripped them by the folds of their shellsuits, and flung them against the wall.

They lay stunned on the stained carpet. Sweat still frothed from Jason's brow, his head still pounded. From somewhere outside there came a loud popping sound, a dull, hollow explosion.

Again he passed out. But this time he did not dream.

EPILOGUE

He awoke lying on his mattress. Flat on his back, legs together, arms by his sides. Still in his clothes. Like you might lay out a corpse. Sun streamed in dustily through the uncurtained window. For the first time in he didn't know how long, his mouth was free of that foul taste. And his headache was gone.

So was the smell of rot and unwashed bodies that had permeated the building. He took a deep breath and for once he didn't gag. He sat up, then got to his feet, and went to the door.

The hall was a scene of confusion. The door to Flat 2a had been smashed in, and the floor inside was littered. A nasty, viscous puddle covered the carpet by the door. Two more glistened by the bay window. A nauseating odour of rot emanated from them, but otherwise, the air was clear.

He went into the bathroom and looked out of the window. No sign of Roger. No sign of anyone. Just another of those viscous puddles in the middle of the lawn; and was that a trace of gossamer drifting past the window, like spores?

He went back down the hall and knocked on the door to the basement flat. No answer. Thoughtfully, he tried it. It was unlocked.

A short flight of steps led down to another door. He

turned the handle and it opened, revealing foul-smelling darkness. His groping hand found a light switch and he flicked it on. A cluttered room met his eyes, piled with old newspapers and cardboard boxes filled with junk. A sickly sweet odour of rot and faeces hung in the air, a bluebottle buzzed monotonously somewhere deeper within, but of Roger, there was no sign. The basement flat was nothing like it had been in his dreams.

He went upstairs to the kitchen. Again no one was about, but the bubbles on the wallpaper were gone. Fragments of wallpaper and wallpaper paste were splattered across the floor. For a long time Jason stood staring at them, his face thoughtful.

Hearing footsteps in the hall, and someone calling his name, he ran back down the stairs. Professor Flint stood there, looking up the stairwell. Beside him was a man about the same age, wearing a shabby tweed jacket.

"Jason!" said Flint. "There you are! This is Doctor Khan, an old friend. He's a GP who took early retirement, although he still works from time to time. I went to see if he could help."

Jason shook the doctor's hand. "Hello," he said.

"Hello Jason," said Khan. "So you're the patient."

"Patient?" said Jason. "I feel fine, doctor. Professor, what's all this about?"

"I found you collapsed on the floor in the first flat," Flint said. "When you didn't turn up for work for weeks on end and never answered the phone I began to worry. I called your ex-girlfriend but she hadn't heard from you in over a month. I came round, and found the door standing open, a terrible mess on the floor, and you lying in there."

He indicated Flat 2a. "In your flat?" asked Jason.

"My flat?" said Flint, perplexed.

Memories ebbed back into Jason's mind. The fight. The other tenants. Roger. "Yes, your flat. They broke down the door! I must have passed out. I was feeling pretty rotten, I can remember that much. My memories are hazy. It's like a dream. Did you take me back to my flat? I woke up feeling as fresh as a daisy."

Flint and Khan exchanged glances. "How about you come back to my house?" said the doctor. "I'd like to give you a very thorough medical examination."

"That's the best offer I've had in a long time," said Jason.

Khan lived in a converted farmhouse on the edge of town with three red setter dogs and a bedbound wife. He examined Jason in his study, where he still had an impressive collection of medical instruments.

"Are you saying you never moved into the bedsit?" Jason was saying to Professor Flint.

Flint shook his head. "I came down today, as I said. You'd not returned my calls, and I was concerned. You've obviously been very ill."

"He has indeed," announced Khan, finishing his examination. "Signs of fungal infection, although it's clear that it is on the mend. Something akin to tinea cruris, with candida albicans to top it off. Also, something else I have yet to identify. I'd like to take a blood sample, Jason, if I may, and get it sent off to the labs. I don't recognise this fungus at all. It's as if it came from another planet."

Jason looked at Flint. "Fungi from Yuggoth?" he asked.

"Unlikely." Flint shook his head. "The folklore maintains that the fungi from Yuggoth are a kind of crustacean. Some traditions link them with the Migou or Mi-Go of Tibetan tradition. The abominable snowman of the popular press."

Jason raised his eyebrows, looked away, looked back. "They're fungus... but they're crustaceans? How can fungal crustaceans be the same thing as the abominable snowman?"

Flint harrumphed. "Such inconsistencies are the daily bread of folklore research," he said. "Moving on, my more mundane research tell me that Roger was by no means a lodger, but in fact, the owner of the house when the meteor struck, back in the Sixties. Shortly afterwards he sold off the rest of it to a landlord but kept the basement flat. He developed a reputation for eccentricity after cutting all family ties."

"He was infected by the fungus from the meteor," Jason surmised. "Everyone who stayed there also became infected. That would explain their behaviour. Mine too. Maybe."

"Maybe," said Doctor Khan absently as he took a blood sample. "I'm going to prescribe a course of clotrimazole and miconazole. Anti-fungal medicine, you see, to treat what remains of your thrush and ringworm, and... hopefully the unidentified fungal infection. I'd also suggest a dandruff shampoo. And speaking as a doctor, albeit semi-retired, I'd suggest you move out of that house. It has a very unhealthy atmosphere."

Over the last twenty years **Gavin Chappell** has been published by Leidstjarna Magazine, Penguin Books, Countyvise, Horrified Press, Nightmare Illustrated, Death Throes Webzine, Spook Show, and the podcast Dark Dreams, among others. He has worked variously as a business analyst, a lecturer, a private tutor, a local historian, a tour guide, an independent film maker, and editor of Schlock! Webzine, Rogue Planet Press, and Lovecraftiana: the Magazine of Eldritch Horror. His influences include Tolkien, Robert E Howard, Michael Moorcock, HP Lovecraft, Lin Carter, and Terrance Dicks. He lives in northern England.

After being sacked from the short-lived Occult Crime Division of the Essex Police Force for reasons he refuses to explain, **Jason Steele** was bullied into setting up a private investigation business by his girlfriend, whose couch he was sleeping on. Despite an abiding scepticism about the occult, he finds himself called upon to investigate a series of strange and sinister crimes. He is ably assisted in his endeavours by independent researcher and former university lecturer, **Professor Flint**.

Both characters were originally conceived for 'One Foul Step From the Abyss', intended for submission for the as-yet-unpublished third instalment of Nordic Press' Doggerland trilogy.

THE PROFESSOR SNOW AFFAIR
ROBERT POYTON

"I hear you are a man to be trusted, Mr Braithwaite. A man who is both open-minded and discrete."

I mumbled a reply and motioned to my visitor to take a chair. We were in my office in Boston, a low-rent premises, considering the fashionable neighbourhood, and correspondingly cramped. The speaker was a young lady in her early twenties, wearing a plaid dress. She removed her bonnet, revealing a fashionably short hairstyle. *Shingling*, I believe it was called, it having recently excited some measure of controversy in the local press. "Please take a seat, Miss…"

"Snow. Eveline Snow. You may have perhaps heard of my father, Professor Arthur Snow?"

"Indeed, I have. In fact, I attended a lecture by him in New York two years ago. If I recall correctly, it was at the Theosophical Lodge in Rochester."

Miss Snow smiled. "Ah, yes. My father had some dealings with that society. Though I believe Madame Blavatsky herself was by that time resident in India."

I sat as she spoke, turning briefly to close the window, shutting out the sounds of the busy, springtime Chestnut Street below. Doing so brought into plain view the burn scars on my neck, despite the high collar I wore. I caught the brief flinch from Miss Snow, a reaction I was used to. To her credit, she passed no comment or asked no question. She waved away my offer of tea and continued. "My father is my reason for being here. That and, as I have stated, your reputation for reliability and sensitivity when it comes to certain… matters. Though, if you will pardon my rudeness, I expected someone a little older."

Now it was my turn to smile. "No offence taken.

I quite agree. Most of those with an interest in the occult sciences tend to be somewhat advanced in years. An interest brought on by an increasing awareness of mortality, perhaps?"

"Mortality," she echoed, her face softening for a moment.

"I apologise, Miss Snow, I did not mean to-"

She waved my apology away. "No need. You are somewhat more forthright than most Englishmen I have known, Mr Braithwaite."

"I have spent some time here in the Colonies." I raised my palms. "Some of that Yankee directness was bound to rub off." I opened the notebook on my desk and sat back in my swivel chair. "How may I be of service?"

"In short, Mr Braithwaite, I wish to hire you to accompany my father on a long journey. To San Francisco, to be precise. The journey is to be undertaken by train, and with all due haste."

"I see. And is your father under threat in some way? I must confess, Miss Snow, I am usually employed for my investigative skills rather than as a bodyguard."

"I understand. Nonetheless, it is primarily as a bodyguard that I require you, although your expertise in other areas may prove useful. And yes, there may be parties involved who wish to... impede my father's journey. Though as to what level of threat they may present I cannot say."

"And once we reach San Francisco?"

"Your services may be required for another day or two. Naturally, all travel expenses will be paid, alongside your fee. Money is not an issue, Mr Braithwaite, I am not without resources."

I took a pencil, jotted down a figure, then pushed the notepad across the desk. "That is my daily fee, Miss Snow." Normally I would have turned down such a job. Body-guarding, as far as I had seen, was a poorly paid and potentially lethal undertaking. However, my current situation was one of mild pecuniary depletion. More than that, the identity of the client and that hint of the *strange* intrigued me. As for danger, well I was confident that my time in the 2nd Warwickshire had equipped me with combative skills sufficient enough to deal with most threats. Miss Snow nodded and reached into her reticule.

"Please be at Boston station by eight tomorrow morning." She handed me a rail ticket. "I will be there, along with my father."

I nodded and rose as she stood. In two steps she was at the door. She paused halfway through it, turning to look at me over her shoulder.

"There is just one other thing you should know, Mr Braithwaite. My father is dead. This is to be his last journey."

I arrived at St James promptly the next morning, just as a large crate was being loaded aboard the train. Miss Snow stood quietly to one side, head bowed, as the porters wheeled away the cart and slid shut the large side door of the van. Shortly thereafter, we were ensconced in our own carriage. My employer had booked a private compartment alongside two sleeping booths in the last passenger coach of the train. Thus, we were positioned directly next to the guard van which, while it could be accessed from our corridor, was not a part of the train that would attract the footfall of regular passengers.

As the whistle blew, I stepped into the van to check all was well. A uniformed rail guard, who introduced himself as Henry, was sat, as arranged in place on a stool next to the pot-bellied stove in the corner. He had the grey, grizzled mutton-chops look of the solid, unflappable type, and I duly noted the coach gun leaning against the wall behind him. I checked the crate, which I now understood to contain the casketed body of the late Professor, and examined all three doors. All was to my satisfaction so, nodding to Henry, I next went to my sleeping berth to unpack my meagre luggage. That done, I returned to the compartment, where Miss Snow sat gazing abstractedly out of the window at the passing scenery. Not wishing to intrude on her meditations, I took a seat opposite, and slipped a thin volume out of my jacket pocket. A few moments later, she broke the silence.

"I see you are a fan of Poe, Mr Braithwaite?"

"Indeed, Miss Snow. Some may find him *outré*. Shocking or fantastical, perhaps. Yet I find that old adage of truth being stranger than fiction often holds true."

I closed the book and returned it to my pocket as she continued "I fully concur. For do not recent events of my own experience prove the veracity of what some may view as a cliché? I thank you again for taking on this task at such short notice, and with such little information. I feel it is only fair that I now avail you of the full facts of the situation. And perhaps the simplest and quickest way to do that is to let you read this."

She handed me an opened envelope, addressed to herself, postmarked *Kingsport, Mass.* The letter inside was dated March 13th 1885 and carried no return address. While the handwriting was clear and legible, it appeared to have been written either in a hurry or under some form of strain. It read as follows:

My Dearest Evie

Circumstances necessitate the brevity of this letter, but I hope it finds you well. I apologise for my somewhat protracted silence but, as you know, my current research has led me to some rather remote areas of the country. In addition, I have succeeded in infiltrating the particular group who were my main focus of interest. That, in itself, also necessitated somewhat my withdrawal from what we might call "normal" society.

Indeed, it is because of this infiltration that I now write. I have been able to make a brief escape from the group in order to pen and post this letter, but shall return to them forthwith. The reason for my return is the approach of a major ceremony or ritual that the group has scheduled for the very near future. It seems that a particular date this March presents the most propitious time for the conduct of this ritual. Its exact details are somewhat vague, though I have been able to piece together certain facts and rumours which, while seemingly incredible in their detail, not to mention disturbing in their implication, nonetheless match with all the other information I have been able to collate. I will not divulge the details of my research to you now, for not only is time short, I also would not burden you with the weight of such knowledge. However, I will say this. Should I not return alive from my travels... should my lifeless body be discovered, I implore, nay beg you to carry out the following instructions implicitly and to the letter. In fact, you can regard this as my last will and testament. I understand that you may find this request unusual, and that some might disregard it as the ramblings of a madman. But I have raised you, I hope, to be as open-minded to possibilities as both I and your dear, late mother. I, therefore, implore again that on recovery of my body, you have it shipped, without delay, to San Francisco. There, you are to seek out Master Kau. He is a Chinese scholar, and more besides, who will know what to do next. I am sorry that I cannot explain further, but can only do my utmost to impress on you that my very soul hangs in the balance, not to mention the looming shadow of a threat that might well spell doom for mankind. I realise this may sound overdramatic, ridiculous even, but there are dark forces at work. Indeed, those forces may even try to intervene to frustrate my request and I urge you to take all good care.

I apologise again for leaving you with such a burden, and truly hope that none of the above will come to pass. The thought of never seeing you again, my dear child, is a source of great pain to me. But please take comfort, at least, in the fact that in the event of my demise, once you carry out my instructions, I shall at last be reunited with my true love.

Yours with all affection
Father

I re-read the letter and sat back. It had obviously been read numerous times and I forbore to comment on the tear-stains that smudged the ink in places, for it would be a cold fish who critiqued a young lady on the death of her father.

"An unusual request, indeed." I handed the letter back to Miss Snow. "What do you know of this Master Kau?"

"Nothing. My father had not mentioned him before."

"I see. And this group he was investigating?"

"A religious cult, as best I can tell. You know my father was something of an anthropologist, with a specific interest in strange religions and occult practices."

"Judging from the postmark, they must be located on the Massachusetts coast, or very close to it." I thought for a while. I had witnessed enough queer goings-on during my time in Africa to restrain any scepticism I may have felt. "And how, if it is not too distressing, did you learn of your father's death, and subsequently come into possession of his remains?"

"I received a telegram from Kingsport police a week after I received the letter. It seems my father had burst into their station in a state of some distress. In fact, they described him as "raving." The police took him in, and secured him for his own protection, but my father apparently died a few hours later, of a seizure, apparently. The officers found a note with my address on it in his wallet and contacted me to make arrangements to return his body to Boston. I am his only surviving family, you see? And so, here we are. As soon as I heard of his death, I began making preparations for this journey. And, given my father's warning, to look for a suitable protector."

I rubbed my chin. "A strange tale, indeed. And were it anyone other than your father, I might, as he indicated, dismiss it as the imaginings of a madman. No, Miss Snow, I think we should take all of this at face value and proceed as your father requested. At worst, we have an uneventful trip to the West Coast. If anything else happens... well, I shall be prepared." I pulled back the flap of my jacket to reveal the Tranter holstered at my hip.

"I also," my companion replied, producing a Remington Derringer from her purse. I must have raised my eyebrows in amusement, as she swiftly retorted, "I have had some practice with it, you now."

"Well, practice makes perfect," I replied, somewhat archly. Then, on seeing her expression added, "I apologise. It is my military background. Her Majesty's forces are ingrained with notions of superiority above all others. We tend to view any other gun wielders as amateurs, at best. I am sure you are most proficient with your pistol, let us hope neither of us are required to put our skills to the test."

Perhaps partly mollified, Miss Snow nonetheless returned to her silent window gazing, and I returned to my Poe.

It was not until the second evening that anything untoward occurred. I checked in with Henry, mentioning I would return post-dinner to relieve him on watch, then Miss Snow and I made our way to the dining car. My own origins are at the more humble end of the social spectrum, nonetheless I was not overly intimidated at finding myself in a luxurious, first-class dining room. Our fellow diners were largely couples, older and definitely of a certain standing. None stood out as posing any threat, in fact, none stood out at all apart from the chap behind us, a most noisy eater. I must admit, the sound of him slurping his soup did set my teeth on edge. The only other disturbance came from a table at the other end of the carriage, where a portly, bearded, garrulous man was holding court. He dominated his group, both in size and volume, and I confess I felt some sympathy for the slight, somewhat worn-looking woman who I took to be his wife.

It was that very same man who was front and centre of the first event. We had joined the diners filing back to their compartments along the narrow corridor, when there was some form of rumpus ahead. It was the large man from the diner, his face even more flushed, from a surfeit of brandy, no doubt. He was actively shouting at his poor wife now, over some perceived misdemeanour. As is the way in polite company, most people looked the other way and pretended it was not happening. But then he raised his hand as if to strike her. His motion was arrested when the upheld arm was gripped from behind. A Chinese fellow, not tall, dressed in a smart, dark grey suit, was the gripper. The corridor fell silent.

"It is not nice to hit a lady," the fellow said quietly.

The larger man flushed even further, his eyes blazed as he attempted to pull his arm free. But the grip held, and I felt a sense that this young Chinese chap was considerably stronger than he looked. Finally, he released his hold, and the bully turned away with a curse. Thanks to my position, I could see what was going to happen next. Hands now concealed by his bulk, the man clenched a large fist and prepared to turn and strike what would no doubt be a devastating blow. I took a step forward and made to shout, but the warning was not required. As though he were moving in slow motion, the young man dropped his weight slightly, the sledgehammer punch sailing over his head. He then pushed his attacker with a curious, two-handed movement, sending the man reeling to crash into a wall close by me. He was seething with rage, snarling as he stood, causing the ladies present to cover their ears with shock at the stream of profanities that issued forth from his mouth. He appeared set to charge again at the Chinese fellow, who stood, quite impassive and unperturbed. Proceedings were interrupted by the arrival of a conductor, demanding to know the cause of the furore. It appeared that the man, even in his drunken state, recognised that nothing trumps the authority of a conductor on a train, and so he stormed off, dragging the poor woman in his wake. The conductor, satisfied that normality had been restored, gestured to the young man.

"Hey, Chinee," he called. "Get back to emigrant class. This section is not for the likes of you"

Once again without emotion, the Chinese chap demurred. His eyes briefly met mine as he turned to leave, and I fancied I saw the glimmer of something there. Recognition? Order restored, I accompanied Miss Snow to her berth, advised her to keep her door locked until morning, then took over Henry's position on the stool in the guard van. I came to with a start. The gentle rocking of the train, the warmth of the stove and that postprandial port had lulled me into sleep. It had been shattered by the usual nightmare... the flames... the smell.... poor Beckett's screams... I received a second start when a face loomed out of the rubrous glow to confront me. It was the young Chinese man. And he was brandishing a knife...

"I am sorry to have startled you," Vincent was seated on another stool, next to me, by the stove. "Well, you certainly did that," I replied. Following my jump, the young man had sheathed his knife and held both palms up. He had introduced himself as Vincent Liu. I lit a paraffin lamp, and we now sat talking. This close I could see I was right about his strength. Though slightly shorter than my own 5' 9", his suit did little to conceal a sturdy, compact frame. His hair was close-cropped to the scalp, his expression open. In age, I guessed him to be similar to my own 26 years, though, unlike me, he seemed rather unmarked by the passage of life and time.

"A bad dream?" he asked and, somewhat embarrassed, I waved the question away. "You have the bearing of a military man," he continued. "And your scars indicate a bad experience."

I felt my face flush, my hand coming up automatically to cover my neck. Here, in the privacy of the guard van, I had loosened my collar. Vincent sat back. "I apologise again. I fear I have offended you." He gave a curt bow of the head.

"It's nothing," I muttered. "Yes, I served for a time."

"I see. Well, if it helps, I too carry scars. Here." He rolled up the sleeves of his jacket and presented his forearms. In the light of the lamp, I could see the burns at the centre of each forearm. But these were not random scars, as my own, these had the form of brands; a stylised tiger on the left arm, a dragon on the right.

"My word!" I exclaimed.

Vincent rolled down his sleeves and smiled. "I would say, however, that mine were voluntary, while yours were not."

"These are of religious significance?" I was reminded of the scars and markings of certain tribes.

"Partly, yes. You might call them a test. A mark of achievement, but also a badge. An insignia."

"And what was it you did to that man? Some form of boxing? Where did you learn that?"

"I was taught by a priest," he replied.

"You learned to fight in a church?" I couldn't help myself from smiling, but then thought of the boxing clubs of my youth, often run by a local vicar.

"More a temple. At least until I met Liang Sifu."

"I have a distinct feeling that you could have caused that man a lot more injury than you did."

The smile faded. "Such an action would not have been in keeping with my beliefs. We have a saying, Mr

Braithwaite. Better to avoid than check, check than hurt, hurt than injure, and injure than kill."

"An admirable sentiment," I replied. "But what if the situation is of the most extreme kind?"

His face remained serious but with a hint of a smile. "Then we return the offender to Heaven, in order that he may be… re-trained."

"And you think we can trust him?"

I poured the tea into Miss Snow's proffered porcelain cup. "Yes, I believe so. I like to think I'm a good judge of character. Besides, he could have slit my throat as I slept. How he got into the guard van without me hearing, I still do not know."

Last night, Vincent had told me something of his background and of his mission. For he was on a mission just as much as I. I was explaining all this to Miss Snow over breakfast. To my annoyance, our slurper neighbour was in full flow behind me.

"He is part of an organisation with a Chinese name - the Heaven and Earth Society in English. Apparently, they have been opposing the cult that your father infiltrated for many years. He described the damage they are doing in China, how they weaken the will of the people with opium and promises of magic. And of more than promises."

"It seems a long way to travel. What brought him here?"

"Certain information he received about the cult's activities. I think it may be connected to the ritual your father wrote of. In fact, he picked up your father's trail at some point, that's why he came to Boston. Still, it is your decision as to whether we accept his help or not."

She sipped her tea and thought for a moment. "If you trust him, then yes. We do not know what threats may await, besides which he may be of help when we arrive in San Francisco. I have the name Master Kau but little else."

"I agree. I will ask him to sit with the guard in the van for now. I'm sure Henry will be pleased of the company."

Following breakfast, I left Miss Snow to check on Henry and Vincent. As I left them, I felt the train slowing. We had entered the environs of Chicago a short while ago, I guessed were now slowing to stop at the station. A conductor confirmed this, saying there would be a thirty-minute stop-over at Great Central Station. I must admit, this amount of sitting and inactivity was making me restless, so I relished the opportunity to stretch my legs. It was as I was making my way back to the train that I saw them. I think what drew my eye was the slurper. I had only spared him the briefest glance in the dining car, but here, as he was leaning out of the train doorway, I got a full glimpse of him. A queer-looking cove, short, rotund, dressed in a rather shabby suit. He was gesticulating toward a group of men coming along the platform, six of them, all of similar appearance to himself. It was then that he glanced up and noticed me watching him. For a second his somewhat protuberant, watery eyes locked on mine. Was there the faintest hint of a smile on his thin lips? Then he disappeared back into the interior of the train. With an inexplicable shiver, I made my way back to my own carriage.

The attack came that night. I had mentioned my odd experience to Miss Snow and Vincent, and we agreed to all keep watch on the Professor's crate that evening. At my request, Henry had provided a cushioned chair, which Miss Snow occupied, a wrap around her shoulders. I periodically stood and paced the van, my restlessness had returned. Vincent sat like a statue on the stool, straight back, eyes closed, though I do not think he was sleeping. For some hours nothing occurred, and I eventually found myself sitting on the floor by the stove, drowsing in its warmth.

The lamp was guttering when a scuffling sound from above jerked me into wakefulness. I glanced up. Vincent's eyes were open but he remained immobile. Miss Snow was snoring softly, I awoke her with a nudge of my foot, signalling her to remain quiet. I slowly rose and took out the Tranter. Vincent likewise stood, rolling his shoulders, and drawing two large knives from within his jacket. At the sound of another scuffle, he pointed to the hatch in the roof. I stood under it, while he moved to the end door. Miss Snow, Derringer in hand, backed into a corner, eyes scanning all angles. Alert though we were, the attack still came as a surprise. There was a guttural cry from above and the hatchway blew in, as if from an explosive charge. Despite flinching against the splinters that rained down, I raised my gun and fired, the noise deafening in the enclosed space. The face that appeared in the hatchway disappeared, but I had no time to congratulate myself on my marksmanship. Another cry, and the end door similarly blew in, its lock bursting, to slam into the wall. Vincent dodged aside, narrowly avoiding being hit, bringing his knives up into a guard position. The doorway was immediately filled with a threatening shape that lashed out with a wickedly-curved gaff hook. Vincent deftly weaved away from it, simultaneously chopping down, eliciting a scream of pain from his attacker. But the man was not alone. Another pushed in behind him, swinging his hook overhead.

I had no time to see what happened next, as a bulky form dropped from above, crashing into me, knocking me down. Suddenly, two clammy hands were squeezing around my throat, a pallid, hate-filled face thrust close to my own, and my senses overwhelmed with a rank odour. I kicked out, but my assailant had his whole weight on me and his grip was devilishly strong. My fingers scrabbled for the Tranter, dropped as I fell, but it lay a few agonising inches beyond my reach. Stars swam in my blackening vision, my heart felt it was about to burst in my chest. Then came the sharp crack of a pistol, a spray of gore, and my assailant dropped like a stone. Above him stood the form of Miss Snow, smoking Derringer in hand.

"I told you I had practised," she coolly observed. I quickly stood and turned to assist Vincent. Truth be told, he needed little help. One attacker sat slumped in a corner, clutching a ruined arm. Another lay motionless in an expanding pool of blood. A third had dropped his hook and had grabbed both of Vincent's wrists in an attempt to control those fearsome knives. I lifted the Tranter to take aim, but Vincent twisted, turned and dropped his weight, sending his attacker head over heels to crash against the crate, where I put two bullets into him. For a second, the three of us stared at each other in silence. Then more footsteps sounded on the roof above, receding. "There were six of them boarded, plus one already here." I moved to the ruined door, gun levelled against any potential threat. The corridor beyond lay empty and quiet.

"I do not think they will attack again tonight," Vincent suggested. "They know we are prepared now."

Miss Snow, a look of profound distaste on her face, nudged one of the bodies with the toe of her boot. I have to say, I admired her grace under pressure. "What do we do with these?" she asked. It was a fair question. We had four bodies on our hands, for the man in the corner had bled to death. Thankfully, it appeared the struggle had gone unnoticed, the nearest passengers being asleep, likewise the staff in the caboose. I ran a hand over my aching neck and croaked, "If we report this, we will likely be detained until we reach San Francisco. And once there, we would be subject to the attentions of the local police. I have no doubt our actions here were lawful, but it could take days to extract ourselves from an investigation."

"Time we don't have." Miss Snow glanced down at the recumbent form again, then up at me. We reached a silent agreement. I unbolted the large side door and slid it open. Cold air immediately filled the carriage. Beyond lay only darkness, with the occasional vague, blurred outline of trees. With Vincent's help, I rolled the bodies across the floor and out into the night. By the time the door was slid shut, Miss Snow was already mopping up the blood, with sawdust from the fire bucket and a broom she had found in a corner. Again, I admired her composure.

"The door and hatch?" Vincent asked, indicating the ruin of each.

"I'll square it with Henry. I'll think of something. Now, Miss Snow, might I suggest you get some sleep? I'll stay here. Vincent, could you keep guard over our compartment?" Vincent nodded. Before they moved off I took a snifter from my hip flask and offered it to him. He declined, but Miss Snow took it and knocked back quite the slug of fiery brandy. She coughed and nodded, then moved towards me, hands raised.

"You should let me examine your throat, Mr Braithwaite. I imagine you'll have some nasty bruising there. I have some medical experience."

"No - no! Thank you, I shall be fine," I protested.

She halted. "Very well, as you wish. I shall see you in the morning, then. And thank you for your work here tonight. Thanks to both of you. I am glad to see the recommendations were justified."

With that the pair left, leaving me to reload the Tranter and take watch once more, this time fully awake with the familiar surge of nervous energy that takes hold post-battle.

Thankfully, we were left unmolested for the rest of the journey. I thought it best to confine ourselves to our compartment and the guard van, arranging to have meals brought to us. I spun Henry a yarn about hobos, and he apologised profusely on behalf of the rail company, both the door and the hatchway being promptly repaired. He also organised an extra guard to keep watch over us. We had quickly searched the bodies before their disposal, but had found nothing on them, save a small amount of cash. Each carried that same peculiar look as the Slurper, indeed they might well have been related. And my only sight of that individual came at the last stop before our destination, Salt Lake City. I took the opportunity to stretch my legs once again, and noticed him exiting the telegraph office on the platform. He half sneered, half cowered on seeing me, before hurrying back onto the train. That did not bode well for our arrival, but I resolved to do my best to protect both Miss Snow and the remains of her late father.

We rolled into San Francisco the next morning, and I got my first taste of the Pacific breeze. Miss Snow had already arranged transportation of the crate to a freight container held in a secure rail shed. At my suggestion, she also arranged for extra guards. The casket secure, we began our search for the mysterious Master Kau. Miss Snow had booked us rooms in the Globe Hotel, on the edge of Chinatown, which, we reasoned, was the most likely location of our quarry. By lunchtime, we were already strolling the streets of the neighbourhood. I noticed that Vincent had changed into more traditional garb, but still, we attracted some odd looks from passersby. I must admit, I found the area fascinating. Whilst being born in a leafy suburb of Birmingham, I had spent some time in London, the beating heart of the Empire. San Francisco appeared as busy and bustling, and many of the buildings here had distinct Chinese features, such as pagoda roofs and colourful banners. We began asking around for Master Kau, but met with blank faces, even, in some cases, thinly veiled hostility.

"It is the Act," Vincent explained. "The Chinese Exclusion Act. It banned Chinese immigration. Also, no Chinese may testify against a white man in court, and there is no right to vote for us here."

Miss Snow snorted at that. "Much the same as women, then. It's an outrage."

I kept my own counsel as Vincent continued. "It has led to a lot of anger amongst my people, for the very rail-road we came in on is built on Chinese bones." We paused at the railings of a large square, somewhat akin to those of London. Vincent pointed to a bench. "Wait there. I may be able to find out more on my own."

Miss Snow and I followed his instructions, sitting patiently on the bench, chatting for the next thirty minutes, or so. We spoke cheerfully enough, but I could sense her tension, her concerns, and so kept to the lightest of subject matters. Vincent duly returned and beckoned us to follow him. He took us off the main streets, and through a maze of back alleys, home to some of the most disreputable-looking characters and establishments I had seen in my travels. He paused on the porch of a single red door, nondescript save for a small sign at its lintel. It was a simple cross, well, more of a plus sign, with a single bar at the end of each arm. I shrugged and raised my hands.

"It is the ancient character for *Wu*. In English it means sorcerer." He smiled and rapped sharply on the shiny wood. A small hatch slid open and an old woman peered out. She muttered something in Chinese and slammed the hatch shut. Vincent sighed and knocked again, speaking in Chinese. The hatch opened once more, and this time Vincent raised his arms, allowing the loose sleeves of his robe to fall away, revealing his arm brands. The hatch slammed shut again, but was this time followed by the sliding back of bolts. We were ushered into a narrow passageway, from thence up a steep flight of steps and into the upper floor of the building.

Despite its squalid outer appearance, the interior, or at least this part of it, was immaculate and richly decorated. The large main room had been converted into some sort of temple. Vincent immediately stepped across to the altar, behind which hung several portraits and a number of statues. A bowl of fruit sat atop the altar, alongside some smoking incense sticks. Vincent lit another stick, held it to his forehead and bowed three times. As he did so, a striking figure in a yellow robe came in through a far door. He gave Miss Snow and I a quick glance, then smiled and hurried across to Vincent, who placed one hand over a fist and bowed. The two began talking quietly in Chinese, and Vincent motioned us over.

"This is Master Kau," he told us. "I have explained our mission. He has agreed to help us. Come, there is tea. Proper Chinese tea!"

We were soon seated in a small room at the side of the temple, around a table on which stood a large teapot and three small cups. Master Kau rolled back his sleeve and poured, giving me a chance to examine him further. He was a stocky man I judged to be in his fifties, though his skin was quite smooth. His eyes, however, seemed much older and sparkled with life. He wore a yellow robe over his clothing, with a curiously shaped black hat atop his head. After pouring, he raised his cup in salute, took a sip, and sat back, stroking his wispy beard.

"Brother Liu tells me you have a serious problem?" He spoke slowly, his accent a little more marked than Vincent's. I let Miss Snow explain, she even showed him her father's letter. Following that, he and Vincent spoke again in Chinese, after which he sighed.

"This is very serious, indeed. And yes, your father had contact with me, and I warned him as I warn you. The cult your father investigated is widespread and dangerous. For many years we have fought them in our own country, and beyond. They have a presence here in San Francisco. That is who I think the man following you was messaging."

"Why do they want the Professor's body?" I asked.

Master Kau poured more tea. "What do you know of the origins of mankind, Mr Braithwaite?"

I shook my head. "Very little. I had a vaguely religious upbringing, I suppose, but nothing beyond that. I am aware of Darwin's work, of course, one could scarce be otherwise given the furore it caused."

"Your Mister Darwin is partly right," Kau continued, "though he only hints at the full truth. In short, there are

~147~

beings that exist beyond the mundane world of humans. These beings date back to days of inconceivable antiquity, way beyond the histories of even my own people."

"I see. They are the gods of old? Of the Ancient Greeks and so on?"

"Older even than that, Mr Braithwaite. But yes, in a sense. They form the root from which the world's mythologies have grown. But such legends are the merest shadow of the reality of the Old Ones. And they are far more terrible than even the wildest imagining of myth."

"And this cult worships them?"

"Worship one, or some of them, yes. They have the belief that bowing before these beings will bring them special favour and knowledge. Perhaps they are right. Though such knowledge is not for the minds of men, our minds are far too fragile for such information. As well try to contain the ocean in a teacup!" He placed his cup on the table as if to emphasise the point. "As to the Professor, his research, and that of Brother Liu, confirms my worst fears. That the cult has conducted a most foul ritual. For the star alignments were certainly right. But back to our origins. It might shock you both to know that humanity was a creation of these Old Ones, or one set of them, at least. The forbidden lore tells us they created a number of servitor races, mankind being one of the lesser. And certain of those servitors survive to this day, in forgotten corners of the world."

"Good God," I uttered. "What are these things?" Then, thinking back to the queer look of our attackers, "And those men, their peculiar features..." An implication gripped me that caused me to shudder.

"Yes," Master Kau nodded. "These cults engage in certain rites of what is the word…? Congress! This results in the type of person you saw on the train. And I suspect the ritual your father was involved in was of similar purpose, though the being, or essence of being, joined with him was something far more ancient and potent than that of your attackers. For the first servitor race were like nothing seen on earth, before or since. It is written that very few survived intact to the modern age, though fragments remain. These fragments might be… introduced…under the right conditions into a human in order to create a hybrid. I believe there is a type of wasp which does something similar. But the result here is the creation of a being with powers beyond the normal, to serve the cult and the god they worship."

Miss Snow gave a small cry and placed a hand over her mouth.

"Forgive me, Miss Snow. I did not mean to upset you. Your father was a wise and humble man, we shall mourn his loss deeply. But I fear we must move swiftly, we have very little time before the process is complete. In short, Miss Snow, we must ritually destroy your father's body."

Master Kau insisted we rest at the temple while he made some arrangements. He spoke of local groups known as Tongs, ostensibly formed to protect the interests of the Chinese populace, though some had fallen into criminal ways. Nonetheless, he assured us they would unite against such a threat. To this end, he had summoned a person known as Little Pete, a man who now stood before us in the temple hall. I had imagined that his sobriquet related to his stature, though he was not particularly diminutive and, that aside, he radiated a confidence that lent him a certain presence. It was also not hard to notice that he sported a chainmail vest and had a gun at each hip! Two burly-looking henchmen, hatchets hanging from their belts, waited over by the door. After introductions had been made, Little Pete spoke to us.

"I will help you. Kau Sifu has explained. These people are dangerous. But I also have my own reasons. For they have begun to interfere in my trade. A man known as Pang Lian appears to be their boss. No-one knows where he came from, few have even seen him. But he is attempting to take over my operations. So," he nodded to Vincent and Master Kau, "as both of these men are my kinsmen from Kwangtong, and for business reasons, I will help. First, we need a safe place for the casket. Here is no good, we could not bring it in unnoticed." He thought for a moment. "My theatre. I recently acquired the Jackson Street theatre, it is closed while we renovate. It will be easy to smuggle a crate in, and my men can easily guard the place. Will this be a suitable place for your ritual, Sifu?"

Master Kau nodded.

"Excellent," Little Pete grinned. "Then it is decided!"

"Well, I always wanted to be on stage," Miss Snow smiled as we trod across the boards. I was glad to see that she had recovered something of her usual verve and hoped that the shock of recent events was a fading memory. Nonetheless, her expression saddened as she laid a hand on the crate now sitting at the centre of the stage. Vincent stood to one side, chatting quietly with Master Kau. Little Pete walked around, giving orders to the various tough-looking men stationed around the stage and auditorium. The place was certainly much grander than I expected, I estimated it could seat several hundred and was as plush as any theatre I had been to in England. Still, it was obvious that decoration was underway, with sheets everywhere. Indeed, it was under such a sheet that the case had been brought in, through the side door and straight up onto the stage. Little Pete had also arranged other lodgings for us, where we could be protected more easily. Vincent came over to me.

"Kau Sifu says he will be ready in a couple of hours. We have to wait for a certain conjunction of the celestial spheres, then the cleansing ritual can begin. In the meantime, all we can do is wait and hope we are not too late."

I nodded, and checked, for the third time, that the Tranter was at my hip. Despite the obvious security in place, I had a small itch at the back of my mind, something I had learned to pay attention to in other, no less dangerous situations. A splintering sound behind me caused me to start, but it was just the Tong men, on Master Kau's orders, opening the crate to reveal the casket within. Shortly the remnants of the crate were cleared away, and the plain, heavy casket placed on a trestle table, stage centre, as if awaiting the start of some performance. Indeed, my mind was cast back to seeing the show of the great John Nevil Maskelyne as a youth in England. It had been his debunking of the Davenport Brothers' so-called "supernatural" feats that had first awoken my interest in this area and led largely to my current occupation. Still, there was no audience here, save some hard-faced hatchet men, and the mood was far from festive or jolly.

Nothing happened for another hour or so, when some of Little Pete's men came onto the stage carrying sacks of rice. Under Master Kau's direction, they began pouring the grains in a circle around the coffin, as he made various chants and hand gestures over it. The theatre lay in increasing gloom as twilight fell. I lit a lamp and hung it on the hook at the side of the stage, other lights were similarly lit, until the coffin was bathed in a circle of light from above that matched the circle of rice on the boards. The air grew strangely still, a hush fell over the theatre. Again I was reminded of that pregnant pause before the performance proper begins. Vincent took up position at the head of the coffin, I noted he carried a long, straight sword. Master Kau brandished a similar weapon, its red tassel waving wildly as he drew shapes or characters with it in the air. The smell of incense from a pair of large censers wafted across to me in the wings. Miss Snow stood at my side, tense but resolute. And then came a shout.

A commotion issued forth from the darkness at the back of the theatre, cries, a gunshot, then more shouts.

Suddenly, faintly illumined by the stage lights, a group of people emerged along the central aisle. Six men, brandishing knives, one with a pistol in his raised hand. The Slurper was with them, along with his remaining companion from the train. And in their midst, leaning on two sticks, wobbled a figure whose lineament and locomotion invited both humour and terror in strangely equal proportions. I have never before, or since, seen such a large man. Large in the sense of rotund, as there was nothing of the athletic about him. He was tall, mind you, looming over his men, but also incredibly round in girth, broad of shoulder, his limbs thick and heavy. He wore a simple shift or robe, stretched tight across his frame, the large bald head atop supported by numerous chins. And the face, his face was… strange. At the time I put it down to a trick of the light, for his features appeared to flicker, to subtly change. At first he appeared Chinese, then more European, then back again. The impression was of a person stood before the screen of a magic lantern show, the features projected onto his face rather than being part of it. And as he drew near their projected from him the most intense chill I have ever felt. Akin, I imagine to that Polar chill described by Nares and the like. He came to a juddering halt just before reaching the stage and looked up at us. A smile opened across the moon-like face and a voice issued forth. If anything, the chill increased. For that voice was how I imagined a thing long dead would sound. There was no air in it, it oozed out of the mouth, like corruption from a wound. Yet, at the same time, there was something musical within it, a certain reediness or fluting that played around its upper registers.

"Well now," the large man said. "What a gathering we have here."

"Pang Lian?" exclaimed Little Pete.

"The very same," came the reply. "How wonderful it is to finally meet you, Fong Ching Toy. But you are not the reason for my presence here today, though I am sure we shall have another meeting in the near future. No, I am here for this." He raised a stubby hand to point at the coffin. "My Innsmouth brethren informed me of your imminent arrival here. How fortuitous, though ironic in the circumstances. Nevertheless, it is most kind of you to deliver this hatchling to me. For birth is a wondrous thing, is it not?"

I found myself moving to the front of the stage as if drawn, Miss Snow beside me. The globose head turned towards us. Behind, I could hear Master Kau continuing his chant, more intently now.

"And here she is," Pang's eyes creased. "The dutiful daughter. I'm sure your father is most proud."

"*Is* proud? "I snapped. "What are you talking about? Professor Snow is deceased!"

The laugh was deep and reminiscent of a mudslide I'd once narrowly escaped in Africa.

"If it comforts you to think so. Yet a living host is required, for sustenance and growth. No, Professor Snow is quite alive and aware, though, to all outward appearances, he has shuffled off this mortal coil."

Miss Snow gave a gasp and sagged against me.

There came another laugh. "You need comforting? I would woo you for my own, your affections to entreat, and bid you come to me alone, such a dainty little treat."

A pallid, slug-like tongue flickered lasciviously over the lardaceous lips.

"You swine!" I cried, withdrawing the Tranter and, without even thinking, firing off two shots, their report echoing around the theatre. Pang's men made to leap forward but, at some invisible signal, stopped. Pang laughed, glancing down at the two bullet holes in his gown. Nothing came forth from them, the impact of the bullets had not even so much as rocked him back. I had heard of bulletproof vests, of course, a recent development I had seen demonstrated in Boston. But even if they protected from the full force of shots at such close range, a man would still be knocked back or over. Pang had merely...*rippled*. The stubby hand shot out again and I found myself as if in the grip of an enormous python or anaconda. With a groan, I dropped the gun and staggered back. I heard Miss Snow cry out as I stumbled into the wall and slumped to the floor. The intense pain squeezed out beads of sweat on my brow, and just as I thought my guts would burst, the sensation disappeared as quickly as it had come. I heaved in breaths, ribs aching as though I had gone ten rounds with the Boston Strong Boy. That voice wormed its way into my ears again.

"You'll find me hard to hurt, young man, though you sting my feelings. Come. Let us be friends, come before me, face to face. I feel you'd change your mind if you'd but submit to my embrace."

I struggled to my feet, with some assistance from Miss Snow, and snarled my defiance. However, I felt most impotent. If bullets could not stop this man, if man he be, then what hope had we? Vincent obviously did not feel the same. He flew past me in a balletic leap off the stage, cut down the henchman wielding the gun, then thrust his blade deep into Pang's blubbery chest. This time there was an effect. Pang let forth a cry of anger or pain, but then surged forward as Vincent withdrew the blade for another strike. The backhand swipe seemed almost nonchalant, yet it knocked Vincent over, he rolled several times before recovering his feet. Master Kau interrupted his chanting to cry out "Liu Kar-Leung, get to the coffin! It is almost time!"

Clutching his chest in pain, Vincent nonetheless complied, running lightly up the steps to position himself at the head of the casket. I noticed the blade of the sword in his hand was smoking, but appeared intact. Little Pete had snapped out of his trance and now ordered his men forward. A battle commenced between Pang's remaining men and the Tong members. Blades flashed, hatchets rose and fell, Pang remained motionless amidst it all, seemingly unconcerned whether his men prevailed or not. There came a lull in the battle, the quiet broken only by the groans of the wounded. It was interrupted by the sound of knocking. I turned, in some confusion, to Vincent.

"Why are you knocking on the coffin?" I asked.

He looked up at me, and for the first time, I saw fear on his face. "I am not, Mr Braithwaite. The knocking is coming from within!"

I'll admit, strange as it may sound, my first thought was of Poe and his references to premature burial. *Could the Professor still be alive?* Yet such fancies swiftly evaporated, for as Master Kau's chanting reached a crescendo, as Pang's oleaginous laughter filled the auditorium, there came a great crash, the coffin lid flying up and out, scattering splinters across the stage. And from within, there rose a thing whose sight, whose mere fact of existence, blasted my mind with the force of a cannonball. For Professor Snow's face arose from the ruins of the casket… but not by conventional means. The grimacing head sat atop a snake-like neck that arose a full six feet above the form below. The face was awful to behold, the weirdly animated rictus of death combined with the natural process of decay lent it a terrible aspect. Miss Snow screamed and threw her hands up to block out the awful sight. I felt rooted to the spot, though somehow managed to raise my gun to snap off three quick shots. Whether any of them hit, or whether they would have achieved anything, I do not know. Vincent had ducked back as the creature burst forth, he now swung his sword wildly, a blow that the glistening column avoided with ophidian ease. Twitching creepers appeared over the lip of the coffin, curiously coloured fronds or tentacles that blindly felt their way down to the floor. Then the whole thing began…. *pouring* itself out of its former resting place.

My recollections of consequent events are somewhat vague. I remember Master Kau throwing a handful of crimson powder, a flash, cries of terror and alarm. I remember Vincent calling to me, as if from a great distance.

"The lantern, Edward! Throw the lantern!"

I remember picking up the hanging lantern and hurling it full force at that blasphemous shape that writhed and screamed in the midst of the red cloud, and the subsequent *whoomp* of the fireball that enveloped it. Still, it screamed, even as it shrivelled and shrank, and blackened and screamed, and writhed and screamed....

I came to with Master Kau holding a cold, damp cloth to my forehead. I sat up quickly, then winced at the pain.

"What - "

"Quiet now," he soothed. "All is well. That... thing... is gone."

Vincent's face appeared over his shoulder. I couldn't help laughing, both his eyebrows were gone. Then I felt the sting of my own skin and, lifting a hand, discovered mine had too.

"I ache all over," I groaned. The smell of burning came to my nostrils and, for a moment I was back in the hospital... that stench, Becket's cries of agony, the moans of the wounded and the dying... The fiery tang of brandy snapped me back to the present, Vincent had poured half the contents of my flask down my throat. I spluttered and rose unsteadily to my feet. We were in a dressing room of the theatre. Outside I could hear gruff voices and general clangour.

"The Fire Department," explained Master Kau. "After the Great Fire, they take even the smallest conflagration most seriously here!"

"Pang?" I wheezed.

"Vanished," said Vincent. "Kau Sifu told me we

were very fortunate. The creature had not quite fully formed as he finished the ritual. Had it got out and made contact with Pang, it could all have been quite different."

"Miss Snow?"

"She is here." Vincent spoke quietly, "Though she has suffered much shock."

Indeed, Miss Snow sat in the corner, a lady from the theatre fussing around her. I went over and crouched in front of her, taking her hand in mine. She looked up, her face pale, her eyes reddened with tears.

"How are you?" was all I could think to say.

She mumbled something and squeezed my tremulous hand. On a whim, I handed her the flask and she drained it of its contents, which appeared to go some way in reviving her spirits.

Mid-afternoon the next day saw us back at the Grand Station, about to board the train for the return trip. Little Pete had arranged a large apartment for us to rest in, guarded by his men. By the time of our leaving, Master Kau was on hand to see us off, Vincent at his side. They informed us that there had been much activity overnight as the Tongs moved hastily against Pang. That man... that creature... had not been seen, though.

"Has Pang gone for good?" Miss Snow asked, shuddering.

"I somehow doubt it," Master Kau replied. "But now he has been exposed, I imagine Little Pete and the rest of the Tongs will do their utmost to track him down and destroy him, with my assistance. Still, a city is an easy place to hide. And there are other cities growing here too. Los Angeles, for example."

The train whistle blew and the guard cried out.

"I shall stay here for a short time," Vincent explained. "To assist Kau Sifu and to learn from him. After that, I shall return to Boston. Perhaps I shall see you there?"

I nodded. "That would be most agreeable, yes." We shook hands. Miss Snow likewise said her farewells and we boarded. She sat sad and silent in our private compartment, not speaking until the train was well underway.

"Do you think that will be the end of it?" she quietly asked.

I sighed. "I could say yes, but I think we both know that would be a lie. I imagine that these cult-types have long memories. And now, we are both known to them." My voice was still hoarse.

Miss Snow said nothing but turned to look out of the window, her face drawn, her expression grave. Eventually, there came a soft whisper. "I fear the same."

I made to respond, but all that came out was a dry croak. My throat had finally given up the ghost. My companion smiled faintly and stood to hand me my own flask. "I forgot to give it back. But here. I had it refilled."

I gratefully accepted it and took a welcome slug. "Why, thank you, Miss Snow," I bowed my head with as much gravity as I could muster.

"Why, you are most welcome, Mister Braithwaite," she replied with a small curtsy. "And why don't you call me Eveline from now on?"

Rob Poyton is a long-time fan of the classic weird fiction authors and set up Innsmouth Gold as an outlet for his musical and publishing projects. To date he has appeared in a number of anthologies, published six Lovecraftian anthologies, and authored around a dozen novels and short story collections.

He is also co-host of the Innsmouth Book Club and Strange Shadows podcasts, and co-organiser of the Innsmouth Literary Festival. A keen musician and martial arts practitioner, originally an East Londoner, Rob has now taken root in rural Bedfordshire, where no-one can hear you scream.

His story in this collection marks the first appearance of **Braithwaite**, **Liu** and **Snow**... it seems likely we shall be meeting them again...

MOTHER OF SERPENTS
GLYNN OWEN BARRASS

The train was nearing his destination, according to the time on Spencer's pocket watch. Currently passing through the Yorkshire Moors, the view beyond his window depicted a beautiful, untamed wilderness. Purple bracken covered the low green hills and valleys, the occasional rock outcropping and stone mound jutting up between the flowers. *This is nature at its most primal*, Spencer thought. There was poetry to be written about this desolation, poetry waiting for a man better with words than him to take pen to paper.

He longed to walk through the moorland plateau, to feel that rough country under his feet. He wondered if he would have time to visit them during his sojourn.

"Not bloody likely," he said under his breath, and instantly regretted it.

"Ah, I see you're admiring our moors. It's very mild there you know, even at this time of year."

Spencer looked to his companion, nodded politely. Although the train was far from full, the gentleman had chosen to join him. He had florid cheeks, a thick blonde moustache going to grey. In his tweed cap, hunting jacket and knickerbockers, the man looked ready for the moors himself. Spencer cringed at the thought of having the insufferable fellow as a companion there.

Stainsby, as he'd introduced himself, appeared to be awaiting an answer. The man had almost talked him to death at the start of their journey. He wasn't going to fall into that trap again.

"The Romans visited the moors, you know?"

It seemed Stainsby would not be perturbed.

"Arrived in AD Seventy-One, built signal stations

all along the coast at Scarborough, Filey, Næddre on the Wold, and Ravenscar."

Spencer's attention pricked up at the mention of Næddre on the Wold, his destination.

"You're quite a fount of knowledge, sir," he replied.

The man grinned, his moustache bristling. "Oh, just a dabbler in local knowledge really. You know the Romans brought Greek practices—"

The carriage door opened behind them.

"Next stop, Næddre on the Wold Peak Station!" the conductor boomed. "All off for Næddre on the Wold."

"Excuse me," Spencer said and stood in his seat. A change of scenery was visible outside. Beyond the untamed moors, he saw uneven cliff edges, and beyond those, the metallic blue of the ocean.

Stainsby, looking out the window himself, said, "You know the name Næddre on the Wold comes from—"

Spencer reached to the luggage holders above his head for the leather suitcase he'd purchased especially for the trip. He retrieved it loudly, drowning out the other man's words.

"Time to dash!" he said, taking the suitcase down. He could tell the train was slowing, both from the vibrations and the view outside. Spencer leant forward, offered his hand, and continued, "A pleasure to meet you sir, pleasant trip."

"A pleasant trip to you too," Stainsby replied. His hand felt warm and moist.

It came as a relief that Stainsby wasn't getting off with him, and Spencer headed quickly to the end of the carriage. The train had slowed significantly now, and soon after lurched to a stop. Spencer saw a conductor enter the vestibule beyond the carriage door.

He braced himself and headed through the door. The conductor was just opening the doors to the station. Spencer smiled, nodded at him, and stepped down onto the platform.

The platform was covered in gravel that crunched underfoot. The stationhouse before him, a large brown, wood-panelled structure, had a ticket booth built into the front wall. A pair of bicycles stood leaning against the booth. An elderly man sat on one of two benches fronting the building, stared at him lazily.

Spencer turned and headed down the platform. A heavy-set, elderly woman was climbing on the train, assisted by a harried-looking porter. She sobbed heavily into a handkerchief.

Curious, Spencer thought, but his real concern was to get directions to Næddre on the Wold.

Beyond the stationhouse a white fence lined the platform. An open gate stood a little ways along, so he decided to head that way.

Hurried footsteps sounded behind him, and a voice shouted, "Sir, sir?"

Spencer turned on his heels. The source proved to be a lad in his teens, wearing an oversized grey flat cap and grey jacket. Beneath matching grey knickerbockers and green socks, his shoes were as white as his beaming smile.

"I was meant to be there greeting you sir." The lad panted as he spoke. "But I was just in the station, using the conveniences. You must be the Scotland Yard man, yes? I can tell by your bearing."

Spencer put his suitcase to the ground and said, "Detective Inspector Edward Spencer, a pleasure to meet you, er…"

"George is the name sir, Georgie for short," the lad said and shook Spencer's proffered hand. "Lord Boynton sent me along sir, to pick you up and take you to the village, I'm his odd-job man and messenger."

Lord Boynton, an old school-friend of his Superintendent and the reason for his presence.

"All right Georgie," Spencer said, "Is it a long walk?"

"Oh no sir," the lad grinned, "There's a car waiting." He stepped forward, took the suitcase, and added, "Follow me."

Georgie rushed past Spencer and headed through the gate. He followed quickly behind him.

Beyond the gate lay a dirt road covered in horse and cart tracks. A large, boxy-looking blue car stood parked nearby, its engine rumbling. The wheels and lower sides were covered in a light brown dust.

"This is the Lord's Triumph," Georgie said as he approached the car. "Pride and joy. I polish her." He patted the paintwork then opened the trunk, depositing Spencer's luggage inside.

Georgie closed the trunk, stepped around the car, and opened a door. He turned to Spencer with a smile. "All aboard!"

Spencer scrutinised his surroundings as he approached the car. A large, whitewashed building, what appeared to be a guesthouse, stood behind the stationhouse. It was the only structure neighbouring the station. A few miles ahead he saw rows of grey slate roofs, their chimneypots pumping smoke into the sky.

Næddre on the Wold, he thought, and nodded to Georgie as he climbed onto the back seat.

The lad closed the door behind him with a slam.

Spencer started in shock. The driver's head looked impossibly large. It took a moment for him to realise the man wore a black turban.

The door to Spencer's left opened, and Georgie climbed in beside him.

"Ah, this is the Lord's chauffeur, Bimalinder. Bimalinder, meet Detective Inspector Edward Spencer."

The Sikh tilted his head. Spencer saw a dark face, a black beard streaked with grey.

"Sir," the man growled. The next moment, the car speeded off, the sudden jolt pushing Spencer back in his seat.

He turned to see Georgie's reaction, but the lad was staring out the window, his expression one of excitement.

Spencer didn't share his enthusiasm. The road beneath the car seemed nothing but potholes and rocks. He planted himself firmly into his seat and looked out the window himself.

They passed hilly scenery for a short while, then a row of low cottages came into view.

Pedestrians stopped what they were doing, stared as the Triumph made its trundling way forward.

Spencer turned to Georgie. "Where am I going first? Police Station?"

"He won't be in," Georgie replied with a thoughtful expression. "Constable Doggett is also our Stationmaster and Postmaster." He pulled a pocket watch from his waistcoat. "Erm… I think he'll be back at the train station. You might want to see the bodies first anyway sir, at the doctor's office."

Spencer raised his eyebrows, wondering what additional occupations the doctor might have.

"You may want to find somewhere to stay too," Georgie continued. "There are three bed and breakfasts. But I recommend the Bawdy Rook, that's the pub, sir. It has the best nosh in the village."

"Bawdy Rook it is then," Spencer replied. A sudden change in direction jolted him in his seat.

The driver tooted his horn. A moment later, Spencer saw a cyclist waving his fist angrily towards them.

"There's the doctor, just heading to his surgery," Georgie said quickly. "Pull up Bimalinder."

The driver grunted, and the car slowed to a stop.

Georgie turned to Spencer. "Best catch him before he goes back out. That's him holding the gun and the dead birds. We'll take your case to the pub, eh?"

"Sure, sure," Spencer replied. "Thank you Georgie, Bimalinder."

The driver mumbled something in a foreign tongue.

Spencer left the car, waved goodbye to Georgie, and stepped onto the dirt road. He barely had time to close the door before the Triumph sped off in a cloud of dust.

He'd been deposited in the village square, an area of flattened dirt with a small hexagonal stone fountain at its centre. Scanning the surroundings, he saw women and children walking past shop fronts, a few bicyclists.

Across the square moved a figure he guessed was

the doctor. Tall and hatless, the man had a thick black beard, a shock of black hair streaked with white. He held a shotgun over one shoulder of his tweed suit. A brace of pheasants dangled from his other hand; the birds strung by their necks. He moved purposefully along the cobbled pavement, then paused before a low, one-story building.

Spencer searched for vehicles before crossing the square. It was an action for the busy thoroughfares of London though, not here.

"Doctor?"

The man turned, watched Spencer's approach with a grimace. He didn't look pleased at the intrusion into his day.

"I'm Detective Inspector Spencer, Scotland Yard," he said, and reaching the pavement, offered his hand.

The other man raised thick eyebrows and smiled. "Oh, yes, yes! You were in the back of that death trap automobile. Follow me please."

The doctor turned, and having ignored Spencer's hand, bustled into the building before them.

Spencer stopped short just inside the door; the other man had paused to stamp his feet on a rug.

The doctor continued forward, and out of politeness, Spencer brushed his own heels against the rug.

The office was large, cosy looking, with a lot of wooden furniture. It had green wallpaper, a varnished wooden floor and ceiling to match. The windows behind Spencer filled the room with afternoon light.

"Bloody nuisance eh?" the doctor said, and deposited the birds and shotgun on the desk facing the window. He removed a pipe from his jacket and placed it in his mouth. Next, he pulled a white lab coat from a coat stand that stood between the front door and the desk.

"Oh, I forget my manners," he said, putting on the lab coat. "I'm Harold Britton-Jones, the town doctor."

They shook hands, the man's grip strong in Spencer's own. Britton-Jones turned and headed towards a door set in the centre of the far wall.

"I have no morgue you'll understand," he continued as he walked, "been storing the dead in the cold room at the butcher's. No disrespect intended. We'd have buried them if you hadn't been summoned." Britton-Jones harrumphed, opened the door, and stepped inside.

The next room had similar dimensions to the first, but quite different decor. Walled with whitewashed bricks, it had a white, wood-panelled ceiling and floor. Two windows, on the north and the east walls, provided illumination. Cabinets and tables lined the walls, white, clean, and filled with surgical instruments and bottles. Spencer's attention went to the two metal tables at the room's centre. The contents of each lay hidden beneath a pristine white sheet. Body-shaped contents, he realised.

"This kind of business never happens here, never," Britton-Jones said, and vigorously shook his head. "That's why Lord Boynton pulled some strings, had a Scotland Yard man come investigate, yes?" He stepped towards the nearest table, paused, and turned to Spencer.

"Yes, the Superintendent chose me for this personally."

Britton-Jones nodded. "We lost some boys in the Great War of course, who didn't? But otherwise, it's been death by natural causes. Until now."

The doctor beckoned Spencer over. As he approached, Britton-Jones pulled back the sheet.

The removal revealed a dead man's face. Clean-shaven, his eyes and cheeks were sunken, the black hair on his head a greasy-looking mop. A pink line along the neck revealed that the man had been choked with something.

Spencer caught the sickly scent of decay. He'd smelled worse, back at the Scotland Yard mortuary.

He removed his hat, out of respect, and clenched it between his hands.

"This poor fellow is Justin Whateley," the doctor said, and removed the pipe from his mouth. "The local tinker he was. Discovered not far from the village one morning, dead as a doornail. Yes?"

Spencer scrutinised the corpse, then dragged the sheet downwards, past the upper arms and shrunken chest. He paused at the start of the forearms, then pulled the sheet further, so both arms and hands were in view. The hands and arms were puffy, swollen, and a greyish blue in colour.

What the? Spencer recognized the swelling. This man had been bitten by something highly toxic.

"His arms, what do you make of this?"

Britton-Jones smiled. He noted the questioning look on Spencer's face and cleared his throat. "Blood pools in strange places when a body dies. I assumed—"

"This man has been bitten. A lot. Do you have poisonous spiders in this locale? Or snakes?"

The doctor looked taken aback. "Well. I've heard talk of adders on the moors, but assumed it hogwash.

You think snake bites? What?"

"Not the trauma to the throat. But otherwise, yes."

Spencer searched his jacket pocket, found his magnifying glass. He leant forward and scrutinised the closest arm using the glass.

They were faint in the bloating, hardly visible to the eye, but magnified, he noted bites all up the arm and spotted the swollen hand. Spencer didn't need to examine the other arm to know it would sport the same.

"The other corpse?" he asked, raising himself.

"Now this one," Britton-Jones said, moving to the next table, "is a real tragedy. Struck down in her prime, yes?"

Britton-Jones pulled the second sheet down, uncovering a young woman's face. She had the same ugly garrote mark as the male corpse.

Spencer grimaced, said, "Right down please."

"This wee girl was found by her mother of all people," Britton-Jones continued, pulling the sheet down past the dead girl's breasts. The arms and hands of this one appeared normal. *No wait there*, Spencer thought. He quickly stepped forward to the doctor's side, leant and examined her left hand. Now these marks were visible even without his glass. Only a pair of them, most certainly bites, however.

" They discovered her stumbling into town last Friday morning, two days before Whateley."

Spencer raised his head and turned to face the doctor.

"Carrie-Anne Fisher was her name," Britton-Jones said. "A maid at The Sunny Nook boarding house."

"You say the girl walked in *this* condition?"

"Yes, yes," according to the mother," the doctor replied, sounding defensive.

Britton-Jones leant past him, began to pull the sheet back over the dead girl's modesty.

Spencer returned the magnifying glass to his pocket and folded his arms. "I would like to see the witness of course, and visit the places these victims were found."

"Oh right." Britton-Jones returned the pipe to his mouth. "Mrs. Fisher is gone I'm afraid, down to Colchester to stay with in-laws."

Spencer recalled the crying woman at the station. *The same one?* "The constable shouldn't have allowed her to leave. Who discovered the other corpse?"

The doctor scratched his beard, tilted his head in thought.

"I don't rightly recall," he replied. "You may have to ask around."

Spencer put his hat back on. "In that case, I'll go ask around. Goodbye, sir."

"Of course, yes. I'll see you out," Britton-Jones replied, and stepped forward.

Spencer shook his head, raised his palms. "No need for that, please."

As he turned to leave the room, he felt Britton-Jones's stare burning into him.

Spencer left the doctor's office in a hurry. He paused outside the building, his eyes not focusing on anything in particular as he considered what he had just learned.

Two people strangled with something. Wire? Rope? But they had also suffered snake bites. Too much of a coincidence that the pair had similar injuries. If snake bites were common, the ignoramus of a doctor would have seen patients with same.

"Adders on the moors," he said aloud, and his gaze paused on a small shop directly across the square. The sign above the glass read "Gentleman's Outfitters." In the window, a dummy stood dressed quite similarly to the man Stainsby on the train.

The clothier might know if there are places on the moors with snakes, he thought, and headed towards the shop.

Half an hour later and Spencer had almost reached Lord Boynton's home. His feet ached, unused to the uneven grounds of this rustic land. Still, he had seen much of the moors, journeying down the path from the village to Boynton House. But now, the scenery around him consisted of trees.

"Just follow the path from town, and you'll find it shortly after," the clothier had said.

Shortly after? Not too shortly, considering. Still, ahead and to the left of the trees he had just caught glimpse of a rooftop. He stepped off the road when he neared the path's left turn, thinking safety might be expedient, should the maniac of a driver come barreling around the corner. The trees were Sycamore, tall and stately, with just a hint of autumn in the hue of the leaves.

Beyond the turn, some fifty feet away, Boynton House stood against a clear afternoon sky. His goal nearly upon him, and despite his fatigued feet, Spencer increased his gait.

Boynton House, stood upon a hill, was three stories high including a small square attic floor and a hipped roof. The west and east wings had bay windows on the first and second floors, a hexagonal tower attached to the west wing. The bricks of the walls were weathered, opportunistic ivy climbing the western corner. Beyond the porch, Spencer saw a stout oak door.

The path terminated, circling around the hill, and beyond its termination, worn, ancient-looking steps ascended the hill to the building. Stone railings flanked the steps, each ending in a tall pedestal bearing a Greek Urn. The urns were new additions he thought, for the white marble appeared less weathered than the pedestals and railings. Spencer looked left and right as he crossed the circling path, reached, and mounted the steps.

"Snakes?" The clothier had scrunched his already wrinkled face. "Not on these moors. The only snakes I know of are Lord Boynton's. He keeps them, those and other reptiles up in his house."

A lead to go on, He had thought earlier. The garotte marks on the victims' necks: he had no idea of. But if snakes had escaped Boynton's home? It was something.

Spencer reached the top of the stairs quickly, found himself on a freshly trimmed lawn. Flanked to the east and west by tall, cone-shaped bushes, a statue stood between every fourth bush. Female, dressed in togas, the statues loomed high on their square pedestals. They seemed to watch Spencer as he crossed the gravel path to the porch.

The oak door had a well-polished brass knocker,

shaped like a devilish face. He rapped four times, and waited. A few seconds later, the door opened. Beyond stood the tall, imposing form of the Sikh manservant, Bimalinder.

"What?" he asked abruptly.

The rudeness took Spencer aback. He composed himself and said: "Lord Boynton, is he available? Scotland Yard business." He added the latter, so the man knew he meant business.

"The Lord is away. On *his* business. The Lady will see you, however. Come inside," Bimalinder said, his stony visage not changing.

"Yes, well. That'll do," Spencer said.

The manservant opened the door further, stepped aside so Spencer could enter.

Beyond the door stood a large, impressive foyer. It had a red colour scheme, from the carpet to the papered walls and ceiling. Red leather padded doors lined the west and east walls. A double staircase stood near its termination, leading to the second-floor balcony. A crystal chandelier hung suspended from the ceiling.

The foyer stood spotlessly clean. Whatever the manservant lacked in manners, he certainly made up for in keeping a clean house.

The door slammed shut, and the man in question said, "Wait," more an order than a request.

Spencer removed his hat, watched Bimalinder head left to the nearest door. He tapped gently then entered, closing it behind him. Left with the silence of the foyer, Spencer stepped quietly towards the door the manservant had entered. Muffled voices issued from within the room, low laughter. He looked away from the door, examined the foyer. Darkness filled the upstairs balcony. Beyond the staircase, he saw a row of glass doors, and beyond them, Trees? A garden this close to the house? *A greenhouse*, he thought to himself, and as footsteps padded through the room, he quickly backstepped towards the entryway. The door opened, and Bimalinder's hulking frame stepped out.

"She will see you. Go inside."

Spencer had to contain a smirk. This man's rudeness was unbelievable. Not only that, he didn't even ask for his hat and coat, a poor show of etiquette from whatever school of butlery this man came from. Spencer smiled politely regardless, and heading back towards the room, stepped through the doorway.

A wall of incense, spicy and exotic, struck him as he entered a room which proved to be a library. Wide, with a single bay window on the south wall, the other walls were lined with ceiling-high bookcases. He stepped across varnished wood, then a Turkish rug, towards a figure with her back to him at a circular table.

"Lady Boynton I presume?"

The woman wore a long black dress with a white lace collar, white lace gloves on her hands. A large white lily flower hung pinned above her left breast. Her red hair had a long pigtail, which trailed down her shoulder.

Lady Boynton turned to him. With her slightly dark skin and large brown eyes, she cut a beautiful, striking figure.

"Ah! You must be the detective my husband brought here. Come, take a seat," she said in a musical voice.

"Yes… um…" Spencer felt fairly taken aback. With Lord Boynton being an old friend of his Supervisor's, he had expected an old man, and Lady Boynton, to be an older woman. He realised he stood lurking, and quickly walked to the table, took the seat opposite her.

As he sat down, he noted maps strewn across the table, a small pile of books with cracked leather spines. He read: *Herodotus - The Histories,* on each spine.

"Just a moment please." Lady Boynton raised a pair of Pince-nez to her eyes. She studied the maps a few moments longer before lowering the glasses to her chest.

"Mexico!" she said with a smile that made Spencer's heart leap. "Lord Boynton and I intend to visit come winter. That is, depending on what occurs during this ghastly business. It is ghastly, isn't it?"

Spencer swallowed. "Yes ma'am. And I've only just arrived here. I will get to the bottom of it, however."

"Yes, yes of course." That smile again. She leant a gloved hand across the table and retrieved a silver bell from behind the book pile. She shook the bell, causing it to tinkle.

Lady Boynton lowered the bell and looked at him expectantly.

"I… I've had opportunity to examine the first two victims. That's why I came here actually. As well as the… garroting that killed them, there also appear to be snake bites."

At that moment, the manservant stepped in. He held a silver tray in his hands, which he brought towards the table.

"Snake bites? My word," Lady Boynton said.

Bimalinder leant between them, lowering the tray. The tray held a crystal decanter of a rich brown liquid, and two glasses.

"Sherry sir?" the man grumbled.

Spencer nodded, continuing his conversation. "Yes. Someone told me in the village that Lord Boynton kept snakes and other reptiles as pets. It's not a lot to go on but—"

"No snakes here," Bimalinder interrupted. He had finished pouring the drinks, and bowing to his mistress, headed back towards the door.

"Ignore him," Lady Boynton said. "No manners to the oaf."

She said it just as Bimalinder closed the door. Did he hear? Did he care? *Probably not*, Spencer thought.

"Snakes? My word no," Lady Boynton continued. "My husband kept some reptiles in the greenhouse, but sent them off to Scarborough Zoo. They didn't adjust to the climate here, you see. I can show you the greenhouse. Should you wish?"

"Ma'am. I didn't mean to suggest your household was the cause of anything. But the victims were certainly bitten."

Lady Boynton took a sip of sherry. Spencer followed suit as she spoke.

"We have trees in the greenhouse now. Torchwood they're called, an import from Arabia. We make incense from the sap!"

She pointed right to an alcove between bookcases.

There were cones of incense smouldering in little copper bowls there. Also, small statues, strange figures with octopoid and demonic faces. He looked back to Lady Boynton, found her gaze probing him.

"The greenhouse?" she repeated.

Did he need to see it? If not, then his business here was done. And he selfishly desired to spend a little more time with this enigmatic woman.

"If it's no trouble?" He fumbled with his hat under the table, feeling sheepish.

"Of course, no trouble, come along," she said and slipped from her seat.

He stood, admiring her graceful gait as she headed for the door.

They left the library. She waited for him, so as they walked through the house they were side by side. The smell of exotic incense clung to the woman as they passed the staircase.

A door stood ajar to their left. Spencer caught the scent of cooking smells. There was a clatter, and a male voice said, "shit."

He looked to Lady Boynton and she smiled, unphased. "You will very much like our trees," she said.

The area behind the staircase looked similar to the entryway: a chandelier, red carpets. Tree limbs pressed against the glass doors lining the south wall.

"All imported, as I said. And a devil to grow here." Lady Boynton stepped forward swiftly, pulled a door open.

"Thank you, ma'am," Spencer said and nodded, walking past her into the greenhouse.

The greenhouse looked huge. Curved wooden rafters, holding the glass in place, met at the ceiling like the insides of a cathedral. Rows of trees lined the greenhouse. Some were low, their bows almost touching the grass. Others were so tall they brushed the ceiling. The greenhouse had a heady, earthy smell. Of reptiles, or any signs of life but the luscious green, no sign was visible.

"This is quite something," Spencer said.

Lady Boynton stepped to his side. "A paradise in the east, flourishing with all sorts of trees," she said, her musical voice filling the greenhouse.

In this place, at this time, beside this beautiful woman. It did indeed feel a little like paradise.

Soon after his business at Boynton House was over, Spencer returned to the village. A lift had been offered, in the Triumph, but Spencer couldn't handle the Sikh's driving twice in one day. Once back he asked around, questioning locals about the deaths, trying to locate witnesses, probing everyone on their theories about the murderer.

"A madman on the moors," proved the most oft-mentioned theory. By late afternoon, he had few if any leads to go on. No suspects to speak of either. It confused Spencer, really. Murder without motivation. It wasn't a thing in London. Lust or hate or money or revenge: they were the reasons that man (or woman)took another life. He saw no motivation like that here. None that he could detect anyway.

I must find something however, Spencer thought that

evening, as he laid himself down to sleep. A return to London empty-handed was not an option. He just needed to see a bigger picture than what he had right now.

It was a deep, contented slumber Spencer awoke from. At first, he thought he was dreaming, the loud rhythmic 'tap tap tap' something his sleep-befuddled mind had difficulty processing.

"Mister Spencer, sir!"

The sound of his name brought his awareness to the fore, and he sat up blinking.

"Sir," the loud, urgent knocking continued.

He left the bed, rushed through the darkened room to the door. Opening it, he saw a young, redheaded girl dressed in a dark blue maid's uniform.

The girl curtseyed and smiled. "Sir I'm so sorry to disturb you but they've found another body in the village and I was told to come find you as all hell is breaking loose and—"

Spencer shushed her. She'd spoken frantically, without taking a breath.

"Where is it?" he asked, speaking calmly in an attempt to put the girl at ease.

She took a deep breath, "Over near the fountain sir. Laid all dead and unwholesome like."

"Alright. Now what's your name?"

"Millie, sir."

"Millie. Can you go there and see about keeping everyone away from it. If Constable Doggett is around, please ask him to make a perimeter."

The girl nodded her head vigorously, her gaze lowered as she absorbed the information. She looked up and said, "But sir, the dead body *is* Constable Doggett."

"Oh bloody—" he began, then stopped himself from finishing the curse. "Just go down and do as I said, I'll be there in five minutes."

The girl nodded, turned, and rushed down the corridor. Spencer left the door ajar and quickly removed his pyjamas. Next, he stepped over to the window, parting the curtains to bring light to the small, rustic-looking room. He dressed quickly, but carefully.

Remaining calm proved an effort, but he knew if he fumbled around it would take even longer.

Once dressed, he headed towards the dresser, splashed water from its basin onto his face. He combed his hair to make his appearance acceptable, wiped his face dry with a cloth, and rushed to the door. A sudden idea turned him on his heels and sent him back towards the bed. He knelt there and pulled out his suitcase. The clasps clicking open at his manipulation, he dug into the neatly folded clothes and found what he desired beneath. The Bulldog revolver fitted snugly into his jacket pocket. He stood, gave the pocket a tap, and returned to the door. Here he grabbed his hat from the hook and headed into the corridor.

A left turn at the corridor's termination took him down a flight of narrow stairs. The bar followed, curtains closed and empty. *What time is it?* As he stepped between the tables and stools, he checked his pocket watch. *Just after ten.* A terribly late start for him, and he recalled asking the landlady to wake him at nine.

There's no time to worry about that now, not with another murder right under my nose. He hated to think of it this way, but a fresh scene might probably be a good thing, at least where finding evidence was concerned.

Spencer reached and opened the entrance door. The bright light beyond made him blink, and it took him a moment to recall his location in the village. He donned his hat and headed right, down a cobbled path in the direction of the fountain. He crossed a street, then cut down a narrow alley. As he neared the alley's termination, a babble of voices reached his ears. Upon entering the square, he found a large crowd assembled before the fountain.

He grimaced at the sight. Onlookers, in his experience, did nothing but damage evidence and spread false rumours.

Some anxious-looking faces spotted him, and the crowd, parting at his approach, left a direct path to the fountain.

A dark shape lay slumped against the fountain's rim.

Millie stood guard before it, scowling at the crowd with her arms folded.

Spencer smiled. As he stepped between the whispering village folk, he saw Georgie stood to the girl's right.

Noticing his approach, Georgie said, "Another corpse sir, a bloody dead body!"

Spencer paused, nodded to Georgie, and turned to Millie.

"Thank you very much. You've done a grand job."

The girl smiled prettily and blushed.

"Now could you go find the doctor, tell him to bring two strong lads and a stretcher?"

Millie nodded and rushed away.

Spencer turned round, raised his arms, and addressed the curious, frightened crowd. "Everyone. I need you to return to your business. Please. I can only deal with this if you give me space."

Heads nodded, and voices muttered reluctant assent. The crowd took off and dispersed into smaller groups

Satisfied he wasn't going to be disturbed, Spencer turned to the fountain.

So, this is Doggett, he thought, and kneeling, scanned the area before him. The dirt floor bore no marks of a struggle. From the corner of his eye, he saw Georgie kneel beside him.

"Looking for clues sir?" the lad asked.

Spencer nodded, then crept forward.

Doggett was a large man, his suit dark grey with a yellow carnation in the lapel. A large, white embroidered handkerchief concealed his face. Spencer guessed either Millie or another onlooker had placed it there for decency. The man's back lay pressed against the fountain, his legs spread. The heels of his black boots were caked in mud.

Noting this, Spencer said, "Georgie, has there been any rain overnight?"

"Showers on the moors, sir, a little patter across the village as I recall."

"Right, ahuh."

He crept closer, braced himself, and removing the handkerchief, placed it on the ground.

"Oh!" Georgie exclaimed.

A pale, weathered face stared blindly forward, the wide eyes clouded and grey. A red mark of strangulation circled his throat. *Would take a large man to overpower this fellow. A large man to carry him here too.* He began searching Doggett's pockets. All were empty but the inside pocket, from which he removed a handful of small objects.

He stood, turned. Georgie's face was as pale as the corpse's.

The square stood empty now, quiet. Movement caught his eye and he saw two men heading down the alley he'd recently used. They bore a stretcher between them. The doctor marched behind the pair, puffing heavily on his pipe.

Britton-Jones waved. Spencer returned the gesture, then turned his attention to his hand. In his palm lay half a dozen small cones, their fragrance reaching his nostrils as he examined them. Incense. He closed his fist around them and cleared his throat.

"Georgie," he said, and the lad stood to face him. "I think we may have found our man."

"Sir?" Georgie said.

Spencer nodded and replied, quietly now, "The manservant at the Boyntons, I'm sure of it. But tell no-one. I'm heading over there now."

Georgie nodded; his face drained of blood.

He turned from Georgie, the corpse, and the fountain, and made his way through the square towards the dirt path that led to Boynton House. He heard raised voices, most likely Britton-Jones's men seeing the corpse, and the man himself shouting for him to return. No. He wouldn't return, not until he had been to Boynton House and arrested Bimalinder.

The man had to be his culprit. He could feel it in his bones.

Spencer left the village, followed the familiar path between the moors. No time now to admire the scenery, no time for anything but concentrate on his goal. The weight of the Bulldog pistol proved a welcome presence in his pocket. The one he intended to arrest might be a handful. Spencer was also thankful his other pocket held a pair of handcuffs.

Clouds started to fill the sky as the woods surrounding Boynton House appeared in the distance. Bloated, bruised, with dark grey patches, the clouds threatened rain. Some minutes of walking later, Spencer reached the woods.

Beneath the sinister, cloudy sky, the trees appeared twisted in grotesque shapes. This added to Spencer's foreboding as he turned the corner to Boynton House. Despite the darkening day, there were no lights on in the mansion. Each window reflected the grey sky, the clouds above the rooftops heavy with the promise of a downpour.

Spencer reached the steps ascending the hill. He dashed up them, rushed forward just as the sky broke. Thick raindrops pelted his head and shoulders as he approached the door. And the door stood open. Darkness within.

This made him halt. What if the manservant had gone crazy? What if Lady Boynton had become another victim? Only one way to find out. He strode through the door, entering the darkened lobby and halting after a few steps.

"Lady Boynton? Are you about?" he asked the shadows. The foyer appeared still, quiet. Sudden footsteps appeared behind him, and before Spencer had an opportunity to turn, something dropped over his head, tightened around his throat.

Spencer screamed, his shock and pain echoing back to him. He grabbed for the object choking him. Thick, metallic, it pressed deep into the flesh of his throat. He clawed at it uselessly, tried digging his fingers into his own flesh in an attempt to pull himself free. Spencer gasped, his vision blurring as the lack of air took effect. Trying a different, desperate tact, he reached to the back of his neck, weakened hands clawing at the fists strangling him with the garotte. No luck. They were like stone. As darkness framed his vision, a figure in white stepped towards him. Beautiful, ethereal, Spencer thought an angel had come for him.

He opened his eyes with a groan, his neck aching. Focusing vision placed him in a small grassy grove surrounded by trees. Some feet ahead stood a weathered stone plinth, an altar of sorts. The noise of heavy rainfall issued far over his head. He tried to move, but his arms were bound by ropes behind his back. He had been tied to something solid. A tree, the quick probing of his fingers discovered.

Looking up past the trees, he saw the glass of a greenhouse. The wet sky was dark there. How long had he been unconscious? Spencer took a deep breath, attempting to calm his growing nerves. He suffered increased pain to his throat for his trouble.

Then, a rustling appeared around him. Spencer examined the low-hanging bows with suspicion. Something, some *things* lurked in the trees.

Footsteps turned his attention right, where he saw two forms approaching.

"So, we meet again," a familiar voice said.

The source filled Spencer with surprise. The man from the train walked toward him, but the hunting gear was gone. In its place, he wore a white toga. It looked patently ridiculous on the chubby old man. Bimalinder walked to his left.

"Stainsby?" Spencer said in confusion.

"I'm usually referred to as Lord Boynton," the one he had known as Stainsby replied, and halted.

Spencer looked from Boynton's self-satisfied face to the manservant.

Bimalinder nodded, smiled widely.

"You. You're the murderers?" He said it as more an accusation than a question.

"I am an acolyte," Lord Boynton said. "You have the most important part to play m'boy. Doesn't he, dear?"

Boynton looked right, and Spencer followed his gaze.

A third figure appeared from beyond the plinth. The angel from earlier, or rather, Lady Boynton, wore a white toga. Whereas Lord Boynton looked a buffoon, she was a thing of beauty incarnate.

Lady Boynton paused beside the plinth and raised her hands.

"For the spice-bearing trees are guarded by small Winged Snakes of varied colour, many around each tree. Come to me now."

From the rustling boughs, from all edges of the grove, strange shapes fluttered. Spencer flinched. *What the?* They were snakes, scores if not a hundred of them. Quite unlike any snake he had seen in London Zoo, each serpent shone a myriad of flashing colours, flew on leathery, bat-like wings. Their flight was a graceful one, and they swarmed around Lady Boynton.

"You know some Greek, yes? My wife just quoted Herodotus, Histories III," Lord Boynton said. "These are the winged serpents of Arabia, guardians to the sacred places of our master, Yig, the Father of Serpents."

Spencer sent him a glare. "What are you talking about? Are you insane?"

"We mean to summon the Father," Lord Boynton said, ignoring the slight. "Though our attempts so far have been singularly unsuccessful."

He thought of the villagers, the girl, the two men found dead.

"You mean the victims?"

"Oh no good fellow," Lord Boynton grinned widely. "Our true victims will never be found. The villagers were just breadcrumbs to lead you in."

"A man of strength, of an iron-clad will," Lady Boynton cut in. "A suitable vessel for our god and master. Your Superintendent sent us a fine specimen."

Spencer saw Lord Boynton's face redden. Could that be jealousy in his expression?

Spencer returned his attention to Lady Boynton, her, and her evil pets.

"You'll never get away with this. People will come looking."

Lady Boynton laughed. A sound he would enjoy in other circumstances.

"And we will be gone. Mexico probably. But wherever our master, in earthly form, desires to go."

Lady Boynton stepped forward, flanked by a guard of hovering snakes.

Spencer noted a silver chain in her hands, with a curiously-shaped amulet dangling from it.

He pushed himself backwards as scores of tiny black eyes glared at him. Spencer expected them to strike at any moment.

"You don't want to do this," he said through gritted teeth.

"Hush fellow. I offer you life eternal," Lady Boynton said upon reaching him.

Her bare flesh looked flawless. The expression on her face appeared benevolent as she dropped the chain over his head.

A few snakes darted closer, their hisses filling him with fear.

"Get those damn things away from me."

"They don't want to bite you," Lady Boynton whispered. "That won't bring forth the Father. But his bite…" The last three words were said loudly. Lady Boynton stepped back, pointed a slender, naked arm towards the two men.

Spencer turned his head slowly, fearing a sudden movement might invoke a snake attack.

Lord Boynton's eyes glared with hatred. Bimalinder cricked his neck, and began to move his head side to side in a strange, rhythmic manner. Spencer's guts turned cold. The Sikh's skin had grown darker, his face riddled in cracks.

No.

Bimalinder's eyes bulged and turned opaque black. A slithering green tongue slipped out between his lips.

Spencer turned away in horror.

Lord Boynton started chanting, a guttural, alien-sounding gibberish. His wife walked back to the altar, accompanied, thankfully, by her winged snakes. When she reached the altar, Lady Boynton turned to face Spencer, then took up the chant herself.

"Sir," the whispered word sounded urgent.

"Georgie?" Spencer whispered back, confused.

"Came back here when you didn't return. My gosh sir. What's going on?"

Spencer felt the rope holding him to the tree loosen.

"Get yourself out of here lad," he said, his whispered voice almost breaking as he caught another glimpse of Bimalinder.

"Not without you sir," Georgie replied.

A moment later, the bonds fell from his wrists.

Spencer climbed to his feet, pulled the Bulldog pistol from his pocket.

Lord Boynton gasped. Bimalinder growled.

Dear God, Spencer thought. More reptile than

human now, Bimalinder stepped forward, his monstrous, wide mouth revealing dripping fangs, a black chasm of a throat.

"Stop where you are," he ordered the abomination.

The manservant charged him, too fast for Spencer to do anything but grit his teeth as his attacker's momentum took them to the ground.

Winded, Spencer struggled as strong hands gripped his already tender throat.

Hot, rancid breath fogged his face. Eyes like the pits of Hell glared down as the snake-faced horror raised its head, ready to strike.

Spencer pulled his gun up, pushed it into Bimalinder's distended mouth.

The following gunshot demolished the back of the monster's head. Blood spattered Spencer's gun and face.

"No!" Boynton cried.

Spencer pulled himself right as his attacker's dead weight collapsed towards him. He wiped blood from his eyes with his sleeve, aimed his gun at Boynton.

The man rushed forward, waving his arms in distress. He fell to his knees at the manservant's side.

"Take the chosen one!" an angry voice shouted.

The flapping of wings followed Lady Boynton's order.

Thinking quickly, Spencer pulled the amulet from his neck, lurched forward, and threw it over Lord Boynton's head.

The man looked at him, eyes wide and bloodshot with terror. A moment later, a veritable cloud of winged snakes was upon Boynton, their massing so thick his struggling form was barely visible.

Spencer stood, backed away from the dead monster and the wailing, flailing lord. He shivered, and turned at a movement nearby.

"He never had what it took," Lady Boynton said. "But you, however."

The woman cut a graceful figure in this place of madness and evil.

"My word. You're shaking. Come here," she continued in a matronly tone, holding a hand out as she approached.

Spencer wanted nothing more than to embrace her. He felt weak, numb, and as Lady Boynton breached the gap between them, a little like a coaxed animal.

"Come with me. We can leave these lands together." Her wide smile revealed perfect white teeth. Her eyes drew him. Deep brown pools, they offered love, companionship.

He barely noticed that Lord Boynton had gone silent. The scent of lilacs and the perfume of this woman's natural odour filled his nostrils.

Lady Boynton placed a hand on his shoulder. Just her touch electrified his body. Her eyes were everything. Her hand brushed his stomach, and he trembled. The woman leant forward for a kiss. "Don't make me chase you," she whispered.

Her face then twisted in rage. A flash of steel revealed a blade in her other hand.

The noise of the discharging Bulldog cracked through the greenhouse. Spencer had pressed it squarely against the woman's chest.

Lady Boynton gasped, staggered backwards. She looked down at the growing red blossom on her toga, then at Spencer. "Clever boy," she said as blood dripped from perfect lips, then she collapsed to the grass.

He stared at her twisted form, numbed by his handiwork. Then, a sudden noise of wings, flapping en-masse, made him turn round. The winged serpents! Their bodies pulsed wildly with colours; their tails flickered. With a hundred hisses they flew towards him. What could he do against such a swarm of horrors? He braced himself, aimed his Bulldog, and shut his eyes.

Wings fluttered against him, gentle, tickling, but no assault followed. Spencer, confused, reopened his eyes.

The snakes had ignored him. Instead, their sole reptilian attention had focused on Lady Boynton. Not to attack, however. Rather, and Spencer felt clueless as to how things without hands could do it, the serpents lifted Lady Boynton up.

He watched fascinated, as they ascended towards the greenhouse ceiling.

"Sir? Are we safe now?" Georgie said from behind him.

Spencer didn't answer, just continued staring at the flapping cloud. Footsteps appeared, and he felt the lad's presence at his side.

The snakes and their charge reached the ceiling, and the glass shattered.

He sent Georgie a look, saw the boy staring at the ceiling, wide-eyed. With a gentle hand, he pushed Georgie backwards as splinters of glass rained down before them.

A few moments later they were beneath the shelter of a tree. The glass had ceased its descent, however, and rain fell in its stead.

"I don't believe it," Georgie said.

Spencer examined the scene before them. Lord Boynton lay dead, his corpse so bloated with venom it seeped from his pores. Bimalinder had returned to his human form, but with most of his head missing, he looked no better for it.

"My boy," he said. "I have trouble believing it myself."

Glynn Owen Barrass lives in the Northeast of England and has been writing since late 2006. He has written over two hundred short stories, novellas, and role-playing game supplements, the majority of which have been published in France, Germany, Japan, Poland, Portugal, the UK, and the USA.

Detective Inspector Edward Spencer was created specifically for this story. The author wanted to create a character used to a big city, unaccustomed to country life. He is also unaccustomed to the horrors he encounters, but faces them boldly, with an inner strength.

GRINDER ROCK
B. HARLAN CRAWFORD

I took stock of the dishevelled young man seated opposite me in the parlour of the Palace Hotel where I rented rooms. He squirmed in his chair in discomfiture, further disrupting his wrinkled tweed suit. He was a tall gangly fellow, the narrowness of his face accentuated by a pencil-thin moustache and his high broad forehead framed by pomaded ringlets. He hastily gulped his brandy, and taking a moment to compose himself, continued to relate to me his difficulties.

"I am at a loss, Mr. Oldridge. I have never heard of Terrence Thorpe. I have no knowledge of what relation he may be to me, nor why he should have bequeathed to me a whole blessed island!"

"Slow down, Pressman." I tried to speak calmly. The lads' hyperactivity was beginning to agitate my nerves. I signalled for another round of drinks. "Tell me again about the telegram you received. This time slowly, make sure you leave nothin' out."

Young Pressman exhaled sharply. I thought for a moment he was going to leap from his armchair and bolt, but then he seemed to deflate and fall back into the deeply quilted upholstery. He began speaking in a more subdued manner.

"The telegram arrived at my sister's house in Providence two weeks ago. I receive all correspondence there as I currently have no fixed abode." This statement verified some of my suspicions, I figured Pressman for a Yankee and a layabout. "It detailed that I was named sole beneficiary of one Terrence Thorpe, and that I am to receive sixty thousand dollars, contingent on my taking possession of Thorpe's California properties,

Specifically Grinder Rock, consisting of the island itself and the buildings built upon it."

"A small cabin and some sort of stone outbuilding, correct?"

"Yes. My sister, my aunt Cecily, and myself, the only extant members of my family line, have investigated this matter most thoroughly, Mr Oldridge, and can find no evidence of a Terrence Thorpe in our lineage. The solicitor who sent the initial telegram, Mr. J. Garnet Hamilton out of Providence, has provided ample documentation of the veracity of this bequeathment, while avoiding any inquiries that do not directly involve my taking possession of the property. My aunt's lawyers in Providence and San Francisco have had no better luck than I in securing further illumination."

"And you think I can wring more information out of this J. Garnet Hamilton?"

Pressman shook his head. The gesture was too vigorous and spoke to the young man's agitation. "I feel a different approach is needed. My friend Percival Unger told me of your discreet handling of his affair in Chinatown. If you could apply similar methods to my case, you may uncover more facts than the more traditional enquiries of my aunt's lawyers"

"We'll have to see about that, Mr. Pressman. Now tell me, since you have travelled across the country to get here, have you been out to Grinder Rock?"

"Not yet. It occurred to me It might be ill-advised to go alone."

"Quite possibly." I finished my bourbon and rose. "What say you and I go out there, say Thursday morning?

In the meantime, I'll make some inquiries and arrange for transit to Grinder Rock. I trust you can have my fee by Thursday morning?"

"Yes, of course. Thank you, Mr Oldridge."

"Best save thanks 'til we see what's what. See you Thursday, Mr Pressman."

My investigations over the following days yielded sparse facts. A perusal of public records and newspaper articles revealed that Grinder Rock was a five-acre lightly wooded island in the San Francisco Bay located just south of San Rafael. It apparently saw some use by the natives, if the low cairn of crude stones piled near its centre was any indication, but there was no record of any archaeological studies there, and records on the native activities in the area yielded truly little save for some half-forgotten references to the island as a place of ill-omen.

It was purchased from the federals in '89 by a group of businessmen for use as a hunting retreat and had a reasonably luxurious cabin erected upon it. These erstwhile outdoorsmen sold the island to another private interest less than a year after the completion of the cabin without ever having made any use of it. The record of who this private interest might have been was so thoroughly vague it suggested deliberate obfuscation.

I tracked down one member of the group, a Mr Dennis Perlmutter, a plump, ruddy-cheeked borax broker with offices on Geary Boulevard. He was disinclined to discuss Grinder Rock overmuch but told me of a miserable evening he spent there.

"I had decided to spend the weekend camping and

bagging a few rabbits," he said. "The cabin was not finished so I brought a tent, supplies for a few nights, and spirits for medicinal purposes. Sometimes the night vapours cause me to have a distemper of the chest."

"I get it, Mr Perlmutter, I suffer from a similar affliction."

"Quite so, Mr Oldridge! At any rate, I set up camp and settled in for a relaxing evening communing with nature. I dozed and was rousted awake about midnight by a horrendous tumult!"

"A tumult you say?"

"I do! Further, my tent was savaged from without by some beast, smashed and shredded while I struggled to maintain my nerves inside! I discharged my shotgun where I thought the thing might stand and fled the tent. I nearly broke my neck stumbling headlong down the rickety wooden steps that traverse the cliff to the pier."

"Did you get a look at the critter?"

"I did not. There is not supposed to be anything larger than a gopher on that island, but this was at least the size of a black bear."

"You ever go back?"

"No. Shortly after that horrid evening, during which I suffered all manner of discomfiture, my fellow investors approached me with the idea of selling the island. My enthusiasm for this idea was such that I agreed to it without enquiring as to whom it would be sold."

I thanked Mr Perlmutter for his time and proceeded to my next avenue of investigation. I arrived at the offices of Professor Ezekiel Wallace around lunchtime on Wednesday. His receptionist Pearl stated he had not yet returned from his morning lecture and would be along directly, and that I should take a seat in the waiting area outside his office.

I was unpleasantly surprised to find lounging on the sofa a bronze giant, a towering Apache whose modern haircut and finely tailored suit accentuated his savage grace rather than obscured it. He was known as Jimmy Bearclaw on the circuit of wild west shows where he performed feats of strength, archery, and riding, but had been called Kuruk among his people. He was no longer a young man, but still hale and vigorous.

Kuruk and I had never crossed paths during those blood-soaked days folk have taken to calling the Apache Wars, but we were both aware of one another's reputations. Our relationship was a cool one. As I entered, Bearclaw had a beatific expression on his face. No doubt having fallen into a brown study. Upon clapping eyes on me, his expression hardened.

"Oldridge," he spoke the name as if it were a curse.

"Jimmy," I replied. And sat opposite him in an exquisitely crafted armchair. Wallace was taking his sweet time returning from his office; thus, Jimmy Bearclaw and I were left sitting in awkward silence for an indeterminable time. I could finally stand it no longer and engaged.

"What brings you to see Professor Wallace today, Jimmy?"

He nudged the carpetbag by his foot.

"He's always keen to have sundry Apache gewgaws. I brought him some."

"Anything genuine?"

"All of it. Wallace knows his stuff. Can't pull the wool over his eyes. Why are you here, Oldridge?"

"I aim to ask him what he knows about that cairn on Grinder Rock. You know much about that cairn on Grinder Rock, Jimmy?"

"Not much, Oldridge. Like you, I ain't from these parts. That would've been built by the Aptos or Uipi maybe. Why you askin'?"

"A job. Boy out of Providence inherited the whole Island, he hired me out to look into it."

Jimmy chuckled. "You one of them Private Eyes now, Oldridge? That's rich. Too old to rob stages and shoot squaws, so now you dig around rock piles fer rich Yankees."

"Bout as rich as you bein' too old to steal horses and scalp women, so now smokem peace pipe and do tricks on horseback fer rich palefaces! I never shot no squaws, Jimmy!"

"Maybe not Oldridge, but I bet you stood by and kept your mouth shut while others did!"

Anyone else might not have noticed, but I sensed Jimmy coiling to strike. Outwardly he looked as serene as before. But there was a change in the air in the room. My hand hovered over my waistcoat pocket where I hid my Webley's Bulldog. Suddenly Jimmy sighed and relaxed.

"We both got a lot to answer for Oldridge."

"I wouldn't argue that."

Wallace showed up then and I was glad of it, I figure Jimmy Bearclaw was too. The little bespectacled ferret of a man enthusiastically greeted us both and ushered us into his cluttered office. I was in a hurry to be gone, so I plied him with my questions about Grinder Rock. Jimmy chimed in with his opinion on who might have reared the cairn, and Wallace had a response.

"Aptos? Uipi? No, no. Those tribes were aware of the cairn, yes, but it predates them. The tribes in the area shunned the place actually. A Lot of fragmented legends about it being a haven for some sort of soul-stealing birds... not birds exactly, maybe some kind of giant moth. The tales were so old they had become a garbled mess by the time I was made privy to them. Do you intend to visit the cairn Oldridge? I had considered mounting an expedition there but I'm getting on in years. If you go and find any interesting artefacts, I will reward you handsomely for them."

I told Wallace I'd keep him in mind and after taking my leave of him and Jimmy Bearclaw, I adjourned to the bar at the Palace Hotel to refresh myself.

I met young Mr Pressman at the waterfront before daybreak on Thursday. Having secured my fee, we two set out in the small boat equipped with one of those new Daimler motors. I had rented the boat at no small expense to Mr Pressman. I had little remorse over this, nor over the exorbitant fee I was extracting from the lad. Though unemployed he was well-heeled enough to afford tailored suits, high-end Yankee lawyers and cross-country train passages, so my paltry expenses shouldn't break him, especially as he stood to come into forty thousand.

It was a short trip, and we arrived at the ramshackle pier on the island shortly after sunup. From the pier, a treacherous wooden staircase wound up the steep rocky cliff to the top of the island. The state of it made me think I should have gotten more money out of Pressman; my bones had grown too old and brittle to take a tumble off those cliffs. I reached into the boat and brought forth a brace of Winchesters, one of which I handed to Pressman.

"Careful with that," I said. "It's from my personal collection and I'd have to bill you for it if you lose it."

Pressman looked at the rifle as if it were a rattler.

"What do we need rifles for?"

"I don't know, Pressman. Maybe we'll bag us a rabbit or two while we're here."

We began the long climb up the stairs. Apart from creaking alarmingly, they were sturdier than one might think upon initial inspection. Reaching the top, we found ourselves on a flat grassy plain within about fifty yards of the cabin, and a hundred of the stone cairns.

"May as well start with the cabin." I said and headed for the low timber building.

The cabin was in remarkably good repair. The doors were locked, and the windows shuttered. I jimmied the lock on the door, and Pressman and I stepped inside. The interior had the look of having been carefully put in order by someone preparing for a long absence.

The furnishings had been tarped over, the shelves emptied, and all the cabinets locked. Of these, we opened a few to find they contained non-perishable items; dishes, flatware, empty whiskey bottles, and linens. A heavy chest in the kitchen contained old rags and a few cans of turpentine or mineral spirits. However, what drew my immediate attention was a fat envelope placed conspicuously on the dining room table, held in place by a soapstone paperweight emblazoned with a peculiar symbol. Examining it I found it addressed to young Mr. Pressman in a spidery hand.

"Here, you are, Pressman," I said, handing the package over to him. In picking up the letter I was forced to handle the paperweight. It had an odd clammy feel to it that put me unaccountably at unease. Pressman took the letter from me, his face twisting up as though I'd offered him a skinned polecat. He pulled a stack of papers from the envelope. His countenance became increasingly disagreeable as he read through them. Most he discarded on the table quickly. These were covered with indecipherable scribblings and esoteric diagrams. The final few sheets he lingered over, his face showing even more distress and confusion. I grew impatient.

"Well, Pressman? What does it say?

"This makes no sense. Why…. This is … "

"C'mon, boy! What does it say?"

Pressman thrust the document into my hands and made for the back door.

"I… I have to get out. I'll be outside, I need air."

I concluded Pressman may be of a type that is wound too tight for anything that veers outside of the commonplace. I read the document. It was written in the same spidery hand that graced the envelope in an archaic flowery style that would have pleased the most erudite of pompous dandies back east. I will not reproduce it here exactly, as the ostentation of the prose obscured the narrative, nor do I still have the original document to refer to.

It took the form of a letter from Terrence Thorpe of Rhode Island to Reginald Pressman. It reiterated young Pressman's rights to Grinder Rock and detailed how Pressman's grandfather was not, in fact, of the Pressman line as young Mr Pressman had believed his whole life, but the illegitimate son of young Pressman's grandmother and a Jerimiah Thorpe from a liaison prior to her marriage. The family concealed this scandalous incident. So, in fact, Terrence Thorpe and Young Pressman were related by virtue of sharing the same biological grandfather.

The next section of the letter was a rambling account of Thorpe's activities. Thorpe entered the federal army at the time of the War Between the States, serving in the telegraph corps. I can only assume his service caused him a great deal of anguish and unhinged the man if that letter was any indication. Thorpe wrote of conducting experiments with telegraph equipment, seeking to boost its effectiveness and to eliminate the need for wire. Through these experiments, he claimed to have contacted a party from "outside." Thorpe maintained contact with this party during and after the war.

Unhinged or no, Thorpe was clever financially. Alluding to varied profitable speculations he engaged in during the so-called reconstruction. This money he poured into his telegraphy projects and secretly purchasing Grinder Rock. The island, suggested to him by the mysterious outsiders, would provide a location where he could work privately and undisturbed.

Thorpe apparently entered an agreement with these outsiders to perform a number of tasks for them, after which they would arrange for him to travel to their "headquarters". The time for this trip had come apparently and it was then he arranged for young Pressman to inherit his estate.

The letter ended with hints at some "great prize" concealed within the cairn, and other flights of fancy that I could only conclude were the ravings of a fanatic or lunatic. There was rambling nonsense about travel "through the black gulfs between the stars," peppered liberally with nonsense words: Yuggoth. R'lyeh. Hastur. Nyarlathotep. Since laying eyes on these outlandish words, they have branded themselves upon my thoughts, and they often come unbidden to my lips in quiet moments when my mind wanders.

I lay down the letter and went out to join Pressman, but he was nowhere to be seen. I was not overly concerned. Considering his reaction to the letter I assumed he may have returned to the boat, intending to leave. I was about to head that way myself when a rifle shot rang out from the direction of the cairn.

I walked toward the low pile of stones, going only a few paces before a second muffled shot rang out. I broke into a run. I am not a young man and the forty-five slug I've carried in my right thigh since Bitter Creek sent waves of agony with every step. Winded, I stopped at the cairn, there was a crude wooden archway framing a man-sized hole in its side. It looked to have been built around the same time as the cabin, maybe a little later. I hesitated to plunge into that dim opening. I peered into it, fidgeting with my rifle.

"Pressman!" I called out. "You in there, boy?

Pressman!" My hail was answered at first by silence, but then a low moan from within came to my ears. Perhaps Pressman was injured. I took a quick swallow from my hip flask to bolster my courage and stepped inside. I followed a damp, downward-sloping tunnel for several yards, making for the ruddy glow emanating at the far end. There were no more gunshots or moans, but a curious irregular buzzing sound grew in volume as I reached the end of the tunnel.

In my day I have seen death and cruelty in all its forms. I have seen men shot, blown apart by cannonballs, skinned alive, choking out their last at the end of ropes presided over by inexpert hangmen. But nothing I have witnessed could have prepared me for what awaited me in that cramped chamber.

Strangely illuminated by rays of sunlight slipping in between gaps in the stone above and by the odd glow emanating from the inscrutable machines arrayed about the floor. I saw young Pressman, strapped securely to a metallic slab. I felt mere moments had passed since I heard those gunshots, but in that brief time, he had been restrained and mutilated with the top portion of his skull neatly cut away. As shocking as this was, the revelation of the disposition of his brain was profoundly traumatic.

The organ in question was held gingerly in the… claws of a thing. While it was the height of a man, it was not a man or any beast that walks the good earth. It was made of a sort of pink, gelatinous pulp, with a multitude of clawed legs that put one in mind of a crayfish. Sail-like growths sprouted from its back. What served it for a head swivelled slowly toward me, a wriggling mass like a fistful of nightcrawlers, pulsing conical orifices poking out here and there producing a buzzing drone.

It seemed that it addressed me, but when I responded only with slack-jawed dumbfoundment, it looked back at the brain in its claws. Reaching out with another of its myriad limbs, it took from a nearby table a hollow metal cylinder. With great care, it slipped the organ inside.

My recollections of the events that followed are suspect. I am not ashamed to say I have known fear in my life, but not the sort of sanity-blasting terror that fell over me in that chamber. Using a rapid-fire technique learned from a New Mexico rancher; I emptied the magazine of my Winchester into the mass of gelid pink. It seemed untroubled by the twelve forty-five slugs ripping through it, and carefully set aside the cylinder with Pressman's brain. It turned toward me and advanced, buzzing infernally.

Wielding the rifle like a club, I belaboured what I assumed to be the thing's head. The stock sank wetly into the mass of writhing tendrils. This seemed to have some negligible effect on the thing, as it retreated slightly. The stock snapped off the rifle after a few blows, and I seized the closest loose object I could lay hands on, another of the metallic cylinders, with this I battered the thing until it recoiled from me.

With this respite from combat, I took to my heels. Fleeing madly back up the tunnel to the open air. I felt I would be safe should I be once more in the daylight. I burst out into the open and sprinted toward the cabin. I would hole up there and take stock of the situation. If there were no pursuit I would make for the stairs and the safety of the bay.

My heart sank as the infernal buzzing sound behind me waxed louder than ever. I stole a glance over my shoulder. The damned thing was pursuing me. Half hopping on its many legs and half flying by clumsily flapping the sail-like growths sprouting from its back. I moaned in despair when a second of the fiends appeared as if by magic beside the first.

My heart pounded like a triphammer, and my breath came in burning ragged gasps. I centred my gaze on the back door of the cabin. if I could only reach it. My vision narrowed and I saw the door as if it were at the end of a dark tunnel like the one I had just fled. I could feel the things closing in behind me. I feared I would pass out before reaching the cabin. A scent like mildew and crushed toadstools filled my nostrils.

The back door of the cabin swung open, revealing Jimmy Bearclaw, wild-eyed and screaming. In his right hand he gripped a Scofield and in his left a bottle with a flaming rag inserted in the neck, which he threw over me. There was a flash and a blast of heat that hurled me face-first to the ground. Jimmy seized my jacket and hauled me upright. Cursing and firing his revolver. We stumbled through the house and out the front of it. I gained a second or third wind and was able to pull my pistol from my waistcoat and engage the creatures as they emerged from the front of the cabin. One was charred and blackened by Jimmy's bottle bomb, damaged but by no means finished. Jimmy emptied his revolver and now struggled against panic to reload as the undamaged creature closed on him buzzing and gesticulating. I distracted it with a few rounds and yelled.

"Jimmy! Make for the boat, for God's sake!"

He nodded and sprinted away, and I followed, blindly firing my revolver at the things until its chambers were empty. I more fell down those old rickety steps than I did climb down them and crawled into the motorboat. The canoe Jimmy had paddled there in was alongside, but he wisely abandoned it in favour of my faster craft.

I do not think those creatures could fly well or they would have easily overtaken us. As I struggled to start the motor, I observed them hopping gingerly down the stairs a little faster than Jimmy and I had negotiated them.

I tore away from the island with every ounce of speed I could coax out of that new-fangled engine. Only when Grinder Rock was out of sight did I slacken my pace to take stock of my situation. My suit was shredded. And I had lost my bowler. I discovered I still held in the crook of my arm the metal cylinder. It was like a narrow hat box, or a tall coffee can, covered in a pink goo which was slowly evaporating before my eyes. The lid clearly screwed on.

"You ain't gonna open that, are ya?" asked Jimmy.

Foolishly I did.

Inside I saw a pinkish convoluted mass that throbbed and pulsated, partially obscured by a web of fine silvery wires. I upended the cylinder. With a sickly sucking noise, the contents spilled out, arrested from falling into the bottom of the craft by the wires that secured it to the cylinder. It hung suspended, throbbing wetly. A small circular disk wired to the mass of tissue vibrated, producing a harsh tinny buzzing that formed words.

"What is happening? Did you obtain Pressman's body? Why have you not made the exchange? Our arrangement was..."

"Goddammit, Oldridge!" Jimmy wailed.

I hurled the whole affair into the bay.

We sat in silence until the waterfront was in sight.

"Why'd you turn up, Jimmy?"

"Well…" he began sheepishly. 'I aimed to kill ya. Figured I'd settle affairs with you and hide your carcass in that cairn."

"What was you gonna do about young Pressman?"

"Dunno. I thought you was alone. Anyways, turned out not to matter!"

"Why didn't ya kill me then?"

Jimmy studied the water churning behind the boat for a space before replying.

"When I saw them things after you it was like… It would have been wrong not to try and stop 'em. You're a white man, but you're still a man. Against those things... You see, it's like all us men, on the earth, we're like one tribe, and them things are another. Anyway, I took your side in that fight, don't get used to it."

"You wanna try and kill me now Jimmy."

"Eh, we ain't in no shape to fight now Oldridge, and them damned things scared me so bad I done forgot what I was mad about. Let's call it square"

"Fair enough."

I had little choice but to report the matter of Mr Pressman to the authorities. Hearing my tale, they assumed I had done away with the young fellow.

Pressman's relations still hold this view and will repeat it to any who cares to listen. An examination of the island by the police yielded nothing. The letter in the cabin had been removed and the entrance to the cairn had been sealed. The police opened it and while they discovered the tunnel and chamber as I had described, it was devoid of any trace of Pressman, dead or otherwise, nor of any habitation by any otherworldly occupant. Jimmy Bearclaw's corroboration of my version of events was roundly ignored due to his being of the Apache persuasion.

Fortunately, there was neither any concrete evidence against me nor any motive I would have for killing Pressman. Further, in my capacity as a discreet consulting detective, I had ingratiated myself with many prominent and influential citizens. Thus, I was exonerated of any wrongdoing. Pressman was declared a missing person and my account of his demise was suppressed.

Keeping the cylinder might have gone a long way in proving my tale, but such a thought did not occur to me.

B. Harlan Crawford is the pen name for a collaboration between the touring evangelist Rev. Dean Conrad Jr. and the Ibakeen Death-God Igraath-Ghulathnragh. From an abandoned TNT plant in southeastern Tennessee the pair have produced multiple works of sword and sorcery and weird fiction containing cognito-hazardous memetics formulated to produce a genocidal rage in the reader.

For more information visit:
https://thelibraryoftheschlocklords.blogspot.com/

"Bitter Creek" Bob Oldridge is a weird western character of my own creation who previously appeared in The Bones of Aneth-Ka published in Witch House #2. At various point in his career he was a bounty hunter, train robber, indian fighter, lawyer, gambler, sherriff, and justice of the peace. At the time of this story he is winding down in his old age and works part time as a consulting detective in San Francisco.

THE MALTESE CTHULHU

A Cthulhu Armageddon story

C.T. PHIPPS

"You want me to find your missing idol," I said, sitting behind my desk and staring at the woman from me.

I had been working as a private detective in the Dreaming City for the better part of a year now and the realities of the business were clear. Most cases dealt with smut, broken trust, missing items, lost relatives, or suspected fraud. A not insignificant portion of them dealt with magic and the best solution in those cases was to consult a wizard or witch.

However, one element of my relationship with my clients was that it was extremely rare any of them could be described as glamorous. In a city of illusions and magic to cover up your horrific true appearance, only a few could afford to be beautiful. This woman was beautiful. Too beautiful in fact.

Standing roughly six-feet-tall in heels, she was "pleasantly shaped" in a way that wasn't quite natural. I'll spare you the private eye ogling and simply state I was no stranger to gorgeous women, but her appearance exceeded all but a handful. Her skin was the colour of coffee, and her eyes were the most magnificent shade of black. She was wearing a red sequin dress that looked more like it was prepared for a party than handling any sort of business in the city. Then there was the wide-brimmed hat that seemed designed to make her seem more exotic and mysterious. She also had a large handbag larger than a lady's usual purse, large enough to carry a gun or wand.

"My missing Cthulhu idol, yes," the woman said. "You can call me Marceline. Marceline de Russy."

An obvious pseudonym.

Marceline de Russy AKA "The Medusa" was a famous Witch Queen of the Pre-Rising Earth down New Orleans way. She had been a Cthulhu cultist who had made the mistake of falling in love with a rich bigoted man who ultimately murdered her before killing himself. The legend, like so many others in the city, had taken a life of its own. It was generally told as a cautionary tale about why members of the Old Great Old Ones and Outer Gods should avoid marrying those who worshipped the Small Gods of Earth. Or just bigoted white men, no matter how rich.

I crossed my arms and tried to avoid looking directly at her. There was something hypnotising about her and that wasn't always a metaphor. "You should know, Ms. de Russy, that I have not the best experience with the Cult of Cthulhu."

"It's a religion like any other," Marceline said.

"One that promises when their god rises, all of their enemies will be destroyed and they will dance on the ashes," I replied.

"So does Christianity," Marceline pointed out.

"Another religion that has tried to kill me a few times," I replied. "Most New God churches in the City consider me a demon."

"Are you?" Marceline asked.

"Demon, jinn, spirit, detective, soldier," I said, shrugging. "It's why I generally don't do religious cases."

The woman reached into her handbag, causing me to reach for my pistol hidden in a holster taped under my desk. Instead, she pulled out a wallet then proceeded to pull out ten crisp century notes before placing them on the desk.

"I am at your disposal ma'am," I replied, dryly.

"Money is all it took?" the woman asked, questioningly.

"What have you heard about me?"

"That detective John Henry Booth is a man of honour, nobility, and willing to walk the mean streets of the City without being mean himself."

I nodded. "Good. Then my publicist is doing his job. As I am none of those things. I am, however, quite willing to do the job for cash."

Capitalism had not been a concept I'd been intimately familiar with when I'd first come to the City. I'd swiftly adapted to the concept when it became clear "credit", paper, and coins were the driving currency (no pun intended) for determining whether a person should live or die. Indeed, I might have avoided many of the people trying to kill me if I'd been rich as well as alien in my nature. It seemed they could get by worshipping alien gods, practising bloody atavistic magic, and consorting with unclean things as an eccentric hobby. It was only the destitute and working class who were considered anathema.

"Good," Marceline said. "The statue is a small clay sculpture, about eight inches tall and depicting an image of the Great Old One's head with a smaller portion of his body. It is several thousand years old and of great value to my family."

"Is it magical in nature?" I asked.

"Absolutely not," Marceline said, obviously lying to me. "Its nature is purely sentimental."

"Mmm-hmm," I replied, deciding to take notes. I took out a pen and began writing on the crisp yellow paper on my desk, the letterhead proudly reading KING PAPER COMPANY. "Do you have any idea who might have absconded with this object?"

"I know *exactly* who has taken the idol," Marceline said.

That was an unexpected and suspicious bit of good fortune. "And who is that?"

"The Ecstatic Order of Shub-Niggurath," Marceline said, frowning her pretty, black lips.

"The *Ecstatic* Order?" I asked.

"It's a sex cult," Marceline said.

"I guessed," I said.

Shub-Niggurath was a less popular cult than the worship of Cthulhu, Yog-Sothoth, or the New Gods but still had a powerful following--for perhaps obvious reasons. A fertility goddess, she was usually worshipped in conjunction with Aphrodite, Bacchus, the Morrigan, Inanna, and Pan. Wild revelries were the order of the day, and it was why her religion was banned even in a city where monsters walked freely.

"They stole it from my family for their rituals," Marceline said.

"And you want me to steal it back," I replied, finally getting down to brass tacks.

"Yes," Marceline said, not denying it or engaging in euphemism. I appreciated that. "There will be an even greater reward for you once you bring it back."

"More money?" I asked.

"Ten times as much," Marceline said, positively slinking over with a not-so-much alluring as predatory movement to her body. "But greater rewards still."

Like a snake.

She pressed herself forward, putting her face-to-face with me before kissing me on the lips. My mind grew somewhat foggy.

"I see," I said, trying but failing to pull away.

"Until next time," Marceline said, departing and leaving me tingling all over.

Oh yeah, she was going to betray me.

Tracking down the Ecstatic Cult of Shub-Niggurath proved easier than expected.

"It's a goddamn sorority?" I asked, staring at the pleasant Victorian building across the well-manicured green lawn.

It was a two-story structure that was sitting in a row of a dozen other structures that formed its own city block. Only the very rich and very gifted could attend college in the City but that didn't prevent people from creating their own little secret societies to help guarantee their futures once past graduation. Notably, the building had iron bars on its windows as well as thick curtains. There was also a large stone wall around the place as well as several wards possessing real magic to them.

In retrospect, I shouldn't have been surprised. A wise but cynical man once said that cults were what big religions called the little one. The truth was a bit more complicated. A cult was, at heart, about secrecy. A religion supposedly was open about its doctrine and truths that it was supposed to share with everyone. A cult, by contrast, was meant to keep its higher truths to devotees that proved themselves worthy of such power.

When magic was involved, inevitably cults formed around the power that its leadership was reluctant to share. Wizards and witches were a surly and jealous lot that always wished to expand their knowledge but were reluctant to share. Apprenticeships were like slavery, and it was the rare conjurer who would let his student learn as much as himself. It was why colleges like New Miskatonic were gathering places for the arcane as a college was meant to share everything, even when it was perhaps better that such truths be kept hidden. Who knew how many secret societies and would-be magicians had found their footing in New Miskatonic's occult library? Many I'd wager.

"I mean, it certainly fills some men's fantasies," Jackie said, staring at the sigh. The muscular redheaded woman was only a bit shorter than me. She was also dressed in a trench coat and fedora which was more men's fashion in the City. Her glamour was slipping a bit today and her teeth were unusually sharp with prominent dog-like canines as befitting a ghoul-human hybrid. Still, she could look like a twenty-year-old and someone who could fit in among these upper-class twits. I admitted I'd expected to find the cult a bit further afield, though.

"Please don't," I muttered, having raised Jackie since she was an adolescent and not able to deal with the fact she was an adult twenty-one years later.

"A good chunk of them are New Miskatonic U cheerleaders too!" Jackie said, giving me an elbow nudge. "Go Squids."

I stared at her. "Please tell me you're joking."

"I never joke for the twenty-five bucks an hour you pay me," Jackie replied. "Two of the ladies here, the Crampton Sisters, are the minds behind the Ecstatic Order. They recruit over the city's internet and host raves through the city that include many after-parties where the drugs and sex flow freely."

"Fascinating," I said, dryly. "The internet is the telephone service that sends pictures and written messages, right?"

Jackie sighed. "We're never going to get you caught up, are we?"

"I don't believe in Yithian science," I said.

Jackie sighed. "You're hopeless, Dad."

"Well now I just have to figure out how to get inside," I muttered. "If they've got the horror in clay then they're probably keeping it in their sacred place--so to speak."

"Yeah," Jackie said. "Are you sure this client is on the level?"

I struggled to throw off thoughts of Marceline. The kiss she'd planted on me had put me under some sort of spell and, worse yet, I knew it. She was an extremely attractive woman, but she hadn't needed to put some sort of geas or curse on me to get me to bring back her idol. I would have done it for the money alone.

Unfortunately, the aftereffects were leaving my blood on fire and thoughts constantly drifting back to the witch. I wanted to bring it to her, and I could tell that unnatural hunger was one imposed on me. I also knew that there was no way it would be a simple transaction and that anyone who used that kind of power on another to control them was someone who intended only to end it in blood.

"John?" Jackie asked, sensing my discomfort.

"No," I answered her earlier question. "She is not. Did you pick up any dangers?"

"You mean are they actually just a pair of party girls or are they genuinely dangerous?" Jackie asked.

"Yes," I replied.

Jackie frowned. "I don't know. It seems like there's easier ways to justify college hedonism than invoking forces mankind does not understand. There's rumours."

"There's always rumours," I said.

"And some of them are even true," Jackie said, slyly. "However, unfortunately, these rumours also come with missing persons reports. Never students of New Miskatonic University but other invitees, poorer and not supposed to be there in the first place. Maybe it's unrelated. Maybe they just ODed."

"Or maybe they're paying a tithe for their pleasures," I said, grunting. "Real magic always has a price."

"And the trick is getting other people to pay it," Jackie said. "The magic in the walls says that at least someone inside this place knows the real deal, though. The cult is only starting out but it's eager to expand its knowledge base."

That gave me an idea.

Laying the breadcrumbs out had only taken a few days but worked like a charm among the more credulous among the city's supernatural enthusiasts. Jackie had created a false profile on the "internet" for me of a reputed bookseller and former student at Miskatonic with a master's degree in Alternative Religion.

"Mr Henri de Marigny" had apparently run into some financial difficulties and was now willing to part with his occult library of originals as well as the translations he'd done. Fragments of the *Necronomicon*, *Book of Eibon*, *Pnakotic Manuscripts*, and so on.

This was already a big warning sign for any serious occult collectors because true practitioners would sell their copies. If you had access to such a treasure trove, you'd rob and kill or make deals before parting with them. It was enough to appeal to amateurs, though, and that was what I was hoping the so-called Crampton Sisters were. We'd received hundreds of inquiries over the next few days. Then our fishes had taken the bait, if you don't mind some Innsmouthtown slang.

"We're so glad to see you, Mr. de Marigny," Babs Crampton said, answering the door in a Miskatonic U sweater and knee-length skirt.

Babs was a beautiful blonde-haired girl with a headband and girl next door looks that nevertheless smouldered with an understated sensuality I couldn't entirely disregard as lingering effects of Marceline's spell. It had been three days and I was still suffering from the effects of it.

"Thank you, madame," I said, affecting an upper-crust City accent. "I am very pleased to make your acquaintance. Is your sister here?"

Disguise wasn't my forte, but it was amazing how a pair of glasses, a change of clothes, and an adjustment to one's demeanour can alter one's entire position in society. In this case, I'd put on a jacket with brown elbow patches, beige pants, and almost slipper-like dress shoes to distract from my bulky muscular form.

"Oh yes," Babs said, cheerfully opening the door to reveal the second of the Crampton sisters.

Raquel Crampton was the opposite of her sister with barely any resemblance between the two, having bright tanned skin and pretty, orange hair with a lime green jacket on. She looked like she'd just stepped in from the rain despite it having been bone dry for several days. Both she and her sister, together, looked like actresses playing college students as opposed to college students themselves.

"I've heard so much about you!" Raquel said, cheerfully. Which was quite impossible given I was a fictitious construct that hadn't existed a week ago.

"You flatter me, madame," I said, smiling as I held tightly to my briefcase. "Will we be alone during this meeting?"

"Why, are we not enough?" Raquel asked, her innuendo-laced joke strangely lacking in sexuality.

"Our sisters are away," Babs said, quickly. "This is a private matter for the leadership of our coven."

"Coven, eh?" I asked, politely.

Babs parted, allowing me to pass. "Oh yes, We teach in the Ecstatic Order of Shub-Niggurath that the word witch is actually a word for the wise. We seek to appropriate it from the patriarchal oppressive religious forces of Yog-Sothoth and Hastorian religious structures. Ones that accent the male idiom over the feminine. Don't you agree?"

I was of the opinion the Great Old Ones did not remotely give a shit about humanity, let alone our genders which probably didn't coordinate with anything their species possessed. I also felt it ridiculous to worship beings that considered us equivalent to termites on a good day but that wasn't going to help my position. "That sounds fascinating, though I admit I am here primarily to discuss our business arrangement. I want my library to find a good home and that requires a face-to-face meeting to hash out our details."

I walked past the sisters and found myself in a stately-looking study with a set of winding stairs leading to the second floor as well as walls full of books, mostly lesser volumes of the occult mixed in with a variety of cheap romance novels for strange contrast. The place had a lot of light coming in from the windows and well-appointed antique (or excellent reproductions of antiques) furniture.

They'd gone to some elaborate lengths to make themselves appear respectable and it was entirely possible they were, at least by City standards. None of that could hide a darker cast to everything, though, as my honed senses detected something unholy beneath me. I could sense a terrible power thrumming underneath the floorboards and guessed it was gathering mystical forces for some nefarious purpose. It always was nefarious with magic. Call me premature but I'd have bet my PI's licence that was where the Cthulhu idol was.

"Of course, Mr. de Marginy," Raquel said. "We just thought you might like to acquaint yourself with the intimacies of our religion since you're someone who is going to help us so greatly--profit motivation or not. Would you care for a drink?"

I smiled, not answering. "I don't drink. Deadens the mind."

How stupid did they think I was?

So, I was an abject moron.

I was presently tied with ropes around my wrists against a Saint Andrew's cross in the middle of the sorority's basement, a large green balefire burning in the centre of the chamber. The walls were covered in a noxious smelling pinkish fungi and smeared with other more identifiable fluids. Both seemed to be feeding strange artery-like vines that crisscrossed the floors, walls, and ceiling.

There was a general sense that the building's foundation was alive, and the foundations had been dug out to allow the unnatural meat-plant growing around me to live. Worse, at least for my peace of mind, were countless animal bones and more human-like ones scattered among the bizarre underground garden. There were a few fresher bodies that looked like they'd been drained of blood with large circular sucker-like wounds on their sides.

How I'd managed to enter this unfortunate situation when I was so cagey and determined to keep the upper hand over the Crampton Sisters is a fascinating story. However, I'm not going to tell it because it makes me look bad and you'll just have to use your imagination. Let's pretend it was something semi-dignified like knocking me over the head with the Cthulhu idol when I wasn't looking.

The Crampton sisters proceeded to move into the chamber, both wearing extraordinarily revealing attire whose sexualized effect was somewhat blunted by the fact they were now hairless nose-less serpent-women. Their bodies were covered in thick scales and eyes of the most malign yellow with long tails sticking out from the lowest point of their back. Which, technically, I suppose made them resemble lizards more than serpents, but taxonomy wasn't my strong suit.

Babs Crampton, I was taking a wild guess as to which sister was which, was holding a purple pillow carrying the Cthulhu idol. It was very different from the way Marceline described it, instead of clay, it was constructed of R'lyehian gold. Perhaps it had been covered in clay and the Crampton Sisters had cleaned it off. Raquel was carrying a large sword with a serrated blade that had a carving of a snake along its side. That was not a good sign.

"You sought to steal from us, Mr Booth," Babs Crampton said, her voice now carrying the inhuman throaty rasp of a serpent woman. "The idol of Great Cthulhu is something that is ours by right of conquest."

"Marceline de Russy disagrees," I replied, working against my bonds as I tested both the wood as well as rope. The rope was strong, but the wood of the cross was old and probably bought for purposes other than bondage—at least for human sacrifices.

"Ha!" Babs sneered. "You don't even know her real name."

"No, I admit I do not," I said, wondering if I had any magic that might aid me down here. I was a hedge wizard and the cost of even the lightest spell was one paid in blood or souls (if such a thing existed), and I was always hesitant to open my mind up to those terrible cosmic forces.

Once there had been a time I could have just torn through them like wet tissue paper, ripping flesh and bone like they were nothing. Being a creature that could have been worshipped by foolish mortals, I'd traded my humanity and, some days, like right now for instance, I wondered if I'd gotten the better part of the deal. Instead, I focused my strength on one spot and hoped I'd be able to break the centre of the cross.

"We were her apprentices," Babs said, pacing the statue at my feet. "She opened our minds up to the true nature of the cosmos but refused to give us the true power. So, we took what was ours!'

"Uh-huh," I said, staring at her. "Was this before or after you became a snake woman?"

Raquel hissed at me, actually hissed. It was *ridiculous*.

"You will die, Mr Booth, and your seed, as well as blood, will be offered up to Shub-Niggurath," Babs said. "The Mother of All and Nothing shall feast upon you, and we shall drink of her ichor."

I was less than impressed with their Pulp magazine villainy and wondered how much their evil witch act was down to how society had educated them that evil priestesses were supposed to act. This was strictly amateur-hour sorcery and they'd obviously ditched Marceline, if she was the real deal, well before they'd learned anything useful.

"The seed part wasn't so bad but there's an unpleasant aftertaste," I replied. "At least now that the beer goggles are off."

Raquel lifted her sword and shouted. "Ia Shub-Niggurath! Yig-Seth! Bla'ata'al mack!"

Raquel was close enough that my recklessness had a small chance of success. Forcing even every bit of stolen strength into my limbs, I snapped the Saint Andrew's cross in half at my back and manoeuvred my body so that the sword buried itself into the wooden beam binding my right arm. Striking it, the area gave way to free my upper arms and I grabbed Raquel before lifting her in the air.

"Ahhh!" Raquel shouted. "What are you—"

Raquel was cut off by my hurling her into the balefire behind her. What followed was a nightmarish scream accompanied by alien, as well as not-so-alien, obscenities. The flames licked at the serpent woman, and she thrashed in its magical flames, the alien forces inside the fire tearing at whatever spells she'd cast upon herself to make her immortal. Raquel reached out to her sister, calling in some ancient tongue to rescue her.

"I can't!" Babs shouted, horrified by her sister's burning. Looking as if she wanted to go into the fire or work some magic to save her, she instead grabbed the Cthulhu idol on the ground before rushing to the door at the other end of the makeshift temple.

"Bitch!" Raquel's final word was entirely understandable. The burning serpent woman then exploded and became a flying spectral will-o-wisp that bolted out of the balefire and rushed out the doorway past Babs. It reminded me of something out of a fantasy barbarian story. The remaining Crampton sister was thrown to the ground and the Cthulhu idol skipped across the ground away from her.

My legs were still bound to the Saint Andrew's cross' remains and that part of the object was bolted to the ground. Reaching down to grab the late Raquel's sword, I proceeded to start cutting myself free. The sword was incredibly sharp and freeing myself was fast but not quite fast enough. Because I noticed the room was *moving*.

The vines on the ground and wall detached themselves, revealing lamprey-like suckers that made disgusting noises as they began to descend upon me. A large tumorous fleshy growth descended from the centre of the roof, revealing the evil heart of the creature the Crampton Sisters had cultivated here.

"The Great Mother's Daughter shall devour you!" Babs shouted, raising the idol in the air. "Feed, mighty one! Feed!"

I proceeded to cut myself free and slashed my way through the vines as they came for me, spilling a noxious foul-smelling ichor where each was struck. Running toward Babs, I proceeded to give her a punch to the jaw that was perhaps not my most chivalrous of actions but still managed to achieve the aim I was hoping for, knocking her flat on her tail. Grabbing the Cthulhu idol from her arms, I made a break for the door as I left the sword clattering on the ground.

"You will never be able to outrun the Great Mother!" Babs shouted at me as I started up the stairs.

"I only have to outrun you!" I shouted back. A quick glance confirmed the vines in the basement were starting to wrap themselves around their former master.

I tried not to listen to the sounds I heard as I reached the first floor. They were infinitely worse than screams.

I grew sicker and weaker with the passing of the days. Within two days, I had lost twenty pounds and every moment I was covered in sweat from a fever that seemed always on the verge of taking my life. I also found myself carrying the Cthulhu idol wherever I went, unable or unwilling to let it leave my sight without the strongest of efforts.

Marceline's spell was more clearly something designed to kill me unless I returned to her the property, she thought was rightfully hers. It was bad client manners and yet I had to admit I only cared that she undoes the magic when I finally arranged for the meeting at the docks near midnight.

I, of course, didn't believe for a second she intended to remove the curse once I'd delivered her property, though. One thing I'd learned about wizards over the years that had held true with virtually each I'd met was this: they were all assholes.

I was standing on the edge of Pier 13, holding a large package wrapped in brown paper with a little wax-covered rope around it. I was once more dressed in my trench coat and fedora, glad to have a set of clothes again even if covering the cost of my lost suit from the guys I'd rented it from would be an enormous pain in the budget. I was armed but I didn't think that would make a large amount of difference with Marceline.

Not if she saw it coming.

"I'm glad to see you're a man of your word," Marceline's voice filled the night air, just a few strokes after midnight. She'd changed from her flamboyant sequin red dress to a blue trench coat that was complimented by a similar blue hat.

"You promised me ten grand," I replied, now shaking with the pain of her presence. I wanted to throw myself on the ground, present the Cthulhu idol to her, and offer my life up for sacrifice. It was behaviour so out of character, I wanted to put a bullet through my brain just to make sure I died as myself.

"I'm afraid that part of our deal is cancelled," Marceline spoke, stretching out her hands. "*Give me the idol.*"

Her voice had a compelling, almost hypnotic quality. "Not until you fix whatever you've done to me."

Marceline's eyes narrowed and she repeated herself. The power behind her words became all-encompassing. "***Give me the idol.***"

Instead, I unwrapped the idol and revealed the Cthulhu idol. It had a grenade wrapped in duct tape around its side. I pulled out the pin and squeezed the safety lever. "I'll happily give you the idol. But unless I'm cured, I guess we'll be finding out if it's explosive proof."

Marceline stared at me.

"Impressive, Booth," Marceline said, her voice sounding familiar. However, I couldn't quite place it. "It seems you haven't lost all of your Wasteland cunning in your time playing acting as a detective."

"Make your choice," I said, struggling for breath. "My hands are really shaky."

Marceline waved her hand over me. "May the dark gods cease feasting on your soul."

I fell to my knees, a sudden sense of relief filling my body. "Thanks."

"Give me the idol," Marceline said, slowly walking forward. "Put the pin--"

Of course, I obeyed her command this time and threw the idol into her arms. Marceline began screaming several commands in a guttural inhuman language before I drew my gun and put three rounds into her head. Her body collapsed into a bunch of writhing snakes that fled into the water beneath the pier. I wasted a few bullets, blowing up as many as I could before they did. I got maybe half in the end, leaving bloody snake parts and bullet holes all over the wooden pier's planks.

Jackie, my backup, ran up to me with a shotgun in hand. "Did you get her?"

"I have no idea," I admitted.

Jackie looked down at the Cthulhu idol and pulled out the wooden grenade I'd carved and painted with shoe polish. "Glad she fell for the bluff."

"I wish I could have acquired the real deal," I muttered. "Either way, I suggest we take this thing down to the nearest foundry and smelt it."

"That'll really piss her off," Jackie muttered.

"I get the impression she already hated me," I muttered. "But hopefully she'll take time to recover."

"Ex-girlfriend?" Jackie joked.

It wasn't funny to me. "To be honest, for a second there, she sounded a lot like my ex-slave master, Katryn. Does no one stay dead anymore?"

I looked down at the Cthulhu idol, whose four ruby-encrusted jewelled eyes twinkled back with the glow of an alien power that would hopefully fade once melted down. A part of me considered keeping it but I knew it would just make me a target for every two-bit magician and wannabe sorcerer in the City. I had enough enemies as it was.

"He's not the one to ask," Jackie said, joking. "He's not dead, only sleeping."

"Yeah, and this world is the stuff dreams are made of."

C.T Phipps is a lifelong student of horror, science fiction, and fantasy. An avid tabletop gamer, he discovered this passion led him to write and turned him into a lifelong geek. He is a regular blogger on "The United Federation of Charles" (http://unitedfederationofcharles. blogspot.com/). He's the author of Agent G, Cthulhu Armageddon, Lucifer's Star, Straight Outta Fangton, and The Supervillainy Saga.

John Henry Booth is the protagonist of "The Maltese Cthulhu" and the star of the Cthulhu Armageddon series.

DEEPEST DARKEST GEOMETRY
JOHN A. DELAUGHTER

My name?

My name is Largekoff, Vincent Largekoff.

One day, Largekoff will be on the lips of every newsperson and every newspaper's masthead nationwide.

For now, my newest home away from home in Arkham is *Charlie's Grub and Pub*.

When you're an "itinerant" newspaperman as I am--I hate the word "vagabond" though there may be some truth to it--you end up with a resume filled with entry-level newspaper jobs.

It also means getting the least expensive place I can afford in each town graced with my presence.

I'm living proof that flophouses aren't just for flops.

Moving around a lot is also a dandy way to stay one step ahead of your creditors.

So, *Charlie's Grub and Pub* is the latest in a string of my "homes away from home—"

The place is filled with smoke; it's loud and alive.

The newest fad in music rocks in the background.

I hate disco.

The food is fair when I remember to eat. Salt is like alcohol and ashes, when it comes to Charlie's cooking.

"Why am I a 'well-travelled' newspaperman?"

"Long ago, the universe stopped setting out the welcome mat for me. Fate smiled down on me in that, almost every time I get a reporter's job in another city, I run into the most incredible, the vilest of horrors."

"I keep telling myself, 'Largekoff, it couldn't happen here. How likely is it to happen again?'"

"But then, it does."

"I've come within a breath of losing limb or life

more than once. As I dig deeper into the stories that most talentless newspaper hacks avoid because things get too messy for their rarefied tastes, well—"

"Where was I?"

"Oh yes, in my world, you'll find a kind of truth more terrifying than fiction. A truth that will shock you!"

"Though not a religious man, I've become a prophet of sorts. My porkpie straw hat, seersucker suit, and white sneakers are not the usual vestments for a holy man. "

"Why do I call myself a prophet?"

"As I dig into the dark basements and dreary graveyards of a story, I run into dark things that folklore, myths, and legends whisper of."

"Like a prophet, when I reveal a truth, the rank and file of humanity disbelieve me and ostracise me. They'd stone me if it were legal."

"I've been run out of more towns on a rail than Amtrak."

"So, what's it all about?"

"I'm talking about the nameless things that ride the wind on stormy nights. They are the nauseous things that squirm in every direction when ancient rocks are turned over in old forests. They are feral and fearsome, sentient and seeking. They worship the Great Old Ones in tottering henges strewn in forgotten corners of the world."

"The dark gods of old are shrouded in primal myths and pretentious legends. The claws and hooves of their inhuman devotees tread the ancient earth long before the rise of man. It's from their forgotten tablets, fabled scrolls, and fanciful petroglyphs that we learn what few details we know about the Old Ones."

"Like I say, I'm lucky to retain life and limbs after run-ins with those things."

"Bartender, would you refresh my drink? Friend, do you want another?"

"What was I talking about?"

"Oh, that's right."

"Do you want to know the truth about the nameless things? They have names, but you can't pronounce them. They're replicated from old languages that defy translation."

"How can you tell if you've chanced upon one of their names? Try standing in the centre of a pentagram, then read aloud from a cursed book."

"Which books?"

"Like the Aramaic version of Ludvig Prinn's dreaded *De Vermis Mysteriis*."

"Did you know that Saint Jerome, the guy who wrote the Latin *Vulgate,* almost translated that devilish book into Latin?"

"That's Old Latin, the one that witches in covens throughout the twilight earth chant during Black Sabbats."

"Hold your horses, I'm getting to my point."

"Jerome was a scholar interested in dusty old scrolls from cob-webbed corners of the world. For some reason, he'd forgotten to employ protective sigils while he was doing the translating. He lost all his hair to hellfire when he accidentally called up an ancient demon while reading the text aloud."

"That's how Friar Tuck's haircut got started."

"You gotta do your research before you go toe-to-toe with the critters. Chutzpah ain't enough. We haven't even talked about the outer gods and the Great Brotherhood of the Countless Galaxies—"

"Charlie, where did my friend go?"

"What am I doing with all the papers in the booth? Your bar is a second office for me.

I'm working on the opening lines of the story that'll win me the Pulitzer. This time, it's a sure thing."

"Here goes, tell me what you think.

'In this world, truth wears many faces.

Sometimes, it takes an Einstein to detect the subtle differences between the clever facades and clear facts in a case—'"

"My opinion," Charlie interrupted, "is that you've had one too many bourbons, Largekoff. Why don't you go home? Forget all the supernatural nonsense. Where has it gotten you in the past?"

"Besides, the bar in closing—"

"Supernatural nonsense? Let me tell you something, Charlie—"

"Oh, it's last call? Well, Charlie, before you go, can you refresh my drink one last time?"

Monday, April 22, 1974, 12:00 PM. *The Steady Acres Funeral Home.*

Bernadette Roads, age thirty-five, a rather smallish woman professional to the core, was wrapping up her work. She was second mortician at the *Steady Acres*

Funeral Home, one of two in the Arkham chain. At the corner of West Derby and Brown, her customers were piled to the ceiling in their refrigerated locker. The reason? The embalming solution supplier, Frigid Fluids, based out of Chicago, was a week behind in delivering the lifeblood of funeral homes.

The delay didn't prevent her from addressing the cosmetic applications that made the dead more presentable to the living. Some clients looked better dead than alive; she was that good at her craft. She wanted to leave the deceased family and friends with the best, "last time I saw them," moment possible.

Bernadette failed to lock the side door of *Steady Acres'* main building, a brick and stucco monstrosity, the kind that was slowly replacing the once teeming sea of gables and gambrels that made Arkham famous.

Two shadows slipped into a hallway not far from the refrigerated storage.

One swung from a side doorway in front of the gurney Ms Roads used to carry her client down the hallway.

"What?" Ms Roads gasped.

"The Master has need of this—" she heard from the shadowed face of her foremost assailant.

Another assailant swung in behind Ms Roads, and twisted off her head, like a twist top from a soda bottle

She fell a trembling mess as her blood spread a crimson pool across the floor.

Later, the Police failed to find her body, nor any of the twenty-five corpses awaiting embalmment. According to a crime scene technician, who I bribed with a bottle of hooch, surveillance cameras caught a dark flash and the headless Ms Roads falling dead amid a shower of blood. Instead of photographing her killers, their forms became shimmering blurs, like flowing subjects in a *Picasso* painting.

Wednesday, April 24, 1974, 7:00 AM. *The Breezy Angels Funeral Parlour.*

I was up early. A reporter's work is never done.

My police scanner crackled with life. The unit sat on my bedside table. From the singular, "Code 487," being broadcast, I almost turned off the noisy thing.

Grand Theft didn't fall under my purview as obituary editor at the *Arkham Purview*, second in circulation to the *Arkham Advertiser*.

It was the business name that got me out of bed, throwing on my clothes, grabbing my camera bag, and heading out the door.

Breezy Angels Funeral Parlour, at East Derby and Federal?

I drove up in my yellow Gremlin, as the crime scene folks broke out their gear, and collected evidence. It was early morning, the sun barely peeking over the horizon. Should I have stayed in bed? The flash of police cameras dotted the threshold and through a few windows in the building.

I got out of my car in the funeral parlour's parking lot and started towards its back door.

Halfway there, an officer turned around from talking

with others and approached me.

"Who are you?" asked the policeman, delegated with the unenviable duty of crowd control.

"Me?" I stopped and looked around innocently, "Me? I'm Vincent Largekoff from the *Arkham Purview*."

"What are you doing here, Largekoff? You're a reporter then? I don't like the *Arkham Purview*. You know why, Mr. Largekoff?"

The officer started to stick me with his pointed finger. I hate 'up close and personal' police work.

"No, why? Officer, officer—" I asked, grasping my camera bag close, hoping it wouldn't be confiscated.

"Officer Chitsworth. You know what the *Purview* wrote about me?" Officer Chitsworth glared at me.

"Chitsworth, Chitsworth. Chitworth? Can't say that it rings a bell—" I replied, stepping back from the Officer.

I practised my own version of 'situational awareness' over the years in the face of fuming policemen.

"One of your 'so-called' reporters did a hit piece on me, alleging I was sleeping in my vehicle, while on duty—" shouted Officer Chitsworth.

"If it weren't for the shenanigans of your buddies, sticking their noses into places they don't belong, I'd still be a Sergeant, with a Sergeant's retirement pay in a few years. Now, I've been demoted to doing trivial duties usually reserved for rookies, not a seasoned veteran like myself."

I was getting nowhere with officer, 'Chip-On-His-Shoulder.' I had to think fast.

I got my tape recorder out and began to ask questions.

"Officer Chitsworth, can I ask you about what

went down here? I mean, 'Grand Theft' isn't normally associated with funeral homes, is it?" I said.

"What does a seasoned veteran like yourself make of this? Did someone steal their hearse?" I said, hoping the words 'seasoned veteran' eased tensions a bit.

Officer Chitsworth's snarl changed to a smile.

"Funny, Largekoff, you should be a comedian," Officer Chitsworth replied.

"That's beside the point," I said. "What in heaven's name do thieves steal from a funeral home?"

Officer Chitsworth smiled.

"I'm not going to play 'twenty questions' with you, Largekoff," Officer Chitsworth replied.

I decided to play my hand and see if that didn't rattle the good officer's cage.

"Ok, you win," I turned, then shot my insider question, "By the way, exactly how many bodies were stolen?"

I paused for effect.

If I didn't win a Pulitzer, at least I could win an Oscar with this performance.

"How many bodies?" Officer Chitworth said, surprised. "How did you know that Largekoff? Were you here when the pervs made off with the deceased?"

"Me?" I said, trying to play up my surprised innocence.

Just then a small, official-looking man in a suit, power-red tie, and wingtips walked out of the building, blathering to someone.

Someone who wasn't there.

The man wasn't looking where he was going and

bumped into Officer Chitsworth.

"Mister Royce?" Officer Chitsworth said.

"Thirty years in the business, thirty years—" Mr Royce replied.

"Who are you, sir? And what happened inside?" I asked, poking my tape recorder toward the small man.

He might spill the beans in the unfiltered moment.

"Me?" Mr Royce said, surprised that other people were around him. "I'm Jonah Royce, owner of *Breezy Angels*. How could they—"

"How could who?" I asked drawing closer to Mr. Royce.

Mr Royce looked at me as if I'd lost my mind.

"The deceased, my clients. What would robbers want with them? That many bodies—"

"How many, sir?" I asked, seizing the moment.

"Thirty—All our inventory, thirty of the departed, gone—" replied Mr Royce.

Another man, burly in build, unkempt in his grooming, wearing an askew tie, wrinkled suit, and scuffed, black shoes stepped out of the building and approached us.

'That's enough, Mr Royce. Don't say anything else until we've completed our investigation," the man said in a commanding manner.

"Sergeant Cole," Officer Chitsworth said, coming to attention.

"Who's this guy?" Sergeant Cole asked.

Sergeant Cole eyed me, I got the feeling he was sizing me up.

"He says his name's Largekoff, a reporter from the *Arkham Purview*—" replied Officer Chitsworth.

"Reporter? The *Arkham Purview*?" Sergeant Cole asked, raising his voice. "Chitsworth, get this scum off my crime scene!"

Officer Chitsworth spun me around, grabbed my right arm, and put it in a hammerlock.

He then pushed me and my scrambling feet toward my Gremlin.

"You'll hear from my Newspaper about this—" I yelled, as Chitsworth opened the car door with one hand, and threw me into it with the other.

The good officer stomped off, leaving me fuming.

I'm no slouch, but I wasn't in the officer's league.

Bruised, all the way down to my ego, I had managed to hold onto my tape recorder. I was puzzled by the pattern that was forming.

Thirty bodies from *Breezy Angels* added to the twenty-five bodies from *Steady Acres*? What did the grave robbers intend to do, open a delicatessen for discerning cannibals?

What other explanation fits the facts of the case?

Wednesday, April 24, 1974, 11:00 PM. *The Other Worldly Journeys Mortuary*.

Another "Code 487" blared over my Police Scanner.

"All available units respond to silent alarm, Code 487 in progress at the *Other Worldly Journeys Mortuary*—"

A half-dozen responders responded with call signs and promises to converge on the crime scene.

I had fallen asleep fully dressed in the easy chair.

The Other Worldly Journeys Mortuary, corner of West Washington and Peabody, was near my humble digs.

I grabbed my camera bag and headed out the door.

Soon, I rolled up on *Other Worldly Journeys*.

Police cars formed a ring around the place. One cruiser was wedged behind an unmarked refrigerated truck, evidently used to carry off the stolen stiffs.

As a side door opened, several police spotlights converged on the assailants. Behind a gurney piled high with sprawled bodies, strode a travesty of human body-parts, sporting arms and legs jutting from random places, and a head with gapping, fanged mouth where its chest should be.

Something also bulging hung around its waist.

It was the thing that should not be, a half-finished, living, breathing Phantasm from *Picasso's War*.

A wedge of officers, brandishing 12-gauge shotguns and .357 magnums, ran toward the monstrosity. The thing pushed its cart aside and met the wedge head-on. The phalanx of officers fired at it from point-blank range.

Meanwhile, I took pictures, circling behind the police cars.

The combined firepower of the police guns drove the thing backwards on its hooves and heels, but it kept on coming forward, baying and barking.

Some officers used their shotguns as bludgeons while others tried to meet the marauding menace, brandishing billy clubs. The thing, a storm of arms and elbows, blocked nightsticks swung by Arkham's finest, while it tossed burly officers aside.

Standing in a ring of decked and dying officers, the thing spotted its chance. I took my last picture, as the beast grabbed the bodies of the gurney, and its wings unfurled from flattened niches in its back.

The thing went airborne with bodies in tow.

The remaining officers behind the squad cars trained a few spotlights on the flying monkey and opened fire.

The thing dropped a cadaver, then its odd belt burst, as it flew into a cloud bank.

A dozen human skulls rained down on me and the others.

Another shifting cesspool of shadows appeared in the doorway and took flight behind its mad twin.

As more police cars arrived, sirens blaring, above there sounded a nightmare whirring and flapping, and a faint, distant baying as of a duo of gigantic hounds.

"Hey, wait a minute—" I yelled, as my left arm was pinned into a hammerlock, and another flash of blue tore the camera from my hand.

I did time in the back of a squad car, while authorities gathered to sort out their stories and attend to the wounded.

Arkham's, "Thin Blue Line," had been ripped to ribbons, perpetrators and whereabouts unknown.

Thursday, April 25, 1974, 10:00 AM. *The Arkham Purview.*

I got up early, to draft a story about the Funeral Home Thefts.

Penelope Ruiz, my boss at the *Arkham Purview*, took one look at my copy and its title, "Modern Graveyard Robbers?" before she tossed it into a trashcan near her desk.

"We can't print this stuff on the obituary page, Mr Largekoff! The families of the deceased are already grieving over their loved ones, without adding unnecessary fearmongering over the theft of their bodies. And all your supernatural mumbo-jumbo about why it's happening?" said Ms Ruiz loudly.

"But you can't argue with the facts—" I replied, buoyed by my own self-righteousness.

"Furthermore, the community should be warned—"

Mr Ruiz then pulled up a newspaper copy off her desk blotter.

I stared at the date and the headline.

It was an early edition of the *Arkham Advertiser*, our top competitor. The headline stuck in my craw, "Local Funeral Freezer goes on Fritz, Families Freak Out."

"Yeah, that's right, Largekoff. While you were wasting time trying to dig up some god-awful angle on the story, someone else scooped us!" Ms. Ruiz shouted at me like I was on the other side of an auditorium.

"I'm not paying you for stories other papers scoop us on. Hell, I'm not paying you for front-page stories either. What the hell am I paying you for, Largekoff? Oh, in case you forget, obituaries! Writing nice, safe and sane fiction about dead people, end of story!" Ms Ruiz said

Luckily, I was beyond her reach.

"Now get out of here before I lose my temper!" Ms Ruiz's nostrils flared in her fury.

She'll change her tune when I scoop the real reason behind the funeral home robberies.

Thursday, April 25, 1974, 5:00 PM. *Arkham Police Headquarters.*

I knew I had to get a handle on things and fast.

The "Official, Party Line" was already being proffered via the *Arkham Advertiser* piece. Arkham's Oligarchy—consisting of city leaders, higher-ups in the police department, the "tried and trusted" TV news, and sanctioned newspaper outlets was unusually thorough in disseminating misinformation about occultic events. Arkham was as notorious as Salem when it came to the midnight world of the macabre.

I attended the official news conference held at Police Headquarters.

Why go to such a "dog and pony show?"

It was my practice to "poke the bear" at such meetings and see what truth might inadvertently slip out.

I entered the small auditorium set aside for such theatrics, as the assembled thespians rolled out their polished polemics.

"And that ladies and gentlemen is the reason for the recent rash of funeral home robberies. When the shortage of embalming chemicals became epidemic, and funeral directors could not hold memorial services, some grieving families tried to take matters into their own hands. The subsequent breakdown of refrigeration units at more than one parlour didn't help matters. Acting irrationally, the families tried to take back their dead and bury the deceased, themselves. Since those methods aren't sanctioned by the Arkham Health Department, we detained the families at the *Arkham Asylum* on code 5150 holds, to evaluate their mental conditions," stated Police Chief, Isaac Standish.

The guy wore a Gold Rolex on his right arm, quite pricey, even on a Chief's salary.

I couldn't miss it, as he waved his arms to emphasise his points.

Others along the table primped themselves before nodding in support, hoping the press cameras got their good sides.

Then, Mayor Alvin Addles took the microphone.

"Now, we'll open the floor to answer your questions."

"Excuse me," I said, rushing to the podium.

"And you are, Mr, er.—" asked the Mayor.

"My name is Largekoff, Vincent Largekoff, and I represent the *Arkham Purview*—" I said, thrusting my chest out to emphasise my importance.

"Largekoff?" laughed the seated Police Chief. "He's the Obituary Gofer I told you about!"

Other members at the table also laughed.

"I was there the other night at the *Other Worldly Journey's Funeral Home*. Arkham's finest, some of them, God rest their souls, confronted a few of your quote-unquote 'grieving family members.' The assailants got away scot-free after manhandling your men," I said, stating the facts.

"And how do you explain when it started raining skulls?"

More laughter, this time the audience joined the panellists.

"Largekoff, the officers on scene said you reeked of alcohol. They detained you for a couple of hours to prevent you from driving home drunk. What you claim you saw were simply, 'pink elephants,'" said the Mayor, in sombre tones.

"I wasn't drunk," I replied. "I hadn't had a drink that day. If anyone wants to check the veracity of my story, they can inspect local hospital registries for officers who were treated for life-threatening injuries that night."

A few whispered in the audience, "Hospitals? Which night was it again?"

The Police Chief stood and motioned to some uniformed officers.

"Take this drunk out of here before I lose my patience," shouted the Police Chief.

Many along the panel began to applaud.

I was roughed up by some officers and tossed out onto the street. I almost yelled, "Police Brutality—" but bit my tongue, for fear of a worse beating.

I adjusted my clothes and dusted myself off.

Even a man like myself has his dignity. A small crowd looked on, as I walked to my Gremlin and sped off.

Nothing new was revealed at the hearing. Perhaps, my charming-self peeked out too soon for there to be an unguarded moment.

Or maybe, some board members were in cahoots with the grave robbers.

How deep did the conspiracy go?

Thursday, April 25, 1974, 11:00 PM. *Offices of Dr Josef J. Nadek the 5th.*

Arkham is an old town steeped in legends.

Legends here blister with teeth and talons, the kind that can chew you up and spit out your bones like an owl in a tree.

One of the first contacts I always try to locate in a new city is the *Twilight Network*, the circle of local occultists that keep track of the goings-on of witches, wizards, and other dark matters.

The theft of so many bodies screamed out an occultic connection.

I decided to try my primary esoteric contact in Arkham, one Josef J. Nadek the 5th, great, great-several times over-grandson of the Mage, Simon Orne, once of Salem, then of Prague.

Josef J. Nadek billed himself as a "Chymist," an old word that described a modern pharmacist or apothecary. He kept business hours between seven and midnight, Wednesday through Saturday nights. The "business" was obviously a front for his operation. I didn't bother to do a background check on a source, especially one that seemed to command forces beyond thuggish henchmen.

Consulting with someone like Nadek is a two-sided

coin. On one hand, he might provide a lead on whomever or whatever was stealing unembalmed bodies. On the other, he might be trafficking in those stolen goods himself, wanting a share of the ill-gotten gain, and whatever occult benefits reaped from a large body count.

Long ago, I became a cynic. I gave up on taking human beings and other things at face-value, that their words constituted unvarnished truth.

Innocence was an evidential thing. Not a play on words used to distract someone from what was really going down.

Dr Nadek had a funny way of looking at me, like I was a frog about to be dissected.

Then there was his pet that wasn't quite feline or canine. The thing hissed and croaked as it slithered between Nadek's legs or circled the old man's throne.

I never got a good look at the thing, as Nadek has a habit of holding his audiences with clients like me in semi-darkness.

Once, Nadek reached down, grabbed the squirming thing by its scruffy collar, hoisted the thing up by the neck, and whispered something in old, barbaric Latin in the thing's ear.

I thought I saw the large, diamond-shaped head of a serpent when he did that. Nadek didn't possess the kind of friendly demeanour that invited one to ask questions.

Come to think of it, I never got a clear picture of what the old man looked like. I just know that when he talked, he wheezed like an old pipe organ.

He might have worn a sloppy mask from what I remember.

I always carried my best weapon against the dark when I visited Nadek. It was a silvered icon of Saint Michael the Archangel, personally blessed by Pope Paul VI. Whether the provenance was true, it acted like a cross or wolfbane to save my eternal soul in a few dark contests. I kept such esoteric weapons in a lead foil-lined pocket in my coat.

Why lead foil? Whatever juju an object possesses is less likely to fade when enveloped by lead.

Look how lead protected the *Man of Steel*.

I also carried a .38 revolver for two-legged predators.

I parked outside the district of Arkham simply known as "the Henge." You didn't bring your wheels into that part of Arkham, especially if you wanted your ride to remain intact.

The Henge sat on one side of the mighty Miskatonic River, Arkham's own dark Styx. Some civil servants who crowed loudest about a clean-up of the Henge simply vanished never to be seen again. Others washed up on its banks, so much flotsam and jetsam in the stream of time.

The Henge was a tumble of back alleys, seldom travelled roads, and intersections overlooked by a few, dysfunctional traffic lights.

I knew the basic direction to Dr Nadek's shop. The moon overhead shone glaring and gibbous. Vagrants eyed me as I passed, their faces shrouded in shifting shadows as clouds drifted by overhead.

An odd neon sign blinked sporadically above Nadek's doorway, spelling out the word, "C-H-Y-M-I-S-T."

A few, high narrow slits for windows announced a business whose proprietor demanded privacy.

The single-story, ramshackle building was otherwise shuttered tight against thieves, the elements, and whatever dark things went bump in the night.

Scrawled on the doorpost in fresh crimson, rode an odd graffiti, written in archaic script.

I walked up a set of creaking stairs, one handrail missing. I knocked two times on the door. Beyond the threshold, I heard padded booted feet, resounding as if they approached through a long, vague hallway.

A hidden peephole appeared in the door facing me.

"I'm Vincent Largekoff of the *Arkham Purview*," I said.

"Largekoff? Ah yes, Dr Nadek is expecting you—" sounded the croaking voice of Nadek's assistant.

I heard other, muffled voices from behind the door, as a series of unlocking sounds fell into place.

The door sounded like a crypt swinging inward on rusty hinges.

Behind it, a single candle flamed to life.

I followed the shambling man through a dusty corridor that seldom saw business. Through one doorway to my right, I caught a quick glance of a glassed-in, but otherwise empty shop counter, the wall behind the stall consisted of a hodge-podge of handmade shelves, populated by dust-covered flasks, beakers, measuring cylinders, test tubes, long-necked Burettes, and crystallizers.

In time, following the flickering candlelight, we stepped down a flight of twisting stairs.

This was a different set-up than my last audience with Nadek. Then, he sat in the dark behind a semi-transparent screen, like a priest taking confessions.

I could see barely Nadek and his animal.

It happened above ground, somewhere else in the building.

At the bottom of the shaft, we arrived at a massive iron door ringed by a concrete arch, hinged like a blast gate. The mousy man pressed a series of numbers on a keypad, niched into a nearby stone wall, stained with age.

The huge door, several inches thick, swung inward. I almost choked on clouds of incense that poured through the doorway.

Despite the incense fires that arose from tripods that littered the hall, the world I entered was cold and damp. An eerie ticking went on in the background, beating out an odd cosmic cadence.

"Ah, Mr Largekoff," rasped a figure sitting atop a fume-shrouded, hexagonal throne.

Was I his stool pigeon or was he mine?

The Chymist's appearance shocked me.

Dr Nadek looked older than Methuselah, a crooked figure bunched beneath a shawl and a tall wizard hat both adorned with arcane glyphs.

Nadek's shambling associate bowed, then left. The vast iron door shut quietly behind him.

"Come forward, so that I may see you better," said the rasping voice.

A glowing pentagram appeared in the swirling miasma ahead. I stepped forward and placed myself within the fallen star.

"You know why I am here, Dr. Nadek?" I asked the huddled Chymist.

I felt a chill up my spine and glanced around the dark room. Nadek's "dog-thing" was nowhere in sight. My hand instinctively went to my pocket, the one with the revolver.

I felt outgunned.

"You have no need for such devices—" Nadek murmured.

Moments later, I felt my gun pocket flatten out.

My revolver was gone. I developed a quick case of the heebie-jeebies.

Nervously, I crossed myself and checked my other pocket. My sacrosanct weapon remained intact.

"You are here, Mr Largekoff, due to the recent rash of body thefts from funeral homes—" replied Nadek, pulling a paper out of thin air. The man deftly swivelled a lighted, magnifying glass across his lap.

"I'll gladly pay you Tuesday, for whatever light you can shed on the matter today," I said, praying I'd live till payday.

The old man appeared to be listening for meanings beyond my words.

"I require remittances other than money. In due time, Largekoff, I will collect my fee from you—" Nadek said.

My god, am I, *Faust*, and this guy, whatever he is, my *Mephistopheles*?

"Well?" I said, knowing there was no way to leave, should Nadek decide to detain me.

The tripods began belching out smoke like a steam locomotive, filling the hall with an iridescent, palatable fog. An enormous, single eye of Dr Nadek, lidless and clouded, stared out into the cosmos. The circular chamber filled with countless cloud nebulas and patterns of different stars forming unknown zodiacs. Novas flashed brilliantly in kaleidoscopic cadence, then faded into cosmic obscurity.

If this were a planetarium floorshow, where the hell was the projector?

"You do well if you ignore these incidents as a series of college initiations gone bad. Miskatonic is well-known in the academic world as a centre of the bizarre," Nadek croaked behind the swirling incense.

"That's not likely to happen—" I said, shaking my head.

A silence fell over the chamber, as the smoke thinned, and the weathered form of the doctor coalesced like an old vulture perched atop his peculiar perch.

"Then further investigation will endanger your soul, Largekoff. There was ever a Mortal Peril for those who traffick with Those Outside—" Dr Nadek droned on, the aimless ramblings of an old man.

"Is that all?" I shouted, losing my cool.

Dr Nadek looked at me.

What the devil stood up behind Nadek? What cast the angular shadows?

"Since you persist in this fool's quest, your best clue is to check the Liturgical Calendar. Look to the day, soon attended by a half-lit moon, that one is holy to both saint and sinner alike," breathed Nadek, like it was his last gasp.

The incense cloud became dense and impassable again. I choked on the smoke, bending over and gagging on my bile.

I wish I hadn't eaten those tamales for lunch.

As I wiped my stinging eyes, I found myself alone on the other side of the blast door.

How'd I get here? Where was Dr Nadek's bumbling associate? Had they slipped a Mickey into the smoke?

And what about my revolver?

Obviously, I wasn't getting anywhere. I think I know how to let myself out.

Up three flights, through a dimly lit hallway, out the front door.

Wait a minute. It's dark down here.

Now, where's that penlight?

Fumbling in my other jacket pockets, I found my torch, breathing a sigh of relief.

Strange, I felt an impression in my gun pocket, not my trusty .38.

I flipped on my flashlight, pulled the thing out of my pocket, and brought it into the light.

The material felt slippery. It was a stone, roughly hexagonal in shape, with a strangely carved glyph, like a flower made up of three stylised sickles fashioned in a yellowish, semi-precious stone.

I thought about putting Nadek's gift into my lead foil-lined pocket. But what if it neutralised my iconoclast weapon?

For now, I put it back into my gun pocket. I eventually found my way out of Nadek's store and the Henge alive.

Funny thing, as I started my Gremlin and reached down to my shift handle. Sitting there stuffed between the seats was my revolver.

How did that get there? Was it a case of Hyperspace

Hypnotism?

I didn't have time for a sanity check; I had a story to pursue. So, I gunned my Gremlin and sped off into the night.

Friday, April 26, 1974, 3:00 AM. *The Lean On Us Funeral Home.*

While I was recovering from my ordeal with Dr Nadek, the *Grand Theft Grave Robbers* struck again at the *Lean On Us Funeral Home*, corner of East High and Zinco.

From the radio chatter, I gather the police got there after the fact. There were fewer uniformed officers on the street due to their last encounter with, dare I say, the flying monkeys? I still had a hard time wrapping my head around what the assailants appeared to be. I didn't ask Nadek about them. I remember those shadows that stood up behind him. The association immediately raised the hackles on the back of my neck.

The Arkham Police immediately went into emergency status. To converse its remaining manpower, they called up all available reservists and called back recent retirees into active duty.

Perhaps Mayor Addles will ask the Governor to call out the state's National Guard. Maybe, they possessed weapons capable of dealing with the flying monkeys.

I still felt Nadek was aware of the occult forces behind the robberies without being an accomplice to the matter. He had given me an occultic weapon, whose use remains uncertain. Through some sleight-of-hand, he also returned my revolver or planted a pre-hypnotic suggestion beforehand that I leave it in the car.

Anyway, though few details were given out over my Police Scanner, I gathered that the Grave Robbers were successful in gathering more bodies.

That was four grand thefts in less than a week. Where was all this leading? Nadek said something about consulting a Liturgical Calendar. A visit to Miskatonic Library should answer that question. There was also the small, but influential Miskatonic School of Medicine. Did the robberies occur because the school needed cadavers?

Now, for some rest, assuming I could turn off my racing brain long enough to catch a catnap.

Saturday, April 27, 1974, 11:00 AM. *Miskatonic University Library*. **Recorded notes.**

I consulted with a librarian at the Miskatonic University Library, a gruff no-nonsense person with no redeeming qualities. It turned out on Liturgical Calendars that April 30th marked the celebration of Saint Walpurgis or alternatively, "May Day Eve" to occultists. Was that what Nadek was referring to?

I ditched the noxious librarian like a bad, blind date.

What did April 30th and Walpurgis Eve have to do with so many dead bodies?

Saturday, April 27, 1974, 9:00 PM. *The Warm Heart Condolences Funeral Home.*

Another "Code 487" blared over my Police Scanner late Saturday night. I had just picked up a Philly Cheese Steak takeout from *Charlie's Grub and Pub* and walked in the door when the Scanner lit on fire. The action was happening at the *Warm Heart Condolences Funeral Home*, corner of Boundary and West High, which meant the other side of town.

I grew concerned. My car could make it.

But I probably couldn't make it on a near-empty tank.

Seven months ago, in October 1973, the Arabs and Israelis went to war. When the Israelis came out on top, it was not the end of hostilities. For America's part in supplying Israel's war machine, OPEC—made up primarily of Arab Oil Producing nations—slapped an oil embargo on the United States.

That meant gasoline shortages. I was coasting on fumes as it was. The government mandated even and odd fill-up days—a type of rationing--based on the last digit on your licence plate. This being April 27 and my licence plate ended in an even number, I was out-of-luck.

Yet, the *Warm Heart Condolences Funeral Home* caper marked the fifth such grave robbery that I knew about.

Sunday, April 28, 1974, 1:00 PM. *The Vincent Largekoff Think Tank and Studio Apartment.*

I needed to spend some time, where I could puzzle out all the details and clues.

I used a chalkboard, a bulletin board with maps, my thoughts garnered postmortem in my tape-recorder, and a pen and paper to aid my brainstorming.

I first wrote out the names of the five known cadaver heists on my chalkboard.

1) Steady Acres Funeral Home.

2) Breezy Angels Funeral Parlour.

3) Other Worldly Journeys Mortuary.

4) Lean On Us Funeral Home.

5) Warm Heart Condolences Funeral Home.

I looked for a pattern in the names. Was their order important? Did flipping the sequence in this fashion or that create a recognizable phrase using the first, second, third, etc. words?

I puzzled through several combinations for over half an hour using my pen and paper. Though the names were catchy, I wadded up pages of random associations and tossed them in a trashcan.

Slam dunk, Largekoff, you missed your true calling.

Next, I tried acrostics. Did the first letter in the first words of each business name spell out anything of consequence? This time, I went with the order of the robberies and worked through a series of possibilities. S-B-O-L-W, no that's not it. I tried the first letter in the second series of words. A-A-W-O-H, no, that's not it either. Working acrostics was getting me nowhere.

Think, Largekoff, think!

I had a map of Arkham thumbtacked to my bulletin board. I also had a dozen-coloured stickpins in the corner, to figure out how to get around in the town I'd just adopted.

How many were there now? Las Vegas, Seattle, Chicago—I had more adventures than Sinbad had Voyages.

Anyway, *Steady Acres* was located across the Miskatonic. Then, *Breezy Angels* was also beyond the river. *Other Worldly Journeys* was down there. *Lean On Us* was off to the east. And finally, *Warm Heart Condolences* was off in the west.

I alternated between using red and blue stickpins. I'm a bit artsy like that.

I stood for a moment, then sat back in my easy chair, eyeing the map and the stickpins.

On the table beneath my bulletin board, sat trophies accumulated from my adventures. Included in that stash was my latest treasure, the *Magic Eight-Ball* with the unknown sigil, care of Dr Nadek.

I sat there and closed my eyes. They were getting tired from all this exertion. I chewed on my thoughts.

What was I missing?

I opened my eyes, trying to capture another angle.

Were the five funeral homes built atop spaces sacred to the local Native Americans or was the ground otherwise cursed?

I abandoned that line of reasoning. Every square inch of Arkham was built on disputed land of some type.

Sometimes the conflict represented a competition between rival cults, jockeying for the favour of the same Great Old One.

My knowledge of that line of dark mumbo-jumbo was shallow and scant.

Then I chanced to look at Nadek's diabolical *Eight-Ball* again. An image flashed in my head. Maybe that's it.

Yes, when I entered Nadek's blast cellar, a pentagram appeared before me to step into. A five-sided star—

Now, where's the yarn that Gladys Taylor gave me when I left my last newspaper gig?

I took the yarn and attached it to one of the stickpins. I then crossed over and used a half-hitch to tie it to each stickpin.

I played with it for a while, until the five funeral home locations meant something. I had formed a rough, inverted pentagram, an ancient sign of the darkness.

Ah, now we're cooking.

OK, I found a pentagram, what of it?

Was there something within the pentagram, one that had some bearing on the story?

I looked up the address of one point of interest in the telephone book.

Within the pentagonal centre, there stood a renovated

house—once rumoured to have been haunted by the likes of the occultist, Keziah Mason--expanded by several wings to accommodate the latest Lodge in town, the *Uncanny Order of Leng*.

I would visit the *Uncanny Order of Leng*'s Lodge on Tuesday evening, to observe Saint Walpurgis Eve with them.

Had Nadek sent me on a wild goose chase?

Tuesday, April 30th, 1974, 11:00 PM. *The Uncanny Order of Leng's Lodge.*

How does one crash a Saint Walpurgis Eve celebration? Was it an exclusive affair or did they use Saint Walpurgis Eve in a membership drive?

I decided to try and blend into a crowd of celebrants as they arrived at the Leng's Lodge. I parked my yellow Gremlin a block away.

The moon above was gibbous and waning. As the clouds slowly drifted by, feral shadows circled overhead, illuminated by faint moonshine. I felt the hairs stand up on the back of my neck, as some muffled, baying echoed in the wind. I remembered the flying monkey that battled the police at the *Other Worldly Journeys Mortuary*. The coincidence rattled me.

There were many passersby in this part of Arkham. I think I'd driven by the Lodge as I pursued other stories.

I carried a few things on my person. It might be a no-photos event and I didn't want to get excluded because of a camera bag.

I came to another corner with the *Uncanny Order of Leng's Lodge* across the street. It took up a city block, and while tall buildings surrounded the complex, they seemed strangely vacant.

Fresh out of my personal razzamatazz voodoo, I took a quick swig of a liquid talisman from my trusty flask, then thought of how to enter the Lodge.

It was a mixture of holy water blessed by a renowned catholic exorcist, forge water from a foundry that black-smithed holy relics, and my trusty bourbon for courage.

A few flocks of the faithful in casual wear approached the Lodge and entered it without much ado. I watched for a mystic handshake between the entrants and the two pale fellas in black suits and ties who stood at the door.

The board signs out front broadcasted a membership drive, "Join Us for Our Walpurgis-Eve Celebration, April 30th!"

I decided my best bet was to identify a group of participants with a fashion sense like mine—casual chaos—and enter the building with them. Not that I could blend into any crowd with my good looks and all-around panache.

But it was worth a try.

I shuffled in, looking this way and that, like a tourist among a crowd that looked like inbred escapees from a forgotten Appalachian Valley.

The ordinary exterior of the Lodge betrayed nothing of its extraordinary, if not bizarre interior. For a newspaperman to be at a loss for words, is unthinkable. But here I shambled among the mesmerised masses, as speechless as they were.

I felt like I'd stepped into a fifth-century mosque or Byzantine cathedral somewhere in southwest Asia, whose scale of architecture made one feel small and insignificant.

The walls appeared to be built around enormous, aged tree trunks, broadening out as the eye was drawn towards the ceiling, networked with thinner boughs and branches, having the appearance of being overlaid with curtains of lace and elegant tapestries. The lace glistened in places, and I swear, I was looking at saliva and not metallic thread.

Was I entering someone's building or something's gullet?

Or perhaps they were the shiny silks of rain-soaked spider's webs?

My head spun with the implications.

The hues of the sky in its varied moods were mimicked everywhere. Moslem arches were repeated in every size and variation among the doorways and the lofty angles above us. The walls seemed alive and vibrant with animation.

The word "Leng" left me with vague forebodings, though where that paranoia arose from, I couldn't remember. Was it the sense of awe and cosmic grandeur that suffused the moment? I felt like I'd stepped through a time portal that took me and the others to another world.

Further in and further up—we climbed a set of stairs fashioned out of solid rock to reach the upper sanctum of the Lodge. The building was built partially into a small hill that arose on the acreage. Here beneath the onion-shaped arches that ran along the outer circumference of the building, there was a profusion of stained-glass windows, dispensing rainbows to mesmerise the faithful. But, instead of beatific scenes, imparting lessons from the lives of famous saints, they bore stylized squids and octopi, some in flight, some in quiet repose, while others displayed unknown beasts in mediaeval scenes.

In Old Latin, Ancient Aramaic, and Koine Greek--I recognized some languages, even though I was not fluent in many—stood the simple phrase, "The Masters."

What a strange pantheon of saints the Brotherhood venerated. Some drifters crossed themselves, while strange sardonic smirks crossed the faces of others. Were these plants who walked with the others, to lull each person into a sense of complacency?

I held my tongue—which is a strange and awkward thing for me.

Then we came to a wall of doors, several of which stood open. They joined onto a large auditorium that could seat perhaps a thousand. Much of the living, glistening latticework continued into this meeting hall, dominated by four large Moslem arches, which supported a canopied ceiling filled with murals of midnight skies and scenes from *Gigeresque* worlds.

The lower echelons of the kaleidoscopic ceilings seem taller at the corners, while the lacey veils and intertwined boughs bulged at the centres seemingly pregnant with secrets.

In the centre behind a transparent steel and glass case, like the walled views at an aquarium, stood a kneeling statue, roughly humanoid in outline. Its head featured a series of iron circles welded together into a sphere, each band bearing dozens of eyes whose piercing gaze seemed to follow the crowd's movement.

It knelt on spindly, hairy, arachnid legs, each ending in a singular, horny talon, not an expected foot pad. Its last two arms, hands clasped in meditative prayer, and upper torso were vaguely human but huge and haunting. Where it should have imitative skin and hair, it had skin, eyes, and grotesque tattoos. It was rust red, as if the statue had been made by other than human hands, and left on a high mountain top somewhere until fledgling humans found it, and worshipped this worshipper of other gods, perhaps, "The Masters," spoken of elsewhere.

Boughs of fresh-leafing oak were handed to each celebrant as they entered the inner sanctum of the Old One. I called it that; the aura of the place was unmistakable. I had been to such lonely places in forgotten caverns under the bustling, teeming cities of man before.

Tall tripods of upraised bowls bore kindling and sprigs of heady incense, ready for small fires to be lit to celebrate Walpurgis Eve. Music began to be piped into the place, which included the intoxicating rhythms of the "Danse Macabre," followed by "Night on Bald Mountain," then "In the Hall of the Mountain King," among others. Spontaneous circles of whirling dancers and those who clapped wildly for them sprung up around me.

The jubilation went on for a good half an hour.

I checked my Timex. Almost 12:00 Midnight, the Witching hour.

A platform, with a hooded shadowy form mimicking

Dickens' *Ghost of Christmas Future*, slowly ascended into sight near the statue.

It raised its arms to attract the attention of the throng of celebrants.

My well-bred reporter's sense started tingling. What was about to go down? Who was this creep?

Or was it that last piece of week-old pizza with anchovies I ate earlier?

"Friends, brothers, and sisters welcome to the Fifth Annual Walpurgis Eve Celebration of the *Uncanny Order of Leng*—"

Random cheers across the auditorium interrupted him.

"Thank you, thank you, you are too kind. Soon, we will light the bonfires to frighten off the spirits from the invisible world and keep evil at bay for another season—"

More spontaneous applause and laughter disrupted the celebration leader.

The mysterious leader raised his arms high overhead to hush the mob.

Wait a minute. What's that on his right arm, a gold Rolex? I had seen such a Rolex before, but where?

"And if the stars are right and given the prescribed sacrifices and your life-giving presence here, we may even have a visitation of one of the gods of old. It may break through the veil from the other side to join us! Commence au festival!" he spoke in tones of seduction and seriousness, a bit out-of-tune with the joyous gathering.

I played a hunch and slowly backed away from the

crowd. I tried, nonchalantly, to head toward the exits, like someone looking for a restroom.

Something was afoot. The ushers lit the upraised bowls that bore kindling and incense, then threw their boughs of leafy oak into the flames. The other celebrants mindlessly followed suit with their boughs, then returned to their pagan jubilation. The same ushers quietly headed to the auditorium doors.

On cue, the vague leader threw a thigh-high switch on his upraised dais, then slowly the platform sunk beneath the floor.

Then I remembered.

The last time I'd seen such an expensive timepiece was on the right arm of the Arkham Police Chief, Isaac Standish.

Why was he here and what did it mean?

Smoke from the incense bowls grew thick, surrounding the celebrants. Some coughed on the fumes, while most stopped, and looked around sheepishly, acquiring a glazed look in their eyes.

Was it gas? I saw the few remaining ushers put something, a small gas mask perhaps, over their mouths and noses.

I had a disposable surgical mask in one of my pockets for times when the stench of rotting dead bodies at crime scenes proved suffocating.

I took my chances and slapped it on; what choice did I have?

The next few moments, I'm still not sure what I saw, had the narcotic fumes affected me too?

A skylight opened over the kneeling god like a starlit

gash in the heavens. A pillar of moonlight descended simultaneously on the otherworldly effigy. The crowd became lost in their own visions, bellowing and writhing in ecstasy among a sea of fiery incense bowls, rearing in pagan exhalation about the noxious god.

On cue, funnelling chutes appeared in the side of the glassed-in-god, while a circle of gaseous flames appeared around its kneeling base.

Unnoticed by the possessed crowd, rag dolls began spilling out of the chutes into the conflagration of flames encircling the huge statue.

A sudden realisation shook me.

Ragdolls? Those weren't rag dolls. They were the bodies stolen by the flying monkeys from the Arkham funeral homes.

What was the *Lodge of Leng* trying to accomplish with the burnt offerings of stolen bodies, bring the kneeling god to life?

The head of the statue creaked audibly above the din of the chanting crowd. I swear on a stack of Bibles, it looked at me.

I staggered back against the wall, trying not to breathe, staring at the crouching god.

Above the dancing, thrashing worshippers, the silky latticework in the ceiling descended, still wrapped around several unknown bundles. As strands of each latticework bundle separated, there slowly emerged enormous, black, and bloated beasts sporting dozens of spindly legs. A swarm of the arachnid-like slugs descended along the blankets of dangling latticework, towards the oblivious celebrants below.

They came to rest scant feet above the revellers, avoiding the still-smouldering incense pots. They attacked the stupefied worshippers with a hail of their spindly, spiked legs. A unison of odd, sucking sounds arose across the auditorium, as many spiked legs found their marks in the multiplied skulls of the celebrants. While some of the bloated spiders enjoyed their feast, others grabbed participants from the crowded floor, spun a web quickly around their prey, and carried each screaming bundle off into the heights of the auditorium for later devouring.

I bolted to the nearest door and slammed it shut, leaving behind a tumult of terror. A single, overwhelming thought seized me as if it were not my own.

I looked around as the milling ushers appeared, recognizing me as an escapee from the Walpurgis pageant. I then fled towards the Lodge roof on a nearby staircase. Behind me, I heard cries of concern, as others ascended the stairs.

I came to the top of the stairs and exited the shaft onto the Lodge roof. I looked around, grabbed a nearby rusty chair, and thrust it under the door handle.

There, safe for now.

To my left and behind me, I heard muffled screams above the hall rocking, "Danse Macabre."

I turned and saw the gibbous moon above some sort of multi-mirrored collectors that gathered shards of moonlight into the singular beam that illuminated the kneeling god below.

I ran to the aperture, walked between the lunar-light collectors, and looked down on the odd statue. The god-awful stench of burning bodies stung my unprotected eyes. I saw strange, occultic outlines—triangles, pentagrams, and sinister sigils—twinkling as starlight as they converged about the many-banded head of the thing, which began to gyrate.

I heard the breaking of a door somewhere and voices shouting curses in the dark.

I glanced back down into the gap.

I swear, I saw dozens of its eyes look upward, and one of its arms flex and extend a seven-fingered hand toward me.

I yelled out nonsensically the words:

> "OGTHROD AI'F
> GEB'L—EE'H
> YOG-SOTHOTH
> 'NGAH'NG AI'Y
> ZHRO—"

Who'd I channel, Bela Lugosi?

At the end of that occultic mumbo-jumbo, I reached into my lead-lined pockets and grabbed my Saint Michael effigy and Nadek's *Magic Eight-Ball*. Knowing this was my only chance, I hurled both into the burning crucible below and backed away from the opening.

A deep rumble shook the building. Through the aperture, Fire and Brimstone exploded, illuminating the night. Amid hundreds of horrific screams, an odd shaft of light shot skyward from the boiling inferno, before the Lodge buckled and collapsed in on itself.

The last thing I remember was the roof giving way, intense heat, and a sensation of falling.

Later, a swirling miasma clouded my mind. I looked down and tried to focus my eyes, as my stomach churned.

My feet had sunk a good foot into a grassy landscape. I occupied one square like a rook on a horizon-spanning chessboard. While some humans of varied dress and social strata stood stoic or animated in nearby squares, others were occupied by noxious things, that either stepped out of centuries-old mausoleums, a steaming primordial sea near the dawn of time, or filtered down from the vast cosmic ether in teeming masses of ill-shaped vermin.

I clung to my anonymity, fearing for my eternal existence. A palpable sense of hunger hung over the board like deadly gases above World War I trenches.

As I stood motionless, my eyes drank in the vast vistas that opened like alternative realities in the shifting horizons.

Then, the quivering outlines of a gaseous god, layered in garish, graveyard hues, arose in the east.

No, that face, it can't be!

My mind became a chaotic mess of cosmic implications.

It was Dr Nadek, no longer in frail, human outlines, but huddled like an immortal titan, his robe a vast night-patterned with glimmering constellations, his eyes like twin calderas of erupting volcanoes, and his face twisted with sardonic glee. His perch was the pinnacle of a black obelisk, set high as the heavens and vast as the foundations of time and space.

Then I glanced in the other direction.

A shield volcano, with columns of erupting lava that spilled down its sides, grew immense and impossibly quick.

Above the Dantesque inferno hovered a disk of rough and glowing stone.

Soon, the disc went vertical and reflected the brilliantly coloured walls of a pristine Egyptian Burial chamber not seen in five thousand years. Living Hieroglyphs spelt out stories in the circular rockface. Eventually, there coalesced the molten face of a wizen Egyptian Pharaoh, wearing a *Khepresh,* the distinct elongated blue crown of war. Its mien was stern and sullen, alien in aspect, broken by a diabolic sneer.

Rivers of rainbows, filled with dead bodies, the eternal flotsam of endless sacrifices, ran down its cheeks and into the fires below.

Flaming pitchforks streaked across the sky above me, hurled in opposite directions by the malformed Titan Nadek, and the Egyptian Demiurge, Lord of the Nile and Netherworlds.

I involuntarily slipped to my knees, grovelling in the gravity of the moment.

Then, I looked up and saw vast bands of cages rotating like the rings of Saturn far above me. Many were filled with humans of every race, gender, or tribe. Some cages were occupied by other things, inhuman, grave and grotesque. And then came individual prisons of the primordial things that should not be, ancient and ageless, ill-formed and irreconcilable to all other beings, save themselves

Then, the continuum of cages shuddered to a halt, like a Ferris wheel stopping to take on passengers.

Through the open door of an empty cage, I saw my world and felt myself take to the wind towards it, drawn like a fly towards flypaper.

I heard the words squarely in my head, as I flew into the prison and the gate slammed shut behind me.

"It is self-evident that truth exists. Living, breathing, cosmic, world-without-end. If anyone denies that truth exists, it is he that does not exist, for truth is eternal, and he is not…"

I didn't know what to think of my nightmares before I awoke in *Arkham General Hospital*.

I felt intense pain from the burns I received when the Lodge caught fire.

The hospital room felt cold, antiseptic, not a friendly face in sight.

Getting back to the time before I awoke. Had I been a pawn in Nadek's hand, a tool used to quash another occult gang-lord in a cosmic turf war?

What of the others in the Lodge? Was I the lone survivor? Was their blood on Nadek's hands, the Arkham Police Chief's, or my own?

And did their deaths feed the ritual I witnessed?

I'll let you, my readers, draw your own conclusions.

I had other things on my mind.

I was experiencing a Déjà vu moment.

Another city. Another angry boss. Another round of being tarred and feathered. Another rail greased and ready to run me out of town on.

For a moment, I experienced a sense of familiarity and with it, peace. I recognized the end of another cycle, another riveting instant in my pointless existence, another momentous moment in a monotonous, meandering series of Groundhog Days.

John A. DeLaughter, M.Div., M.S. is a Data Security Analyst.

His non-fiction work has appeared in the Lovecraft eZine, in the Vampire Anthology, The Vampiricon (2023), and the Candlemas edition of Lovecraftiana (2023).

His fiction has or will appear in the Novella Anthology, "Eldritch Prisoners" (2023), the Horror Detective Anthology "The Culture Cult Casebook," (2023), Eerie River Publishing's "Cosmic Horror" Anthology (2023), in the Halloween Anthology of Lovecraftiana (2023), Innsmouth Gold's Lovecraftian Anthology, "The Pickman Papers" (2023), Nordic Press's 'Eldritch Investigations" anthology (2023), and Skywatcher Press's "The Depths: Unleashed, Book 2" anthology (2023).

John lives in Pennsylvania with his wife, Heidi, and their two dogs, Jasper and Daisy May.

Paranormal Investigative Reporter, **Vincent Largekoff** first appeared in the story, "The Madness in the Mirror," which is featured in the Horror Detective Anthology "The Culture Cult Casebook," (2023) available on Lulu.

HARLAN CORMELL &
THE CULT OF BYAKHEE

JASIAH WITKOFSKY

San Francisco, the City of Love and boy do I love it! Carefully extracting myself from the dead weight of Cindy's drunken arm, I gently massage the fog that rolled in from the Bay straight into my eardrums. Well, now that memory creeps back in, I do recall the mist salting my mouth came from countless shots of Jacky Ds. Spying half a Marb plugged firmly into the ashtray upon the nightstand, I flick a Bic to replace last night's tang with the funk taste of a stale relight.

Finishing the smouldering butt all too soon, I grunt my way to the bathroom to piss like a racehorse and splash cold pipe water upon my five o'clock shadow. Looking into the cracked corner mirror, I slick my near-black pompadour into shape to the best of my addled abilities. My hair, eyes, and skin tone come from my mother's side... and sure did wonders with the ladyfolk. Her Sicilian heritage also left me enough dough to house upon the coastline, pay for a downtown office, and allow me enough Benjamins to discard like toilet paper. Some whispered of familial Mafia ties, but that is one topic I refuse to investigate.

I didn't get much from my father, Sergeant Harry, of good Anglo stock who went MIA during the Korean fiasco, but a solid steel case of rifles and various handguns - that and a spinoff of his name. Now, I assume my mom joined the poor bastard after her failed bout with lung cancer some years previous. So, in honour of her memory, I picked up her disgusting habit of puffing like a chimney and mumbling a quick Catholic prayer after each cig... well, almost.

Taking one last opportunity to admire the razor-sharp cut of my sideburns (Damn, baby! I could almost fly with these raven wings.), I pull on my bootcut jeans and throw a tweed over my slightly soiled wifebeater. Sneaking Cindy's dial-up into the bathroom, I phone in my trusty valet to pick me up in Richmond, I'd be waiting on the curb. A final look at the dirty blonde's dishevelled mop and I resist the urge tightening my zipline. Slipping on my Italian leather half-boots, I leave a calling card on the bed after sketching a heart on it with a wayward stick of cherry-red lip gloss.

Harlan Cormell

Discoteca Detective

Mr Makoto arrives exactly on time, per usual. The gentle purr of my 76 Buiy LeSabre eases to the pullout inches from the toes of my polished boots. Flinging a smouldering filter between the sidewalk and gutter, I open the shotgun door and slide into the plush interior with the practised ease of a gull landing the nest. My driver, and so much more, Mr Davey Makoto, with his tacky Giant's cap, greets me upon entry.

"*Konnichi wa*, Harlan-san. It being Sunday, I assume you wish to attend church, or to be delivered straight back to your domicile?"

I groan at the mention of services and direct my manservant home as I recline to a more suitable angle. Rolling the window to catch a breeze, I drift into half-consciousness through the traffic and winding stretch of asphalt.

Upon the comfort of my favourite sedan chair overlooking the Pacific pastels, I sip a well-iced bourbon, recovering from the bustle of the previous two nights. Scratching habitually at Canny's head, my valiant Great Dane, I slip into a comfortable doze. I awake when the setting sun forces my eyelids to attention like a soldier aroused by the blare of the bugle. A late Sunday afternoon, always an odd time for me, where the dusk of party life heralds the dawn of a new workday. By rote, I march to the shower to scrub the nefarious weekend from my pores before entering the kitchen where Kara ladles a bowl of her spiced lentils. Like Davey, Karina possesses impeccable timing, one of many reasons I retain her services after Mama's passage. Cracking dual steins, one amber, one tan, I make way for the boob tube to idle at pointless sitcoms before sleep overwhelms me yet again.

Deposited at my second favourite java shop, I tip for my scalding styrofoams and waltz my routine gait to the business district housing the quaint exterior of my agency. My secretary greets me with mahogany eyes hovering above her specs as I hand off a brew before swinging my dun overcoat upon the ageing coat rack. Stacey is an office seven, a pretty face in a nerdy kind of way, but her body could best be described as twiggy. I should know after the case of the wharf's boat theft where we celebrated with a bottle of bootleg and a tryst upon her desktop – an affair neither of us discuss.

"No new updates or calls over the weekend, Mr Cormell." Stacey relays in her nasally monotone. "Nothing the police haven't dealt with according to the dispatch receiver."

I placate her disappointment with a smile and a knowing shrug, thanking her for her diligence as I slip into my private cubby to light a Red and sip gingerly on my coffee. Sifting through the bills and receipts that litter my drawers and tabletop, I quickly grow tired of the monotony of paperwork and what isn't discarded is hastily swiped into an overstuffed file cabinet away from my immediate concern. Kicking my feet upon the desk, I resign myself to the sedation of banal tedium.

Upon the following day, an agitated pipsqueak barges into the building to badger poor Stacey with a barrage of inquiries and wild demands. Springing from my swivel chair, I burst into the main room to confront the pudgy mofo leaning over my secretary in an attempt to browbeat some intel out of her. Startling the suit with my abrupt appearance, the well-dressed man recovers quickly to give me his full attention.

"Mr. Cormell, I presume?" The little chud offers me a soft, clammy hand in greeting. "I am Gerald Potts of the Hamilton and Potts law firm… may we speak in private?"

Ignoring the quivering palm, I wave the attorney into my chambers, informing Stace to hold my calls. Dusting off a seat that hasn't seen any use in well over a season, I plop down on the other side of the desk, brusquely motioning the high-end fink to continue. Noticing his palpable distress, I open a pack of Marbs and offer one to the quaking Jello-mould of a man. Retrieving his own fancy slims from an interior pocket, I light our smokes with an old-timey butane switch. After some awkward inhalations, Mr Potts gets to the point of his visitation.

"Please forgive my unseemly arrival, I am not one to make an unprofessional entrance." A few more nervous puffs and he begins. "I will be honest, I am a desperate man with nowhere else to turn. My only child, Lynda... well, no longer a child, has gone missing and I fear foul play."

He pulls a picture from his breast pocket and slides it my way. I study the sepia print of a wavy-haired brunette smiling innocently, but with a sly cast to her eyes. Medium of height and thinly built, I listen to the father who passed little of his piggish genes onto the hapless lass.

"As most parents experience, my little doll is going through, well, a rebellious phase. It started out with weekend excursions and no calls home. I tried to put my foot down on this worrisome behaviour, but this only drove her to become more obstinate. Soon, she no longer spent nights at home and any words shared were cold and hurtful. After a week's absence, I hired one Jason Falscelatto, a private investigator, to scout out her whereabouts and was soon able to ascertain her favourite haunts, the premiere hangout being the Golden Dive.

"Thrilled at his results, yet still unsatisfied, I sent Mr Falscelatto to find out where she was spending her nights. That was over half a month ago and I have not heard back from him since." Gerald's jowls began shaking as he braced himself to finish his monologue.

"Please, Mr Cromell, I have nowhere else to turn! I would do anything to have my daughter returned to me. After her mother passed, she is all that I have left. I grant you this as an initial fee if you choose to accept and you can expect tenfold when she is safely in my arms."

A stuffed envelope slides my way as I snuff the last dregs of my cig in a dingy ashtray. Flipping through the contents, I count a minimum of one thousand big ones. Mulling over the prospects laid in my paws, I appear thoughtful to watch this corp-pig sweat. Money's not an absolute necessity, but that's not why I float the bills to keep the lights on. Besides, Stace is growing restless and it's my responsibility to keep her lively. Slapping the wad upon the hardwood, I offer my hand to my future employer for the first time.

"I will do all that I can, but I require all reports gathered by your previous investigator, along with any pertinent information regarding your daughter. I will keep this for any expenditures required for this venture." I slip the photograph into the envelope before standing. "Expect a call in the morning."

I wait till Friday evening before approaching the Golden Dive, a trendy, two-story dance bar that borders on the sheikh and the affordable nestled in the sweaty armpit of the city. A perfect club for rich kids wanting to be bad and struggling college students wanting a break. For this initial leg of my investigation, I decided to invite Deshawn to hop along as my wingman for the night. My best friend since high school during the peak of the race riots and the Black Panther Movement, me and Deshawn have been through it all and there is no one I could trust more.

Getting a drop off at the end of the block, I tell Davey to wait on the road, feeling guilty that I can't invite my valet in for the fun and games. Turning, it takes no time at all to find Deshawn J. Franco's towering afro amidst the line trickling into the establishment. Looking spiffy in his night-black stretch shirt and bellbottom Levis, I give a slight nod to my Afro-American compadre when I catch his eye. I'm rocking it pretty sharp myself. Cream-white trousers tucking in a Hawaiian button-up beneath a sequin blazer that screams jetsetter. Striding to the rear of the partygoers, I keep my distance from Deshawn so no one associates the two of us together.

Entering the Golden Dive, the dark, high-vaulted interior is lit by a plethora of tiny, multi-hued lights reflecting off a gyrating disco ball dangling from the epicentre of the ceiling. The D.J. is on a tear which is apparent by a dancefloor packed like sardines with writhing studs and nubiles seeking to impress or attract one another. Deshawn is there in the action, his lanky frame sliding between the masses with the fluidity of a cobra. Popping my collar, I bob my head to the bass and slurring hi-hat, edging closer to the bar.

Spinning out a stool, I order a Bud, giving me time to sip on the beverage while scouring the faces of the inhabitants and ingratiating myself with the bartender. After the half hour mark nears and a couple of generous tips, I cut to the chase with Darnell, the well-oiled barkeep.

"Have you seen Lynda around? She was supposed to meet me at seven-thirty, she's never this late…"

"Who?" Darnell double fists vodka and soda water into a tall glass.

I pull out her picture and steady it before his gaze. "Lynda Potts. We meet here every month… some of the regulars."

The keep shrugs, handing off the mixed drink to an impatient customer. "To be honest, I haven't been here that long. Just moved in from Omaha till I can line up a mechanic gig. Don't know no Lynda 'round these parts."

Out of the corner of my vision, I spy a lady sitting next to me shifting about nervously, uncrossing and recrossing her legs barely sheathed by a dark pleather skirt. Swivelling nonchalantly, I inhale her cheap perfume, taking in her getup and bleach-blonde bangs hovering above a pair of heavily mascaraed eyes. Upon closer inspection, I could discern the crow's feet and bags belying a woman attempting to mask her years. She was probably closer to my age, but I wore it better.

"How 'bout you, missy? See Lynda around lately." I dangle the photo in front of her.

She gives me a blank stare before shifting out of her stool to bolt full speed towards the rear of the building. Damn, how did she sprint so fast in those heels? Flopping a bill on the narrow counter I take off after her, almost nosediving on an alcohol spill smearing the floorboards. Recovering, I set fingers to my lips, piping out a hallmark whistle over the thumping speakers, pivoting Deshawn's head in my direction. Raising my hand to point at the back of the room, I race after the broad trying to give me the slip.

Shoulder-to-shoulder, we crash through a swinging door, weaving past the kitchen staff into the storage locker. The dimly lit cooler could not conceal the toppled boxes settling around a cellar entrance echoing the clatter of stiletto heels. Taking the lead, Deshawn dives down cement steps alit with sputtering bulbs from a bygone era. High-stepping the murk that dampens the slates of the tunnels, we burst through an ailing door at the end of the stretch.

Our way is blocked by a broad-shouldered meathead, the kind of two-brain-celled jock that found his greatest joys depositing dweebs into trashcans or guzzling their way to the bottom of a keg. Not one to be intimidated, Deshawn shuffles forward to engage the bruiser. Being a fan of Bruce Lee and Sammo Hung flicks, my buddy kicks out a riveting roundhouse to boot the door guard square in the chest. Whooping out the contents of his lungs, the bull of a man falls to the floor. Straddling his opponent, D-Jay hamfists the bouncer's temple rendering the poor lug comatose.

Skirting the brawl, I advance on the hussy huddling in a weeping mass against the far corner. Reaching down, I hoist the waif of a woman to her knees, glaring daggers into her makeup-streaked mug.

"What's your name? Where's Lynda?" I scream inches from her face, spittle flicking her ruined eyeliner.

"I don't know! I swear! The Priest wanted her, that's all I know." She squirms and squeals in my clutches.

"What Priest? Tell me!" I wrench her micro-purse

from its spaghetti-strap, extracting an ID.

"The Priest of Byakhee. That's all I can say." She cries like a baby, barely comprehensible.

Finished with his ass-whooping, Deshawn glances around the dank, candlelit room and shudders. "What kinda Voodoo heebee-geebee shit is this?"

Looking about, I take stock of the tiny shelf lined with a handful of books and occult trinkets. Bizarre and undecipherable runes were roughly hewn into the walls of what may have once been an underground opium den during the Chinese migration more than a century prior. Whirling back to the floozy bawling at my feet, I stow her licence away for future utilisation.

"Well, Miss Deana Ellsworth, if you remember any information regarding dear Lynda, I will be expecting a call." Flipping my card on her lap, I scoop up a couple of books from the collection, ushering my cohort from the eerie confines of the underworld.

Inhaling a deep breath, I reluctantly push through the entrance of *Sarasvati's Store of the Surreal*. The musk of foreign incense smoke wages war with my nostrils as I penetrate the beaded curtain dividing the outside world from the stuffy atmosphere of the New Age curios shop. Resisting the urge to light a cigarette to counterbalance the heady rush of burnt curry and sweat bonded together with a heaping wad of elephant dung, I step around the mass-produced dreamcatchers and cheap crystal charms, waving my way past a limp-haired cashier to cross into the backrooms barred to the general public. Waiting outside the black curtains, I stifle my laughter at the séance taking place within.

When an awestruck couple finally parts the veil to exit the store, quickly forgetting the crystal ball hogwash purchased by the minute, I brush aside the sheets to tromp inside like I own the place, and in many ways I do. Calmly shifting her gaze in that infuriating manner of pomposity and spiritual elitism as if I reek of Hell's Brimstone, the scarved woman rises to accost me.

"How dare you defile my inner sanctum with the file taint of your presence! This purified chamber is for paying customers and true believers only!"

Scoffing at the tired rant, I adjust my eyes to the candles and wavering blacklights. "You can dispense with the Broadway performance. I'm here for business, which will benefit you as well." I slam my briefcase upon the circular table for emphasis.

Rolling her eyes, the fortuneteller replies in salty tones. "You know full well that material wealth and possessions hold no sway for one who has pierced into the realms beyond."

"How presumptuous of you to think I offer mere cash, although what keeps this sham operation afloat?" I stare hard at the shawled proprietor, egging her on with a heightened sense of the mysterious.

"Why should I care what you have to offer, you muck-sucking worm?" She plants her hands firmly upon her jaunty hips in a show of defiance.

"Are you not curious what I have to say, hag?" I counter the spiritualist with an appeal to her undying curiosity by tapping the lid of my briefcase. As long as an intriguing unknown was in my possession, I held the high card.

"You degenerate pimp!"

"Worthless hippie."

Darting around the table, the willowy female embraces me in a ferocious bear hug. "Oh, baby brother, it's been too long."

"Hey, sis." I pat her on the back reassuringly. "It has been a while."

My older sibling offers me a seat then takes her own, smiling wide like a kid in a candy store. Shuffling the tools of her trade from the table, Sarah (not Sarasvati) folds her hands before her, eagerly awaiting my proposition.

Sarah Cromell's long hair is dark like mine, but her hazel-green gaze comes from our father, a bewitching trait she took full advantage of during her spiritual grift. Flashing my one-sided grin, I let her know I possess my own charms to counter her own. Popping the latches of my briefcase, I add to the suspense by keeping its contents from view.

"I confess, I come to you in need of your particular skill set. But I have something you may find of great interest, in addition to payment for your services." I extract two books and a bundled wad of bills. "I've been hired by some bigwig to track down his daughter and my search has led me to this…"

I push the archaic hardbacks her way, keeping the money as bait. I see I've peaked her interest when her eyes grow wide, flipping through the pages with gaudy fingernails. "The first tome translates as *The Book of the Dead*…" Pausing to skim the larger of the leatherbound manuscripts, she mulls over the arcane sketches before responding. "This unnamed volume reminds me of the Keys of Solomon – an encyclopaedia of demonic entities, none of which appears familiar to me." Breaking from her fixation, she stares pointedly at me. "Where did you find these? These are no mass-produced, dime store reprints, but one-of-a-kind originals."

"Beneath some dance club near the Tenderloin." I shrug, leaving any unnecessary details as vague as possible. "Some old-timey under lair built by the Chinese, I believe. Recently converted into the remnants of some cult the bar tried to keep hidden."

"And did you catch the name of this cult?" My elder pries further, ever thirsty for knowledge of the esoteric.

"B-Lockey… Babayagi… I'm sorry. My ear for languages is nowhere near your own. The people I interrogated seemed largely ignorant of the Satanic shitshow they became embroiled in." Sister Sarah spent the vast majority of her inheritance travelling the globe where she picked up a smattering of foreign lingos and a vast array of trivial tidbits that she would hold over your head whenever the opportunity arose. The income she accrued from her shiny trinkets could not pay the rent regularly, so it was often up to me to cover the bills. She could hold her own against any professor when it came to cultural studies, but no savvy businesswoman be my sister.

Agitated at the standstill I found myself in, I pull out a cig and add my own aroma to the flavours that permeate the backroom. Eyeing me in annoyance, I tap the stack of greenbacks letting my dear sister know who held sway within her own chambers. Exhaling, I cut to the heart of the deal. "These books are yours if you give them a thorough reading and fill me in on any insights you glimpse. I gotta stay on the prowl, so I'm relying on you for any research in this matter."

"I will keep my feelers out and peruse every page for you, just like I read to you when you were a baby." She smiles coyly.

I drop the cash and my card (I'm sure she trashed the last one) in front of her steepled hands and move to the drapes. "You know where to find me, Wicked Witch of the West."

A week passes and I find myself no closer to the whereabouts of Lynda Potts than the day I took on this miserable assignment. No call from my sister or any word from the skateboarder I paid to scope out the comings and goings of the Golden Dive. In pure frustration, I snatch the keys from Mr Makoto and cruise my tangerine LeSabre around the entire Bay, crossing the Golden Gate as the setting sun purples the coastal clouds over my left shoulder. Far from clearing my head, I find my thoughts spiralling despondently as I circle the waters that lap the shores of California's heartland. Pulling onto my driveway under a full array of blinking stars, I return my wheels to the care of my manservant, trudging my sorry ass into the familiar confines of my gilded flat.

I am instantly assaulted by the complex spices of Kara's Persian cuisine, but tonight I'm not interested... I'll get my calories from a bottle or two. Snagging a fifth of pricey vodka, I pour a hasty Moscow Mule, down it, and take the handle to pug straight.

Wandering into the garage where Davey-boy is obsessively scouring the interior of my Buick, whisking clear the stray ash and foul butts littering every crevice my lazy hide could offload into. Sliding a KC cassette into the boom box, I offer the water of life to my Japanese sidekick. Ranting and railing to my dutiful chauffeur, I slowly come to terms that my presence is nothing more than a hindrance to my loyal mechanic. Slipping him a hundo, I insist he take the wheels out for a night on the town and enjoy himself for once, free of any burdens.

Slinking into my study, I crack into my personal liquor cabinet and rifle through the slim files courtesy of Fascelatto's prior investigations. Blurry of mind and hazy of vision, I haphazardly gather the strewn paperwork with no rhyme or reason. Staring at a blank desktop, I retrieve the curling photograph of the missing woman from my wallet to permeate her image into my sloshing braincells by way of osmosis. Pretty by any standards, I look past the gentle swoops of her hair and snug turtleneck to read into those crafty eyes. Sly, fun-loving, and up to no good, I gaze deeply into her lidded orbs, guzzling distilled Russian grain until sepia fades black.

I'm shaken to skull-rattling consciousness having fallen into a self-imposed oblivion upon my chair. Kara's concerned features hover over me as I swallow the gorge building up in my throat. Thankfully, I forged my stomach into an iron furnace to avoid spewing my guts. Grinding the saline buildup from my eye sockets, I peer at my housekeeper who looks in horror at the spilt booze and broken glass strewn about the private office. Recovering her bearing, Kara lays a gentle hand upon my shoulder.

"Sir… Harlan. Your sister is here. I let her into the living room. She has an urgent message for you."

Jumping to my feet, I sway like a sailboat in a tempest and rush to the toilet. Dousing my face with an overdose of cologne and slipping on a satin reading jacket, I jaunt downstairs to greet my sibling.

"Sister Sarah! How long has it been since you've graced us with your presence?" I tease, playing off the jealousy of one sharing rent in a downtown apartment. Too excited to be thrown off guard, she raises her kerchiefed head in a rush to bombard me with the latest scoop.

"Baby brother! I have something that should please you…" Reaching into her oversized satchel, Sis pulls out a black and white Polaroid from the endless clutter of her fringed leather purse. The image printed on the waxy film conveys a portrait of a male face, finely sculpted features tapering off into a tight, dark ponytail with a freshly trimmed Vandyke beard surrounding firm lips.

"Apologies for the quality of the shot, but if there was ever a person devoid of colour, here he is." Sarah gloats as she fingers the picture authoritatively. "He goes by Sebastian Seville, but in my profession, that's probably a pseudonym. He came into my store looking for a lexicon of demonology. After telling him I only dealt in white magick, he invited me to his new moon gathering off the coast of Canyon Ranch, attempting to seduce me into his flock. I left my response ambivalent, so he claimed he would return after giving me time to deliberate on his proposition. He also left me a contact number." She leans in, flashing a calling card and a confident grin below heavily painted eyelid. "So, Mr. Detective… I believe I found your Priest."

Springing from the sofa, I rub my hands together in glee, thrilled to finally have some cornerstone, no matter how tenuous, to build upon. "Excellent work, dear Sister! This calls for a celebration. Kara, daiquiris for the two of us!"

Recognizing the look of disapproval on my maid's expression, I flash a smile to assuage her rational misgivings. "No need to fuss, sweet Karina. Sister here is absolutely sober, and nothing cures a hangover like a nicely chilled splash of fresh spirits. Counter poison with poison as they say."

In no time at all, we are clinking glasses in a toast to a long-awaited commencement point that may finally lead to the discovery of the wayward girl I've been hired to locate. Lounging back upon the downy cushions, I relay the instructions that will further the next steps of my… *our* trek.

"Sarah, I want you to accept the invitation. You've trotted the globe and I trust your ability to handle your own, come what may." She glowers at me with all the vitriol of the experienced looking down on an uppity youngin, mistaking my words as condescension. My tongue scrambles to rectify any misgivings my touchy sister may have gleaned from our dialogue. "But this wet behind the ears lil' girlie needs all the help we can muster… and that is why we need you." I look square into her dual jade orbs. "I would never throw you in harm's way, yet I can't think of anyone better to infiltrate this dark cabal. And I'm not sending you alone, dear Sister… we'll be right behind you."

Sarah's lunar charts kept us keen to the limited amount of time we have to set up the operation. For the first time in years, me and sis have bonded to a degree nearly as tight as our teenage standing when she would send out her boy toys to save my gangly freshman ass from cannings or outright beatdowns. Despite all our disagreements and petty infighting, I know dear sis has always had my back. That is why I feel an intrinsic need to pay back a debt that I shall forever owe. With that in mind, I send out Mr Makoto to chauffeur Sarah to the ritual and follow her from a distance.

Meanwhile, I rev up the combustion engine of my motorboat as Deshawn loads the wave-skimmer with all essentials. Giving me the salute, we launch from the dock house with the sea breeze coursing through our hair. Cutting the waves like a katana against hot butter, I slice the surface of the waters, skipping the swells like a dolphin.

Cresting the southern end of the bay's northwestern peninsula as night encroaches, I slow the speed of the boat as we near our destination. Eyes adjusting to the vanishing sun, I switch off the lights to glide across the cove with all the stealth of a submarine. Having the topography seared into my memory banks and all too familiar with the coastlines of my hometown, we glide across the inlet to the picturesque crags lining the Canyon Ranch reserve.

Amplified situational awareness allows our night-ready eyes to make out bobbing flashlights and lanterns hovering alongside the brink from a quarter mile out. Shutting down the engine, we drift silently to a narrow washout severing the rocky shoals that made up much of the Pacific edge of Northern California. Situating our gear and artillery, Deshawn and I crash through the shrubs that wall us off from the obscured trail. Barging onto the narrow pathway, the two of us toe our way at a quick yet quiet trot, following the direction of the departed lights.

After a span, we come across an expansive crevice that could not quite be considered a cave, but a gigantic dugout carved by aeons of unrelenting tides slamming against the soft bedrock. Two shrouded figures stand vigil at the entrance to the great depression, so I motion Deshawn to quietly ascend the top of the rise. At the apex of the wooded peak, we come across Mr Makoto levelling his small handgun at us. Recognizing who we are, he motions us over to look down a narrow chasm growing wider as it penetrates deeper into the bowels of the subterranean hollow.

Tying a length of cord to the nearest conifer trunk, Deshawn flashes me a thumbs up giving us the go to slowly lower down to the opposite end of the rope. Being the smallest, Davey is the first to make the descent which does not take long as we feel the slack signalling his offloading. I follow behind, using a simple belay clip to relieve the wear and tear on my hands. The tight confines of the precarious entry allows me to utilise my legs along the ravaged walls until the chamber widens drastically forcing me to climb down hand by hand. Finally, Deshawn drops to our level, spinning the semiautomatic rifle from his back, ready for action.

Circling the cordage around a stalagmite near the far wall, I whisper for Davey to stay put to take care of the two watchmen guarding the entrance if shit hits the fan. Drawing my revolver, I wave Deshawn to my side, advancing along the sandy corridor deeper into the chasm. Our way is lit by the eerie radiance of tall red candles spaced along wave-shaped rocks lining the walls. The underground passage is not long and when a formal baritone reverberates throughout the cavern, we scurry for opposite sides of the tunnel.

Edging carefully onward, we halt our progress behind several dozen people, all eyes upon the back wall in heightened anticipation. Robed acolytes dump aged driftwood upon dual fires illuminating the focal point of the ritual with flickering gouts rising higher and higher. Upon a large slab shed from the eroded culmination of the natural carveout, a hooded figure stands before a veiled enigma in poised reverence. Turning towards his devotees, the cloaked figure raises his arms to begin his oration.

"Welcome, brave souls willing to shred through the paltry veneers of society, followers of an untrod path leading forward towards a new tomorrow. As we ready ourselves to traverse into the darkness, we do so knowing full well that those who persevere shall breach all obstacles to a new dawn. In this undertaking, sacrifices must be made by those who spearhead the movement. A move towards a resplendent world that will rejoice in your presence and grant you the power to fulfil your greatest ambitions.

"In these endeavours, I will act as a bridge between you and your grandest desires. I do so in the spirit of true reciprocity, for I have been gifted a mere taste of the infinite wonders that lie beyond and recognize the boundless potential to be shared with all those found worthy for such an undertaking. Those with the fortitude to pierce the threshold shall be heralds leading the way into a higher dimension. To this end, I reveal the manifestation of the divine interlocutor to the mundane realm."

On cue, one of the fire-tenders steps upon the makeshift stage to rip the covering from the central object it conceals. Beneath the cloth stands a life-size figure etched into dark, igneous rock. Looking past the ceremonial spokesman who I now recognize from Sarah's Polaroid as Sebastian Seville with his pretentious goatee, I squint against the light of the shifting flames to pick out the details of the statuesque caricature. In the middle of the jagged display, a rendition of a grotesque and demonic being, absolutely lifelike in its terrifying posture and agony, though I am no art aficionado. The most startling features being the batlike wings spread horizontally across the hardened lava, spanning farther than the height of the creature's length. Clawed, skeletal limbs, frozen in motion, protrude from a nondescript body topped by a narrow head with the snout of a shrew. Its jewelled eyes shone like segmented rubies, bringing to mind something quite insectile or chameleonesque.

Turning my attention to the spectators, I am sickened by the enraptured sheep all too eager to be willing dupes for this scam operation. My sister is shifting her head left and right, visibly uneasy with the situation she found herself enmeshed within. Turning to Deshawn, I see his eyes glowing wide as he mouths *What the - - - -* at the unholy shitfest taking place before us. I pivot my gaze back centerstage when the long winded rant begins anew.

"Behold! The Fallen Angel! Do not be frightened my children, for he signifies the descent of the previous aeon, but holds the key for the escalation back to Paradise. An ascension we shall claim as our own... but first, we must awaken the Messenger with an offering of flesh and blood."

From a concealed location, cowled, monk-like attendants parade out a maiden clothed in sheer white material leaving little to the imagination. Even from this distance and the abysmal lighting, I can make out the drugged-up features of Lynda Potts, docile as a lamb to the slaughter. Led to the feet of the ringleader, Sebastian takes her hand, assisting her to stand above the brainwashed masses.

"Our earlier rituals have done much to stir the soul of the Savior. As you all can see, his eyes glow radiant with the vibrancy of life from previous sacrifices. Yet the sins and doubting natures of prior victims have hitherto failed to fully awaken the Demigod. In the hopes of rectifying such failures, I bring to you the very essence of purity itself. A virginal (doubtful) bride to free our host from its centuries of imprisonment. One whose soul will transcend alongside the Deliverer to a world void of boundaries and superficial concerns. So, step forth, beloved, and kiss he who shall redeem us all from the constraints of the illusory world."

As the vile con artist turns his back to his mindless fanbase, I realise this is my last opportunity to rescue the girl from whatever dangers she's gotten herself into. Checking my ammo rounds, I slap my revolver closed and hiss to my ally across the corridor.

"Deej, cover me."

Edging along the striated wall, I nearly fall flat on my face, tripping over the corpse of some poor sap dragged out of view behind a tumble of boulders. Staring down at the unfortunate stiff, I gasp in horror at the withered husk wearing an olive-green peacoat. The greyish flesh is completely drained of fluids to the point I would have mistaken it for a mummy if not for the modern wardrobe. Instinct tells me that I just discovered the fate of Jason Fascelatto, the P.I. sent in before me to uncover the whereabouts of the attorney's daughter.

Looking away in revulsion, I curse my frightened outburst when I spot a handful of cultists shifting about, looking around in annoyance for the source of the noise that interrupts their freakshow. When plans go to shit, I'm left with no choice but to go with my gut. Lunging from my hiding place, I sprint forward, springing above the heads of the seated observers as I run full bore towards Lynda and Sebastian. Launching upon the giant slate that supports the Hellish monument, I sock the High Priest solidly on the kisser without slowing my momentum.

Damn! I gotta remember to use the butt of my gun next time as I can barely move my knuckles. Spitting on the unconscious prick, I grab Lynda by her limp arm and slap her across the cheek.

"Snap out of it, tootsie. Your pop's is paying me the big ones to get you to safety and I'm not letting you out of my sight."

Spinning around, I find my way obstructed by an angry mob of fanatics. No way I was going to be dragging out an opiated damsel in distress through this seething mass, so I raise my fingers to my lips and bleat out a shrill note that reverberates throughout the faux cavern.

"Alright, you sons of bitches! Party's over!"

Deshawn punctuates his words with a wild burst from his Kalashnikov into the naturally formed ceiling. At the echoing uproar of rapid gunfire, the vast majority of the gathering panics and flees out the way they came. I don't blame them or give chase. I ain't no copper and these poor fools are nothing more than indoctrinated pawns from all walks of life – empty-suit yuppies, the homeless, desperate churchgoers who have lost their faith, and disaffected youth who could no longer believe in their parents or failed institutions, those seeking a different route to navigate a sordid world bereft of morality and a deeper logic.

Tugging Lynda by the hand, we drop from our raised vantage attempting to clear the path by kicking the nearest aggressor directly on the ballsack. The look on the poor sap's face brings a wicked grin to my lips. Pulling the addled young woman behind me, I frantically scramble to avoid the remaining diehards seeking to hinder our escape. Recognizing our plight, Deshawn advances to lay down another brutal salvo far above the heads of everyone involved in this debacle. When chunks of debris began to rain down from the fragile cavern top, the last of the devotees took to their heels to run for their dear lives.

Following the stampeding horde desperate to save their skins, I half-carry Miss Potts from the crumbling chamber, dodging dust and cascading rocks falling along our precarious path. I reach sight of the moonless exterior meeting up with Davey, D-Jay, and Sarah at the mouth of the collapsing sanctum. Panting to my driver, I lay out a terse series of orders preparing to divide my crafty contingent.

"Get sis and Deej safely back to their homes. We will reconvene once I have the girl safely back to her father. Go!"

I stir from my scattered bedsheets in near-total darkness, the morning sun still unshed deep below the eastern horizon. In the dimmest of lights, I can make out the outline of Lynda's lithe figure breathing gently beneath the down comforter of my four-post bed. Delicately shifting a stray lock of hair from her soft features, I reach for whatever glass of liquid remains on my nightstand, mulling over the climactic wrap-up of my weeks-long case.

Discreetly lighting a Red to not awaken my dreaming guest, I ponder the fate of Sebastian, the cult leader last seen lying unconscious upon the floor of the now destroyed ritual chamber of the Devil worshippers. If the manipulative scam artist made it out alive or not, I couldn't give a shit. If he did manage to slither out of the doomed hollow, he best think twice before attempting to abduct any impressionable young women in my city. As for the strange and twisted sculpture, never has there been a work of art more worthy to be discarded into the waste bin of history.

The first traces of dawn hint the coming of a new day as I extinguish my second cigarette. Gulping down the final dregs of my oversized shot glass, I gaze wistfully at the lass who shares my bedding, the rising sun caressing her cheekbones and long lashes which slowly begin to flutter. Upon our boat ride back to my coastal property, I provided the young Miss Potts full use of my abode. After a long, steaming shower, she reappeared wrapped in a skimpy bath towel, dampened hair curling about her bare shoulders. I offered one of my various guestrooms, but after a couple of soothing drinks, we ended up here. A little young for my liking... still, her hair smelled sweet and our lids grew heavy. Duty may have dictated that I return her immediately to her father, but the hour had grown late and I felt it would have been rude to rouse my employer after hours.

Rolling over to her side of the bed, I snuggle in to suavely initiate my trademark wake-up call.

Deep beneath the bowels of the ruined cavity that edges the shoreline of San Francisco's northern coast, a residual tremble shifts the altered landscape. Deep underneath the freshly dislodged rubble, a trapped being rouses to a full awakening. The tumultuous upheaval that caused the depression cracked the hardened magma that encased the otherworldly traveller within a millennia-long imprisonment - an initial glimmer of freedom withheld for an indefinite amount of time.

Crimson, fractal eyes radiate with a noxious glow, sending a beacon permeating tons of granite and silicate to scour the stars, giving missive to the Outer Ones. Caught in a limbo of materialist gravity and petrification, the obstruction could no longer contain the transmission from the thousand eyes of the All-Watching nor the ears of the All-Hearing – synesthesia in the truest sense.

Too impatient to await a response, the blackest of claws rends through the final coat of molten bonds freeing the alien presence to tear passage through the collapse. Piercing the top layer of natural detritus, the darksome being unfurls its wings to full extension to break the stratosphere. When the density of the veil thinned enough, space folds to allow entrance into the Void.

Jasiah Witkofsky is a philosopher-gardener who spends his off-hours penning dark speculative fiction and swashbuckling tales of daring and adventure. He resides at the foothill base of the magical Sierra Nevadas of Northern California with his merry band of rascals and rapscallions. His works can be found in more than ten publishers, magazines, and journal companies from all over the English-speaking world.

Find him under

http://www.facebook.com/jasiahwitkofskyauthorpage

Harlan Cormell is an original creation of the author

THE FUNG MYSTERY

An Andrew Doran Story

MATTHEW DAVENPORT

CHAPTER 1

As I sat in my apartment, smaller than most hotel rooms that I have stayed in, and stared at the stack of last-minute assignments, I couldn't get past one single thought.

I hate grading papers.

The thought of summoning a school-destroying alien god from another dimension just so I could avoid grading them was a serious consideration.

Instead, I stood, walked across to the small dining area that had been taken over by interdimensional maps drawn by madmen over three hundred years ago and removed several trinkets in the shapes of various animal gods whose roles were reportedly in the divination of magical pathways between worlds. All to find the bottle of whiskey sitting near the window. I poured a small glass, added water from the tap, and sipped.

My apartment was nothing special. There was the main room that acted as my office, my living area, and my kitchen, a bedroom that would be better described as a closet, and a bathroom. The size of my place, as well as the mess, were all a result of my never being there. My role might have changed at Miskatonic University from Dean to Professor of Anthropology, but my life's purpose had yet to shift course.

I was fighting a silent war against the horrors that

wished to invade our world through magical or scientific means while the rest of the world dealt with a global conflict the likes of which hadn't been seen in over twenty years.

Oh, and I also graded papers.

My door was suddenly shaking as someone slammed a fist into it repeatedly. I started, almost spilling my drink. I looked at my clothes, a white undershirt untucked from my brown pants, and then I looked to my watch. It was a little after midnight.

My pistol was somewhere back in my bedroom. I decided against going for it. Whoever was pounding on the door could have just kicked it in if they were looking for a fight. Instead, they were frantic.

A turn of the lock and I had the door open but my foot in front of it, allowing me a relatively safe look at who was outside.

She wasn't short, that much was certain. The woman on the other side of the door was dressed in a blouse and a long jacket. She had shoulder-length auburn hair and a manic look on her face.

The jacket and the skin that I could see were covered in blood.

That was all I saw before she lunged at the door, forced my foot back, and sent me bouncing away on the one foot that hadn't been trampled by the door.

"Ow," I said it like a barb aimed at my attacker.

In my life, I had made a lot of enemies and I was suddenly more aware of my lack of a pistol than I had been previously.

I slammed the door shut and turned toward the

woman, standing in the centre of my small apartment. The emotions on her face were all over the place.

My pain subsided, leaving only the uncomfortable feeling of someone having invaded my personal space.

"Who the hell are you and what are you doing here?" I demanded.

Her face was mostly angles and I figured that if she hadn't been covered in blood and whatever trauma had put it on her, then she might look like someone who was familiar with being in charge. She reminded me of my secretary.

She moved past me and to the door. Opening it and peering out into the hallway. After a moment of her head twisting back and forth, she shut it again, softer than I did, and pressed her back against it.

Her eyes were still closed when she answered me.

"Camilla," her voice was quiet but solid, which surprised me. "Camilla Rhodes. I am being hunted."

"By what?" I asked immediately.

"What do you mean 'what?'" Her eyes opened and she looked at me, studying me for the first time.

"Are you hurt?" I asked instead of answering her question with the obvious answer of 'monsters.'

She put her hands into her jacket pockets and looked at herself. "This isn't my blood."

"Who is hunting you?" I asked. "Who's blood is it?"

"Are you Andrew Doran?"

My curiosity was only growing, as was that itch for my pistol.

"You're in my place," I gave as an answer. "I think I'll be the one asking the questions. Whose blood?"

Camilla's eyes were darting all over my place. She looked like she was searching for an escape, but as she was still leaning on the door, perhaps she was looking for something to defend herself with.

"Do you know Larry Henton?" she asked.

The name was familiar to me. "Journalist for the Arkham Herald," I answered. "He exposed a campus gambling ring and many students and several teachers were arrested. They call him the 'man who made campus football honest again.'"

Camilla nodded. "It's his blood. About," she looked at a man's watch on her wrist, didn't like what she saw, smacked it and continued, "I don't know, an hour ago, maybe. About an hour ago, I woke up to his mutilated body with no idea how I got there or what had happened to him."

Assuming she was telling the truth, that explained the blood.

"Who is hunting you?" I asked.

She let out a slow breath and forced herself to calm down. "Not long after I woke up, police sirens and flashlights were lighting up the place."

"The police?" I demanded. "You are being hunted by the police and you chose to hide at a random college professor's house?"

Camilla's face contorted with confusion. "What? Wait. You're a teacher? Are you Doran?"

I stepped toward her slowly and guided her to the chair where I had been grading the papers. I pulled it away from the desk. Adding blood next to a failing grade was just adding insult to injury.

"Yes," I confirmed. "I am Dr Andrew Doran. How do you know of me?"

She started to cry. Slow and silent sobs left her as she said, "I don't even know how Larry and I got there. When I woke up, or before that, I guess, a very clear voice told me your name and this address." Tears turned to a frown as she stared at her blood-stained hands. "Why would I dream that?" Then she looked at me. "And how could you be real?"

This was turning out to be more complicated than a woman running from a murder charge. I always took dreams seriously. Some of my best friends were dreams.

I moved to the window and looked out onto the night street. In the distance, I could see the spire of the Registrar building at Miskatonic University, where I worked. Arkham streets held more nightmares at night than during the day, but currently, nothing outside seemed interested in my visitor.

The sink had a dishtowel sitting by it. After it was wet, I gave it to Camilla to let her clean herself up a bit.

"I am a professor of archaeology and anthropology at Miskatonic, but," I tried to explain, "that's like saying you're just a laundry basket's worst nightmare. In both situations, there's much more to the story."

Camilla stopped wiping herself off and looked up at me, fear returning to her face. "Are you saying that … you … hurt Larry?"

That took me by surprise. "What? No! Besides, if you look like that, the killer probably looks worse." I picked up my drink and offered it to Camilla. She downed it one gulp and handed the glass back. I didn't pour her another.

"How did you know Larry?" I asked.

Camilla wiped her face as she answered. "We met at work. Officially, I'm his secretary, but I help Larry do his investigations and type up most of his articles." She stopped before adding, "We just started going steady."

"Other than the obvious," I said, nodding toward her clothes, "why do you think that the police are looking for you? Did they see you as you left the scene?"

Camilla shook her head. "I heard them say my name. To 'circle around' and to keep an eye out for the 'Rhodes girl,' or something close to that."

"You don't know how you got there but the police expected you before they had even identified the body?" This was too convenient. "Someone, likely the real killer, phoned it in. That means they knew you, or at least Larry. Did anyone have a reason to hurt him?"

She snort-laughed, but there was no real mirth in it. "One article got how many students and teachers arrested? He wrote dozens."

"You ran, but why?" I asked. "Aside from the obvious, they could have just had a few questions."

Camilla scoffed and held up the dishtowel, now soaked in blood. "I doubt they would have seen me and chosen the path of polite gentlemen with their questions."

I conceded the point.

"Besides," she continued, "you didn't see Larry. He was torn to pieces." Her face took on an almost blank look as emotions left her. People had different demeanours they could take on to handle different situations. I wouldn't use the same tone to speak with my peers as I would to my students. It seemed to me that whatever her professional demeanour was for dealing with the dark underside of Arkham that she and Larry wrote about, she was wearing it now. "He was shredded, and I was standing in the middle of it. Even I thought I looked guilty."

I grabbed another glass from the counter and finally decided to pour myself another one.

"And the voice clearly said my name?"

Camilla nodded. "Clear as day. I thought that it was real until I woke up. Wait a second," she paused, "are you saying that you believe me about the voice?"

My mind was racing with the names of people that I knew who could communicate psychically. Not only people who could communicate, but who also knew me and would be involved in the death of a journalist. I was so preoccupied that it took me a moment to realise that when I didn't answer her, Camilla's journalistic curiosity drew her eyes to the tattoo on my inner forearm.

The tattoo was half of an anchor and a date, cut off by a scar where the skin colour of my arm abruptly stopped being the tan of my hand and became the paler look of someone who had lived in Arkham for a few years.

I grabbed a dress shirt from the back of a nearby chair and put it on to cover up the tattoo. I didn't want to talk about it as there was never anything worth saying. Either I lied, unconvincingly, about how I got it and threatened the trust my visitor was willing to put in me, or I told the truth and that never went over well.

Oh, this? Well, I was killed by a god of nightmares from an alien world and he cut off my arm. Some nice military folks with arcane tools at their disposal resurrected me and put me back together with pieces from one of their dead friends.

That was without diving into how the god of chaos, Nyarlathotep, might have used the entire experience to try and leash me to his will as one of his avatars.

See? It was too complicated, so I put on the shirt.

Camilla opened her mouth to speak, but I cut her off to keep the conversation on topic.

"Let's just say that this isn't the first time that someone has reached out to me through dreams," I said as an explanation.

Camilla took a slow breath. "Well, it is new to me. The idea that you are a real person is almost as scary as Larry's death."

She was doing investigative journalism in Arkham and the idea of someone communicating through dreams seemed odd to her. Camilla was surprisingly new to this. It was one thing to ignore all the weird things that happened in Arkham, it was another to be taken entirely by surprise with them.

"A little bit of advice," I offered, "when you get a message from a dream, or anything seemingly impossible happens to you, do everything in your power to not dismiss it." I stopped and then quickly added, "Especially in Arkham."

"What does that mean?" Camilla started scrubbing at her clothes. The blood only smeared, but she wasn't willing to give up on the saturated towel. "I have lived here my entire life and nothing like this has ever happened to me before."

I went to my room to retrieve my holster and jacket. Not long ago, I used a holster that hung at my hip, much like a cowboy. This new holster, a gift from an old friend, was meant for hiding the pistol under my coat. I strapped it on and returned to Camilla.

"What are you doing?" She was no longer in the chair. The towel was in the sink, and she had done a decent job of getting her boyfriend's gore off her skin. "Where are you going?"

"I listen when dreams talk, and we are going to figure out what's going on." I tossed her a coat that wasn't covered in blood. It wouldn't do much to hide her state, but at a distance, she might be able to avoid passing glances. "Besides, I didn't want to grade papers anyway."

CHAPTER 2

"Where are we going?" Camilla repeated from the passenger side of the pickup that I was not supposed to have.

For various reasons, I didn't have an automobile of my own. I had taken to borrowing the campus trucks from the maintenance shed whenever I needed a ride. When I was the dean of Miskatonic University, that had been considered a perk. Now that I had been reduced to a professor in a department that I wasn't even head of, borrowing required more bribery than before.

You likely would not be surprised to know that underpaid staff tend to be easily convinced to loan you campus materials for a bottle of scotch. It left me concerned about campus security, but it also left me with wheels.

Instead of answering Camilla's question directly, I led with a question of my own.

"Do you know how to send messages from the Dream Lands?"

Camilla baulked at the question. "The Dream Lands? What? No. I have never heard the term before you said it."

"Exactly," I said as I turned the rusted clunker around a surprisingly empty Arkham street. Even for being the middle of the night, Arkham was emptier than expected. In any other town, I wouldn't have noticed, but everything in this city felt like an omen. "Most people don't. I don't, not really. But I do know two things about messages from the Dream Lands."

Camilla didn't appreciate my not getting directly to the point. "And that would be?"

"The first is that the easiest way to send a message is through the weak spots. Places where the Dream Lands touch our world. Those places are rare and mostly unknown to people. I think Larry was killed in one of those places."

Camilla nodded, still emotionally torn from Larry's death. "And the second?"

I waved my hand in the air to dismiss the question. "Later. Right now, tell me what you remember before waking up."

She rubbed her eyes, the physical act seemingly sending her mind back in time. "Larry had just picked me up. From my home. Well, it was my parents' place. I have been taking classes at night and saving to get my own place."

"You're a student?" My ears perked up at that. Perhaps Larry's assailant was a disgruntled gambler. "Not archaeology, then?"

Camilla smirked. "Journalism, sorry." I waved it off.

"Picked you up?" I pressed. "For what?"

"Dinner," she answered. "Larry is always working on a story, and he wanted to tell me about the big break that he made."

"What kind of story?"

"Someone has been moving an unlicensed pharmaceutical through Arkham. Not everyone who takes it wakes up," Camilla explained.

An illicit drug being passed around a college town was not a huge surprise. The fact that people weren't waking up in enough numbers to catch the attention of Larry Henton was surprising. Even more so was that a campus professor, myself, hadn't heard anything about this.

While the existence of drugs in Arkham was not a surprise, it was still something of note. We didn't have the number of issues the bigger cities would get.

Which, given the city's usual inclination toward the darker aspects of nature, was a small blessing.

"What did he find out?" I asked.

"Before dinner," Camilla said, "we had been at a dead end. Everything we investigated couldn't even be confirmed. There wasn't anything we could find out that not every other student in town already knew."

"I'll leave it to your imagination how frequently the students tell their professors about their drug use," I said.

Camilla acknowledged my point. "They call it Fung, but I don't know why. Larry said that it looks like a purple powder that shimmers."

That caught my interest as we turned onto another main road in town. "Shimmers? How?"

"That was the odd thing," she explained. "Larry said that it only shimmers in the moonlight."

"What does Fung do? Why are people taking it?" I asked.

She shrugged. "Nothing entirely exciting, which is part of the mystery. Everything in my research showed that it helped with sleep. Larry, on the other hand, heard from someone that it is supposed to give you dreams beyond your wildest imagination."

I was beginning to wonder how Larry knew so much about this drug that his research assistant couldn't find anywhere. It was likely that he had tried some.

"What kind of dreams?"

"Great dreams. Addicting dreams. So addicting that Fung doesn't need to be. People don't take it because the absence of it makes them crave it, they take it to get back to those dreams."

If Fung was not native to our reality it could be several things that I was aware of and about a billion that I wasn't. If I could find out what kind of 'great dreams' the Fung users were having it would help narrow it down. I knew of several herbs and flowers from other realms that could induce a sort of time travel, allowing users to imagine their lives differently by changing one thing. There were others that allowed the user to develop entire realities, though temporary, from their greatest fantasies. There were some that could even transport your consciousness into alien bodies for a short time, but those were mostly outlawed across reality by ancient races.

Throughout my inner debate on what Fung was, Camilla continued to talk, explaining a relatively normal evening between two people who were both interested in each other and the same subject matter. The restaurant that he took her to, Giovanni's, was a small Italian place that was frequented by the staff of Miskatonic University, but not so much by the students due to the cost.

Camilla remembered ordering dessert, but she did not remember anything past that until she woke.

"Where did you wake up?" I asked.

I knew this would be the harder part of the conversation, and even in the dim light of the streetlamps I could see her get a little paler as she recalled the details.

"I think it was a boat house," she said quietly. "But there were no boats."

That didn't make sense. "The river is miles from Giovanni's. Would you be able to take me back there?"

It was obvious she didn't like that idea, but she didn't back down. "I think so."

We turned the truck down a small alley and slowed down as we neared a painted, wooden sign that only read "Psychic." There was a light above the sign, but it was flickering on the verge of failure.

"A psychic?" Doubt and mistrust returned to the young journalist's face. "You don't believe in that kind of thing, do you?"

I frowned at her. "Someone put my address into your head." Realisation dawned on Camilla, and she sighed. "Besides, Madame Skai is the real thing. She can help us get a few answers."

Camilla reached for the door handle of the beat-up maintenance truck, but I held up my hand, stopping her.

"Not yet. What did Larry find out? Whoever is putting Fung into the hands of students is likely responsible for his death. I needed to know what he knew."

Camilla nodded. "He told me who his informant was, but not who was providing the informant with the Fung."

"Who?" This was a bigger lead than anything else she had told me, and I didn't understand why I was just hearing about it.

"You have to understand," Camilla explained with more energy than I had expected, "as journalists, our informants are everything. They trust us. If I tell you, I am breaking that trust."

I tried not to roll my eyes. "After he told you who his informant was, you woke up next to his dead body. The informant is likely the best possible person to answer what happened to Larry."

She sighed. "A man named Lumley."

I didn't recognize the name, but that was no big surprise. I hadn't been out buying drugs recently.

I put that information away in the back of my mind as we climbed out of the car.

As I reached to knock on Madame Skai's door, it

flew open.

"Andrew, darling." I was pulled into a tight hug faster than I could react to the door opening. "I knew you would be here tonight."

Madame Skai dressed in all black, but there was nothing formal about her clothing. She wore a long dress that seemed made of silks and transparent materials. If the lighting in her home had been any brighter she wouldn't have needed to wear any clothes. Even so, in the dimness of the room she pulled us into, it was easy to make out her figure. Camilla, to her credit, took it all in stride. Skai was older than me by at least ten years, but she had the energy of someone half my age combined with the quiet demeanour of someone of great wisdom.

"Madame Skai," I pulled from the hug and turned my attention to Camilla. "This is Camilla Rhodes." To Camilla, I said, "Skai plays up the psychic thing a little much, but she is the real thing. Since I know that, and I know she gets her information from her walks in the Dream Lands, who told you we were coming?"

Skai smiled knowingly. "Your guardian angel, of course. A Monsieur Dubois."

I had assumed as much but hearing that my old friend was still looking out for me warmed my once-dead heart.

Leo Dubois had joined me on many adventures at one time. Unfortunately, he had been murdered by those same adventures. At the time, I was able to save him by moving his spirit into the Dream Lands. He was forever lost to our world, but at least he could live out a long and, hopefully, happy existence there.

Madame Skai led us deeper into her small home.

We entered what looked like a Victorian living room. Bookshelves lined the walls. Instead of books, they were covered with small jars of different coloured powders and elixirs. It looked like something from Sherlock Holmes' apothecary. We both took a seat on an antique sofa that felt uncomfortable enough to likely be an original. Then she sat in a high-backed chair across from us, crossing her legs and placing her hands in her lap.

"You're here about Larry Henton's death?"

"What didn't Leo tell you about?" I asked. "Yes. Camilla was with him, but she doesn't remember anything."

I explained everything that Camilla had told me, checking with her regularly to make sure that I didn't confuse the facts. I let Camilla describe Fung.

"This Fung sounds much like the types of chemicals that I deal in." Skai turned her attention to Camilla. "You see, dear, I use natural means, plants and minerals, to project my consciousness into another world. The Dream Lands. It is an entire world, peopled by the thoughts and wishes of a billion races from a billion times as many realities. If you dream, you go to the Dream Lands, and if there, you can trade for anything. The only thing worth trading for outside of the Dream Lands, though, is information. This makes it very good to be a psychic."

"Do you ever let others use those chemicals?" I asked.

Madame Skai nodded. "For a fee, I can act as a guide and take others with me." She held up a finger at Camilla's attempt to ask a question. "Never without my guests knowing the dangers, though."

"Dangers?" Camilla asked. I could see the journalist's curiosity piquing. "Like people not waking up?"

Skai nodded. "When you go the Dream Lands, or project your mind anywhere, really, there's always a chance, just as in our world, that you could get lost, hurt, or worse. If that happens, you would not return to your body, this reality." Her eyes lit up. "Perhaps the users of Fung are going to the Dream Lands, or somewhere like that, without a guide." She waved a hand at herself. "Without a guide, the odds of returning home safely are greatly diminished."

"Skai," I said, "Larry thought he might have figured out where people were getting Fung, and I'm thinking that if I pull on that string it will lead us to who killed him."

"You are also curious as to what Fung really is." It wasn't a question.

I gave a short nod.

For all my talk of Skai being useful, I did not enjoy psychics. They knew too much about things that I didn't prefer to share. As if bidden by my acknowledgement, Skai explained to Camilla.

"You see, Camilla, dearest Andrew has lost much in his life. At one time, he was a person of great power, though he would not admit it. Now he is mostly powerless, protected only by his wits. When he lost that power, he lost something else, as well. It is his hope to learn the secret of opening paths to other worlds so that he may reclaim some of what he lost."

"A girl, right?" Camilla smirked. "It is almost always a girl."

"Anyway," I needed the subject to change, "I am here to stop people from dying over a drug. Do you know more about Fung or what it actually does?"

"Andrew," Skai was having fun with us and it made me uncomfortable, "are you getting bored with your whiskeys? Monsieur Dubois will be so disappointed."

I allowed a smile to creep at the reminder of drinks with my friend. "No, I have my vice. I just don't want any more people to die." My mirth vanished. "Also, I am less worried about where these people are going so much as what they might be leaving the door open for."

I was referring to the empty bodies of those who hadn't returned from wherever the Fung had taken them. With their bodies empty, it was only a matter of time until something found its way inside. If we were lucky, it would be some mindless entity that didn't know the first thing about using a human body.

We were almost never that lucky.

"You see, dear?" Skai had returned her attention to Camilla. "Leo sent you to the correct man. Andrew is a man, as I feel you are already beginning to see, who puts the protection of our reality above all else." She returned her attention to me. 'How can I help?"

"Not so fast," I said, catching her statement about Leo. My old friend was at the top of my list of suspects who might have spoken to Camilla in her dreams, but he wasn't my only suspect. "What makes you think it was Leo?"

Madame Skai shrugged. "He was the one who told me you were coming. The last thing I knew, he did not have any powers to see into our reality. How might he know if he hadn't been the one to send the girl to you?"

"Woman," Camilla corrected.

Skai nodded, "Apologies, Ms Rhodes. At this point in my lengthy journey to the grave, everyone looks like a child."

As I had mentioned earlier, Madame Skai wasn't that much older than me. Either she was smoother than silk, or she had just said we were old. I decided to believe the former.

She was right, though. Given that she knew of our coming, Leo was the only real person who could have told Camilla about me.

"You can help by telling us if you know anything about Fung," I answered. "A purple powder that shimmers only in the moonlight."

"Without properly examining it, I would only be guessing," she said.

"Please guess," I encouraged.

Camilla interrupted before Madame Skai could offer her thoughts.

"How is any of this hoodoo witchcraft going to get the police off of me and onto the real killer?"

I gently placed my hand on Camilla's. "It does us no good to find out who killed Larry if we don't have a motive," or the means, but I kept that to myself. Going unconscious and then being torn to shreds miles from your last memory made no sense. "If we go to the police with a story and no proof, you are still the most likely suspect as the person who saw him last."

Madame Skai's voice was quiet, but it cut through everything with her tone. "Andrew will help you. It is what he does."

It takes a moment, but Camilla nodes, accepting this fact.

Madame Skai stood up. "Come with me, darling. Let's get you out of those clothes."

Camilla followed Skai out of the room. I stood and began examining the shelves, looking for anything that looked like it might fit the description of the Fung powder.

I was comparing bottles of different shades of purple powder when Skai returned.

"She is a charming girl." She nodded back the way she came. "I have left her to get dressed."

"And your guess? About the Fung?"

A thoughtful look crossed her face. "The colour is likely inconsequential, but the sparkle only in the moonlight is unique. Given all the realities and infinite potential, it could be anything, but I feel the name might also be a clue. There is a powder that can be made from a red fungus that grows in the Enchanted Wood."

"In the Dream Lands," I said, recognizing the name of the place.

Skai nodded. "To venture into the Enchanted Wood to collect it is beyond foolish and bordering on suicidal unless you are familiar with the Dream Lands."

"You're referencing the Zoogs," I said and an image of what a man torn to shreds might look like came to my mind.

The Enchanted Wood, though a very generic and almost fairy-tale name, was well known to the people of the Dream Lands. Of all the places in all realities that might touch the Dream Lands, they only touched in the Enchanted Wood. It would be the only place for anything to cross between the two. That included Dreamers. Most Dreamers entered the Dream Lands through the Enchanted Wood, and it was mostly safe as long as you stayed on the trail.

It was when someone strayed from the trails that they encountered the violent species native to the Enchanted Wood.

Normally, Zoogs were small creatures, only barely larger than rats, with large eyes and gaping mouths of too-many teeth. They have hands and can use weapons, but rarely need them. Mostly hairless, they stick to the forest and act like piranhas when something ventures too far from the path.

"If someone has discovered how to collect that specific fungus then they are someone who has learned to avoid or perhaps repel the zoog." Madame Skai seemed almost impressed. "They would be someone of great power."

It was at that moment when Camilla returned. She wore a buttoned shirt and slacks. It was a very different look than what she had on previously, but at least she was in something more practical and with less blood.

"Does the name Lumley mean anything to you?" I asked Skai.

Her eyes lit up at the name. "Perhaps Clark Lumley?" She shook her head. "Navigating outside of the path of the Enchanted Wood is beyond him. He is a weak dreamer at best, and mostly dreams to paint with the moving pigments from the markets in Hatheg. He's a simple-minded artist. Murder seems beneath him."

I shrugged. "Either way, we think he might know something. Do you know where we could find him?"

She nodded. "Sometimes he comes here to do his dreaming, but mostly he prefers the apartment he lets above the Rawlik Pharmacy."

Camilla touched my arm. "I know where that is."

We thanked Madame Skai and returned to the truck.

CHAPTER 3

"I want you to stay in the car."

"That is not the way this is going to go, Andrew." Camilla shook her head. "As soon as you leave, I will be right behind you."

"No," I shook my head and wanted to say more but she cut me off.

"If this is about protecting me, then you can put that right out the window, sir." She was getting heated. "I might be a woman, but I am not some delicate flower. Might I remind you that I only recently discovered the body of a man who was very dear to me and have managed to take the majority of tonight's revelations without going faint or weeping uncontrollably? Perhaps you would do well to remember that."

A sigh escaped my lips and it was obvious she didn't like that.

"Because you do not know me, I understand why

you would think that. You don't know me, though, and you don't know that most of the fights that I have been in have been with warrior women by my side. What they had that you do not, and the only reason that I am asking you to stay in the car, is a gun."

Camilla's grin was attempting to offend me. "No worries." She pulled a small pistol from the pocket of her trousers. "Your psychic friend loaned me this."

I rolled my eyes. "Let's go then."

We were two steps from the car when a man in a thick coat and stocking cap burst from the door that led to the apartments above the Rawlik Pharmacy.

He was backing out and aiming a shotgun at the entrance.

"No, you beasties," he shouted. "Back! Leave me be." He fired twice. That was when I realised it was a double-barrel shotgun, as he had to stop and reload after the second shot. His fear made him clumsy, and he took longer to load the gun than he should have.

The appearance of the man and his gun made Camilla and I dive back behind the truck.

"Clark Lumley?" I shouted from the relative safety behind the truck. "Are you Clark Lumley?"

My timing was horrible, as he had only just snapped the shotgun closed when I called out. He spun, aiming into the night and too close to our direction for comfort.

"Who are you? Did she send you?"

I decided to try and reason with his logic.

"Look at the truck," I said, hoping he would see the name of the school printed on the side. "We're from the university. I just wanted to ask you some questions."

To his credit and given the circumstances that Camilla and I had walked in on, Lumley's face was filled with confusion, and I couldn't blame him. A noise from the doorway, something like a cat trying to talk, drew Lumley's attention again.

He spun back toward the doorway.

"No! Get back!" He fired the gun again.

Something in the dark leapt out at Lumley while he tried again to reload. It hit him square in the chest and drove him to the ground.

It was too dark to make out what it was, but it wasn't much bigger than a cat.

When Lumley hit the pavement, his shotgun clattered away. Camilla and I both took that moment to run to the man's side.

We hadn't taken a step when the thing on his chest saw us and darted away into the night.

We took positions on each side of him. Large swaths of flesh had been torn from his neck and chest. His shirt was in tatters. Blood poured from his neck. He didn't have long.

"What did this?" I demanded.

Blood bubbled on his lips as he answered, "She did." He said it but he wasn't looking at Camilla. Then he noticed her for what seemed like the first time.

"Who is she?" Camilla demanded. "Did she kill Larry Henton?"

"She controls the zoogs. The people, she sells them to keep her power over the Wood." Blood sprayed from his mouth as he tried to cough. "Power. People for power."

He mumbled something else that I didn't catch and

then he died.

I turned and sprinted after the thing that killed Lumley. I didn't get far before deciding it was too late and that the thing was long gone.

"Did you get that last bit?" I asked when I returned. "What did he say?"

"River," Camilla had tears on her face. "He said something about a river."

I touched her shoulder.

"What is going on?" Her question was aimed at no one. "Why is all of this happening?"

My voice was soft. "I don't know yet, but I think something is beginning to make itself clearer. Can you wait in the truck? I want to go look in his apartment."

I helped her up, and this time she gave no arguments about waiting as she climbed back into the truck.

The apartment was a mess in the way that every painter's studio has papers and paints and whatever strewn about. I didn't expect to find much, but within minutes I had located a bag with a palm-sized glass jar of purple powder.

To be certain, I had to tear newspaper from the window to hold it up to the small bit of light the moon was shining onto Arkham.

It sparkled like broken glass.

When I climbed back into the truck, Camilla looked angry and her eyes were dry. She held Madame Skai's pistol in her hand tight enough to make her knuckles white.

"How are you doing?" I asked. It was a dumb question, but it was the kind of question that you couldn't avoid asking.

"I am ready to put an end to this zoog woman."

I wasn't about to correct her on how this wasn't a zoog woman so much as a person who controlled zoogs.

"Me too," I said. "Take us to the boat house."

It was about twenty minutes later when we pulled into the docks along the Miskatonic River that gave the school its name.

The boat house that Camilla was taking us to had a police car with two officers inside parked out front.

I didn't want to get their attention, so I circled the truck around and went to the far end of the docks and buildings before I found a Marsh Shipping warehouse. I left Camilla in the car as I ran inside and then ran right back to the truck.

Then I returned to a clever spot in the shadows not far from the boat house we wanted to get inside.

"What was that about? What's going on?" Camilla asked.

I couldn't have given a better answer than the resulting explosion that destroyed the Marsh Shipping warehouse.

We watched as the cops radioed and then took off toward the fire.

"That should buy us some time," I said.

"Time for what?" Her voice got quieter. "I don't know that I want to go back in there."

"If we want to figure any of this out, you are going to have to." I expected her to be hesitant. I was and I hadn't even known the reporter. "After everything that we have seen tonight, I think that in there is not only the answer to who murdered Larry but also the solution to getting rid of Fung in Arkham. Your next byline will be about how Larry Henton died solving the biggest drug case in Arkham history."

That got her out of the truck. With only minor prodding, she directed me back into the building the same way that she had exited.

It was clever of her and also surprising that she hadn't been caught. The end of the boat house was open to the river. She had used the panelling on the walls to shimmy around the outside and to the shore, never touching the river. If the police had thought to circle the building, she would never have gotten away.

Once we were inside, the carnage was clearly visible. Whatever had happened to Larry, it looked like he had exploded. His parts and fluids covered almost everything.

Camilla gasped before clenching her jaw and taking shallow breaths.

"If I gave you some really weird stuff to focus on, would that help?"

Camilla closed her eyes and sighed as if she were dealing with an especially tiring toddler. "I don't think that it could hurt."

The boat house had two bays open to the river with platforms surrounding each area where boats should have been but weren't. We were on the left platform if you were looking out at the river from the front of the boat house.

The side opposite us, further back and closer to the river, looked to be where the police had removed whatever larger pieces of Larry had still existed. Even from across the boat house, I could see the small dry spot that must have been where Camilla had woken up.

"Weird stuff, right," I said distractedly as I took the scene in. "So, when someone enters the Dream Lands, they almost always enter through the Enchanted Wood."

Camilla nodded and we started to move deeper into the building. "Both Skai and Lumley mentioned it. What do you mean by 'almost always'?"

I shrugged, but she was too distracted to see it. "There are infinite means to enter infinite realities. I'm mostly hedging my bets." That wasn't a lie to comfort her, either. There was a time when I would use the power of different peoples to call upon the Night Gaunts to take me into the Dream Lands. When I did that, I never stepped into the Enchanted Woods. Camilla didn't need to know about Night Gaunts. Not today anyway.

"The Enchanted Wood is the dream that everyone recognizes. Built from our fantasies and stories, or maybe our fantasies come from it. Either way, that makes it the most real place in the Dream Lands." We were moving slowly toward where Larry's body had been found. That was where we would find our answers. "The Enchanted Wood is real enough that it has been known to touch our reality, creating rare places where things can cross from the Dream Lands to our world."

That made Camilla's eyes grow wide. "Things can come here?"

Nodding, I continued explaining. "The Dream Lands are home to the things of our nightmares, too. We don't want those things on our side." I shiver ran down my spine as I thought about my recent encounter with a god of nightmares. He could summon those same nightmares directly from the Dream Lands and the entire world almost fell to him. "That's why these places that touch the Enchanted Wood stay unknown. Sometimes the best defence is not knowing you need one." I took a deep breath. "Except, I think Larry found one."

"Here." It wasn't a question. Camilla had reached the same conclusion.

"Lumley said that someone was controlling zoogs. Zoogs only exist in the Enchanted Wood. Sometime between your dinner and when you woke up, this person, the one who provides the Fung, met you both here. She somehow knocked you both out and-"

"Brought zoogs here to kill Larry," she finished my sentence. "What is a zoog that it can do this?" We had finally reached where she had woken up. She was right in that this looked like more carnage than anything should be able to create. Zoogs weren't just anything, though.

"Zoogs are usually cat-sized with tentacles and teeth for a mouth. They don't hunt people but have been known to eat them. Elder zoogs can get big, but most don't live long enough to get that size. Not to mention the political ramifications if the cats learn that the zoogs are killing outside of the Wood."

"Cats?" I was only confusing her again.

"Never mind," I said. Then I pulled out Lumley's bottle.

"We're here to answer what the second thing is that I know about messages from the Dream Lands."

Camilla had mostly forgotten about the conversation, but at my reminder, her eyes lit up.

"Oh, right! What is it?"

"The second thing that I know about sending messages from the Dream Lands is that they don't generally send them to us about things happening in our world. So, if you were told in a dream to come and seek me out, it probably wasn't about what you woke up to. Not directly."

"Something is happening in the Dream Lands." Camilla put it together.

"Bingo," I confirmed and then held up the jar. "We would normally mix this with water, I think, but I didn't bring anything that didn't taste like river."

The journalist held out her palm and I poured an unspecified amount of the powder into it. I poured the same amount into my own palm and looked at Camilla.

The woman who had only recently been woken up to the horrific mess of her dismembered boyfriend and had seen horrors beyond human understanding this same evening didn't hesitate to pour the powder into her mouth. She started chewing and then gagged.

"Don't chew it."

That woman was either going to go insane or was made of stronger stuff than most of humanity.

I poured the powder into my own mouth and coughed at the taste. It was surprisingly moist for what seemed like entirely dry dust. The taste was the worst. I imagined that the waste product of a golem of earth and rot would taste similar.

"Hold my hand," I told her. "We should enter at the same place as long as we're together.

CHAPTER 4

It wasn't long before we were asleep and in the Dream Lands. I could only assume that Fung put us to sleep and that the particles of the plant it was created from used our brains as a way of trying to return to the reality that they preferred. Or, maybe it was magic. I don't know.

We stood in a dark forest that I knew had to be the Enchanted Wood. Camilla still held my hand and was examining the path that we stood on. It was a dirt path that seemed entirely out of place in the very green and dark place.

I turned around and directed Camilla to do the same.

Behind us was a window into the real world. This was the place where the Enchanted Wood touched Arkham and through it, we could see our sleeping bodies lying on the floor of the boat house.

We turned back to the path and I let Camilla's hand go.

"Whatever you do, stay on the path."

Camilla nodded before mouthing, "Zoogs."

Aside from the fear of dismemberment at the alien hands of cat-like creatures, it was almost fun seeing the light and excitement mixed with curiosity that was Camilla discovering an alien reality for the first time.

It made me miss being that blissfully ignorant.

We started down the path, but we didn't make it a hundred yards when we came across a camp just off the path. The fire was lit and it burned every colour and more. There was a small tent, but we could not see anyone.

Given the events of the evening, I had a decent idea of who owned the campsite.

"Hello to camp," I spoke.

Inside the tent, I heard a familiar voice curse.

"Merde! You took your sweet time, American."

From the tent crawled a dark-skinned Frenchman named Leo Dubois.

We pulled each other into a tight hug and then stepped back.

"Camilla, this is my friend, Leo. He sent you the message."

She shook his hand and remained quiet. She seemed surprised to see a person here. Or, I realised, she was seeing her last shred of hope that the voice in her dreams had only been a figment of her mind. Now, everything that had happened was becoming more and more terrifyingly real.

"I am glad that you came," Leo said. "Someone has been using the Dream Lands to traffic dreamers."

"Dreamers?" Camilla asked.

"People like Lumley and Madame Skai," I answered. "Folks who do this regularly enough to not need chemicals all of the time." I turned my attention back to Leo. "That ties into what we've been seeing." Then I filled my old friend in on all the events that had led us to his camp.

"Our culprit gives this powder to children, then takes

them when they get here. To what end?" Leo asked.

"A man that we think was involved," I said, "Clark Lumley, said that it was to gain power over the zoogs."

"And you believed him?" Leo looked unconvinced.

"We watched one kill him," Camilla's voice was barely audible.

Leo cursed again. "Stupid! If the cats believed the zoogs were being organised, or worse, weaponized, there would be war. The war would be too big for only one world."

"The cats?" Camilla asked.

Leo gave his most gentle smile. "Sorry, mademoiselle. The cats and zoogs are natural enemies. In the Dream Lands, they are, er ... chattier than in your reality."

"I think they want to exercise that control in our world. Some have already crossed over." I told him.

Leo shook his head in disbelief.

"How did you find out about the people being traded?" Camilla asked.

"My daughter," Leo said. "She is what is known here as a timeless child. Sometimes, children born in the Dream Lands get her condition. Time does not affect her, or perhaps it affects her too much. She travels to Ulthar for treatment. The cats hold timeless children in high regard. They found a lost soul during a raid and he spoke to them about what had happened. Naturally, he knew nothing about what was really happening, but the cats are clever. They asked my girl to pay attention. She told me and together we tracked down three people we think were trafficked." He waved at us. "And now we know how."

"Do you know who it could be?" I asked.

Leo frowned. "No, but whoever it is must be from your world or our psychics would have found her."

Camilla's mind had turned away from the alien environment and the horrors of the night and I could see the journalist working hard behind her eyes.

"Lumley said something about a river right before she died. Does that mean anything to you?

"The only river-" Leo stopped abruptly. "What was that?"

A mix of hisses and growls came from the shadows of the forest around us.

At the same time, all of us said, "Zoogs."

Leo spun back to his tent and dove inside. When he came back out, he was carrying a turquoise-coloured whip.

"I can hold them off, but you must go," Leo said. "If what you say is true, your bodies are unprotected."

"Quickly," I said to my friend. "The river?"

Camilla was pulling on my arm to leave as Leo said it quickly to me. I almost didn't catch it, yet once my mind had understood what he said, everything became clearer.

Over our shoulders, I heard Leo shouting at us. "Stick to the path! Even enthralled, they will not want to touch it."

Zoogs leapt at us as we cut through the bush and back to the path.

I could tell when Camilla finally got her first good look at one because her gasp was almost a scream.

The creatures, small though they were, were the

most real monster that she had ever seen. Their mouths of tentacles and teeth, their human eyes and hands, and the wild look in their eyes was all something that was both foreign and familiar to her.

It was terrifying.

As spectacularly scary as it was, I had no fear for my friend's safety. A former soldier of the French Resistance and a man who had spent who-knew-how-many nights in the Enchanted Woods, he was more than capable of surviving.

Fear of the path or not, Leo hadn't been correct about the zoogs not attacking us on the path. Only that they didn't plan on touching it.

Camilla and I were ducking and diving just to stop the zoogs that had learned to jump from leaping across the path and onto us. We had no weapons here and avoidance was our best option.

Finally, we saw the window onto the boat house. We ran and dove through it.

We woke up next to each other and still holding hands.

We were surrounded by zoogs. Legions of them were in the boat house, standing on every surface and staring at us with an unmatched hunger.

They weren't moving.

Camilla was the first to talk.

"Why aren't they attacking?"

"Because," I answered, "she's showboating."

"Who?" Camilla hadn't heard the last piece of the puzzle that Leo had provided. She hadn't been able to piece the entire tableau together.

"I should have seen it sooner," I said. "How did someone so stupid get a doctorate in anthropology? If Leo hadn't told me, I would never have pieced it together."

"Told you what?" Camilla was getting frustrated.

"That the only river that runs through the Enchanted Wood-

"-is the River Skai." Madame Skai walked in from the door we had chosen to ignore on our way in.

Camilla was so confused and shocked at the same time that she was stuttering.

"Y-you? Why?"

Skai shrugged. "Fortune-telling doesn't quite pay like I hoped that it would. Our dear Mr Lumley made a comment about how well my powders would sell if I found the right buyers. At first, it was going well, but then demand went up and I needed a way to get the fungus I needed that wasn't as dangerous. Travelling to the Dream Lands once every few months was one thing, but more was too dangerous."

"Too dangerous unless you can control the zoogs," I said.

Skai nodded. "I knew of this place from years ago." She sighed. "Time is different there. I spent six years there before I found a man in the southern sea who knew how to repel them. When I returned, only a night had passed."

"You control them, you don't repel them," Camilla noticed.

"The slave trader in Illarnek told me that I could bend them to my will and that he could provide me with that power," Skai continued. "I only needed to provide him with slaves that had no traceable connections. People from here that no one over there would miss." She raised her wrist and showed a bracelet made of black wood. "And for that, he would give me this."

All of this was nonsense and a waste of time, in my opinion. I was more concerned with whether she planned on using the zoogs to eliminate two other witnesses.

"What is your real name?" I demanded.

Madame Skai rolled her eyes and crossed her arms. She still wore the thin black clothes and looked like an annoyed teacher at an all-vampire school.

"How can you, of all people, ask me such a boring question?" She forced a smile. "I would like to thank you, though, Andrew. When Lumley squealed to that reporter, it wasn't easy to get him here. I had to drug Ms Rhodes and then let the zoogs take care of him. One short phone call later and she was wanted for his murder." She mocked a shocked look. "Arkham's most famous reporter and then the former Dean of Miskatonic University? It would seem that we have a habitual killer on our hands."

"You monster!" Camilla was shouting. Likely in some hopeful attempt to get the attention of the police.

Except, I had given them something else to worry about.

Skai waved her hand at Camilla. "Scooch closer, darling. It will sell better if you're covered in his blood, too. I mean you're already wearing his clothes. Remember those, Andrew? The night you left them at my place?" She laughed at our futility. "I wonder what the papers will say. Woman Twice Scorned Murders Two?" She nodded. "I like that."

Whether the death all around her, the monsters from other dimensions, the magics, the horror, the long night, or all of it, Camilla finally snapped.

It was as if she could no longer see the dozens of zoogs or the mad psychic with her magic bracelet. She raised her pistol, the one given to her by Madame Skai to endear her to the woman, and she ran at the witch.

Every step she took, she pulled the trigger.

I was taken by surprise almost as much as Madame Skai had been. Skai let out a yelp of pain and surprise as a bullet hit her leg. She thrust her hand at Camilla.

The zoogs rushed us.

Back in my own body, I had my gun with me. The zoogs didn't care about me, so I fired on them without any concerns. This freed up Camilla and she was free to continue firing on Skai.

Skai was riddled with holes but was somehow still standing.

Camilla finally reached her and tackled Skai to the ground. The gun was just clicking now as the hammer had no bullets to fire. Camilla never stopped attacking. When she realised that the gun was empty, Camilla began using it to hit Skai. The zoogs had thinned out and I wasn't going to try and stop Camilla.

That was when I noticed the cats.

First, there were only one or two on the rafters. Then they were swarming in through every entrance. They were a wave of murder that crashed onto the zoog shore.

Claws and fur and flesh flew everywhere. The zoogs

got a few good hits in, but they were outnumbered.

It was at that point when, bracelet or not, the zoogs decided to retreat. They grabbed at Skai from under Camilla and dragged her away. The cats halted their attack at the first sign of zoog surrender and we all watched as the monsters dragged their controller toward the wall and then faded from our reality.

As if by design, the black bracelet didn't go with Skai. It clattered to the floor when she had completely faded.

When the zoogs were gone, the cats slipped away and back into the night taking the corpses of allies and enemies with them.

Camilla was gasping and grunting for air as her shock and panic tried to make sense of where she was. I took the pistol away from her and pulled her into my arms where she finally let her emotions catch up to her.

The next day was filled with surprises.

The fire at the Marsh Shipping warehouse had claimed multiple buildings.

Oops.

It went all the way to an abandoned boat house.

The papers claimed that Larry Henton had died in an evening car accident on his way to pick up his girlfriend for an evening out.

When the police had shown up to the boat house, they found Madame Skai's name carved into the wood near Larry's graphic death.

When they arrived at Madame Skai's business and home, they would find a confession in both Larry's death and Clark Lumley's.

I didn't know what to say about how they died, so I added a line about taking her pet tiger, Felix, with her and running away.

When Camilla saw the police next, she asked if it was alright if she spared Larry's family the horrible news of his death and wrote about a car accident instead.

The police prefer nice stories that make sense in Arkham, especially when they offer to write themselves.

I waited a few days before going to check on Camilla. For obvious reasons, she wasn't quite ready to talk to me. She was alright, though. As far as I could tell, all of her horrific things, at least the ones from outside of normalcy, had been shoved somewhere deep inside Camilla, and she was better for it.

I was going to keep an eye on her, at least from a distance. I knew, better than anyone, that the horrible parts of the world, this one or the others, couldn't be buried forever. When it did come out, and Camilla was torn by her tragedy or forged into a terror of her own, I would be there.

Matthew Davenport hails from Des Moines, Iowa where he lives with his wife, Ren, and daughter, Willow. When his scattered author brain isn't earning weird looks from the ladies of his life, he enjoys reading sci-fi and horror, tinkering with electronics, and doing escape rooms.

Matt is the author of the **Andrew Doran** series, the Broken Nights series (along with his brother, Michael), The Trials of Obed Marsh, and Satan's Salesman among other titles.

He's also a self-styled student of the Cthulhu Mythos and exercises that influence in his stories and as an editor at the blog Shoggoth.net

You can keep track of Matthew through his twitter account @spazenport.

You can also support him and get regular chapter and novel postings at
http://patreon.com/matthewdavenport

THE HORROR OF ANGOVE HALL
TIM MENDEES

As a thick London Particular coiled around the intermittent electric lighting lining the Embankment, I freely admit to feeling a twinge of apprehension. It had been two months since I had last heard from Carnacki, and the card inviting me to dinner had caught me somewhat off-guard. It wasn't what was written on the card that gave concern, nor the late hour of its arrival, instead, it was the way in which it had been written. Normally so precise in his handwriting, my friend's script had become a barely legible scrawl. It was as though written with a tremulous hand, which in itself was troubling. Carnacki was never one to suffer from an attack of the nerves, even when confronted by those things he dubbed the *abnatural*.

Approaching 427, Cheyne Walk, I gave three sharp raps with the wrought iron knocker. As the door opened, I was cheered to see that the other guests, Taylor, Arkright and Jessop, had already arrived and were waiting in the foyer for our esteemed host. As it happened, we didn't have long to wait. Carnacki appeared on the landing almost instantly and after a minimal greeting, ushered us up the stairs and through to the dining room, as was his way.

As was traditional on these occasions, he breathed not a word about his recent escapades while we tucked into succulent helpings of grouse. Knowing our host's ways, none of us broached the subject, and instead chatted amiably about current events and the new shotgun that Arkright had purchased for hunting. It was a perfectly relaxed meal, yet I couldn't shake my gnawing unease. Though outwardly fine, Carnacki's eyes seemed to have lost some of their lustre. The sharpness that defined them was somehow dulled and he appeared nervous, at one point flinching when Taylor dropped his knife against the side of his plate. He seemed, for want of a better term, haunted.

After the plates were cleared, it was at last time to find out what had kept our host so busy over the intervening weeks since our last soiree. I freely confess to being on tenterhooks. Following tradition, we furnished ourselves with wine and cigars then made ourselves comfortable in our favourite spots while he filled his pipe and got settled into his big chair. Once he had inhaled a lungful, Carnacki wet his lips with a mouthful of brandy, sat back in his seat, and began.

"Over the past few weeks, I have been engaged in a case that, I confess, has had me in something of a funk. It has taken me the best part of a month of research to mentally recover from an encounter with a force so malevolent that should it be unleashed on the world, I fear madness and destruction would follow in its wake. The implications of this latest escapade are wide-reaching, and I thought it wise to find out as much as I could about the threat before returning home.

"It all started one evening in late September. I had dined at a private club in Pall Mall and as I was leaving, I ran into an old acquaintance, a Naval officer by the name of Tremayne. I was cheered to see him after so many years so I readily agreed to join him in the bar. We had been thrown together during a case involving a haunting at a sea fort many years ago. It was one of my first cases and he proved to be a superb ally. His keen analytical mind was the anchor I needed as I attempted to navigate the stormy seas of the uncanny.

"We chatted about his career and, after our tongues had been loosened by the warming liquor, moved on to some of my more memorable cases. He sat quietly as I regaled him with the story of the Invisible Horse, hanging on my every word. It was clear to me that this case, above all others, had piqued his interest. When I had concluded my narrative, the cause of his rapture became clear.

"'An interesting tale,' he began, 'that puts me in mind of a conversation I recently conducted at a charity ball in Boscastle, Cornwall. Tell me, are you acquainted with Colonel Arthur Angove?' I couldn't say that I was, leading Tremayne to explain that the Colonel was the owner of Angove Hall outside the village of Hollowhills on Bodmin Moor and that, of late, his home had been plagued by disturbances along the same lines of the Phantom Horse of Hisgins. Unexplained presences charging up and down the corridors, strange sounds in the walls, you understand?

"Tremayne took a sip of brandy and a puff on his cigar before explaining that the disturbances started in late spring during the renovation of a cottage on the manor grounds. Colonel Angove's daughter was with child and due any moment. Her husband, a Major in the Army, was away on a tour of duty so Mrs Angove thought it best to have her within earshot, as it were, in the event of any complications. It certainly made more sense than to have her rattling around their draughty London townhouse at the mercy of the hired help.

"In any case, during the renovation work, a mummified cat was discovered in the foundations of the dilapidated cottage by a couple of local labourers. When they informed the Colonel's eldest son, Eugene, of their grisly discovery, he told them to get rid of it. The men protested, talking of witchcraft and other such notions to which the young man was dismissive. In the end, he removed it himself and deposited the desiccated moggy in the gardener's incinerator atop a pyre of burning privet clippings.

"This concluded Tremayne's introduction to the horrors that had beset Angove Hall since the removal of the feline remains. I confess that my interest had peaked since the first mention of the late animal. I have heard of this singular tradition being practised in many places in West Suffolk as a kind of defence against witchcraft. Though, I had never heard any mention of this being enacted as far West as Cornwall and hitherto thought it a curious local custom borne of hysteria following the Bury St Edmunds witch trials of 1645.

"In regard to the mummified felines, it was believed that the unfortunate creature, when walled up in the foundation, acted as a guardian against those practising the dark arts and can ward off the *evil eye*. Many local manor houses and public buildings in the Suffolk area are said to have taken this precaution through fear of reprisals from beyond the grave from those executed on Thingoe Hill. Indeed, a public house in Bury St Edmunds found one such sacrifice while undertaking expansion work in the cellar. The cat was removed and now hangs in a small curiosity shop at the end of The Traverse. As an interesting side note, the public house in question is now believed to be haunted by a grey lady. Make of that what you will.

"When Tremayne had concluded his narrative, he asked if it would be a case that I would consider investigating. I readily accepted. The presence of the cat in a county so far removed from Suffolk, together with his description of the nocturnal disturbances sounded like something I could really get my teeth into. I was in the process of making certain adjustments to my electric pentangle, and I had been itching for an opportunity to test my equipment. The way he had described the phenomena made it seem like nobody was in any immediate danger making it the perfect time for a test run, as it were. As it turns out, we were both misguided on that assumption.

"Upon leaving the club, I told Tremayne to put Colonel Angove in contact with me and I would make preparations. This he did with alacrity and by the first week of October, I was on a train Westbound from London. I took an overnight train on the Great Western, knowing that the journey would be long and dreary. Angove Hall is in an isolated spot high on the moors near a small mining village. No trains go anywhere near it so I had to leave the relative comfort of the railway at Truro and then take a coach to Betyls Cove, the closest town, where I would wait at a local Inn to be met by his son, Eugene.

"It was a stormy Wednesday when I arrived in that small fishing town and my spirits were instantly dampened by the driving rain and bitter winds whipping in off the Celtic Sea. I had the coachman deposit me and my trunk of equipment outside the Ancient Mariner, a former coaching Inn on the esplanade, as directed. I found myself around an hour early for my rendezvous, so I hastened inside, ordered a rather pleasant local ale and awaited the arrival of one Eugene Angove.

"First impressions are important, and I am rarely wrong when judging character. To say that I was less than impressed with the eldest of the Angove offspring, would be a great understatement. For starters, the man was over an hour late and appeared to have been drinking. His ruddy cheeks and glassy eyes certainly hinted that he had been imbibing something far stronger than apple juice. The dark circles around his eyes told me that he was a man familiar with burning the midnight oil.

"Eugene Angove stood around six feet tall and was dressed in an ill-fitting tweed suit. He looked uncomfortable in the garment. I later found out that his mother had insisted he wears one of his father's cast-offs in an attempt to make a good impression. As a student of archaeology, he practically lived in unpressed linen and mud-caked boots.

"Holding out a clammy paw he introduced himself and enquired whether I'd had a pleasant journey thus far before starting to carry my bags out to his conveyance. The horses stamped impatiently while Eugene made a meal of securing my trunk to the rear shelf of the carriage. It was a cramped affair that was in dire need of essential maintenance. I later learned that this was Eugene's personal vehicle and that he showed it about as much care as he gave to his appearance. We barely exchanged a handful of words as he thundered around the narrow cobbled streets. Soon, we were leaving the relative civilisation of Betyls Cove and climbing the winding lanes onto Bodmin Moor."

Carnacki paused to relight his pipe with a smouldering Lucifer. Once the ember was glowing nicely, he took a series of deep inhalations and sunk back into the upholstery. This appeared to be his method of coping with what appeared to be a stressful memory.

"Angove drove like a blasted lunatic," he exclaimed, showing rather more emotion than we were accustomed to, "by the time we reached the ornate iron gates separating the road from Angove Hall, my nerves were shot. I'm not usually given to bouts of travel sickness, as you well know, but the way he threw the carriage around the tight bends had me feeling sick to my stomach. Angove stuck two fingers into his maw and gave a shrill wolf whistle. It was answered by a stout-looking groundsman who appeared from a nearby shrub clutching a pair of rusty secateurs. The gate groaned and grumbled as the man swiftly drew back the latch and drew the left-hand gate inwards to allow us ingress.

"If I thought the worst of the ordeal was over, I was sadly mistaken. The driveway was riddled with holes making the remainder of our journey punishing on the posterior, to say the least. The leather seats were cracked and had lost most of their padding, meaning that we were in essence sitting on a wooden plank. One plus to the fellow's reckless driving style was that we were in the yard in no time. Well-manicured lawns, vibrant flower beds, and impressively-sculpted hedges passed in a blur as we rattled on towards our final destination.

"Drawing the cart to a halt in the yard to the western side of the hall next to the stables, Eugene clapped me on the shoulder with a bulky paw and motioned for me to alight. I must say, it was a blessed relief to climb down onto solid ground and stretch the kink from my spine. Angove hopped down, grinning inanely, and was met by a tired-looking valet of advanced years and a rosy-cheeked footman.

"'Take Mr Carnacki's luggage through to the guest room, Barker, there's a good chap,' he directed to the youngster before turning to the valet. "'I dare say our guest is in need of a brandy, Andrews, I know I am!'

"The valet looked to me for confirmation, I readily nodded my approval to this notion. As you know, I like to keep a clear head while investigating the uncanny, but I judged these to be special circumstances. The long journey coupled with the foul weather and Eugene Angove's sloppy navigation skills had left me weary, do you understand?

"'Come along, dear fellow,' Eugene grinned, directing me to the tradesman's entrance to the side of the hall. 'Father will be in his study, fretting over curses and whatnot. I swear he gets dafter by the day. Andrews, go up and tell the old devil that his esteemed guest has arrived. I'll take him through to the drawing room and sort us both out with a tipple.'

"Andrews nodded, rolled his eyes when he knew

Eugene wasn't looking and scuttled off up the cramped staircase just inside the hall. I was impressed, the old gent displayed a nimbleness I would scarcely have expected from one of his age. When he was out of earshot, I turned to Eugene and raised an eyebrow. 'Am I to take it from your comments that you don't believe anything is amiss here at the hall?'

"'No, it's just a load of local twaddle, if you ask me. They're a superstitious bunch around here. They are full of yarns about witches, sirens, and little people in the hills. Spend an hour in any of the taverns in the area and you'll soon have your fill of spooks and spectres. You should have heard some of the cussings when I burned that wretched cat. Up in ruddy arms, they were. By the way they acted, you'd reckon I'd just set fire to their grandmother's undergarments... The daft lot.'

"'Have you not experienced any of the phenomena your Father recorded in his missive?'

"Eugene shrugged and held the door leading to the grand staircase and entrance hall. 'All I've *experienced* is some blasted rats in the walls, scurrying about in the dead of night, making a right ruckus. If you ask me, you've been led on a wild goose chase. I reckon we stirred up a nest doing the renovation work on the old cottage and they have moved inside to get out of the way of the workers. One of the Irish chaps we have working for us lopped one clean in half with a shovel. Big bugger, it was too. To my mind, there's nothing supernatural about any of it. Just nature doing what nature does.'

"'And what is that?' I asked.

"'Whatever it bloody well likes!' Eugene guffawed

~368~

and directed me towards a door that hung to the left of the stairs. 'In there. I'll go and fetch a bottle of the good stuff, we don't want any of that swill Father keeps in the decanter for when the vicar pays us a visit. The only thing that's good for is getting the bird muck off the South-facing windows.'

"Portraits of Angoves' past leered down at me from fading paintings as I skirted a mighty aspidistra on my way to the drawing room. All of the men had been painted in a uniform of some sort. Evidently, they were one of the families that had served the crown for generations. One couldn't help but speculate that Eugene was bucking a trend by following an academic path and wondered how this would affect his relationship with Colonel Angove. It was at that moment that I entertained the possibility of Eugene Angove being something of a black sheep.

"Stepping into the drawing-room, I was instantly hit by a disquieting feeling. This was strange as the lavish surroundings should have put me at ease. It was a light and airy room with a fire crackling in the grate of a grand fireplace. Above it hung a portrait of the current lord of the manor, looking resplendent in his dress uniform. The furnishing consisted of a collection of antique wing-back chairs and tables that blended nicely with the oak panelling. A vase of fresh flows sitting atop a decorative lace doily added to the overall homely feeling. It was a lovely room and yet I felt the crawl of some malign force. I shook myself to try and rid myself of these feelings, put it down to my general malaise, and turned my attention to the décor.

"As I gazed half-aware at the paintings of the local

area that adorned the south-facing wall opposite the two bay windows, I was again aware of a presence. This time, I was in no doubt that I was indeed being observed. A scuffle to my left alerted me to its source. There was something behind the panelling. Crouching down onto my haunches, I searched for an opening that could have been used by a furtive rodent. There was none. I had started to tap along the wood with my knuckle when Eugene Angove returned.

"'I see you've met our furry friends?' He asked as he strode past me to the drinks globe that sat next to the fireplace. Producing a couple of glasses from the shelf below, he proceeded to pour me a generous measure, and himself an even larger one. 'Blasted pests,' he continued as he took a sip and brought mine over to me. 'No offence meant, but father would have been better off calling that piper chap from Hamelin than your good self. He'd have had more joy, I'd wager. Here, this will see you right.'

"'Thank you,' I muttered as I stood up and took the drink. I had quickly realised that I wasn't going to get much in the way of useful information out of Eugene in relation to the disturbances, so I decided to change tack. 'So, how is your sister? Is the baby due soon?'

"'Due? It's already bloody arrived. Did father not tell you? She popped the little perisher out three nights since!'

"'That's no way to speak about your nephew," a voice boomed from the doorway. It was Colonel Angove looking red in the face, his mighty moustache aflutter. As he marched into the room to confront his son, I was struck by the facial similarity between the duo, they even had matching luggage under their eyes. Clearly, the elder Angove hadn't been sleeping soundly of late either. 'Drinking already, are you? Isn't it a bit early... even for you?'

"Eugene shrugged, this was obviously an oft-repeated rebuke. 'I was getting one for our guest, he's had a long journey. It seemed rude not to join him.'

"'I'll bet,' Colonel Angove harrumphed before lifting his frown and greeting me warmly with a firm handshake. 'Mr Carnacki, my dear fellow. Thank you for coming all this way. I fear things have *escalated* somewhat over the last couple of days.' At this point, Eugene gave a snort of derision that drew the ire of my host. 'Pay no attention to this lout, Mr Carnacki, have you nothing better to do than loaf around making the place look untidy?'

"Eugene bristled, knocking back his drink and charging towards the door. 'Don't worry, Father, I won't keep you from your ghosts and goblins. If you need a break from this lunacy,' he said, addressing me, 'I'll be out at the cottage. Come find me and I'll give you a tour of the local beauty spots... such as The Rat and Raven in Hollowhills.' As his sire gave a sharp intake of breath, he gave me a bawdy wink, grinned, and sloped out of the room, slamming the door in his wake.

"Colonel Angove shook his head. 'I'm sorry, Mr Carnacki, I feel I must apologise for my son. The fellow can be a blithering imbecile at times. I had hoped to straighten him out with a stint in the Army like his brother. Alas, my wife, bless her, talked me into funding his archaeological pursuits instead. Much good it has done him so far. Sadly, he treats University as one long party, he's seldom without a drink in his hand' as he spoke, Colonel Angove had gone over to the drinks globe and poured himself a glass. I had to stifle a grin. I'd wager the two were more similar than either would admit. Probably why they constantly butted heads like a pair of tweed-encased stags.

"I have little interest in family drama, as you know, so I decided to steer the conversation to more pressing matters. 'I believe congratulations are in order, upon your becoming a grandfather?'

"'Indeed. A lively bouncing boy. Did you not get my telegram? I sent it the morning after the birth.'

"'I'm afraid not, Colonel,' I confessed, 'I had taken a trip to Bury St Edmunds to look into the history of mummified cats and witchcraft. From there, I caught the train directly on my return to London. I fancy my housekeeper neglected to put it in my valise.'

Carnacki broke from his narrative to produce a telegram from his inside jacket pocket. He opened it, sniffed, and then passed it to Taylor. Our mutual friend scanned its contents before raising a startled eyebrow at Carnacki.

"As you can see, it's a shame I hadn't received it. I would have been treating the situation a lot less lightly than I was at that time. I confess that by this point, I was beginning to wonder if Eugene Angove was not indeed correct. The presence of rats and mice can play havoc with one's nerves. This, combined with the birth, would have everyone in a state of high anxiety. Under these circumstances, it is easy to imagine peril and perfidy around every corner. Alas, I was wrong in this assumption, as you will see.

"In the absence of the letter, Colonel Angove proceeded to appraise me of recent events. Thomas Carrington, the new fruit on the family tree, was born at roughly six pm on the Sunday prior to my visit. A midwife from the nearby village had aided the delivery and it went without a hitch. Both mother and child were visited by the local physician and deemed fit and healthy. All was well, so Colonel Angove retired to his study for a brandy to *wet the baby's head*. Exhausted by the birth and by the recent disturbances, he fell into a deep slumber where he found himself in a nightmare which he can't recall. As the grandfather clock in the library chimed for midnight, he was awoken by a blood-curdling scream.

"Leaping from his chair, he charged down the corridor towards his daughter's chamber. Upon reaching it, he barged in, startling Eleanor Angove awake. Confused, he asked if all was well. She assured him it was before falling back into slumber. The doctor had given her a little something to aid her sleep, you understand?

"Angove was on the verge of leaving when he realised that something was missing. The baby. As he moved towards the bed to shake Eleanor awake so he could question her further, a hand fell upon his shoulder. Just about jumping out of his britches, he turned to find his wife, Lady Margaret Angove, looking just as ashen as he was. She too had heard the scream and gone to investigate. Upon inquiring about young Thomas, Lady Angove informed him that Jenny, Eleanor's maid, had taken him to a makeshift nursery they had set up in Eugene's old room so the weary mother could get some well-needed rest.

"The Colonel and Mrs Angove took the corner to the west wing and hurried towards the end room. Around halfway down the corridor, Mrs Angove let out a yelp of alarm, freezing on the spot and clutching her chest. Colonel Angove asked her what was the matter. A sensation akin to a blast of Arctic wind had fallen upon her. She could only describe it as if something had passed through her leaving her with a feeling of emptiness and acute confusion. The Colonel, impatient to discover the source of the scream, gave her his arm and urged her on towards the nursery.

"As they took a step towards their destination, the door crept open without apparent agency. Mrs Angove gasped again and placed a hand on the decorative paper that lined the walls in an effort to steady herself. Faced with inexplicable dizziness, Mrs Angove was unable to continue and, with mounting dread, instructed her husband to continue. This he did. Reaching the door, he recalled sensing *something* on the other side of the oak. He called out for the maid, yet got no reply. Gritting his teeth and steeling his nerves, the old soldier pushed the door open and stepped inside.

"By the column of pale moonlight that flooded from the end gable window, Colonel Angove took in the crib with its precious bundle. On the cusp of breathing a sigh of relief, his eyes followed the path of lambent silver, he found the maid, Jenny, sprawled on the floor in an untidy heap. As one of his slippered feet crossed the threshold into the surprisingly cold room, the walls became alive with the sound of scurrying.

"Colonel Angove struggled to describe the hellish din. He could only compare it to the sound of a hundred rats being chased by a gale-force wind. It started in the far corner of the room, over by the cradle, and spread around all four walls in a matter of heartbeats. The movement manifested itself in a foot-deep wave that Moved swiftly towards him. Raising his hands to ward off the invisible attack, he was knocked off balance by the intensity of the sound as it passed over and through him, leaving him breathless and *empty*. It didn't stop there, however. The ghastly phenomena raced through the door, and towards his nigh-hysterical spouse. As the wave washed over her, she wobbled and slumped against the wall, before sliding down it to a seated position with her head in her hands.

"As you would imagine, Colonel Angove was shaken and in something of a dilemma. He wanted to check on Mrs Angove, but also Jenny and young Thomas. He called out to his wife to ensure she was as well as could be expected and if he should aid the maid and check on the baby first. To her eternal credit, despite, I later learned, feeling as though all life had been sucked from her body, she replied with a simple wave of the hand, directing him to check on Jenny. Feeling some trepidation, he entered the nursery.

"To his relief, Colonel Angove found the baby's chest falling rhythmically and apparently sleeping soundly swaddled in blankets. Jenny, on the other hand, was out cold. The first thing he noticed was her hands. They were outstretched as though trying to cling onto something, presumably the mahogany-framed cot. She looked to have been leaning on the heavy item and then keeled over backwards. Her eyelids fluttered as he crouched down to attempt to rouse her. She made no response to his words, so he decided to lift her head to slide a pillow under it. This is when he discovered the blood.

"The back of Jenny's head looked to have been dealt a heavy blow that had split her scalp. Now, whether this had been done before or after she crumpled to the floor was up for debate. The injury could most certainly have been caused by impact with the bare floorboards, though, Angove suspected that the blow was the cause of the fall in the first place. The Colonel suspected foul play though who could have done such a thing was a mystery. More so than who, was why? What purpose would clubbing a lowly ladies-maid serve to someone with nefarious designs? Nothing had been disturbed, aside from poor Jenny, and, to his knowledge, nothing had been stolen. Still, Angove was now convinced there was an interloper on the premises.

"By now, Mrs Angove had recovered sufficiently to have appeared in the doorway. The Colonel instructed her to take over with Jenny while he went to retrieve his revolver from the study. Faced by what he deemed a tangible threat, Colonel Angove became galvanised into action. As a man with the Army in his blood, strange noises and feelings were things he had no idea how to deal with. A flesh and blood enemy, on the other hand, well... this was his bread and butter. He had felt uncommonly impotent over the weeks leading up to this event, unable to find a rational explanation or to offer any kind of reassurance to his wife and daughter. Now, he'd sort things out with a bullet!."

Carnacki paused in his narrative to finish his glass and reach for the decanter. As he poured himself another measure, I could see that his hands were trembling. My face must have given this knowledge away, as he met my eyes and smiled joylessly. "Of course," he continued, "it wasn't to be that simple."

"Taking his Webley from the upper-left draw of his document-strewn desk, he checked the chambers were loaded before exiting. Upon reaching the landing, he decided to go room by room in pursuit of the phantom intruder. It is worth noting at this juncture that Colonel Angove made no mention of the auditory and spiritual disturbance. I questioned him later as to why this was the case, to which he replied, 'I had convinced myself at the moment that it was all trickery designed to leave us vulnerable.' This made sense that he would think this way, after all, terror tactics have long been a part of the arts of war dating back to the death whistles of the Aztecs.

"Approaching the door nearest to the nursery, a small room cluttered with generations worth of bric-a-brac in dusty boxes, another scream drew his attention to the library on the ground floor. Hurrying along the corridor and down the stairs, he barged into the room, gun drawn, to find his son thrashing around in the camp bed he had set up while his own was used for the newborn. That he had chosen the library over one of the guest rooms is a curious fact that I will return to later.

"Rousing his son from his nightmare, Colonel Angove dragooned Eugene into aiding his search for any ne'er-do-wells. By now, the staff had been awoken and had assembled on the grand staircase looking bewildered. They too were conscripted to their cause. I won't bore you with the details of their exhaustive search, it went on until the cook served breakfast and proved to be utterly fruitless. This concluded Colonel Angove's tale. A repeat of the auditory phenomenon had since occurred every night around the same time and was always followed by Eugene screaming in the library. It seemed that the alcohol and, I later learned, laudanum the young man consumed were not the only cause of the bags under his eyes.

"Before making a start on my investigations, I asked about the maid, Jenny, to which Angove assured me she was well and staying with her parents in the village. No permanent damage had been done but she had been left shaken, as you would expect. She came around with no memory of the events that led to her being rendered unconscious. One moment she was standing at the foot of the crib watching over the child, the next, she was flat on her back with an aching head, staring up at Mrs Angove.

"I thanked the Colonel for his time and advised him to get some rest. I fully intended to put an end to the horrors that plagued Angove Hall and warned him that the next few nights could prove somewhat arduous. He nodded and told me to enlist Andrews to aid in my investigations. The old fellow had been in the family service for generations and what he didn't know about the house and its surroundings wasn't worth knowing.

"I Left the drawing room and interviewed both Mrs

Angove and her daughter. They were unable to add more details than the Colonel had already given; save for one important observation. When the disturbances began, they seemed to encapsulate the fullness of the property. Since the birth, however, they seem to be focussed on the west wing corridor alone. This was troubling news and I feared I had little time to avert an escalation in the troubling events. I immediately sought out Andrews and asked him to lead me to where it all began... the old cottage in the woods."

Carnacki reached into his jacket and produced a series of photographs. As we waited silently, he riffled through them, drawing three and placing the rest face down on the table next to his glass. After scrutinising each one, he passed them to Taylor, telling him to pass them on once he was finished. Each picture showed a densely overgrown wood with a rough track leading to a door. This was the only part of the cottage visible from the garden, and, only because the workers had trampled down the weeds.

"As you can see," Carnacki said once we had all looked at the photographs, "the cottage is aptly named. The juxtaposition between the well-maintained lawns and this area of wilful neglect was startling. Andrews informed me that it was no accident that the cottage was out of view from the house. 'Out of sight, out of mind,' is how he put it. I asked him to explain and was unsurprised to hear that the cottage had been vacant since long before his time. The Angove family put it down to its dilapidated condition but was told by an old woman in Hollowhills when he was a boy that it had a reputation for being haunted.

"The cottage was of early eighteenth-century design, like the rest of the manor and outbuildings. It was originally intended as a gamekeeper or groundsman's cottage but saw extension work not long after the completion to provide a home for a family in service to the Angoves in residence at the time. Sir George Angove, being a man blessed with a charitable disposition, took pity on the couple when the woman, a maid named Susan Mothersole, found herself with child by one of the gardeners. As you would expect, due to the woman being unmarried, there was something of a scandal.

"'Tell me,' I cut in, 'Miss Mothersole wasn't a local, was she?'

"'No, sir,' Andrews replied, 'she had been taken in by the rector of St Mary's in Hollowhills as a girl of around twelve. She was an orphan. How did you know?'

"'The family name, you see? It is local to a small village north of Bury St Edmunds. I came across it while researching the tradition of placing mummified cats in the foundation of houses.'

"'And, you think it was her that entombed the poor creature?'

"'It's certainly possible,' I said before urging him to continue with his tale. Andrews went on to explain that once the rector got wind of a child about to be born outside of wedlock, she found herself out on her ear. Sir George, having lost a daughter to tuberculosis had grown fond of the young lady and decided to step in. All was well until six months after the birth when another young lady appeared on the property. It turned out that Susan Mothersole had an elder sister.

"At this point in the story, details became hazy. All Andrews knew was that there was some kind of tragedy that left Susan Mothersole the sole survivor. She later took her own life. From that moment on, the cottage had remained empty. The locals believed it to be haunted by the wretched girl's restless spirit. When pressed for more details on said tragedy, the valet could only shrug. He was sorry, but that was all that he knew. I made a mental note to visit the library in Betyls Cove before my return to London to see what I could dig up on the subject.

"By now, we had reached the wooded area that bordered the estate. We had been lucky in one respect, the rain had finally stopped. That didn't stop the lawn from becoming a quagmire as we trudged onwards. The bottoms of my trousers were soaked and my shoes were caked in the loamy gleys of Bodmin. Sharp winds cut at our bodies as we approached the foreboding treeline. Ancient yew trees stretched out their tangled limbs like spindly arachnids awaiting a juicy bluebottle. The area had a singular atmosphere. One that seemed to exude malice.

"The door of the cottage stood ajar and the interior was illuminated by the sickly flicker of an oil lamp. The workers hadn't returned since news of what befell Jenny reached the flapping ears and wagging tongues of the denizens of Hollowhills. This left the cottage with one sole occupant, Eugene Angove. From the extension built upon the western side of the property, I could hear the scrape of a trowel against stone and a bawdy sea shanty being delivered with gusto. I looked to Andrews with a bemused expression creasing my features. He returned it with another well-rehearsed rolling of the eyes.

"'Ah, there you are, Carnacki,' Eugene grinned through the dirt that streaked his cheeks, 'I was hoping you would pop by Take a look at this, I think you will find it most interesting.'

"I joined him in the far corner of a cramped room where he was crouched in the exposed foundations clearing soil from around a peculiar piece of architecture that seemed to have nothing at all to do with the stability of the property. At first glance, it looked to be a haphazard arrangement of strangely angled stones, nothing more than discarded building materials. I voiced this observation to Mr Angove.

"'That's what I thought at first,' he admitted, 'but, on closer inspection, it appears to be a tiny room built under the floorboards. Whoever constructed it was no architect, I'll tell you that much. The angles are all *wrong*.'

"'Wrong? What do you mean, *wrong*?'

"Eugene stood and took a dented hip flask from his pocket. The peaty aroma of fine Scotch whiskey escaped from the container as he unscrewed the lid and took a nip. 'Take a look for yourself,' he shrugged, offering me the flask. I abstained. 'Suit yourself. No sane person builds like this. I'm no mathematician, but, I believe they would call it, *non-Euclidean*.'

"I crouched to take a closer look at his excavation. 'Hmm, it certainly is of a strange design. It makes my eyes hurt to look at it.'

"'Indeed. It had been purposefully filled in, with some haste, I will add. Take a look at that,' he pointed to a mound of earth, ashes, and other detritus. 'That's what had been used. Hardly standard building materials.'

"Nudging the mound with the toe of my boot, I had no option but to concur with his observation. Amongst the filth were balls of screwed-up paper, singed scraps of fabric, and several charred sticks. 'Looks like the contents of a fire grate.'

"'I'll tell you something else,' Eugene returned to a crouched position, 'that mummified pussycat that caused such a palaver, it was found right here, on top of all that rubbish. Almost like...'

"'Almost like it was put there to stop something getting out?'"

"'Got it in one, old chap!'"

"I was starting to warm to Eugene by this point. His brashness aside, he had a keen mind and could possibly evolve into being a good investigator one day. He evidently had a knack for archaeology and, providing he doesn't pickle his brain before maturity can set in, he had a bright future in one of the Empire's esteemed universities. However, it was now that I discovered his other vice... laudanum. "

"I began questioning Eugene about the nightmare he had suffered on the night of the birth but he insisted that he remembered nothing aside from a profound feeling of emptiness. I was certain that it was somehow related to the disturbances so I kept digging. He brushed off my concerns, informing me that he had suffered nightmares since he was a child and that his doctor, quack more like, prescribed him a potent tincture of laudanum to help him sleep. He showed me the little blue bottle and mused that he must have neglected to take his dose on that occasion. I didn't want to get into the perils of opiates at that juncture so I changed the subject, asked him to let me know if he found anything interesting amongst the foundations, and continued on with my investigations.

"Upon leaving the cottage, I sought directions to the village and took a leisurely stroll across the moor. The wind had dropped by now and it had brightened into a not-unpleasant afternoon. The fresh air was a tonic after the stifling atmosphere of the cottage. It was well that I was in high spirits by the time I reached Hollowhills as my venture proved to be ultimately fruitless. Aside from some campfire tales relating to the cottage, I could find no more useful information about the Mothersole tragedy.

"The only thing of note to be gleaned from chatting to the patrons of The Rat and Raven public house was that Eugene's nightmares seemed to have started after he and his elder brother had dared each other to spend a night under its sagging roof. Eugene did so through sheer stubbornness while his brother fled upon hearing the hoot of a nearby owl. It was clear to me that whatever malign presence haunted the Angove family, the source was the cottage. I returned to the hall, ate a substantial luncheon and retired to the guest room to prepare for the night ahead..."

Taking advantage of the natural break in his narrative, Carnacki banged out his pipe and refilled it as we sat in a state of rapt anticipation with only the crackle of the fire breaking the silence. Once this ritual was complete, he picked up his photographs and sorted through them. Putting one of them back into his pocket, the original, he explained, he gave us each a picture face down. Telling us not to turn them over until he gave the word, he struck a match and resumed.

"I have to say, that Andrews chap really was a credit to the Junior Ganymede Club, that shadowy brotherhood of valets and butlers. He cheerfully helped me transport the trunk containing my electric pentangle out to the cottage and even went so far as to take a stroll to the nearby river to fetch a bucket of water to fill the bowls that sat in the valleys. Eugene, on the other hand, was less than helpful. Choosing instead to smirk to himself and mutter less than favourable words about my craft. He did, however, find something of note amongst the strangely warped foundations."

Carnacki pulled a small item wrapped in an oil skin from his pocket. Unwrapping it, he showed us a small green stone on a decaying leather thong. He explained that it was soapstone carved with a five-pointed star design that had, he assumed, been strung around the dead cat's neck as a sort of collar. Eugene handed it to him and he placed it into the inside pocket of his heavy overcoat. He said no more of it at this time and placed it next to his glass of brandy before continuing.

"I instructed Andrews to allow nobody to come near the cottage under any circumstances and locked the door behind him and Mr Angove. The household had been told to carry on as normal but to be prepared for any eventuality. I feel I must confess that I was confident of bringing the matter to a satisfactory end. I had deduced that the presence had something to do with the bizarre stonework under the foundation and believed that by using the pentangle in conjunction with *The Saaamaaa Ritual* and other defensive measures, I would be able to close what I understood to be a gateway.

"Nightfall in that part of West Cornwall can be bitterly cold so I had taken the precaution of bundling up against the elements. Still, I felt a distinct chill as I watched the two men become engulfed by the darkness as they made their way to the hall. After they had gone, I sealed the doors to that oppressive back room with wax and baby ribbon. I then smudged a circle of garlic around the perimeter of the electric pentangle which I had set up around the *gateway*. This done, I engaged the current and retreated to a far corner where I had set up my camera along with a powerful flash bulb. Suitably prepared, I made myself comfortable and began to wait.

"The hours ticked by uneventfully towards the witching hour. As is often the case, as soon as the hands on my wristwatch reached midnight an air of disquiet set in. I felt a preternatural cold sweep the room like the creeping hand of death as I fought to remain still as cramps assailed my calf muscles. I had been sitting in the same position for so long that my body was fatigued. As it turned out, I wouldn't have much longer to wait before things built to a terrifying crescendo.

"It started with a shift in the atmosphere above the

blue glow of the pentangle's vacuum tubes. It is hard to put into words but I would describe it as an inhalation, as though the universe took a deep breath and held it. The already thick air became almost unbearable but I forced myself to keep my vigil and deny the urge to flee into the night. That's when the scrabbling started.

"What began as an almost imperceptible scratching against the floorboards quickly built to an ear-shredding din as the sound of a hundred phantom rats burst forth from the aether. It was hard to pinpoint the source of the sound due to the sheer volume, but I managed to discern that it emanated from the oddly-angled stonework, radiating out as far as the perimeter of the pentangle. My defence was holding. I had the disturbance contained. All I had to do was find a way to seal the gateway. I was confident that some of the more powerful incantations at my disposal would suffice and reached into my inside pocket for my notebook. It was then that disaster struck.

"Taking advantage of my momentary distraction, a furtive form, large, black, and hairy, shot from the far corner of the room and attacked the wires connecting the battery to the pentangle with tooth and claw. I shot to my feet but was knocked back by a kind of elemental shockwave as my defences failed and the spectral rats burst forth. As my back collided with the wall, my hand jerked around the trigger to the flashbulb that I had kept within my grasp. The burst of dazzling white light whipped the presence into a frenzy and left me momentarily blinded.

"As one, the phantom rats shrieked and spat before rushing towards me. I thought my number had been called, as a funk unlike any I have ever encountered fell over me. As the invisible horde came within scratching distance, I suddenly felt a sharp burning pain against my breast."

Carnacki tapped the cat's collar with his index finger. "This *talisman*, which I now know to be an *Elder Sign*, saved my life. The powerful magic contained within its design repelled the horde, diverting them away from my person and out into the night." He paused and turned to us, "Gentlemen, I ask you now to turn over your photograph. It is an enlargement and quite blurred, but I'm confident you will be able to see what I was up against.

Doing so, we gasped in unison. "By Jove," I managed to sputter after a second of stunned silence, "this rat... it has a human face!"

"Quite," Carnacki nodded, "the foul creature was the last to leave. I couldn't see it, but I *heard* it. Can you believe, the abomination cursed me and left me with a vow to 'get the child.' As you can imagine, I was frantic. I felt along the wall for the door, unlocked it, and followed them out into the entranceway. A sliver of moonlight had fallen through the fan-shaped transom above the warped front door providing me with a guide. My vision was still impaired but I managed to hurry to the door and exit the cottage.

"The gnarled and sinister trees thrashed as though beset by gale-force winds as the phantom colony of rats and its ghastly emissary made its way towards the lawn. I was forced to delay my pursuit as I blinked and rubbed the vision back into my optics. It would have been foolhardy in the extreme to attempt navigation of the raised serpentine roots without full possession of my faculties. I would have broken my neck, do you understand?

"As the demoniac scrabbling and screeching receded into the distance, I cursed my overconfidence. I was so sure of my success that I lowered my guard for a second. A second that may have proved disastrous. The rat-thing's awful words made everything click into place like some grotesque jigsaw. The child was the target. I have since read of dark witch-cults that deliver a newborn to *The Black Man* to receive the boon of forbidden knowledge and passage between realities... but, I am getting ahead of myself.

"My vision restored, I plunged into a breathless sprint towards Angove Hall. The sodden grass negated my speed and I nearly lost my footing a number of times. By the time I reached the rear entrance, I could no longer hear the sound of the rats. All appeared calm and still. Any comfort this silence may have brought was quickly shattered by a roar of primal terror from the direction of the library. I bolted through the kitchen, overturning a bucket of vegetable peelings intended for the compost heap as I went. Circumnavigating the bottom of the staircase, I was hit once again by an overwhelming feeling of oppression. The malignant presence was in the library and I was certain that the rats and their leader were just the tips of the iceberg.

"I stepped into the library to find Eugene Angove standing by a lone flickering candle, the heels of his hands pressed against his eye sockets as he babbled forth a stream of guttural syllables. 'Eugene,' I called out, crossing the room in haste, 'what the devil happened?' His hands dropped to reveal two glistening white orbs. He was either asleep or under some form of hypnosis. I made to approach him but was halted by that same furry abomination from the cottage. It chittered and giggled as it leapt from the back of a wing-back chair onto Eugene's shoulder.

"'What do you want with him?' I asked, trying to control my movements so as not to startle it into doing something rash. The beast possessed a pair of savage-looking fangs that were far too close to Eugene Angove's jugular for comfort. It didn't grace me with a response, it merely chittered once more and pointed towards one of the ceremonial swords that hung above the fireplace along the far wall. I instantly saw what it was about. It intended to use Eugene as its personal instrument of death. The target... the newborn child in the nursery.

"Eugene made spasmodic movements as he took a step towards the hearth, his fingers jerking and twitching like a sufferer of St Vitus' Dance. From the upper floor, I could hear the rats and the subsequent commotion amongst the household staff. I knew I had little time and had to act. Reaching for the heaviest tome to hand, which ironically turned out to be a book on veterinary medicine, I took a step to my left and hurled it with all my might at the rat-thing. The book struck Eugene in the shoulder, knocking the rat from its perch. Without thinking, I launched several volumes of the Encyclopaedia Britannica at the brute. It screeched a string of invective that I will not repeat at me as it ducked the projectiles and rushed for the door.

"Seemingly from out of nowhere, Colonel Angove appeared in the doorway clutching his trusty service revolver. Displaying the sharp reflexes and fighting spirit that had earned him a string of commendations, he took one look at the creature and unleashed a volley of three shots. Two struck the parquet flooring, splintering the wood, while the third connected with the animal. It let out an ear-splitting shriek as it was sent spinning under the legs of a chaise longue.

"'What in God's name was that thing?' The Colonel cried as he levelled the barrel of his weapon at the dark space under the seating. 'Did that rodent have a blasted human face?' I nodded in the affirmative and turned my attention back to Eugene. When the creature had been hit, he had dropped to the floor like a marionette with its strings cut. As I rushed to his aid, Colonel Angove gingerly approached the chaise longue and moved it aside just in time to see the creature dissolve into a sticky protoplasmic globule.

"The Colonel let out a yelp of disgust as it began to undulate and swell, forcing the bullet from its body. It hit the wooden floor with a jarring tinkle. Preparing to unload another series of shots, he watched in horror as the *thing* started to vibrate and manifest a collection of baleful eyes and pseudopods. Seeing that he was frozen to the spot, I did the first thing that came to mind. I picked up the heavy book of veterinary medicine and brought it down on the entity with a sickening splat.

"As it seeped into the cracks between the wooden tiles, dead at last, the house erupted into a frenzy of noise and vibration. The invisible horde was going to attempt to finish the job. As the room shook violently, sending books and ornaments tumbling from the mighty oak shelving, Eugene suddenly sat bolt upright unleashing a torrent of language unknown to me. To the best of my recall, it was something along these lines, 'Cahf ah nafl mglw'nafh hh' ahor syha'h ah'legeth, ng llll or'azath syha'hnahh n'ghftephai n'gha ahornah ah'mglw'nafh.'

As Carnacki spoke those horrific words, I felt a shudder trace itself like a cold finger along my spine. He noticed my discomfort and smiled. "I later learned that the language is Aklo, the tongue of The Great Old Ones. Roughly translated, it means, 'That is not dead which can eternal lie, and with strange aeons, even death may die.'

"I hurried over to Eugene and asked him what he could see. It was futile, he was under the will of something far more powerful than I have ever encountered. He let out another litany, this time including a name... Nyarlathotep. Even whispering it fills me with such a dreadful feeling. As he did so, the movement inside the walls began to increase tenfold. A howl of wind burst from the chimney breast filling the room with discordant piping. At once, all light in Angove Hall was extinguished as something from *outside* started to force its way into reality.

"Panic almost got the better of me until serendipity struck for a second time. Once more, the cat's collar started to burn with a strange unearthly heat. I whipped it from my pocket and held it in my palm. It glowed with a comforting green radiance and in that second, I found a still point amidst the chaos around me. I felt the presence of cats. Not those of our Earthly plain, but those that inhabit the land of dreams. It all finally made perfect sense. I knew why the citizens of Bury St Edmunds used mummified cats to ward off witches.

I must have raised an eyebrow because Carnacki turned and addressed me directly. "You see, dear fellow, if the witches of Suffolk were, in fact, a cult in the service of Nyarlathotep, then it made sense to use the powers of those that oppose him to counteract his influence. Nyarlathotep resides on the *outside* between the land of dreams and our waking reality. I learned later that a race of felines from a city called Ulthar in The Dreamlands are natural enemies of The Crawling Chaos... one of Nyarlathotep's many epithets. In Ancient Egypt, when Nyarlathotep came amongst us in the form of the Dark Pharaoh, Nephren-Ka, his followers were plunged into war with those who served Bastet. For whatever reason, cats are anathema to this *Outer God*.

"Feeling the protective force of these feline guardians, I sprung towards Eugene and placed my palm against his heart. As soon as the Elder Sign connected, he let out a strangled gasp as his body arced and buckled. The Colonel cried out for me to stop, but the convulsion subsided after a second. At once, the sound of the rats and the vibration ceased. Eugene's eyes rolled the right way around and gave me a look of thanks before his lids fell closed.

"Time was of the essence, I instructed the Colonel to keep the stone against his son's breast until I gave him the word. If he let it drop for a second, the connection could be restored. I left the library and sought out Andrews and several other members of the staff. Working as quickly as we could, I had my electric pentangle transported from the cottage, erected around the cot, and repaired the chewed wires. Once the child was protected, I returned to the cottage with Andrews. Once inside, we dismantled the gateway stone-by-stone and performed several rituals outlined in *The Sigsand Manuscript,* sealing the rift. Forever, I hope."

Carnacki finished his brandy. The sign that his narrative was almost at an end. I had many questions but knew better than to ask them. As I sat and waited, he produced several scraps of charred paper from his pocket. "Eugene made a speedy recovery. He remembered little the following day and I gave him only the briefest of outlines. I'd wager, he will be less dismissive of the abnatural from now on. Before I left Angove Hall, he found me in my room and handed me these. They are scraps of letters between Susan Mothersole, the tragic mother from the cottage, and her sister, Maud.

"While only fragments, I was able to glean much information from them Most of which I backed up by consulting parish records both in Suffolk and Cornwall and certain texts in the restricted section of Cambridge library. Susan, it is documented, was living with her maiden aunt when her mother came under investigation for witchcraft. A plague of infanticide had blighted Suffolk leading to harsh measures being taken. Many feared the return of a Matthew Hopkins-type witchfinder and Susan's mother and elder sister fled the country before they could be tried. The aunt moved to Cornwall with Susan to start a new life but died soon after from a mysterious wasting sickness leading the child to be taken in by the rector's wife in Hollowhills.

"After fleeing Suffolk, Susan's mother ended up in The New World where she settled in Arkham, Massachusetts. As Nyarlathotep's influence over her grew, she instructed her daughter to track down Susan and return her to the fold. One born into the service of the Great Old Ones can never leave, you understand?

"In the letters, Susan pleaded with Maud to leave her be. Saying that she was happy and considered the aunt to have been her mother, not the wicked creature that spawned her. Maud took this as a betrayal and returned to England to enact revenge on behalf of her matriarch. It was she who constructed the gateway and called on the powers of her master. I can only surmise that she did this while Susan was at her work.

"The conduit complete, she sacrificed Susan's child to Nyarlathotep before fleeing back to North America. The father was taken by the local magistrate and hung on Ravenroost Hill for infanticide. Before taking her own life, Susan must have uncovered the gateway. Upon putting two-and-two together, she did what the superstitious folk of Suffolk would have done. She entombed a feral cat she found in the woods together with the Elder Sign her aunt had given her to ward off the influence of her evil mother's unearthly benefactor. This held the forces of the beyond at bay until a young boy with a vivid imagination fell asleep above the gate one night while taking part in a childish dare...

"You see, I postulate that Eugene must have somehow entered the Dreamlands that night and a link, albeit a weak one, was forged. This explains his nightmares and the residual *haunting* that had plagued the cottage. I hope that free from the connection, Eugene can give up the laudanum and concentrate on his studies. As I mentioned, despite his many faults, he has a keen mind that, given the correct nurturing, could prove formidable in his chosen profession.

"When I left Angove Hall, everything seemed well. No sounds had been heard and I performed another vigil in the cottage just to make sure. I didn't return directly to London, instead conducting the research I have mentioned. It was during this research that I came to a conclusion about The Hog. I now believe that monstrous power to be another of these *Great Old Ones*. Indeed, I have learned that there are many such malign forces and multitudes that worship them. I have decided to dedicate my future endeavours to stamping out their baleful influence."

His story concluded, Carnacki rose from his chair and addressed us in his customary manner. "Right, out you go!" In a few short minutes, I was standing on the embankment staring at the languid waters. I had many unanswered questions but felt satisfied that, knowing Thomas Carnacki, he would answer them in due course. As I meandered homeward, my mind spun with the implications of his tale. It was no wonder he looked haunted. After all, he now had intimate knowledge of things that no man should ever hope to encounter. My only comfort was that I couldn't think of a single soul better equipped to deal with these forces than he. I dread to think about what will happen when he is no longer with us. Who will take on the fight against the forces of *The Beyond* in his place?

I pray that whoever becomes his successor proves to be up to the challenge...

Tim Mendees is a rather odd chap. He's a horror writer from Macclesfield in the North-West of England that specialises in cosmic horror and weird fiction. A lifelong fan of classic weird tales, Tim set out to bring the pulp horror of yesteryear into the 21st Century and give it a distinctly British flavour. His work has been described as the lovechild of H.P. Lovecraft and P.G. Wodehouse and is often peppered with a wry sense of humour that acts as a counterpoint to the unnerving, and often disturbing, narratives.

Tim is the author of over one hundred published short stories and novelettes, nine novellas, and two short story collections. He has also curated and edited several cosmic horror-themed anthologies such as *The Nookienomicon, Musketeers VS Cthulhu,* and *The Shadow over Doggerland.*

When he is not arguing with the spellchecker, Tim is a goth DJ with a weekly radio show, co-organiser of The Innsmouth Literary Festival, and the co-presenter of the Innsmouth Book Club Podcast & Strange Shadows: The Clark Ashton Smith Podcast. He currently lives in Brighton & Hove with his pet crab, Gerald, and an ever-increasing army of stuffed octopods.

www.timmendeeswriter.wordpress.com/

Thomas Carnacki is the creation of weird fiction legend **William Hope Hodgeson** and stars in a series of short stories collected as *Carnacki the Ghostfinder.*.

In his later years **Eugene Angove** stars in a series

of novelettes by the author. Ably assisted by his faithful valet, **Hampton**, he is often pitted against the machinations of the Great Old Ones and their Earthly agents. This is his *origins* story.

THE O'CONNOR FILES: THE CULTS

CHARLES REIS

With a glass of whisky nearby, I read the newspaper. I sat in my dimly lit office with my feet placed on my desk. I shook my head reading about the mass suicide that happened in San Diego last week by a group called Heaven's Gate. Thirty-nine misguided souls were lost. Taking in this information had my face burning up and my teeth grinding. I had come in contact with many cults since I started this job four years ago. I tapped my feet together and listened to the thud of my leather dress shoes. I'd started tapping my feet, whether it was the tips or the heels, together to calm my anxiety since my service in the Gulf War. One sip of the whiskey helped too.

Since my small office was located in East Harlem, horns from cars and the chattering of people bombarded my ears. So, I had the radio on. "I Want You" by Savage Garden drowned out the noise. As I sang along, a loud knock at my door interrupted the flow.

"One moment!" Time to get professional. I kicked my feet off the desk and dropped the newspaper on it. I placed my glass of whiskey into a drawer right next to the bottle. On the sidewall next to a stack of books rested a small mirror, so I glanced into it. I wanted to be sure my tie was tight, the lapel on my suit was straight, and my short red hair was perfect. I snapped my finger, pointed at the mirror, and then winked; I was ready.

I turned the radio off. "Come in."

The door creaked as it opened, and a woman peeked in. "Hi, um, are you Detective Bryan O'Connor?"

"I am. Please, come in."

A woman wearing a blue sweatshirt and stonewashed

jeans entered. I guessed she was about ten years younger than me, so about twenty or twenty-one. She kept her head low as she came closer.

"I'm Gabrielle Rojas." Her face cracked a smile, then it returned to a stoic position. I gestured for her to have a seat in the chair in front of the desk.

"How may I help you?"

Pushing back the long ponytail of her black hair, Gabrielle took a deep breath as she sat. "I need your help finding my brother."

I raised my brow. "You do know I'm a special kind of detective, right? What makes you think I'm the right person for the job?" I'd done missing person cases before, but they had to have vanished by unusual circumstances.

Her dark eyes looked into my green ones, and she replied with a raised voice, "He went missing in Innsmouth."

Innsmouth. That name had graced my ears many times. The town of dark forces and black magic. A town overrun with strange cultists and xenophobes. My work had led me to many strange towns, but never there. Looked like that was about to change.

I leaned back in my chair. "Okay. Continue."

She reached into her pocket and took out a photo. "His name is Hector. He and his friend, Mitch, vanished in that town less than a month ago." Gabrielle handed the photo to me. It displayed a thin, clean-cut young man, late teens, dressed in a dark suit. Although I couldn't read it, I recognized the type of name tag on his suit.

"Mormon?"

She nodded. "My parents and Hector are devotees.

My siblings and I are, you may say, non-practising."

"I get it, I'm a non-practising Catholic," I pointed around my office, "For obvious reasons." Pictures of occult symbols and horrendous creatures dotted the walls. Stacks of texts on ancient gods and rituals mixed in with some Hemingway novels created a little city. In the corner, I kept one grimoire, bound in boar skin and written in a language that only I could read, in a glass case on top of a pedestal. It was the first one I ever got.

My traditional Irish family disapproved of my job relating to the occult. Along with my sexual orientation, I had been disowned by everyone, except for my sister. I wondered what they would have done if they knew of my ability?

I handed the picture back. "What were they doing there? Even the Mormon Church knows better than to send missionaries to that godforsaken place."

"He and Mitch were doing their mission in Ipswich. One night, my brother called me and said he wanted to proselytise the heathens of Innsmouth. He went against the advice of the Church Elders, as he believed it was God calling him to do it. I told him he was crazy." A glint of tears formed in her eyes. "He convinced Mitch to go with him. That was the last time we talked."

I squeezed my lips to hold my tongue. I remembered that their disappearance was reported on the national news. Back then, I said to myself that they were idiots to go there. I wanted to blurt out that sentiment now. Instead, I let my compassion oppress my words.

She wiped her eyes. "No one will help us."

"Let me guess, the Innsmouth Police investigated

and claimed that Hector was never in their town?" She nodded. Innsmouth PD had that kind of reputation for cover-ups. "I know the state police won't enter Innsmouth unless they had to, and after what happened in Waco four years ago, the FBI was reluctant to go after another cult." I crossed my arms. "I gather I'm your last resort?"

She lowered her head. "That town's notoriety has kept everyone from taking the job. The last guy I asked was, uh, Malone, I think?"

"Ya, I know him, out in Red Hook." Ah, Greg Malone. My best friend of ten years. We try to meet up at least once a week for lunch or a drink. His family had a long tradition of detective work in the city that went back over a hundred years. I guess I should thank him for the recommendation.

"Yes, he's the one. He gave me your information and said you would be a better fit for this job."

"Well, I'll agree with that. A case involving the occult needs someone with knowledge of it." I placed my hands on my desk. "And anything involving Innsmouth would involve the occult." I took a deep breath. When I started this job in '93, I vowed to help anyone affected by the occult, no matter where it led me. Besides, I handled Iraq, so I could easily handle Innsmouth.

"My fee is twenty-five thousand upfront, and another twenty-five once I solve it."

She remained silent for a few seconds. "My family, we're desperate. But I don't want to be taken advantage of. I want to believe that you're worth every penny."

Desperation didn't cloud her scepticism. I admired that. I opened the drawer with the whiskey and took out the half full-bottle. I placed it in the centre of my desk. Gabrielle tilted her head and looked at it with a blank expression. Maybe I was being childish, but I couldn't wait to see her face.

"What are you doing?"

I grinned. "Watch." I focused my eyes on the bottle and I balled my hands. A chill went through my spine, then into my body, but I didn't shiver. I had become used to this sensation over the past few years. I didn't blink as I remained focused on the bottle. The trickling sounds of water entered my ears, but only I could hear them.

The bottle vibrated. The alcohol fizzed. It wasn't the bottle I controlled, but the water within the whiskey. Magic uses emotions to make it work if done by a human. This was a minor trick, so the excitement I had of showing off was good enough. A second later, the bottle launched towards me and I caught it like a baseball. Damn, I was good.

Gabrielle jumped out of her seat. "Dios mío!" She placed her hand over her chest, which rapidly rose up and down. "How-how di-did you do that?"

Upon sitting down, I placed the bottle on the table. "Let's just say it's a gift that I picked up during my service in the Gulf." For the past six months, I had used my powers a few times in front of others. When the stories came out, some people labelled me a fake and a con artist, while others feared me and damned me to Hell. (I'd been told worse throughout my life.) A few times, it landed me a paying gig.

I opened the drawer and took out the whiskey glass. "So, am I worth the price?" Smirking, I opened the bottle and poured myself a drink.

She stood there for a few moments. Her breathing returned to normal and she placed her hands by her sides. "I don't care if your powers came from God or the Devil. I just want to know what happened to my brother." She sighed. "I'll convince my family you're worth the price."

I got the call less than two hours later. The Rojas family hired me. Although several members were reluctant to hire an "occult detective", Gabrielle convinced them by saying I was a veteran. She left out that I had powers, as she thought that would send them over the edge.

Hector's missionary companion was an eighteen-year-old from Utah named Mitch Delissen. I contacted his family, but they refused my help, citing my profession in the occult. Moments after, Mitch's aunt and uncle contacted me, saying they would go against the family and wanted my help. I gave them the same deal as the Rojas. By the end of the day, both families wired me the down payments. Five thousand dollars. Not bad for one day.

The next morning, I cruised along the back roads of central Massachusetts towards Innsmouth. The sun rose over the mountains. Acres of dark forest covered the landscape. The pine surrounded the maple trees that sprouted with early spring leaf growth. An occasional house or shack dotted the landscape, but it was mainly untouched.

The roars of my black '68 Ford Mustang's engine

shattered the quiet. I named my girl "McQueen". I inherited her from my father, who died soon after I came back from deployment. He never knew my orientation, but if he did, I was convinced he would have accepted me. She was my good luck charm, and she makes me look cooler. Her roars grew louder as I pushed her along at top speeds.

I turned on the radio. "Life Is A Highway" by Tom Cochrane played, so I turned it up and sang along. Although "Highway to Hell" would be more appropriate.

I checked into a hotel in Newburyport, as I would never stay in Innsmouth overnight. Besides, there hadn't been a hotel there since the 1920s. Although I didn't want to bring McQueen into the town, no buses or trains were going there anymore. Also, no taxi services would help either. I had no choice but to bring my girl there.

With the help of Greg, I did some research the night before. The town's history of hostility to outsiders went back to the 1840s. Back then, residents would sneer and ignore visitors, but now they used intimidation to drive them out. Although violence was rare, there had been a few assaults reported over the years.

Add in cults and black magic, and that place wasn't welcoming. What the fuck were Hector and Mitch thinking? Could they have joined a cult there? That wasn't out of the question. The world was a complicated place, so I had to be prepared for anything.

The main road to Innsmouth passed through salt marshes that stretched for miles. I noticed a small village that stood in the middle of one among the flat, dark landscape of tall grass. While it lay within the municipality of the town, I ignored it for now. A little after ten in the morning, I entered the belly of the beast.

The sun struggled to pierce through the grey clouds. I was told that the weather was like this half the time. The rest was either rain or snow. Some superstitious people believed this was the result of sea creatures called the Deep Ones that rested off the coast. It wouldn't surprise me if that were true.

I turned on Water Street and reached the fishing harbour that consisted of a breakwater. In 1954, Hurricanes Carol and Edna struck New England, and Innsmouth was hit hard. While the Town Square and further inland fared well, most of the structures along the harbour were destroyed. At the tip of the breakwater stretched a white tower of the lighthouse with its light glaring. Since the 50s, it had been repaired and was fully automated.

The cabins and dories were gone, leaving behind a bare sandy tongue with a few pieces of wood sticking out from the ground. A large, light blue two-floored cabin did survive the hurricanes. It had been repaired and turned into a local bar with a neon sign on the roof that read "Gilman's Tavern". I thought about stopping here, but I didn't think it was wise to interact with drunk assholes. I drove past it.

The old 18th-century homes along the street were washed away. In their place stood brick mid-century modern tract housing with butterfly or pyramid roofs. Two dozen brick warehouses replaced the wood ones destroyed along the shoreline, and the half dozen wharves were now made of concrete. There were no boats to be seen, so they were likely out fishing.

A couple of cars parked along the street and a few residents walked about. The older folks dressed conservatively. The men wore dark suits and fedoras and the women had on dark-coloured dresses and veils. The younger people were more up-to-date with style, wearing stuff such as leather jackets, jeans, and sweatshirts.

A few stopped and stared at me. Some snarled and spat. Most cussed out at me. One man in his twenties shouted out, "Leave our town, you dirty Blaireau!" I had no clue what that meant, but I was sure it wasn't a compliment.

"Love you too!" I said as I flipped him off. Hemingway said that "The only thing that could spoil a day was people." That was an understatement.

Beyond the harbour stood a large church made of grey brick with a bell tower that was about fifty feet tall. Black wood made up the material of the roof and the tower's gable. It sat at the end of a concrete wharf that stretched into the water about five hundred feet and thick pilings held everything. Small waves passed under it and crashed into the moss-covered stone shoreline. No matter what hostilities I may face, I had a job to do, so I might as well start there.

Several people watched as I turned onto the wharf. Its width accommodated McQueen, but it had no guardrails so I drove slowly. I kept my eyes on the church; I hardly blinked. The tower acted like a claw stretching itself up from the ground. My imagination was in overdrive as the church welcomed me with malicious intent. Throughout my life, both in the military and personally, I had been to places that felt like they greeted me with hate. Especially churches.

I parked McQueen a few feet from the entrance. Maybe I was stupid for not being discrete, but I believed a direct approach would be useful. The people didn't want me here, but it would be worse if they saw me sneaking around. It was the difference between getting screamed at or getting the shit beat out of me.

On another note, while these people could give me as many bruises as they wanted, they better not scratch McQueen. Inside the glove compartment rested a small idol. The three-inch bronze statue depicted a figure with the head of a woman wearing a headdress, the wings of a bird, and a long body. She represented the protective deity, Lamma. I created her several years ago with the knowledge from my special grimoire. Many times before, she made sure no one messed with my baby, so she would stay here. She saved Greg once, but that's another story.

I glanced into the rearview mirror. I fixed my tie and hair, then snapped my finger, pointed, and gave a wink. Whiskey would be nice now, but I never drank while on a case. Under my suit jacket was my shoulder holster that held a Glock 17 pistol, a gift from Greg. My military training taught me to be prepared for anything. Time to investigate, so I exited McQueen.

The sea salt air pleasantly interacted with my sense of smell. The crashing of waves against the shore and the calling of seagulls greeted me. The wind chilled my skin, so I tied the belt on my leather trench coat. Once I put on my fedora, I walked up to the church.

Three stone steps led to the red-arched double doors. A small bronze plaque on the side read, "The Order of Dagon Hall." Damn, The Esoteric Order of Dagon. A few cults operated within Innsmouth, but the Order was the oldest and the most powerful. A year back, I had a case involving ritualistic murders that happened in Nashua, New Hampshire. The people who did it were part of an offshoot of the group. Most members of the Order didn't commit murder, but I also didn't want to deal with them if I didn't have to. But if anyone in this town knew where the boys were, it would be them.

I knocked. Almost a minute passed with no answer. I knocked again; the same thing. I yelled out a hello, then I tried to open them. Locked. I examined the keyhole below the brass handle. It would be easy to open it. What kind of detective would I be if I didn't know how to lock pick? The boys may be here, they may not be, but that was an option best left on the table for now. So I walked around to the side.

The wind blew in my face. A couple of seagulls fled into the air once they saw me. A few feet separated the church from the edge of the wharf. I glanced up to examine the large circular stained glass windows. Each one portrayed a large starfish with wiggly arms and a large eye in the centre of the body. While they each had their unique colour patterns, they portrayed the same figure. It was one of the symbols that represented the Order. The ones in Nashua carved into the chest of their victim.

Towards the back was a small arch door. I rushed over and grabbed the handle. Locked, of course. Again, it would be easy to pick it, but I was still reluctant. I didn't think the residents would appreciate my trespassing within their sanctuary. I wasn't going to do it… yet.

As I filled my lungs with the cold air, I looked out at the grey wrinkly sea surface with its white tips. The ocean stretched to the horizon and it murmured around me. The dark clouds remained still like a painting. I remembered that the government destroyed a reef off the coast back in the 1920s. Maybe the ruins of it were still out there? I bet Santiago from *The Old Man and the Sea* would hate this place. Anyway, this place was a dud. I decided to head back and try my luck at Gilman's Tavern before I do anything else. I walked back.

I turned the corner and stopped in my tracks. "A little early for Halloween, isn't it?"

Six men carrying metal bats surrounded McQueen. Four were dressed in suits, while the others, including one that leaned against my girl, had on jeans and leather jackets. They hid their faces using white makeshift paper masks in the shape of a fish. Black ink was used to draw out large almond-shaped eyes and a wide mouth. The eyes did have small cut-out circles.

The man leaning on McQueen, who had his bat hoisted over his shoulder, looked at me. "You came to the wrong place, Blaireau."

My muscles tensed and my heart raced. "Hold on," I took a step forward with my hands held up. "I'm a detective from New York. I've been hired to find out what happened to the missionaries who came here recently."

The same man chuckled. "Those faggots? They were here, but they're long gone." I clenched my jaw. This guy was the worst kind of dickweed. I had been on the receiving end of homophobia many times. My patience for such shit was limited.

"Where did they go?" I stared at my baby. "Could you get your ass off my car?"

"It's all good." The dickweed got off and then glided his hand over McQueen's hood. "We got nothing against this fine-looking vehicle." He then pointed his bat at me. "As for those boys, we drove their asses out of our town."

I placed my hands down and balled them. "Did you hurt them?" The anger in me rose like a firestorm. I tapped my heels together. A chill went down my spine and into my body. The trickling water echoed in my ears. I remained focused.

The men walked towards me. "We allowed them to leave without harming a single hair on them," said the dickweed. "You'll not be getting the same consideration."

They surrounded me like a pack of wild dogs. It brought back memories of a gay-bashing incident in '85 involving my friends and me. Six men attacked us late at night near Central Park, calling us various names as they beat us with their fists. We got a few cuts and bruises, and one of my friends got a broken arm, but it could have been worse. It happened a week before my enlistment into the army, but it didn't affect that since I kept the attack hush-hush. With so much water around me, I used that memory as a focal point to increase my anger. The stronger the emotion, the stronger my powers.

As the men came closer, the water sounds grew louder. My body got colder. I could control any water source, except for water found in living organisms. The men focused on me and were unaware of the increase in the ocean's roars. Some water splashed onto the wharf. I clenched my jaw to the point my teeth ached. The men took a stance with their weapons as if they were going to hit a baseball. If they wanted to bring violence, then I would open up a can of whoop-ass.

A wave that towered over us crashed onto the wharf, bringing with it thousands of gallons of seawater. The deluge covered from a few feet in front of the church to about forty feet back. The wave passed over myself and McQueen since we were cloaked with an invisible barrier. Dark waters surrounded me. The ocean mist tickled my skin. The men screamed as the wave swept across. With the men in tow, the water reached the opposite side and returned to the sea. I didn't want to kill them, just teach them a lesson. I had to do this last year when I was visiting Long Island and a punk threatened me with a knife. I taught him a lesson too.

The drenched wharf had seaweed scattered about, but Lamma protected McQueen, and I remained untouched. I blinked and took several deep breaths. Although exhausted, I still let out a short burst of laughter. Releasing such strong magic did physically drain a human. The more powerful the magic, the worse the exhaustion was. I could create a tsunami that would wipe out Innsmouth, but that would kill me.

I walked to the edge and gazed at the water. "Good day for a dip, isn't it?" Smiling, I watched with great pleasure as the men flailed their arms and legs as they headed to shore. Normal waves pushed them along. I better leave before they came back.

"Impressive," said a feminine voice behind me, "You have our attention."

I turned to meet my new visitors. Standing by the open church doors were a man and woman wearing black robes. The short woman had smooth skin and long, silky black hair, while the tall man had a trimmed beard and buzzed blond hair.

"I'm Detective O'Connor. And who the hell are you?"

The woman spoke. "Haggith Dupont." She glanced over at the man. "That's my husband, Malachi."

"We are the leaders of the Order of Dagon," Malachi said. The couple walked off the steps.

I crossed my arms and snickered. "Oh, you allow women to be leaders now?" My research stated that the Order had a history of misogynistic views that stated women were only vessels for making babies.

Haggith smiled. "It's the 90s. We've updated our views."

"But not all of it."

"Well, you aren't here for a philosophical debate, now, are you?"

"Obviously."

She took a step closer and put her hands behind her back. "We'll tell you what we know if you tell us how you got such powers. We're intrigued." Magic was far more common than most people realised. Since Haggith and Malachi weren't shocked by my ability, they likely witnessed some form of it before.

Anyway, they wanted tit for tat for knowledge. That

was easy to do. I told them what happened six years ago when I first learned about the world of the supernatural.

March 3rd, 1991. Southern Iraq. I was a Sergeant in the 24th Infantry Division. Despite President Bush declaring a ceasefire a few days earlier, the Battle of Rumaila commenced on March 2nd, in which the 24th Division was involved. After the fighting, I learned that a hospital bus with wounded Iraqi soldiers that had already surrendered was destroyed by gunfire from my unit. Several people died. It wasn't intentional, but I couldn't escape the guilt that weighed me down over those deaths.

The next day, during a routine patrol near Basra, I spotted an old beggar sitting along the highway. The man had a long dirty white beard, torn and ragged clothes, and blistered skin. He sat there with his hands out and begged for food and water in Arabic (I learned a lot of the language during my time there). Hemingway wrote in *A Farewell to Arms* that "The world breaks everyone and afterward many are strong at the broken places." This man and I were broken in our own way. It wouldn't exalt my guilt, but I stopped and gave him all the rations I had in my possession. The man smiled, showing a mouth missing teeth, and thanked me.

That night, I had an amazing dream. I stood on top of an intact multi-level ziggurat in the desert. Bright sand stretched to the horizon. Wind and pebbles pelted my face. The sun glared down from the clear blue sky. My lungs filled up with hot air. The stairs ramp before me leads down to the outer walls and the domed gate. When I turned around, I saw the old man, who stood at the entrance to a small square structure.

He smiled and revealed bright white teeth. He had a clean shiny beard, tailored clothes, and smooth skin. I felt safe but confused. The man spoke using perfect English. He told me his name was Enki, the Sumerian God of water, knowledge, and creation. The compassion I showed pleased him, and he rewarded me with the power over water. Enki again thanked me and placed his cold hand on my head.

When I woke up, the knowledge of my power was implanted in my brain. I used it instantly when I sent a canteen flying across my tent. Enki also left an old grimoire bound in boar skin in my duffle bag. The grimoire was on Sumerian magic and rituals written in the ancient language that somehow I could read. Today, I kept it in the glass case back at my office. After leaving the army, I dedicated my life to helping others with the use of my magic.

My story took a few minutes to tell, but Malachi and Haggith listened with stoic faces. They didn't react to my talks of ancient gods and magical items.

Malachi shook his head. "There are too many gods in this damn universe."

"Your tale is as old as our world. So many people have been gifted powers in similar ways." Haggith said. "I've seen people control fire and wind, but never water until today."

I took a step forward. "I've told you my story. Now tell me what happened to those missionaries."

Haggith squeezed her lips. "When they came here, they tried to hand out their little book in the middle of

Town Square." She smirked. "I give the little shits credit, they were brave."

"And?"

"They were harassed until they were driven north."

"Did anyone hurt them?"

"No one from our group laid a finger on them. Can you imagine what kind of attention our town would get if we attacked some young missionaries?"

I laughed. "Well, you got the attention anyway."

"But no one hurt them," Malachi said. "Our command was to drive those boys out of town, but not to physically harm them. They obeyed."

"You sure? I was almost attacked."

"You were snooping at one of our sanctuaries. You deserved it," he paused for a few seconds, "No one in the Order disobeys us. But not everyone here is one of us."

I uncrossed my arms. "You're telling me one of the Cthulhu cults did something to them?" Through my research, I learned that Cthulhu cults were common in Innsmouth. Ever since I started this job, I had come across them throughout the Northeast. In my experience, they were capable of doing something to those boys. While I remained sceptical, I had to be open-minded that someone else was involved.

"Unlikely. Our Order and Cthulhu's followers have an understanding. They wouldn't go against us either."

Haggith interrupted, "We believed The Disciples of Azathoth had something to do with their disappearances."

I rolled my eyes. "What is this place, the United Nations of Jonestown?" Azathoth, the Blind Idiot God, an Outer God. Malachi was correct, there were too many damn gods in this universe. It seemed like I learned about a new cult every week. "So, who are they?"

"Ten years ago, a small meteor crashed into the salt marshes north of the town. No one here made an issue of it, but we kept it a secret so as not to attract the media."

Malachi added, "But a man named Josiah Allemand took it as a sign from the Outer Gods. He was a known practitioner of the black arts, but he kept to himself up until then. Afterwards, he and dozens of his followers claimed the marshes as their own and set up a village."

That must be the village that I saw earlier.

"Can I safely assume that the Order and the Disciples don't see eye to eye?" An age-old tale: religions with different opinions fighting each other. Conflicts between followers of the Great Old Ones (such as Cthulhu and Dagon) and the Outer Gods (such as Azathoth) were uncommon, but not unheard of.

Haggith smiled. "You assume correctly. There's been a lot of tension between our people. Three years ago, a fight broke out between the Order and the Disciples, resulting in deaths on both sides. We now have an agreement: they stay out of our town and we stay out of their marshes."

"The missionaries were in their territory when they vanished. They are the ones you should investigate," Malachi said.

I stood there. With my hands behind my back, I tilted my head back and took a deep breath. Their openness took me aback. Even using magic wouldn't cause anyone in Innsmouth to help so quickly. I believed they wanted something.

"Why are you helping me? You want something, don't you?"

She smiled. "You're smart. The Mormon Church is pressuring the governor and FBI to take action against our town."

I sneered. "Which means you'll have plenty of unwanted attention soon. And none of you would confront the Disciples because that would violate the agreement. So after I impressed you with my power, you realised you can just send me to do the dirty work."

"Again, you're smart."

"Will I be attacked again?"

"No, we'll make sure of it."

I turned and walked away. "Good." McQueen was in my sight as I reached my hand out for the door.

"Do you know where you're going, Blaireau?" Haggith shouted. That fuckin' word again.

"Yes." I glanced at her and smiled. "Remember, I'm smart, Chelb." The couple gave me a dazed look. I'd learned a lot of insults in Arabic, so I had plenty of words to hurl back at these people. While I wasn't sure if I could trust them, I had no other leads. Next stop, the village.

My instincts told me I had to be stealthy this time. My military training went into full gear. Due to where I was heading, I changed out of my suit and into my old Army woodland camo uniform. Tan combat boots replaced my shoes, and a utility cap replaced my fedora.

My utility belt had my gun, a combat knife, binoculars, and a flashlight. Once the sun had set, I scoped out the location.

The village wasn't hidden and a dirt road that led to it allowed for easy access. I believed that when Mitch and Hector left Innsmouth, they saw this place and decided to try their luck here. Although using the road would be easier, I took a less direct route. With McQueen parked two miles away and protected by Lamma, I trekked through the marshes.

My boots sank into the mud as I crouched and walked about the tall cordgrass and shrubs. Crickets chirped around me. With the new moon phase, the additional darkness helped cloak me. The Hale-Bopp comet shone among the stars with its bright white body and white and blue tail. As I glanced at it, I thought about the incident in San Diego. I hate cults!

I stopped about twenty yards from the village and took out my binoculars. Located on the dry edge of the marsh flats, this place had fifteen wood homes. Each had a brick chimney that spewed smoke. Some had cars and trucks parked near them. A vigorous buzzing came from a large barn, which I believed housed a generator.

In the middle of the village stood a white wood church with a short belfry that contained a large bell. A thick pole in the shape of a cross stood several feet from the front of the church. Something like a statue was attached to it. Knowing this place, it wasn't of Jesus. I couldn't make out what it was due to distance and the obstructions from the homes.

So far, I'd seen five adults walking around. They

were in their twenties and wore matching grey pants, shirts, and jackets. It was quiet, so I put my binoculars away and moved in. As I crept in, I remained as low as possible.

It took some time to reach the backside of a long and narrow house. Like all the buildings, it was well-constructed with its pinewood structure and black shingle roof. A brand new Lincoln Cadillac rested nearby. There were several fancy vehicles here, such as BMWs. This begged the question: where did their money come from?

I inched my way towards a square window that had light coming from it. From the corner, I peeked through it. It led to a dining room. Five adults, four women and one man sat around a rectangular wood table. A large gold candelabra on the table lit up the room. A black and white artwork of an eight-pointed star with a gold frame hung on the wall behind them. Several cups, plates, and utensils lined the table, all made of gold.

A grey-haired pudgy woman with a wrinkly face slouched over in a chair at the head of the table. The others were much younger with thinner bodies, healthy smooth skin, and shiny hair. They looked like they belonged in *Vogue* magazine. A big, open book rested on the table before the old woman. Her hands shook as she used a feather quill to write on the yellow page. Once she finished, she smiled and placed the quill on the table.

A sixth person, a muscular young man with short black hair and a moustache, walked into the room while holding a small chalice, which was made of gold. He stood next to the older woman and shut the book. As expected, the cover was made of gold. Where the hell were they getting all that from?

"Judith Blouin, you have completed your initiation. The Disciples have accepted you into our group." He held the chalice in one hand while placing the other on her forehead. "Now accept your reward."

The old woman said in a weak voice. "Praise be to Azathoth." The man pushed her head back, and she opened her mouth. He held the chalice over her and poured a green liquid into her mouth. Some of it splashed out of her mouth and spilled on the side of her cheeks. As it did, the liquid splattered over her shirt.

If what occurred next happened before I'd met Enki, my eyes would be bulging. Instead, I kept calm as I observed the old lady transform into a young, thin woman with long curly blond hair and smooth, toned skin. I'd seen people levitate, control minds, and create zombies, so a youth elixir wasn't out of the ordinary.

I had read about restoring one's youth many times. The one fact that had my stomach churning was that the elixir required the blood of an immortal being or a creature with longevity. Something like that had to be lurking around. (Maybe Hector and Mitch fell victim to it?) I had to be on guard for whatever creature may be here. As the people in the house chanted "Praise be to Azathoth", I sneaked away.

I remained crouching as I went down an alley between two homes. While I heard talking from within the houses, I haven't seen anyone else walking around. The goosebumps and the chill on my spine informed me that might be too good to be true. I took it slow and looked around when I could. Light shined at the end of the alley where two metal barrels resided. I rushed over and used them for cover. I grabbed my binoculars to observe what was up ahead.

The village's centre was lit up by a series of torches. Before the church stood a twenty-foot-tall cross made of logs. Attached to it answered the question of where the Disciples got the blood for their elixirs.

A reddish-black insect-like creature, about eight-feet tall, was strapped to the cross. Wrapped around its arms, legs, and torso were fat gold chains. Dozens of locks kept everything tight. Its thick, long arms with thin fingers and grey claws were stretched out in a Christ-like pose. The head resembled a stag beetle with oversized mandible appendages for a mouth and small black eyes. The thin, long antenna drooped to the side as it kept its head bowed down. The rest of its body had a human shape with thick legs and a muscular body. The torso expanded and contrasted, so it was alive.

A few feet from the front of the cross was a twenty-foot crater. I couldn't see what was in it from my angle, but I recalled Haggith telling me about a meteor that crashed into these marshes. Could this be my first encounter with an alien? It wouldn't be the first time an alien arrived by a meteor. I recalled a report stored at Miskatonic University about a meteor that crashed west of Arkham back in the 1880s. What came with it was a multi-coloured, illuminated organism that vanished soon after it appeared. Other texts I owned detailed encounters with other alien species such as the Greys and The Mi-Gos. While it could be something else, I was betting it was an alien.

A normal person would run in terror, but I had seen more hideous creatures than this: zombies, banshees, and more. Hell, a few months ago I met some ghouls. Now, I wasn't without fear, with my stomach fluttering and heart racing, since I would be stupid if I wasn't. Fear, when used properly, helped me make a smart decision. The real question now was this creature friendly or hostile?

I spotted a missionary. With a potato sack over his head, he was bound with a thick rope to a smaller cross that was erected to the right of the crater. Despite these shitheads' worship of Azathoth, they had something for Christ poses, as the boy was tied in one too. I didn't know if he was alive, or where the other one was. I drew my gun and moved in closer.

I zigzag my way to my target, stopping at any barrel, crate, or car to remain hidden. The shadows cloaked me as I avoided as much of the light from the torches as I could. It took time, but it was safer. As I moved past the crater, I peeked into it. Chunks of purple rock, red metal scraps, and green wires lined the bottom. The meteor that crashed wasn't natural, but rather some type of vehicle.

Something was up. It was too quiet. No cult member was around and it was easy to get to my target. This might be a trap, but what choice did I have? The boy needed my help.

I reached him. Empty bottles of water and baby food jars littered the ground around him. It read "Elder Rojas" on the name tag. The stench of piss and shit filled the air. His suit was torn and dirty with brown stains soiled the grey trousers. These bastards must have kept him on the cross the entire time and made him go in his pants!

"Hector, can you hear me?" I said in a soft voice.

His body twitched and he groaned out, "Help, I want my mom." I wasn't surprised at what he said. I heard many brave men call for their moms on the battlefield.

"Your family sent me, kid. Take it easy, and keep quiet." I put my gun back in the holster and grabbed the knife.

"Release me," said a deep, buzzing voice. I turned around and saw the alien, its head and antennas rose, looking at me. "Release me." The mandible appendages moved as it spoke.

"You speak English."

"No. You speak my language." Ever since Enki gave me this gift, I gained the ability to understand certain ancient or otherworldly languages. To my ears, the alien spoke English, but to its ears, I spoke its native tongue. If only it worked with common languages like Spanish or Chinese.

As I used the knife to cut Hector's rope, I said, "Tell me what happened to you?" This wasn't the first time I'd talked to a creature. Not all were malicious, but I needed to be sure first.

"My world was destroyed by a supernova, and my people fled. I crashed onto this world years ago. Josiah found me when I was weak. I asked for help, but he bound me and harvested my blood for youth and gold."

The ropes came off little by little. Glancing back, I noticed long yellow tubing attached to the alien's arms where its blood was drawn. Josiah was the real deal with his magic since he had mastered alchemy. That man could be more dangerous than the alien.

The last piece of rope came off and Hector fell into my arms. I gently placed him on the dirt. The stench assaulted my sense of smell, but I adapted to it. I took the sack off and revealed the poor boy's sunken and pale face. His breaths were shallow as he moaned and curled into a ball. No doubt, he would be too weak to walk. Now, where was Mitch?

"I'll be right back, kid." I put the knife away. Standing up, I looked at the alien. As I focused on it, I went in closer. I wasn't scared, as this was normal for my job, just very cautious. Although a victim too, I wasn't sure if I should set it free, but it remained an option.

"Can't you just break free?"

"My strength did return, but Josiah keeps me bound." It moved its arms and the chains rattled. "They are cursed, both locks and chains. I want revenge against these people, but especially Josiah. You know magic, I can see it. You can release me." Some otherworldly species could detect others with magical abilities.

I got in closer. Examining the locks, I wanted to see if it was possible to pick them. The five-inch, square locks didn't have keyholes. Instead, an inverted triangle with six dots inside it was etched on each lock. I scratched my chin; the symbol was ancient Sumerian and meant something like 'shackle'. These enchanted items had been used for centuries to capture and hinder the powers of otherworldly creatures. Only someone with magical knowledge could control these locks, so the alien needed me. I better decide what I would do, and soon.

"Lo-look out," mumbled Hector. The crunching of

dirt and the murmuring of people sprung from behind me. I snapped my head back to witness several dozen cult members surrounding the area. Many carried weapons like axes and bats, but a few possessed rifles. Several mocked me with words like "Infidel", or "Blaireau." This was stupid of me; I put my guard down and now I was surrounded. With the distance and the amount of water nearby, I would be physically drained to the point of death to take them out. I could draw my gun, but I was outnumbered.

The crowd parted like the Red Sea as the man with the moustache walked towards me. He smiled and kept his hands behind his back. The others looked, smiled, and even bowed to him as he passed. He stopped a few feet away.

"You must be Josiah?"

"I am," he laughed. "Did you think you could enter our sanctuary unnoticed?" Josiah pointed at my belt. "Toss the gun and knife on the ground." My nostrils flared and my lips tightened. Irritation shook my body and clenched my jaw. Giving up my Glock wasn't something I wanted to do.

"Now!"

Taking a deep breath, I grabbed my weapons and tossed them on the ground. A tall blond-haired man ran over and grabbed them. With a smile on his face, he walked and stood beside Josiah. I focused my eyes so much on him that if I was Superman, my heat vision would burn that man. I wished Enki had gifted me that ability.

Damn, I wished I brought the Lamma.

Josiah glanced up at the alien. "You've seen our great gift."

"I don't think it sees itself as a gift."

"That doesn't matter. Azathoth gave it to us, and we're blessed because of it."

I snickered. "Whatever. You're all fuckin' nuts." Then again, this was a psychotic universe we lived in. Maybe we're all a little nuts. The members jeered, but Josiah raised his hand, and they went silent.

He lowered his hand. "We handled the Order, so it's no problem handling you."

I pointed to Hector. "Just like you handled them?" My body tensed up, so I tapped my heels.

"They came with their blasphemous language and saw our gift. We couldn't let them leave, so we gave them a choice: Pledge their allegiance to Azathoth, or remain bound until they do."

I balled my hands. "What happened to the other one?"

Josiah smiled with a wide grin. "He refused, and he succumbed to the elements. That will happen to you too if you don't pledge."

Hate was a poison that harmed everyone. A chill went through my body. The trickling water returned. My face burned as my hatred rose. Mitch never got the chance to live. The emotions that boiled inside me would be enough to create a powerful magic that would wipe out his town, but that would kill me. It would be worth it though.

"Release me," the alien said.

I turned my head towards it. "How do I know I can

fuckin' trust you?"

The crowd gasped, so I looked back at them. Many had their mouths wide open. A few rapidly shook their heads. Some took a few steps back. Josiah's eyes were wide and his hand was over his mouth. I let out a short laugh, as I loved seeing their fear. They now knew I was no ordinary person.

"He speaks the same language as the gift," someone in the crowd shouted. When I spoke to it, it sounded like English to me, but to the alien and the others, I spoke the other language. Magic was a weird bedfellow. After six years, it still surprised me.

As the comet travelled above the village, I recalled the words to undo the locks thanks to the grimoire. This might be a risk to me, but it was worth taking. A few men pointed their guns, so I ducked and shouted, "Tar-kud!", which meant something like "destroy". Simultaneously, the locks fell off like rain. Loud clanking accompanied the chains hitting the ground. The alien dropped down, creating a loud bang and a small tremor as it hit the ground. A few seconds passed, and then it hoisted its body up. Cracking resonated from its joints as it stretched its arms, legs, and back. It moved its head in a circle. Hissing spewed from its mouth as it stood straight up and clapped its mandibles.

Josiah took several steps back, then ran and vanished into the darkness. Several others joined him, but most stood there with trembling bodies. Several perspired and soaked their faces.

Long, black, semi-translucent wings, like that of a dragonfly, sprung from its back. The alien formed a loud hiss that had everyone covering their ears. Its wings flapped, and it sounded like a stampede of horses. It launched into the air and flew over me. The cult scattered like roaches, screaming as they did. Some men fired their guns. The alien dive bombed and hit the blond man as he tried to run. It remained on his back as the man fell onto the ground. Then, it raised its arm and balled its hand. Hissing, it slammed its fist into the man's head. The pop of the cracking skull was heard over the screams.

Another man with long brown hair ran up and shot the creature's head at close range with a magnum. The bullet ricocheted, and the alien swiped its claws at the man's neck. A river of blood gushed from the wide cut in the throat, turning his clothes red while he tumbled over. "Josiah!" The alien screeched as it flew back into the air. The night sky cloaked it, with only the noise of its flapping wings and loud hisses indicating its whereabouts. I ran to Hector while crouched over.

Once I reached him, I knelt and said, "Kid, I'll get you out of here." The boy moaned, so I placed my hand on his forehead and felt it burning. A round, dark object rolled by like a soccer ball a few feet in front of me. I gasped, realising it was a severed head. "No matter what, keep your eyes closed!" I launched myself up and got into action.

It was war. My heart throbbed as I ran to retrieve my weapons. Gunfire and screaming raged from everywhere. From the corner of my eyes, I saw the members running and screaming as panic ensued. A fancy blue truck drove by with the lights off. The alien, its wings almost invisible due to how fast they flapped and slammed into the truck's hood. A loud metallic bang accompanied the crushing of the front as the truck stopped. Three people's heads smashed into the windshield. Blood splashed over the glass. It flipped the vehicle onto its side. Ten years of pent-up rage gave that creature strength.

"Josiah!" It returned to the sky.

My sense of time slowed down. I huddle over the blond man's body; his crushed head spilt out brains. As I searched his pockets as sweat formed on my face, I held back my guilt. Their death screams echoed into my ears, but I ignored them. These people, although disgusting, were being slaughtered because of me. From what happened in Rumaila to now, my guilt manifested as a boulder that weighed me down. It exhausted and hindered my body. Like many times before, I pushed that feeling aside to get back to normal.

I found my gun and knife in the man's front pocket and put them back on my belt. I had killed before, but I had been saved. I had shown hate, but also mercy, even to those who didn't deserve it. Now, it was time for me to save. I took a deep breath through my mouth, filling my lungs. I exhaled and ran back to Hector.

I put my arms under his knees and back. "Hang on, kid." Adrenaline pumped through my muscles which had my body burning. Hector was already light from weight loss, but when I lifted him, it was like holding a pillow. His strong stench had me breathing through my mouth to make it tolerable. I was ready to run, but instead, I stopped in my place.

The alien enacted swift vengeance.

There were no more screams, gunfire, or crunching

metal. Just the sound of crickets doing their nighttime melody. Glancing around, I saw dozens of dead bodies. They looked like grey mounds of grass that dotted the dark landscape. A small house in the distance lit up the darkness as fire and smoke billowed from the windows.

We had to get out of here. I believed we were safe, as the alien had the chance to attack us but didn't. But I wasn't going to stick around to find out for sure. Gripping the boy, I cradled him in my arms. Far up ahead, the dirt road led into the darkness of the wilderness. As I made my way for it, I tried to stay focused on the path ahead.

I walked fast past a red car that was flipped onto its roof. While I sidestepped a tall man's body with the spine torn out, my boots splashed into a blood puddle. A severed arm rested nearby. Perspiration formed on my face and stopped in my place. A flashback took me back to the war, to the "Highway of Death". My unit patrolled along the six-lane Highway 80 on the outskirts of Al Jahra, Kuwait. Thousands of wrecked cars, buses, and military vehicles cluttered the sides of the road. In and around these vehicles were many mangled and bloated bodies. I blinked my eyes and tapped my heels to return myself to the present. I questioned if I did the right thing in freeing the alien.

Several yards away was a green truck with the engine running and the passenger's side door opened. While I could easily carry the boy to McQueen, I knew it was quicker to take a vehicle. I rushed to it while I stayed focused on the truck to avoid seeing more carnage.

Upon placing Hector on the seat, he moaned, laid on his side, and curled into a ball. Poor boy. I pushed his feet in as I shut the door. I took a deep breath and walked around the front of the truck. A few feet from there lay the upper half of a woman's torso. Intestines spilled on the ground into a small pile. Blood splattered over her face. Along with green stains on her shirt, I knew she was Judith. She participated in horrible things to become young again and this was how she ended up. I shook my head, thinking what a waste.

With the door unlocked, I sat down in the driver's seat. Luckily, I knew how to hotwire a car. I removed the plastic cover on the steering column and did my thing. It took me about a minute, but with the help of my knife, I got the truck roaring.

"We're out of here, kid." I slammed my foot on the peddle. The tires kicked up dirt and rocks as I drove out of the village.

As I sat in my office late at night with whisky in hand, I finished up my report on what happened over the past week. When I reached McQueen, I used her to drive Hector at top speed to a hospital in Newburyport. He suffered from dehydration and malnutrition, but he was expected to make a full recovery. He was transferred to Boston, and His family was currently at his bedside.

The authorities in Innsmouth swept through the village. Sixty-eight people were part of the Disciples, but only sixty-seven bodies were discovered. Josiah was nowhere to be found and was assumed to have gone into hiding. As for the alien, it also wasn't there. When I told the Order about the alien, they nodded and wanted more details. I couldn't help but laugh. I was sure they had seen many other creatures before. I wonder what kind?

It took a few days, but Mitch's body was discovered in a shallow grave a few yards outside the village. It was estimated that he had been dead for two weeks. While the Rojas saw me as a hero, I didn't feel like it. I informed Mitch's aunt and uncle to keep the rest of the payment and asked the Rojas to donate their remaining balance to the Delissen family.

Innsmouth's talent for cover-ups was in full force with their version of events. The massacre became a copycat mass suicide of Heaven's Gate that Mitch and Hector tried to stop it. The members attacked the boys, killing Mitch, and Josiah held Hector captive. With the help of sympathisers, the incident was reported as happening in Newburyport. I got to admit, I was impressed with them.

Hector had no memory of his time in the village; I used a little magic to make sure of that. The Order wanted me to corroborate their story, so I made them a deal. If they delivered Mitch's body to his family, I would go along with their story. They agreed. Before I left, Haggith told me she hoped to never see me again. With my job, I believe we will cross paths once more.

As I closed this case, I thought about Mitch, and I wished I saved him. A night of whiskey and Hemingway was required. As I opened up *The Sun Also Rises* and drank, I thought about Josiah. There was no way he got away from the alien. Since the killings, there had been reports of people hearing a man's screams coming from the marshes at night.

I snickered. The alien was still enacting his brutal revenge.

Charles Reis was born and raised in Coventry, Rhode Island, but currently lives in nearby West Warwick. He graduated from the University of Rhode Island with a BA in English Literature in 2012. He's had several short stories published, appearing in various anthologies such as One Night in Salem, Cursed, and More Lore for the Mythos. Besides writing, he also has an interest in travel, history, horror films, the outdoors, and the paranormal.

Detective Bryan O'Connor is an original creation influenced by magical characters like Harry Dresden and John Constantine. This story will be his first appearance, but likely not his last. He joins a "shared universe" that mixes the Cthulhu mythos with various mythologies and historic events.

THE YELLOW DOOR
MARK RANKIN

"I'm looking for a Mr Charlie Durant."

The voice emanated from beside the door that bears that name. I hadn't heard it swing open, but it was still early and I needed a drink.

"Then congratulations, you've found her."

The declaration gave the well-dressed man standing in the doorway a moment of pause. He screwed his eyes into a suspicion-filled glare for a moment and then strode more fully into the office, closing the door behind him with an amber-headed cane and removing his Homburg.

"I'm led to believe," he said, clutching the hat as he dusted down the chair we reserve for clients, "that the title of 'Mr.' is usually reserved for the male gender, Ms....?"

"Durant," I tried to keep the resigned amusement from my voice. "Charlotte Amalie Durant.—Private Detective—at your service."

"Right." Finishing with the chair, he sat down and flashed a tight, humourless smile. "Well, if it's all the same to you Ms....Durant, I think I'd rather bypass this attempt at humour and speak to the gentleman in charge. I'm sure as his secretary, or assistant, or whatever, your skills are formidable, but this is a matter of some import and, I fear, not entirely suitable for a member of the fairer sex."

I think it says a lot about the powers of restraint I've been so carefully building over the years that I didn't make a feast of the guy, or at the very least throw him out and send his cane flying after him. Instead, I raised one eyebrow and searched my pockets for a cigarette.

"Let me tell you something Mr...?"

"Broderick. Charles Emerson Broderick"

"Well, Mr Broderick, your 'request' is one I've heard more than a few times before, and I'm going to give you the same answer I gave the rest. You see, I've dealt with everything kind of lowlife this town has to offer Mr. Broderick. I've pursued murderers, played mind games with both crime lords and creeps. I've seen things that would make your toes curl and your guts drop." I waited for the grimace of disgust and wasn't disappointed. "So, you'll forgive me if this 'member of the fairer sex' doesn't give a rat's hairy ass if what you have to say is 'suitable'. You either say it, or you get out. It's that simple."

Charles Emerson Broderick sat back and smoothed his waxed moustache with the knuckle of his right index finger, his gaze never leaving my face.

"Very well," he said. "If that is indeed the way of things. Allow me to say, however, that the details I am about to furnish you with may seem not only unseemly, but also rather fantastic.

I lit my smoke, and met his scrutiny head-on. "Then you've come to the right place."

"So I was told."

I arched the eyebrow again. My reputation for handling the weird and not-so-wonderful was an almost open secret in the city of St. Germain. The reason I was so successful? Well that wasn't. It made me wonder how much Charles Emerson Broderick knew, and who might have given him my name.

"Then why don't we stop with the pissing contest and get to work. Tell me everything you can about this

'Emily Stern' you want me to find. Start at the beginning, don't leave anything out."

"This is Emily," he said, across my desk pushing a colourized photograph of a girl with red hair, green eyes, and a sardonic smile hovering above a strong chin. "She is my god-daughter. A young woman, with all of life ahead of her, and an upbringing that gave her the means and connections to build that life whichever way she chose."

"Rich?"

"In today's terms. This so-called 'Great Depression' America finds itself in has not been kind to anyone's wealth, but the family is most certainly comfortable. Had Emily opted for the unadventurous life, she would have wanted for very little."

"But?"

Broderick flashed me a keen glance. "But the child was gifted with both fierce curiosity and a somewhat wilful independence. Admirable traits, I'm sure you'll agree, but, when entwined with her artistic sensibilities, they led her down a dark and dangerous path. She wished to explore life, you see—wanted to taste it—to feel it— and experience all the darker, less fortunate side of St. Germain had to offer. Toward this end, she rented a room in the slums I believe some call 'The Warren'. Her plan, to live among the poor and the desperate, supporting herself in whatever way she could."

It was a tale I'd heard before. The rich kid, keen to

rebel against their privilege and immerse themselves in manufactured poverty, cutting themselves free of the life they were born into in order to explore the seedier side of the world—safe, all the while, in the knowledge they can quit the game at any time, and race home to the moneyed arms of mom and dad.

"I guess it was inevitable she would fall into a bad crowd," Broderick continued. "The 'employment' she secured was with a man called Dorian Brookes, a mountebank if ever there was. Brookes is the owner of two bars in downtown St. Germain, both of which started life as Prohibition speakeasies, and it was in one of these, an establishment called The Blind Pig, that Emily began her adventure. I can only piece together the details from the letters she sent her parents, and the accounts of the people who worked there, but it appears it wasn't long before Brookes, ever a man for a pretty face, introduced himself to her. That was when the real adventure began.

I could sense the hesitation behind his words, but I kept my counsel and let the heavy silence do my urging for me.

"Brookes was a rich man, thanks to the black market profits he made during Congressman Volstead's puritanical crusade. It was that money which allowed him to set up a more salubrious establishment north of the river. A club he named 'The Yellow Door'. On the face of it, it was a sanctuary of good whiskey, fine cigars and hushed conversation—but there had been rumours. Nothing substantial, you understand—nothing overt— but persistent whispers that something wasn't quite right. I think that might have been the reason Emily accepted

Brookes' invitation to trade in her barmaid's apron for a job at The Yellow Door. On paper she was to work as a 'hostess' greeting the members of the club on arrival, making sure their spirits were kept high and their wallets loose, but my guess is she fancied herself a sleuth, on the verge of uncovering some great conspiracy." Broderick let a pointed gaze rest upon the tie tucked into the vest of my trouser suit for a pointed second. "I don't know what she found, if anything, but I know Dorian Brookes is not the kind of man to tolerate such wild fancies— Within five weeks of accepting her post, Emily Stern disappeared into thin air."

I flicked ash from my cigarette onto a small saucer I keep for that purpose, watching the grey-white flakes fall like unclean snow. "And you believe this Brookes character is the man behind her disappearance?"

"You catch on quick Ms. Durant. The thing is, Brooks is connected. Politicians; bankers; even the chief of police—all are rumoured to frequent The Yellow Door, but suddenly, no-one is talking, and no-one shows any enthusiasm for investigation. Almost as if rumours are true. So when I heard awe-filled whispers of a private detective—One who gets results, no matter who or what they're up against—it sounded too good to be true. The trouble is I still think It might."

"And yet here we are."

"Desperate times call for desperate measures, Ms Durant."

I extinguished my cigarette and let the implied insult slide.

"My rates are non-negotiable, and I don't do days,"

I said. " I won't make you any promises, Mr. Broderick. You know I can't. But, if Emily Stern is to be found then I'll tear this city apart until I do. You might have heard rumours, Mr Broderick, but rest assured, you don't know the half of it. If there's anyone in this city who can find your goddaughter, then you're looking at her. That's the one promise I can make."

With a smooth of his moustache, and a curt nod, Charles Emerson Broderick rose and extended his hand toward me.

"Then I believe we have a deal Ms Durant."

"You heard, I take it?"

I posed the question to the empty air and wasn't entirely surprised when it answered.

"Of course, I heard. I'm dead, not deaf." I felt a chill pass through me, and, a second later, the ghost of Tamara Quinn materialised in the chair Charles Emerson Broderick had so recently vacated.

"And what do you think?"

"Of our Mr. Broderick?" Her ethereal face contorted like she'd eaten dirt. "I can't say I took to him."

"Me neither." I walked to the window that allowed me a view of the night-shrouded street below, my hand automatically falling to my pocket in search of a smoke. "I meant the story though, not the man."

"Right. Well, in that case, I think our client has more or less the right idea. The Stern girl disappearing so soon after coming into contact with a lowlife like Dorian

Brookes is a coincidence too far."

"You know the guy?"

"I know of him. Dad had an 'encounter' with him back when Brookes was in the bootlegging business. The way he told it, he was a nasty little creep, even then. The type of guy who'd drag his grandmother over broken glass to clear his path to a dollar."

I kept my eyes on the road and let a slow, deliberate nod do my talking. Tamara's dad, A man of legendary morality and a mean right hook, had been a beat cop. A foot-soldier in the war against intoxication, and a need to live up to that legend had formed part of her reason for helping me found Charlie Durant Investigations. The values he installed in her, saved what might generously be called my life—and cost Tamara her own. If Thomas Quinn, that paragon of integrity, backed the opinion of Charles Emerson Broderick, then I wasn't going to argue. The task now was to find out exactly how right he was.

"So, what's the play?" Tamara's question echoed my thoughts. If 'The Yellow Door' had half the clientele Broderick claimed, then security would be on the ironclad. I chewed on my lip for a while then started my thinking out loud.

"I could get myself hired at The Blind Pig, and see where that leads me. The trouble is, we both know I don't have the patience for undercover work."

Tamara conceded the point with a knowing smirk "And that's before we get to your other 'restrictions'. I mean, daylight wouldn't be a factor, but bars have been known to contain the odd reflective surface. One mirror, one polished piece of brass, one bottle angled just the right way, and your cover is as dead as the two of us. Besides, who'd fix your hair and make-up?"

It was a fair point. One of the less well-publicised downsides of being a vampire is the lack of a mirror in which to make oneself presentable. It didn't pose much of a problem in my chosen career—most of the time—but it didn't lend itself to playing the sweet, innocent *ingénue,* either.

"Then I guess I play to my strengths." I turned from the road and met Tamara's gaze. "A full-frontal assault gets us nowhere, but, assuming they're not expecting me, I should be able to head to The Yellow Door at first dark tomorrow and hopefully bamboozle Brookes' security detail long enough to find a back way in."

"And then?"

I snatched up a book of matches lying by the phone and lit my cigarette. "Then, nothing." I blew out a stream of smoke. "I get in, get the lay of the land, and get out. No muss. No fuss, just a chance to find a few facts."

"And if you happen to stumble across the cold dead body of Emily Stern?"

"Then I guess we'll know the facts."

The Yellow Door was remarkable in its obscurity. A row of three brownstones that had been co-opted into one building, it was marked only by its eponymous portal, sitting beneath a shallow yellow awning, and two sombre-looking characters in ill-fitting suits lurking on its steps.

As I watched, a big, black car pulled up to the curb, and one of the men descended to street level to open its back door. The man who exited was white of hair and stiff of bearing, but his suit was tailor-made, and the herring-bone overcoat he wore to keep out the evening chill was pure dense wool, Alpaca or something equally exotic. Everything about the scene screamed money and privilege. It looked like I was about to breathe some rarified air.

Not that I actually breathe, being of the undead and all. I can still take air into these old lungs, though—can still take time to smell the roses. It just doesn't do anything else. Not since I died.

Some two hundred-and-change years ago I made a deal with a man who turned out to be a vampire. It didn't go well. Since then? Well, let's just say my life—or un-life—got a lot more interesting. The private dick gig? That's more recent, but it turns out, being supernaturally built for stealthy, violent encounters by the pale moonlight can be a hell of a boon for a humble gumshoe, especially in a town like St. Germain.

"That's not the way in." The voice that brought me back to the moment came from just behind my right shoulder. I didn't need to look around to see who spoke.

"I thought you haunted the office."

"I do." There was an undercurrent of wry humour in Tamara's words "Check your pockets."

I did as prompted and, in the right-hand pocket of my coat, nestled beside a pack of smokes and the notepad I keep as an *aide-mémoir*, found an object at once familiar and completely out of place.

"Am inkwell?"

"Yup, your inkwell, to be precise. Part of the decorative set Mr Callaghan donated to the office after the Dalton case. Remember?"

I did. Patrick Callaghan, the man who owned a solid half of the city's less legitimate enterprises, had been grateful in the extreme after we'd tracked down the light-fingered employee who'd pilfered a week's worth of numbers-take before he could spend his ill-gotten gains. The twin set of inkwells flanking a fountain pen too expensive to use had been his expression of that gratitude. A gift given on top of our usual, generous fee.

"I do."

"Well, Mr. Callaghan didn't present it to you, or me, but the office, which makes it an integral part of said office, and, therefore, hauntable."

"And that logic holds?"

"Apparently so. Anyway, in case you hadn't noticed, both the man helping Councilman Delaney from his car and his friend up the stairs are armed and on full alert. We're going to need to find a back door."

She was, of course, correct. In the face of the potential for lethal, and more importantly, noisy gun-fire, a degree of surreption seemed in order. I pushed myself away from the wall and sauntered down the street, giving the guards a wide berth until I found the side street that led to the club's rear.

Here, the facade of genteel civility was exposed to be just that. A facade. The brownstone and its two adjoining properties so clearly knocked together to make one were exposed, and the guts of the club were plain to see. Here were the pipes, the black painted fire-escape, and a large dumpster, overflowing with shattered bottles, and the corpses of half-eaten meals. Here the paintwork was chipped. Here the steps were unclean and the air rich with ripe odours of rotting meat, souring creamy sauces, and the rich, sharp scent of alcohol rising from the gathered trash. As I watched on, hidden in the shadows, a young woman, her short skirt covered by an off-white apron, opened a small and far less impressive door and emptied a box onto the dumpster's noisome contents with a clatter of breaking glass.

"That could be our in." Tamara's disembodied voice whispered in my ear.

"No." My eyes narrowed as I entertained a speculative thought. "There's too many staff. Even with my skills', fooling all of them would be impossible. Someone would see me. Someone would raise the alarm. No, if we're going to avoid a fight, we need to be aiming a little higher."

"The fire-escape!" As she followed the direction of my gaze, Tamara couldn't disguise the excitement in her voice. "But how do we know that leads anywhere better?"

"Because it has to." I said. "When you're entertaining the money and power we saw leaving a chauffeur-driven limousine out front, you keep up to code, but what you don't entertain is the thought of letting your 'guests' know such unpleasant necessities exist. No, the way I see it, those rungs lead to some secluded window in some seldom used backroom."

"And if it doesn't."

Then it can hardly be much worse than a crowded kitchen, with its knives and cleavers can it?"

Tamara pursed her lips. "I guess not."

"Then up we go."

I waited until I was sure the coast was clear, bending every one of my senses to my immediate surroundings. Beyond the closed kitchen door, I heard the sizzle of pans, the fall of a knife through something beguilingly organic, and the off-tune whistle of someone actually happy to work in such a hot and frantic environment.

All of this and more filled the air, augmented by rich aromas of mushrooms and steak being seared in butter, dancing tantalisingly, above the stench of the nearby dumpster, but none of it was aimed my way. It seemed that now was as good a chance as any to make my ascent.

I covered the ground in seven quick and silent steps and looked up at the ladder which would be my means of ingress. The bottom rung hung well out of reach, with only the operation of a catch halfway along its length allowing the bottom half to slide toward the ground. A common measure taken to prevent the kind of burglary I was about to partake in, but one which didn't factor in the unusual athleticism of the undead. On my first leap, my fingers barely brushed the rusted metal, but a second did the trick. As my hands made contact with the cold steel, I hung on hard and swung my legs until one booted foot found purchase on the reddish-brown bricks.

The application of some muscle and hustle allowed me to climb aboard the ladder more fully, and, as my foot found purchase, began to climb. Within the space of a minute or so, I found myself peering through the large second-floor window to which the ladder led.

"Looks like you were right." Tamara Quinn whispered in my ear. The disembodied voice, almost making me lose my grip on the rain-slick metal. "There's nothing inside but a few boxes and a discarded clipboard.

I nodded to the empty air, and examined the window frame. It was obviously designed to be opened from the inside, which meant accessing the catches securing it was impossible without breaking the glass. Something that could well cause an attentive ear to become curious.

"We need a distraction." It was as if Tamara had read my mind. "Something to get people listening the other way."

"Any suggestions?"

Before she could reply, a gong sounded from the area of the club that lay beyond the room we were surveilling. A sound followed by a collection of whooping cries, and the swell of music.

"Well, that works. Be quick, though.."

Before Tamara's words had time to settle in my mind, I was already aiming my left elbow at the pane of glass. One sharp impact and the musical sound of glass hitting polished floorboards, and the window was open. I cleared away the shards still clinging to the window frame, being careful not to allow the sharp edges to dig into my flesh. Blood being spilled, even my own, would be…disruptive, bringing the risk of the passions I'd worked so hard to keep in check being released—and it was too soon for that. I took a deep breath, born more of habit than need, and waited a long second for The thirst for blood and The hunger for death, the twin passions that rule me, to lay dormant once more. Then I climbed inside.

It wasn't a storeroom. To be honest, It wasn't any kind of room. Stood without purpose or title, it might seem as if the club's owner had simply run of ideas for the empty shell, if not for the metal steps that lurked outside its now broken window.

"The noise is coming from through there," Tamara's voice informed me. "It sounds as if they're having a party."

It was true. Beyond the walls, the jubilant cries, birthed at the sound of the gong were continuing apace, and had been joined by the sound of music. Not the jazzy swing beats of this modern era, but a pulsing, tribal, rhythm, overlaid with a screeching, discordant melody. A combination harsh enough to raise the hairs on the back of my neck, and send a shiver racing down my spine.

"It sure sounds like a high old time," I said. "What say we crash the party before someone gets hurt." Without waiting, I slipped through the doorway and into the room beyond.

The people I found myself staring at were almost exclusively of middling years, their dinner suits and gowns made of the finest materials, and their fingers and necks dripping in ostentation. They were also masked.

It couldn't have been for the sake of anonymity, as even with the slim, silk, domino masks in place the celebrants gathered in loose groups, their easy conversation peppered with low chuckles and shy, complicit, smiles that screamed of familiarity. I let my gaze wander across the room for a moment longer, idle speculation as to identity and connection rising in my mind, and, unseen, pushed away from the doorway.

There's a trick that Vampires can pull off. One that doesn't get mentioned in the stories and the lore. Not in any detail. We can become invisible.

Well, that's not completely true. Not in the strictest sense of the word.

No, as I circled the room, keeping my back to the wall, and giving the gathered throng as wide a berth as I could, not one single pair of eyes that glanced my way could fail to pick out the slow-moving form of the twenty-four-year-old girl who died a couple of centuries ago. I forget what she looks like these days, but dressed in my street clothes, I must surely have struck an incongruous figure against the forest of formal wear. But still, every errant glance simply slid away without once alerting the onlooker's brain of my presence.

It's a neat trick, one my race has perfected over the centuries. If you read the stories closely, it could go some way to explaining vampires turning into wolves, or bats, or even clouds of smoke. Of course, it's harder to convince someone of your non-existence when they've already recognised your presence, but with a momentary break in the line of sight it's still possible. You'd be amazed at the stories people are willing to tell themselves

"Ladies and Gentleman, if I may have your attention." The booming, golden-brown voice ripped me from my reverie just in time to see its owner, a tall, square-shouldered figure dressed in a long, hooded yellow robe, loosely fastened above a razor-sharp suit, appear in a doorway opposite the one through which we'd entered the room.

"Brookes?" I asked Tamara.

"The one and only," she replied. "Although, in the photos Dad showed me, he was dressed a tad more conventionally"

"Ladies and Gentlemen," Brookes repeated. "Friends. I want to thank you for your attendance tonight, and for observing the necessary, uh, dress code in such wonderful style" It wasn't a joke, but a ripple of nervous laughter ran through the crowd all the same. "Now, if you would all care to finish your drinks, and make whatever preparations you deem necessary, the altar awaits, and in ten short minutes the ceremony will begin." He spread his hand wide, palms open." *Nilgh'ri vulgtlagln Hastur!*

"Vulgtlagln Hastur.Ahornah h' ah mgepvulgtmah!" The crowd answered. Brookes took a moment to acknowledge their response, then turned on his heel and disappeared back through the open door.

"An altar?" I could almost see the expression lurking behind Tamara's words. "As in 'sacrificial'?"

"I think it's a safe assumption. It might not be unreasonable to guess the name of the sacrifice, either."

"Emily Stern?"

"If we don't get to her first."

"And will your invisibility gimmick be enough to get us close enough?"

It was a fair question. One I couldn't readily answer. Fooling a group of socially lubricated cultists was one thing, but fooling them well enough to snatch Emily Stern from under a ceremonial blade while they looked on was another. I let my gaze wander across the gathered luminaries, my mind working, and found my attention taken by a slim woman with iron-grey hair as she whispered a few words in the ear of the woman next to her, and wheeled away.

"Maybe not, but I think I've just found plan B," I said. "Assuming we can find the facilities."

As I expected the woman needed to exercise her nervous excitement in a way vampires never do. I followed her progress through the milling throng, making sure to give each loose group enough space to ignore my presence and soon found myself hovering outside the powder room.

The slim woman had just walked in, but I waited, keeping a watching brief until not one, but two of the women who'd beaten her to the draw exited. My target may not have been alone in there, but the way I figured it, now was the only time I had. Swallowing a little, I pushed through the door and into a cloud of citrus and white florals cut through with the chlorine-tinged scent of bleach.

The grey-haired broad had already availed herself of one of the three cubicles, so I hovered by the tiled wall opposite the sink and waited for her to answer nature's call. It didn't take long before the water closet flushed and a scrape of metal upon metal announced a bolt being drawn.

As I expected she turned straight to the sink to wash up and adjust her wardrobe, smoothing down her black dress and straightening the shoulders of the matching jacket before turning her attention to her tightly gathered hair. A rite performed in front of a generously proportioned mirror which, in usual circumstances, would provide her with a clearer view of any threats lurking behind her. Luckily my circumstances are anything but usual.

Most of the things people 'know' about vampires are wrong, to one degree or another. Not the reflection thing, though. No, that one's dead on the money, and meant that as I crept on silent feet toward the preening woman, she saw nothing in the mirror before her to tip her off. As my hands closed around her throat, cutting off her supply of oxygen, her eyes bulged with shock and fear. She struggled some, who wouldn't, but it still took only a matter of seconds to put her on the ground in a graceless and, more importantly, unconscious heap.

Conscious of interruptions, I moved fast. The mask was the most important thing. Without that, my chances of blending in with the ceremony's attendees would rely solely on my not being seen. With it, and the addition of the black dress which looked not too far from my size, it wouldn't matter. I'd be just one more masked face in the crowd.

"You gonna leave her like that?" The voice of conscience that was Tamara Quinn asked.

"You think I should dress her?

"Well—No. You might at least lend her your coat, though."

I glanced back at the unconscious woman propped up against the cistern of the toilet in stall number three, and conceded the point. Her situation wasn't filled with dignity, but I still owed it to her to lend her the little I could. As I might have mentioned before, I may be a vampire, but I'm not a complete monster.

"Good enough?"

"Yeah, I think that covers her." I could hear the smile in Tamara's voice. "Now what say we leave the lady to her toilet and take in a satanic ritual.?"

It wasn't a satanic ritual.

Not in the strictest sense, anyway. There were still the tall pillar candles complete with dramatic drips of wax, flanking a raised dais upon which an oversized effigy stared down at the chanting celebrants before it with barely disguised malevolence. But that was where the similarities ended.

Instead of the horned, leering monster so often depicted as the focus of such a ritual, the graven image, carved from stone and standing a full eight feet, was of a spare figure dressed in yellow robes, its right arm outstretched toward its congregation as if to proffer them the orb grasped in its claw-tipped hand, the other holding open a book. A deep hood hid the face of whatever lurked below, but from the way the skirt of the robes billowed and swelled, lending its folds a decidedly serpentine aspect, I guessed it wasn't even faintly human.

Mgr'luh, o uh'eog! C' mgr'luh goka! Sup ot c' orr'ee

The alien words were intoned in a muffled, sing-song voice, and my gaze dropped to a figure in yellow robes This time the hood was up. From within its shadow the smooth contours of an off-white, full-face mask could just be glimpsed.

C' ah soth. Nilgh'ri ymg' ah! The congregation answered in unison *C' ahph'nglui llll ymg' orr'eog*

The figure in the white mask raised its arms in a gesture of rapturous acceptance, picking a knife and a golden chalice from the altar.

"Behold." the rasped word spilled forth from the lipless visage with unmistakable authority "Behold the form of our lord and master. Hastur, great and ancient prince. Feaster from afar. He who dwells in the halls of lost Carcosa and whispers dreams of dark and terrible purpose."

"Behold him!"

"Bear witness to the majesty, before which we are nought and less than nought. See his immaculate design, revealed only so that we might serve in its fulmination."

"Witness. Witness."

"For though our lord is mighty, his foes many, and he has gifted us with glorious servitude so we might aid in bringing them to heel. For all must know his glory and his vengeful mercy. He has called us, and we answer.

Starting now. With our offering—of blood!"

A euphoric wail overtook the masked figures, of whom I was one. Whipped into a frenzy of unthinking adoration and dark, animalistic hungers, long sublimated by their higher selves, they capered and danced; some falling to their knees, others openly weeping tears of pure joy. A charge ran through this adoring throng, and ran through me, too. A baying, howling call to lash out—To feed...To maim...To kill. As the thirst for blood and the Hunger for destruction built to an undeniable crescendo. I felt my brow fall, my cheeks sink and the ragged fangs of the vampire begin to force my lips apart as...

"You are not this monster, Charlie. Not this—thing. You are Charlotte Amelie Durant—the woman who beat the vampire and can beat it again! Remember! Remember who you are!"

The voice of the closest I've had to true friendship echoed in the vaulted halls of my mind, penetrating the inferno of rage and desire raging through me to reach what lay beneath. The quiet place. The centre. It was small now, and shrinking with every needful moment, but it persisted, and as Tamara's words found it, responded, unfurling with tentative care—to test the fire surrounding it—pushing through where it could, and retreating where the flames burned too hot. It took longer than I would have liked,, but gradually I felt my control—a control I'd worked so long to develop, and so hard to maintain—return. I closed my eyes for a moment and clenched and stretched my fingers as the last vestiges of desire fueling the beastly transformation flickered and dimmed. I felt bone and sinew shift as the visage of the vampire melted from my face and I returned to me again. The me I wanted to be.

"Impressive."

The single word voiced in a deep, rough rasp, was the last thing I heard before something hard slammed into my left temple and turned out the lights.

"She's coming round."

This voice, unmistakably female, came from a place that seemed a million miles away, under a thick layer of gauze. I opened my eyes and blinked a few times until something like focus returned. I was in the same room, the inner-sanctum of the urban temple hidden behind The Yellow Door, but the congregation was gone, and I was tied to a chair.

"Check the ropes again." The honeyed tones of Dorian Brookes made the order sound far more like a suggestion. "If she moves, you have my permission to shoot her, but for god's sake aim low. The kneecap should suffice."

I felt movement behind me as someone did as Brookes asked. The rope securing my torso to the chair and my bound hands behind me were both given a firm tug, and then the unseen rope-tester scrambled back to the safety of their master.

"But you said I couldn't hurt her," the female voice opined. "You said she needed to be whole. Unsullied."

"Which was before I knew she could hear us." Brookes sauntered into my field of vision. He'd changed out of his hooded robe and was adjusting his tie. "And, in the main, to get you to shut the hell up." He flashed me a rueful smile. "I apologise for Mrs Inneson. Ever since you knocked her out and stole her clothes she's been a little testy. You must tell me how you got the drop on her, by the way. Oh, and, while we're in a sharing mood, exactly who and what you are, how you got in, who sent you, and for what particular purpose."

I kept my gaze low, avoiding his eyes, and let my tongue slide across my teeth and push at the inside of my cheek, by my first molar. Brookes was shooting for some kind of chummy urbanity. The type that could turn vicious on a dime. He thought he had me in his power. It was time to take both thought and power away.

"Alright, I said. "I'll talk. But not to you. If I'm going to 'share' then I need to talk to your superior."

"Oh, I think you'll find I'm the man in charge here."

"Of the club, maybe, but we're not talking about the club. You cut an imposing figure Mr Brookes, and you look good in yellow, but it would take a fool not to notice you stand a good three inches taller than the masked preacher who delivered such a fiery sermon. A little bulkier, too, despite how concealing those robes must be. No, Mr Brookes, you might be the public front of whatever this racket may be, but the power? Well, that lies with the person behind that pallid mask. So if you don't mind, that's who I'll do my talking to."

"Nice, Charlie. That one slipped by me." Tamara Quinn whispered in the vaults of my mind. It was good to know she was still there.

The speech was a touch heavier on the melodrama

than I'd intended, but it had the desired effect. Dorian Brookes stood in slack-jawed amazement, his veneer of calm control lost. He made to stride forward, but the action was arrested by a slow round of applause from the dead angle behind me.

"Very nicely done." The voice contained that same muffled quality I'd heard earlier, although the sing-song cadence had been dialled back to a low monotone. "I have to admit, I was getting a little tired of Mr Brookes' bravado myself, although I would value some answers to his questions."

"I'm sure." I kept my eyes fixed on Brookes' and flashed him a grin. "And you would be?."

"Careful Charlie. Let's remember our comparative situation here, shall we?"

Tamara had a point. At least one person in the room was armed, judging by the way Bnookes' suit bulged at the hip, and, to the best of my knowledge, It was only myself who was currently tied to a chair.

"Me? Why, I would be the person you asked so eloquently to speak to." The speaker slowly walked into my periphery to see our friend from the dais. "The person whose nefarious schemes you no doubt came here to stop—Now regarding those questions?"

"Okay, well, let's see.. My name is Charlotte Amelie Durant. Most people call me Charlie, I scratch a living as a Private Investigator of sorts, I got in via the badly guarded fire escape to the rear of the premises. Oh, and I'm here to locate a young girl, her name is Emily Stern. You might have heard of her."

"And the rest?"

"Rest?"

"Yes, Ms. Durant, the rest. The truth of what you are."

"Oh, right, the vampire thing. I guess you caught that, huh?" Again, I saw the colour drain from Brookes cheeks. "Don't worry, I won't bite. Not as long as I get the answers I want, anyway. Starting, I think, with what the hell is going on here."

"In time, perhaps, the truth of things will be revealed." The rough voice was still calm and controlled despite the revelation and the implied threat I'd followed it with. "And on that day, perhaps you too will come to know the all-consuming majesty of the one we serve, and give your own offering. Perhaps then you will come to see the subtle intricacies of his designs. The glory and power which are in his gift, and his alone, to bestow."

"And until I do?"

"You will stay here, under lock, key, and all the traditional wards your type is said to be vulnerable to. Do not mistake me, Ms Durant, a vampire, as you call yourself, will make a fine and powerful ally to our cause, but until you see, until you are made to understand, that cause cannot be put in jeopardy."

"And if I decide to put it in jeopardy?"

"That would be…unfortunate, but the altar is always hungry for fresh sacrifice, and one way or another you will be made to serve. Emily Stern could bear witness to that—were she still alive." I didn't see the smile, but I could hear its echoes among the muffled words. "Yes, Ms Durant, If you came here on a rescue mission, I'm afraid you're a little late. Your 'Emily Stern' is dead, her excuse for a life taken by these hands, and her body burned in offering to the glory of Hastur. Such is the price of defiance.

I looked up into the green eyes behind the expressionless visage of the mask; eyes that held not one iota of recognisable emotion, and thought for a while.

"No." I said. "No, I don't think so. I don't think the body of Emily Stern ever tasted the flames. Her mind? That might be a different matter, because a mind like hers? One thirsting for knowledge and experience? Well, that's an easy thing to burn. isn't it…Emily?"

"How did you know?"

The question, voiced in a rough, halting whisper, broke the stunned silence which exploded through the room.

"A thousand things. A million. All nagging away at me, ever since you delivered your sermon. But in the main? Your eyes."

"My eyes?"

"Yes, your eyes. The same green eyes I saw glaring with proud intelligence and endless curiosity from a picture Charles Emerson Broderick showed me. Yes, That was the cincher."

"And the rest?"

"Well, there's the matter of your height, and the way you speak, not the muffled, distorted thing— Although why would that even be necessary if there wasn't something to disguise—but the vocabulary and mannerisms. That told me you were educated, and, when I added it to your hands, opened up the possibility you were female, too."

"What about my hands?"

"Small." I let my gaze drop there now. "Kinda delicate, too. I mean, the gloves help, but from my experience, there aren't all that many men with hands like that. Some, yeah, but not many."

"Small hands, green eyes, and an education. Right. And that was enough."

"Well not quite. You see, I know, I know what it's like to be overlooked and undervalued—What it's like to have a brain and be told not to use it. Back when I was young, being pretty and doing what you were told was all there was. A lot has changed since those days, but I still know a cry for freedom and agency when I hear it. Your godfather thought that's all your adventure was, as he spoke of your intelligence, your willfulness, and your curiosity, traits I'm pretty familiar with myself, but we both know there was more."

The masked figure I now knew as Emily Stern reached up and lowered the hood of her robe, shaking loose her auburn locks, and pulled the ceramic mask from her face. The features below were undoubtedly those of the ironically smiling girl in the photograph Charles Emerson Broderick had shared with me, but made hardened by whatever The Yellow door had shaped her into. The green of her eyes was flat and lifeless, her skin thin and drawn across sharply defined cheekbones. On her left cheek, the brand of a trisected glyph burned in a sickeningly organic way, as if the livid scars might move and reform at any given moment.

"And what do you know, *vampire*?" Free of the mask, Emily's voice was lighter in tone, but an angry, bitter edge still dragged within it. "What do you know of those that seek and find something greater than themselves and the small world they inhabit? Not the empty promises of religion, or the straitjacket of societal expectation. Not money and unearned privilege. Power, Ms. Durant. Sheer, unfettered power which, when unleashed upon this world, will change everything, forever. What do you know about that?"

The words pulled me back to a different place and a different time. To the halls of Versailles, and a day when an unthinking, *ingénue* of a girl was presented with a choice and a price not fully explained. If only that day could be reclaimed..."

"I know it's not worth it." My voice welled with restrained emotion. "You might think you've found something here, Emily. A way to escape the bonds of expectation. A way to be seen. To show the world the intelligent, resourceful woman who, given the chance, could be so much more than she's ever been allowed to be. You may think you've found redemption, Emily, but trust me, the path you've set your feet on only leads to a more insidious servitude, and it's a path you need to turn away from, and now."

"I found the glory of Hastur, Ms Durant. That's what I found. I found Hastur, and he found me. Hastur showed me what it was to be powerful—what it was to be feared—and I knelt before him, pledging my soul, my very being, to his cause, in a sacrifice of everything

I am. The people you saw gathered here today may make their offerings—filling the cup with their mingled blood and drinking deep, but I dedicated all that was of Emily Stern, and it is through me that the full might, the full reality of his majesty, will be unleashed upon this world—Through me that all will be called to worship and bleed and die for him as The Feaster comes, bring all Carcosa with him, Ms Durant. There is no turning from that."

"Okay, Charlie, I think we've heard enough. Any time you want to get with the busting out and start doing what you do best, I'm with you."

I glanced again at Emily Stern, my unbeaten heart bursting with recognition and sympathy. "Not yet."

"Oh?" A sudden fire blazed in the depth of Emily Stern's eyes, as she mistook the meaning of my words. "You think you can somehow delay what is surely inevitable? You think you stand a chance? Let me show you a glimpse of what you've decided to put yourself in the way of."

She stood back, half turning toward the statue on the plinth, and raised her arms, wide, the fingers of each hand splayed.

"Uh'eog Hastur, l' mgah'n'ghft fahf hlirgh ymg' orr'eog!"

The air around me thickened. Shadows poured from every corner of the room, coating it in tenebrous tones. Above me, the electric lights flickered and spat.

"Charlie." The disembodied voice of Tamara Quinn was shrill. *"I don't like this. Come on, girl. Action time!"*

I looked once more toward Emily, she still stood in

the exact same position, her arms extended in adoration, and her scarred face illuminated with a beatific smile. Tamara was right, it was time to move. But I had to give Emily Stern one last chance. The chance denied to me. I owed her that. Owed it to her, and to myself.

"Emily," I shouted. "Emily, stop. Please. Don't do this!"

Her only reply was to turn and extend one hand toward me.

"Hastur, h'mggoka!"

At once I felt the pressure around me rise. A chill wind, blowing from nowhere in particular, tore at my clothes, whipping my coat from my shoulders. In the depths of the growing murk, sparks of electricity bloomed and died, the blue-white flashes accompanied by a scrabbling, scurrying, as if a thousand chitinous legs were finding purchase in the dark.

"Charlie!"

I rose, taking the wooden chair on which I'd seemingly been so securely detained with me, and threw myself backwards. It was a bold move, perhaps a stupid one, considering the jagged, stake-like shards the chair exploded into underneath my weight, but it was the fastest way to get me free. Ridding myself of the last vestiges of rope and wood, I rolled to my feet and, with a kick to the face, stopped the progress of the onrushing guard in a very definite way.

"Stop her!" Dorian Brookes screamed. The last vestiges of his cool demeanour falling from him. "Must I do everything myself?"

Two more guards, the men who I'd seen on the steps

of the old brownstone, rushed toward me, fumbling for weapons, but a right cross, followed by a spinning back-fist sent their guns skittering across the parquet flooring and their prone bodies tumbling after. As the second man fell, I stooped, letting my momentum carry me and launched a length of chair leg at Emily Stern, catching her a glancing blow across the left temple and shutting down her chanting. Then I turned my attention to Brookes.

The tall man had rescued the gun I'd suspected the presence of during our earlier interaction. An ugly, snub-nosed thing of blackened metal and lethal utility. Not that guns and bullets hold much danger for a creature like me, not without a little moderation to the payload, or a very careful aim. Being shot still hurts like hell, though, and a well-placed shot would slow me down some. Lifting my eyes from the gun I flashed Brookes a challenge-filled smile that was still on my lips as he squeezed the trigger.

What happened next took less time than the telling. In a routine perfected over long years in our sordid little business, Tamara read the situation and made herself visible. Her spirit, diaphanous as smoke, wavered into existence in the empty air two feet to my right and two feet to my fore. It was enough to split Brookes' attention for a fraction of a second and give him a new target to aim at. The first bullet hit nothing. Taking advantage, I closed the distance and broke his nose with a left hook, sending him sprawling to the floor, to join his unconscious goons.

"Impressive." The word echoed back to a room surging with vicious energy and a blow from behind which knocked me out. I looked up to see Emily Stern regaining her feet, a slow dribble of blood running from a small cut where the chair leg caught her. " But in the end? Pointless. You cannot stop this, Ms Durant, no matter how quick or strong you are. Hastur is inevitable. He will have this world and every world that follows— no matter what you do here. You—" Her words came to a sudden halt as her eyes grew distant. As if some unheard voice had interrupted her. "—You are too late, Ms Durant—Too little—But your continued meddling cannot be permitted, no matter how inconsequential it might be." She turned back to the statue of the yellow-clad figure holding the book and the orb. "Hastur, My King! I call upon your almighty power! Lend me your might that I might rid this world of those that would defy you. *Vulgtmah Hastur. N'gha l' hlirghh!.*"

The last words, screamed in the same alien language I'd been hearing all night, a language that bore no relation to any I knew, echoed through the room. As if in answer I once again heard skittering, scurrying sounds from beneath my feet, and looked down, but there were no insects, no spiders, nothing.

"Charlie, look! The statue!"

I followed Tamara's words and fixed my eyes upon the effigy standing behind the altar. Something was writhing beneath and within its carved robes.

Earlier, when I had first set eyes upon the dread idol who, I assumed, represented 'Hastur', I'd thought the shape of its robes suggestive of something serpentine lurking within. Now, as the insectile chitters grew in volume, and the cloak of shadows rose, that snake-like aspect took on new life as if a thousand snakes, each of a different length and girth, churned against each other. From the skirt of the statue's robes, a black ooze dripped, the unctuous mass separating into distinct tendrils that writhed and crawled with unholy grace from the dais toward me.Darkness took me as the oily tentacles approached, filling my mind with everything I hated of myself. Images of torn flesh, and lives destroyed—Of sundered throats, and the fear and agony of the dying, all with myself, standing fierce, proud, and hungry, as the author of the carnage around me. Destruction wrought in the glorious name of Hastur.

As the droning chatter and the inexorable approach of the oozing tentacles continued, the shards of memory and invention intensified—The grim picture show joined by the thirst for blood and the hunger for destruction that framed so much of my life. I felt the hunger for destruction flare inside me, and the insatiable bloodthirst erupt. A silent voice that might have come from within me cried out, begging me to let go. To surrender. To be.

"Charlie! No!" Tamara's alarmed voice called in the halls of my mind with just enough force to break through the baying howls of vampiric need. *"Fight it. You're better than this thing. You know you are. You can't let it corrupt you."*

As faint as the words came to me, they rang with an iron-cast certainty that what they said was true. I tore my gaze from the effigy of Hastur, the entity who had so efficiently infected my mind, took three quick steps back from the questing, serpentine, feelers and let the reality of those words seep into my consciousness. As before, when the strange energy which swept over the gathered worshipers unleashed the side of me I kept imprisoned so well, I sought my way to that small, still place within me.

Among those frenzied supplicants, I had used the sanctity of that place to quell the urgent fire raging within me, but now my needs were different. I took hold of the fire—the raging need to consume and destroy and channelled it—using the needful fire to forge a steel-clad purpose, directing the hollow passions back to the thing that had unleashed them.

With an inhuman roar, I launched myself at the carved image of the demonic god, letting needful fury propel me past the grasping tentacles to barrel, with all my weight, into the statue. It was tall, and it was heavy, but under the undeniable force of the attack, it still shifted unsteadily on its base.

"No!" Emily cried out. "No, this is impossible. You can't…"

"Well, I am," I snarled, as the bestial visage of the monster I truly am contorted my features. Again, I seized hold of the power the unquenchable urges granted me, using their fury to ram my shoulder against the graven semblance of Hastur. If Emily was so alarmed at the thought of her god's image falling, then fall it would.

"No!" She cried again, stumbling toward me in an unsteady lurch, her hands outstretched, her eyes brimming with tears "Stop! Stop or…or I'll stop you!" Beneath her feet, the oozing, writhing mass thrashed in concert with her desperate state and the serpentine shapes within the statue answered. The solid surface of the idol, a lifeless thing of stone, was suddenly alive. The painted folds of its robes gave way beneath my weight, welcoming me into a permanent, deadly embrace.

It might have ended there and then, but for Tamara. Her voice had been a constant companion throughout the evening's adventures, and her more visible intervention in my face-off with Dorian Brookes had surely saved me from a world of pain, if not worse. Now, with immaculate timing, she showed herself again. Tall, athletic and dark-haired in life, in death she was taller still and suffused with a pale blue-ish light that shimmered and shifted like reflected smoke. I think what struck Emily Stern the most, however. were her eyes. They glowed with a sultry, charcoal, light, like darkness on fire. A baleful stare locked squarely upon Emily's face as she hovered toward the red-haired girl, one arm outstretched

It shouldn't have worked. After all, Emily had seen so much in her tenure as high priestess of whatever abomination Hastur was. Somehow, however, the vengeful ghost of Tamara Quinn, and the unreal aura that surrounded her, surpassed even those horrors, tipping the delicate balance of her sanity past the point of return

With a whimper she fell to her knees, her eyes wide and her lips trembling in absolute terror As she sank to the ground, her control over the effigy of her god and all it in turn controlled, began to slip. The long, slug-like appendages fell, lifeless, into the viscous muck that formed them, the ooze retreating in turn back into the base of the statue of Hastur.

"Now Charlie!" Tamara's voice was hollow and distant. *"Do it now!"*

In response to her urging, I put my shoulder to the now rock-solid effigy and, summoning all my hatred, all my hunger, and every iota of my supernatural strength, pushed. With an agonised crack, reminiscent of a pained scream, the statue swayed and, with one last shove, began to fall.

A bitter scream escaped the throat of Emily Stern. She raced forward, her arms outstretched, and a manic light dancing in her eyes, but it was too late, both for the statue and indeed, for her. With a sickening crunch, the idol fell through the insubstantial form of Tamara Quinn and smashed into the far more corporeal body of the young woman who served it so well.

"So, what's the play?"

We were back in the offices of Charlie Durant Investigations. I was applying a little ice to a sore shoulder, and Tamara was asking a very pertinent question.

"Well," I said, "The Yellow door and whatever it led to, are history, and I guess the news of its demise must be pretty common knowledge by now. That makes a visit from the delightful Mr Broderick pretty imminent in my eyes.

"Sure, but what are you going to tell him?"

It was another good question, and one I didn't have a ready answer for. Emily Stern's family, including her godfather, had to have received word of the mysterious fire which had claimed the recently opened club so completely. And surely, if so, they must have suspicions regarding the fate of Emily. It was up to me to confirm or deny those suspicions. Up to me to reveal just how complicit I'd been in the arson. Or perhaps not.

"It wasn't her fault." I continued my thinking aloud. "I mean, yes, she was headstrong and needy. Yes, she was angry, but I understand why. All her life Emily Stern was told she wasn't good enough—Wasn't clever enough—Wasn't strong enough. She was ripe for corruption—"

"—And if that corruption was by some eldritch force—"

"—She stood no chance at all."

"Sounds kind of familiar, doesn't it?"

Tamara was talking about me of course, and I had to admit she had a point. It was more than possible that the sympathy I felt for Emily Stern had its roots in my own sordid history. Something which didn't make my decision any easier.

"So," Tamara repeated, "what's the play?"

Ignoring her for a moment, I turned to the window, letting my attention drift to the traffic below while I thought it through.

"The family need closure," I said, chewing each word over. "They need a memory to bury. I don't see any reason to deny them that. Nor do I see a reason to taint that memory with the truth. Charles Emerson Broderick thought his goddaughter was playing the sleuth. What if she was? What if she found his great conspiracy? What if, in the act of stopping it, she died, her body consumed by her own righteous fire?"

"Making her the hero of the piece."

"Maybe." My hands dropped to my jacket pocket in search of a cigarette. "Better that than what she became.

"And you?"

"I'll claim my fee, maybe offer a discount, and move on. The Yellow Door might be closed, but the thing it led to? This 'Hastur'? I think that's far from done."

Based in West Yorkshire, England, **Mark Rankin** is a writer who loves exploring the supernatural
His debut novel The Heart That Died now out for query, he writes a personal blog and frequents several online writers' groups when not being really, really bad at video games.

Mark is a full-time wheelchair user on an ongoing and mainly successful mission to not run over his cats.
Charlie Durant & Tamara Quinn are original creations, who feature in the yet to be published debut novel The Heart That Died, as does the entire fictitious city of St. Germain.

THE DEATH OF MANY EYES

JONATHAN INBODY

It had been a long time since anyone had received one of Carnacki's famous invitations promising dinner and a story from his travels, but I wasn't one to turn down either when the opportunity arose. When I arrived at No. 427 Cheyne Walk, it took him a little longer to get to the door than it used to, and the lines on his face when he smiled seemed deeper than ever in the soft yellow light. Contrary to all I'd ever believed about the man, Thomas Carnacki was finally getting old.

The five of us caught up over dinner. Jessop and Arkright were just the same as in my memories, give or take a few grey hairs, but Taylor was quiet, withdrawn. When he excused himself during dinner, Arkright told me in a hushed tone that Taylor had lost his son last year to an automobile accident, although to my eyes the pain on his face had looked as fresh as ever.

Then Jessop told us tales of the sea - glorious ghost stories of the Sargasso - always glancing at Carnacki to make sure he wasn't cross that someone else was the centre of attention, but the gleam in the detective's eye and the curled-up corner of his mouth showed only his usual warmth.

Through it all, though, I was curious. I had thought Carnacki retired from the world of mysteries and monsters, of ghost-finding and electric pentacles. I knew I couldn't ask over dinner, not without a smirking rebuke and a teasing-but-serious instruction to wait until we'd finished eating, but the question burned in my mind.

We settled into the study after dinner for tea, though I took brandy, then found our places in our favourite chairs and looked expectantly at our host. Carnacki smiled, taking our faces in with eyes glittering in the firelight, and lit his pipe.

"You must forgive me," he said through a cloud of smoke. "It's been entirely too long and entirely my fault. I feel I've missed so much of you, and I needed a moment to enjoy your presence. To simply *be*, you understand. But I owe you all a story, and I fear it may be the last."

He cleared his throat, then puffed again at his pipe and began.

"Have any of you heard of the Liquid Death?"

I nodded, then looked over at Arkright to see him nodding too. Taylor raised an eyebrow, and Jessop crossed himself.

"It's a pox, isn't it?" I asked. "Some new disease?"

"Very good, Dodgson," Carnacki said with a smile.

"Half of London's been in a panic," Arkright added. "Ever since the pictures got out. That poor woman."

Jessop scoffed. "I've heard folks saying it's come from India, brought in at the docks, but if it were I'd know. And the state of the bodies? There's no pox from here to Hell that does the likes of that."

"You may soon find that an unwise turn of phrase," Carnacki replied. "The pictures speak for themselves, but without knowing what you *don't* know, I ought to start from the beginning."

"The first victim went to the doctor complaining of a rash and bumps underneath the skin, but by the time they'd started to examine him, he was already dying. His muscles were putrefying, you see, almost rotting off the bone, and when the doctor pressed the stethoscope against his chest it sank straight through. Mercifully, the man died when his heart collapsed, but not before his skin began to dissolve. By the time he had been dead for ten minutes, his body had melted into such a pile of loathsome putrescence that the doctor's office was abandoned for the better part of a week."

"When I read about the case in the paper, I couldn't help but be reminded of the case of Francis Leicester and the so-called Mystery of the White Powder, along with that Valdemar hoax out of New York. And while the latter could never be verified, despite the apparent throng of medical doctors as witnesses, I spent some time researching the former. As it turned out, the Leicester case had been the simple result of the wrong ingredient mixed into medicine - namely the powdered sacrament of the Witches' Sabbath - which resulted in the regression of the human form into the most hideous form of primordial corruption. My colleague Doctor Haberden, who had pronounced the pitiable man dead, was even consulted on the state of the new body in the doctor's office only a few weeks before they consulted me, but eventually, it was deemed that any similarity was mere coincidence."

"The next body put all of that to rest, you see - the woman, the one whose picture was splashed across every newspaper in London. The symptoms came on faster this time, and even more extreme. She had just finished preparing dinner when her husband spied a lump swelling on the side of her neck, and as he reached out to touch it she began to shake. Her hair began to fall out as she staggered forward and clutched the side of her pot of stew, trembling with pain, and as her fingers smoked on the burning metal her husband tried to pull her away."

"When he tugged her backwards, her shoulders separated from her arms… and the torn-apart muscle that dangled down from inside her sockets was black with rot. The pox lumps spread across her face as her husband watched, then down her neck, and finally swelled to such a size that it closed her throat."

I shivered and took another swig of brandy. My host nodded sadly.

"You have heard about more of the victims, no doubt," Carnacki continued. "Some nine as of the most recent count. But there was a tenth victim, or rather the third, whose death was hidden from the public due to its… irregular circumstances."

Taylor perked up. "What sort of irregular?"

"Well, the symptoms took longer to come on for the third victim, and doctors were able to examine him for the better part of a day before he finally died. Given the state of the man, I have no doubt that it was a day more harrowing and agonising than any of us have yet faced. The fingers rotted first, you see, along with the toes, and the doctors could hardly cut pieces off quickly enough to keep them as samples. At the same time, the pox lumps spread until they covered most of the man's face and grew almost impossibly swollen, crowding out his eyes and mouth until the nurses forced a straw into his shrivelled nose to make sure he could continue breathing."

"Finally, one of the doctors decided to take a sample of pus from inside a lump and lanced one to try and get at it. But there wasn't any pus, you see - only clear, viscous liquid - and no one understood why until the skin of the first boil split and opened to reveal a ring of blue around a black circle."

"They were *eyes*; every last one. Some were swollen shut, and some lids never tore, but every lump on the man's head had an iris and a pupil inside sitting atop a misshapen mound of clear jelly."

"Would they have worked? Could they have seen? No one can say for certain. Before one could be removed to check for an optical nerve attached at the back, the man's head sagged and fell in like a rotted pumpkin. In a few more minutes, the entire body was nothing but a stain."

"So you see, to call it the Liquid Death is half true, but the other half is all the more disturbing. Luckily for the authorities, none of the witnesses to the other deaths seem to have seen what lies inside the boils... or at least admitted it out loud... so they may be able to suppress a panic as long as the condition doesn't spread."

"Condition?" I asked. "So you don't believe it's a disease?"

"All of the victims but one knew each other; the police have put together that much. But none of them had been out of the country, and none of them worked in a hospital or prison, so the cause of the illness remains unknown... or should I say, '*remained*' unknown."

I furrowed my brow. "The victim that didn't know the others... What was their profession?"

"She was a professional medium," Carnacki replied with a gleam in his eye. "Unfortunately, I was a few days from putting the puzzle together when someone arranged the pieces for me. I was called out to a manor house in the countryside by a man called Winfield, and when I arrived I found the place outfitted for war. An armed man stood posted at each entrance, and a grey-haired groundskeeper circled the grounds with a pair of hunting dogs eagerly pulling at their leashes. I was shown inside and up to the library, where my host was waiting with a comfortable seat and an expensive bottle of American whiskey."

"It was there that he told me a story - a strange story, but one I believed. Or at least, I believed that *he* believed it. He said that there, almost two years ago at his manor house, there had been held a séance, and that every victim of the Liquid Death currently known had been in attendance. They'd connected to something that night, he said - some shadow out of time he called the Great Race."

"'They were long since dead, forgotten conquerors of vast primordia,' Winfield told me, 'But their consciousnesses remained. They had projected their souls outward before, traded bodies with far inferior races on distant worlds to save their own kind from extinction... and let the minds of their inferiors die in the bodies the Great Race had abandoned.'"

"I nodded then. 'I've read something of that before; old legends given half a reference in the Sigsand Manuscript or fragments of the Necronomicon. If I remember correctly, I believe they called themselves the Yith... at least if you believe the stories.'"

"He beamed at me then, and when he opened his mouth again his voice was trembling. He told me that the Great Race had finally died, aeons old and trapped in millennia distant, and that their disembodied minds had been swept back and forth across the vast reaches of the universe by the hurricane of cosmic time."

"'But somehow, we'd found them,' Winfield continued. 'Our souls had reached out and grasped them, galaxies away, and while we struggled to keep our minds from shattering they began to claw their way in. They couldn't steal our bodies, or *trade* them as they called it, without bodies of their own to deposit us into, and although we tried to close the gateway I'm afraid our medium ended the séance only a moment too late. They were inside us now; their ancient, alien minds stirred into ours like milk in tea.'"

"'I've had their dreams,' the old man said, turning to look out the window. 'I've seen impossible worlds, *been* impossible things - I've felt the bodies of a thousand disparate creatures from the inside looking out. I have knowledge that could threaten the world, Carnacki. Perhaps all worlds.'"

"I questioned him further," Carnacki said, puffing on his pipe. "Asked him for as many details as he could give of his so-called alien experiences. With each answer, he grew more pale, more distant, as though the mere memory of it drained him. And while it was fantastic - garishly, absurdly fantastic - his words carried no deception in them. He believed it, as firmly and fervently as a man might swear by the church."

"But it *is* absurd!" I interjected. "A possession by alien spirits? It's nonsense."

Carnacki narrowed his eyes. "I thought much the

same when I first heard it. I thought perhaps he'd gone mad, in part or in whole because of the terrible death of so many of his friends, but he assured me that every word was the truth."

Jessop scoffed. "The assurances of a madman."

"He said he'd read about me in the newspaper," Carnacki continued unabated, "And wondered if I could help him using my knowledge of the occult sciences."

"Help him do what?" Arkright asked. "Separate the spirit from his own? Was that what was killing the others - some incompatible biology?"

"No," Carnacki replied flatly. "At least, not in that sense. There was a rival, he said, another race responsible for the destruction of the Yith. He had dreamed of them - some squamous, polypian things with no set form - and he feared that they knew somehow that the Yith had returned. He thought they could sense it somehow."

"'The deaths of my friends, my *people*, is no plague,' that's what Winfield told me, 'And certainly no accident. They've been murdered at the rival's hand, using some ancient weapon. I've shut myself up at the manor, surrounded myself with paid protectors and bloodhounds and taken every precaution, but something inside me can *feel* that it isn't enough. The rival is near, I know it, and so is my end... unless you can help me.'"

"'Please, Carnacki,' the old man pleaded, 'Your electric pentacle, that mad and brilliant device you've used to ward off foul spirits... can't you use it to protect me?'"

"'Not if your rival is indeed material,' I told him. 'It can keep out the things invisible and intangible that seek to invade our world, but it cannot repel the knife or the bullet of a living foe in flesh.'"

"'Detective, *please*,' the man begged. 'If you can protect me - if you can save my life - I can teach you the arcane secrets of a thousand worlds. I can- I can show you how to be young again, to be *eternal*; to transport your mind from one body to another like the Yith.'"

"I wish I could say I denied him outright, that I left on general principle, or that it was only curiosity that kept me in his employ… but it wasn't. I hope you all can understand; the older I grow, the more I fear the end. The things I've seen, the creatures that I've witnessed try to break into our world… what if their own eldritch realms are where our souls pass onto?'"

"You can't be serious," Taylor said darkly.

"I can't be *sure*," Carnacki replied. "And although I am no coward, Winfield's promise tempted me. To live without the fear of death? The fear of age? What man that can feel their mind dim day after day could deny desiring it?"

"Your mind isn't dimming, old friend," I said supportively. "You're as brilliant as ever."

Carnacki bristled, irritated at my pity. "Nonetheless, I stayed at the manor for some days, doing my best to assuage the old man's fears. He bade me perform the ritual of SaaaMaaa to focus the house's energies, and although I thought it pointless I acquiesced. There were no spiritual disturbances at all, at least as much as I could figure, but if it brought him comfort and passed the time I had little room to complain."

"His servants saw to all of my needs and seemed

relieved to see their master keeping company again. It was clear that there hadn't been a guest allowed in for some time, and that any staff that had quit since the deaths began hadn't been replaced for fear of the rival's intrusion."

"One of his servants, a man called Phillip, was the only one he trusted to bring him his meals, and Phillip had been instructed to carefully watch the kitchen staff as they prepared it. As near as I could figure, he performed his job with silent, loyal precision."

"Then, one night, just after Phillip brought Winfield his dinner, a scream echoed down the staircase. I rushed from my room with my revolver drawn, convinced my host was under attack, but upon entering the room I found him in a different state entirely."

"Winfield was chalk-white, staring down at the floor next to his dropped tray of food and a spilt teacup, where Phillip was rolling and twitching on the floor in twisted agony. With each violent shake, another hideous boil pressed out of his head, red and pulsing."

"Was it the Liquid Death?" I interrupted, leaning forward.

Carnacki nodded. "In as hideous a form as it was ever seen. His limbs were steaming, dissolving like sugar in water as he screamed and writhed, and when he opened his mouth to scream only black tar poured out. The boils on his head pulled themselves open, and countless eyes darted back and forth in a dying, desperate panic as he gurgled and shook."

"I tried to will myself to raise the revolver, to do the dying man one last favour, but my hand wouldn't move.

We simply watched, Winfield and I, as he melted. The man's suffering was over in no more than a minute, but trust me when I say that it was a minute I shall never forget. The eyes were the last to rot, you see - and they stared until the very end."

"Finally, once the vacant horror had washed away, leaving only the pure, animal disgust at the sight and smell of the remains, Winfield managed to bring himself to speak. He'd had Phillip secretly tasting all of his food before he ate it, you understand, for fear of poison... and unfortunately, the loyal fellow served his purpose."

"So it really *isn't* a disease!" Jessop interjected excitedly.

"No, indeed," Carnacki replied. "Now friends, you must let me finish my story without another interruption, for if you bid me stop even for an instant to explain, I shall seem a madman. What I am about to describe, it defies... Hm."

He paused and slowly scanned our faces. "Just know that when I am through, you will know exactly as much as I do - nothing less and nothing more. And further explanations, though they must exist, are so far lost to me that I may as well be a hog learning arithmetic."

None of us spoke, and after a long moment, Carnacki cleared his throat and started again, refocused.

"The manservant Phillip was dead, and Winfield had just told me why and how, leaving only the question of '*at whose hand*' remaining. I told Winfield to lock the door and ran downstairs, revolver drawn, ready to confront whoever I might find in the kitchen. Fortunately, the men on guard outside had not heard the scream, so I could maintain the element of surprise. Unfortunately, however, as I crossed the dining room a maid exited the hall and collided with me. I fell headlong into a cabinet of glassware, much of which toppled and fell, and after the loud shattering there were a few seconds of silence as I stared at the kitchen door."

"Finally I rushed in, pistol raised, just in time to see a broad-shouldered chef disappear through the back door. The rest of the staff shouted and ran as I shoved my way through, yelling at any staff up ahead to apprehend the man fleeing. This seemed to finally set the guards outside into motion, though they were crucial seconds behind."

"I pursued my quarry into the hall and took a shot at his shoulder as he ducked behind a heavy door. I swore I hit him, but he didn't stop, so I tried to close the distance. I realised when I got to the door that I was standing at the top of a narrow stone staircase leading into the cellar. As I hurried down it, I didn't have time to think if he had fled there on purpose - intent on escaping through some hidden passage or waiting to strike me in the dark - or if he'd accidentally cornered himself in a mad dash away from his pursuer."

"At the bottom of the stairs, the room opened up into an ancient wine cellar, with two opposite walls lined with massive wooden casks. The whole place was draped in shadow, and after half a moment of listening for movement I realised he must have been hiding somewhere."

"I crept forward with as much stealth as my shoes could afford me, eyeing the long shadows that filled every nook and corner. He was here, I knew as much, and he must have known too that we shared the room."

"I must have passed his hiding place, for in a second he was at my back, wrapping his burly arms around my neck in an attempt to choke me. I raised the gun and he swatted it out of my hand, but with a well-placed stomp to his foot I got myself free and scrambled after it. I dove for the gun, grasped it, and rolled over, blind-firing two shots into his chest as he charged after me."

"The man swayed, but didn't fall. Then - and I swear this is the truth, if only the truth of a flickering basement light - his face rippled as though it were water. Other faces flashed, all unfamiliar to me, before it settled again and I looked down. The bullet holes in his chest seemed only to ooze some thick, yellow ichor, and when he raised his hand to the wounds it sank into his chest as if it was mud."

"This thing - the rival, the polyp - reached into his chest and withdrew the bullets. He tossed them aside and started back for the stairs, only pausing when I sent another shot whizzing into the back of his leg. It, too, only oozed, but he staggered and seemed to fall."

"I heard the soft clatter of something glass drop to the floor, then watched a small vial roll from his side over to one of the wine casks. There was... *liquid*... inside; black as pitch and wriggling with life. But what gave me pause - what chilled my blood - were the floating eyes suspended within."

"The vial rolled to a stop, and I could just make out a thin crack on its surface in the basement's dim light. The rival turned to look at it, then bolted for the stairs in a blind panic. I tried to follow, only to find I hadn't yet regained my balance after his savage attack, and could only listen and catch my breath as his heavy footsteps faded."

"Suddenly, the glass vial burst and the loathsome thing inside slithered out, bulging and expanding in seconds like a mountain of yeasting rot. Countless, squirming tendrils lashed out, covered in eyes and toothy mouths, and the squamous bulk of the thing seemed to grow with each shuddering movement."

"A tentacle, if that's what they were, smashed through the side of the cask and wine poured out onto the floor, instantly steaming and boiling as it came into contact with the living mound of black plasma. I ran for my life, then, and as I desperately ascended the stairs I could hear it bubbling up to follow me."

"In the hall, I shouted for anyone who remained in the manor to flee, even as the men with rifles finally arrived, and as I tried to instruct them the ever-growing creature rolled out of the basement and began to spread across the floor. And the eyes - the *eyes*."

"I rushed back through the kitchen and towards the stairs as the riflemen fired, trying my best to ignore the sounds of straining wood, smashing walls, and screams, but fate wouldn't have me get back to Winfield. As I rounded the corner, a massive black tentacle crashed through the wall and up to the roof, pulling down tons of wood to cover the stairs. At the eye-covered tentacle's end, the pulsing, shuddering bulk of the hideous thing was still growing, rolling outward like a waterfall of black mud that threatened to fill the entire manor house."

"With sudden horror, I realised that the guns of the

guards had long since gone silent."

"In a blind panic, I ran for the nearest fireplace and dashed the burning wood across the floor with the poker, taking care to kick a piece as close to the velvet curtains as I could manage. Luckily, they took, and in an instant, the place was burning."

"It was only after I made it outside, half-singed and coughing from the smoke, that I remembered the cellar was full of alcohol. I stood on the lawn, nearly mad, surrounded by the horrified staff of the Winfield house as the manor burned. For a time, I could hear the gigantic, monstrous thing shrieking inside, gurgling and piping madly as it tried in futility to escape the blazing inferno, but eventually, it fell silent."

"My God, Carnacki," I marvelled. "What was it? And what happened to Winfield?"

Carnacki exhaled. "The creature? In the Necronomicon, the Mad Arab would have called it a 'shoggoth,' I think - a living weapon created by an elder race long since dormant. Perhaps the rival knew how to make one… or where to find one already made."

"And Winfield?" I asked again.

"I'll return to that," Carnacki answered.

"But there's still so much left only to guess at!" Jessop said. "What about the murders? How were they done?"

"Admittedly," Carnacki said with a gleam in his eye, "Winfield's rival had a touch of mad brilliance. Though I can't say for certain, I believe he managed to remove parts of his pet creature - back when it could be contained in a vial - by some form of tanning or freezing, and when he had created the shavings he had only to slip them into his victims' food. Infiltration and extraction were no object, given the rival's changing appearance."

"Then, it was only a simple matter of… what did you call it before, Arkright? Ah, yes, 'incompatible biology.' Perhaps he experimented with the dosage, sometimes too little and sometimes too much, but I daresay merely a cell of that loathsome creature would eventually be enough to kill anyone. It always grew, you see; tried to assimilate the new tissue but only managed to dissolve it."

"It's genius," Taylor whispered.

Arkright nodded. "Is the killer still out there, do you think?"

"I expect I shall find out soon," Carnacki replied grimly. "Winfield's rival doesn't strike me as a thing to be crossed without the risk of retaliation."

"My God, man," Jessop said, aghast. "Where do you get your groceries? What if your dinner was poisoned?"

"I doubt he'd try that," Carnacki said. "He'd want to question me first, determine Winfield's whereabouts. Besides, I have dangerous knowledge that he'd need to ensure wasn't passed on - I know a fair bit more about his specific method than I've admitted. Think about it, fellows, what can virtually everyone in London be known to consume?"

He waited to see if any of us would answer, then continued with a smirk. "He poisoned their tea - I haven't drank any for days, in any case."

Taylor looked down at his empty teacup, then over at Jessop and Arkright. They exchanged a panicked look, then stared down at their cups as their faces went white. After only a moment, Jessop's face twisted with fury and he leapt from his chair.

"You knew that and you let us drink the tea?!" Jessop shouted, jabbing a finger at Carnacki.

"Quite," Carnacki replied with a smile. "There's no danger - because I know for a fact I poisoned the brandy."

He turned to look in my direction, and the rest of the room followed his gaze to the empty glass on the side table next to me.

"W-what?" I stammered. "Why would you-?"

"Because you knew to avoid the tea," Carnacki replied flatly. "And because Dodgson doesn't drink. You gave yourself away in a thousand small ways - words, gestures, even expressions - but it hardly matters. No doubt you found out my name, and anyone that knows me knows about my invitations, my dinner parties with the promise of a story. I knew you couldn't pass up the opportunity. All I had to do was hold a party and watch closely - watch men I've loved like brothers to discover which one was already dead. I knew, too, that it was only a minor risk to the others. You'd have to wait to kill me until it was just you and I; too many prying eyes would only risk further exposure."

The edge of his lip curled slightly up. "And there was just enough of your creature left after the fire, as it happened - just enough to use the way you used it. I could hardly think of a more fitting end."

"You've lost your mind!" I shouted, throwing the brandy glass against the wall. "Don't you understand? You've killed me!"

"Perhaps there is some Dodgson left inside you," Carnacki replied mournfully. "Some film, some smear of memories and thoughts. If so… I'm sorry, old friend; but you must know I've set you free. There was no other way."

Searing pain spread out across my forehead and I fell to my knees, grabbing my face with both hands in agony as red, swollen lumps began to press up from underneath my skin. In seconds, steam began to pour out of my mouth as I screamed.

"Do you know what you've done, Carnacki?!" I shrieked, yellow ichor spilling out around my rotting fingernails. "You've protected a race of killers older than the universe! They're body snatchers, life stealers - nothing more! *They* deserve to die! Not me! *Not me!*"

I felt my legs wither and sag beneath me, burning like coals as the muscle peeled away and liquified. The pain on my head radiated outward, and I felt the thin flesh rip and spread as countless dying eyes tore themselves open.

Carnacki walked over and stood above me, silently puffing his pipe. One of Dodgson's stray memories floated into my head just as my skull caved in - some scant familiarity of one last custom. And as my face sank in and my brain boiled above a cavernous, dissolving chest, a look of recognition came over the detective's well-worn face. He knew just what I expected him to say - the same thing he said at the end of every dinner party - and as a hundred eyes went black I finally heard him utter it, as grim and melancholy as if it were a eulogy.

"Out you go."

Jonathan Inbody is an author, podcaster, and filmmaker from Buffalo, New York. He is an avid reader of 20th century Weird Fiction and a lover of monster movies. His full-cast audio drama Gray Matter: An Acid Horror Anthology Podcast, which features original stories and adaptations of classic horror tales, can be found on Apple Podcasts and all major platforms, with a new episode released each month.

Carnacki the Ghost-Finder, created by author William Hope Hodgson, stands as one of the early examples of the occult detective template in fiction. Taking cues from Blackwood's John Silence and Le Fanu's Dr. Hesselius, Thomas Carnacki is a detective and a professional debunker driven by a combination of gadgetry and the scientific method. Unlike those detectives, however, Carnacki's cases - which he tells as stories to his four friends at a series of dinner parties - turn out to be hoaxes almost as often as they turn out to be genuine manifestations of the supernatural. Without the action-horror adventures of Thomas Carnacki, there may never have been The X-Files… or even Scooby-Doo.

MORE FROM MYTHOS